I AM NOT
THIRTEEN

ISBN 978-1-7328360-1-3 (Paperback Edition)
ISBN 978-1-7328360-0-6 (Digital Edition)

Library of Congress Control Number 2018967550

Some characters and events in this book are fictitious. Any similarities to real persons, living or dead, is coincidental and not intended by the author.

Cover and interior design by Damonza

Printed and bound in the United States of America
First printing January 2019

Published by
Calhoun Press
1050 Johnnie Dodds Blvd.
#1404
Mt Pleasant, SC 29465

www.calhounpress.net

I AM NOT THIRTEEN

A.O. MONK

CHAPTER ONE
2016

THE TIP OF the knife presses into my throat.

"Don't scream," my sister says. She's the one holding the knife. We're in the church vestibule, my back pressed against the wall. I can't see the knife, but I know it's big—the kind you use to skin a deer. Or a younger sister.

"Leah," I say. "Leah, look at me."

"I'm looking right at you," Leah says. Her eyes, huge in her hollow-cheeked face, flit over me without ever meeting my eyes. The tip of the knife presses in.

"Let's go inside. We can talk about this."

"You're not going anywhere till I get my money."

A bead of blood slides down my neck.

"Yeah," I hear myself say, "I know. Let me get my wallet, okay?"

I'll give you the money after you're clean, I used to say. *Go to rehab, get in a sober house, do ninety days.* That's what the interventionist said—no support until she gets sober. That's what's best for your sister.

But my sister never pulled a knife on me before.

A woman passes us without a glance. My hand, deep in my

purse, won't hold steady. The wallet flips and dances out of my grasp. The knife presses in.

"Hurry *up*."

Two minutes ago, I was lighting a candle to my father's memory, trying and failing to pray. Thirty seconds ago, I was deciding what to cook for dinner, what kind of leftovers would last the longest. When I first saw my sister standing by the outer door, I thought, *Here we go.* And now I'm going to die, and she'll use my money to score.

My phone vibrates in the belly of my purse. I can feel it through the fabric. Must have slipped behind that hole in the lining. My hand closes around the wallet. I lift it, shaking, out of the bag. Somewhere above us, prerecorded bells ring out. *Dah duhh dah-duhhh...duh-dah da-duhhh.*

Leah snatches the wallet out of my hand. The knife comes away from my neck, hovering in front of me. It really is big. A slick of dark blood glints on its tip. Her gaze wanders my face as she tucks the wallet in her hoodie's front pocket.

The deep brass bell rings eight times overhead. Shit. I'm already late for work.

"Bank. Let's go." Leah grabs my free arm and pulls me forward.

We march down the steps together. Leah holds the knife underneath my jacket, pressing just below my ribcage. Her other hand clasps my arm at the elbow. I watch myself walk down Mission Street, watch the purse dangling from my hand, feel nothing but the knife at my rib. I eyeball every passerby, trying to catch their attention. Can't they see the blood dribbling down my neck? A man, staring glass-eyed at his phone, bumps into me.

"Sorry," I hear myself mumble. He doesn't look up.

This isn't normal, an inner voice insists. *Most muggings last a couple minutes, if that. If she's taking you somewhere, it's to hurt you, kill you, or sell you. Run.*

The light turns green before we reach the crosswalk. We've stepped into the street when the white pedestrian turns to a red hand. The numbers count down: *10, 9, 8...*My pulse pumps against the knifepoint.

"ATM," I say.

"Where?"

"We passed it."

Leah turns. Her grip loosens. The knife drops a centimeter or two. I bolt, wrenching my arm out of her grasp. I run into the street.

You're dead, stupid. You should have turned back.

A horn blares. A bumper taps my legs, hard enough to throw me to the ground.

I look up. Leah's running down the street. There's a large canvas patch on the back of her hoodie, showing a black sphere with a white halo. Her own artwork—I'd recognize it anywhere. Pain, radiating out from my side, overtakes me. Reality grays out, like a radio station fading into static.

I come to as the paramedics strap me into a gurney.

"What's your name?"

"—hasn't lost too much—"

"Honey, is this your purse? Where's your—"

"What's the date, hon?"

I hear my own voice answer. "August...nineteenth? I'm not sure, sorry."

"What year is it?"

"2016. As if I could forget."

The paramedic above me smiles grimly and looks away.

The hospital is a blur of fluorescent tubes, hallways, MRIs, blood draws, people talking overhead. Sharp pain throbs at my side. A nurse sews stitches into my neck. Mina Sirota, my boss, wails over the phone; there's a new diagonal crack across its screen. My crown braid slips out of place. Someone tells me I'm lucky. "One millimeter this way or that, we'd be cutting you open downstairs."

Lucky indeed. I have a broken rib, which only hurts every time I move or laugh or talk or breathe, and stitches along my neck and my side. There's also the splitting headache that makes the world throb with every heartbeat. Stars wink and burst open in my eyes.

Officer Rampling, a forty-something cop with a red-gold ponytail, takes my statement. Officer Kwan shifts from foot to foot as we talk, his face set in a frown. I tell them everything that happened, from the church to the ambulance.

"How much older is your sister?" Officer Rampling asks.

"Almost five years. She'll be thirty...no, thirty-one this December."

"Has she ever stolen from you before?"

"Only my college fund."

"Any other issues between you two?"

"We're sisters. What do you think?"

Not even a courtesy laugh. Officer Rampling watches me, pen hovering over her notepad.

"She got clean, once," I say, to break the silence. "I got her a job at a café, set up a website for her paintings, helped her register for classes. I really thought she was gonna make it. Then she met this prince of a guy at Narcotics Anonymous. He shot her full of drugs, pimped her out, locked her in his apartment..." I sneeze. A starburst of pain explodes from my ribs to my eyeballs. I curl up on the bed, trying to find a comfortable position. There is none.

"What happened to him?"

"Jail. For five seconds. He pleaded down to…misdemeanor assault, some petty shit."

"What's his name?"

"I don't remember. Kind of repressed it, you know? It went to court in, ah, San Rafael. Maybe four years ago." Rampling writes in her notebook.

"After he got arrested, Leah went around the bend. She told everybody I stole money from her website. The number gets bigger every time I see her."

Rampling asks with her eyes.

"Not one cent. No good deed, right?" I laugh, then wish I hadn't. "Maybe I should have. I had to take out an emergency student loan because of her. Do you have any idea what the interest is on an emergency student loan?"

"You guys keep in touch?"

"No. Last I heard, she was down in Santa Cruz."

"When was that?"

"When I last heard? A year ago, maybe two. I assumed she was dead."

"How'd she seem to you today?"

"Dead. Like something was wearing her body and walking it around town."

"Any reason she'd visit you now?"

I rub my eyes, watching the kaleidoscopic patterns swirl. "The money, I guess? Maybe she's reliving her glory days. She used to stand on Lombard Street with this sign: *Majored in English, Anything Helps.*"

"*That's* where I know her from," Officer Kwan says. He turns to Rampling, beaming. "'The English Major.' Did you know her?"

"I read about her. She sold drawings, right?"

"Yeah. Good ones. I told her, these should be in a gallery downtown. She drew me once—it was me as the Hulk, with huge green muscles." He laughs. "I always wondered what happened to her."

"Now you know."

Silence, punctuated by Rampling's pen gliding across her notebook. Kwan looks out the window. I will myself to breathe deeply, like the doctor told me to.

"If you can, leave the city for a little while," Rampling says. "Don't post anything on Facebook, don't tell people where you are."

"What about my mom?"

"Where's your mom?"

"Woodacre. It's in Marin, uh, west of Fairfax."

Rampling smiles to herself. Kwan frowns absently at me. I wonder if he's comparing my face to Leah's, looking for similarities, wondering what separates us.

"I'll call West Marin P.D.," Rampling says. "They can station a car outside your mom's house. I'm sure they can spare someone." A knowing smile flits across her face. "Does your mom, ah, talk to your sister, give her money—"

"No."

Rampling and Kwan hand me their cards.

"Call us if you want to add anything to your statement, okay?"

"Hang in there, Amy."

A few minutes later, a nurse comes in. He asks me if I want acupuncture, for the pain. I do.

The acupuncture helps a little. I wait for the doctor to come back; he got weird when I asked for "non-opiate painkillers." "My sister's a junkie," I explained, which didn't help. I still haven't called Mom. What would I say? "Hey, you know my older sister, who we don't talk about anymore? Well, she tried to kill me. She almost did."

A cough comes, harder for my attempts to make it go away. Pain shoots out from my rib, winding me. I'm still crying when my phone rings.

Tom Templeton, mobile says the screen, next to a picture of Tom's smiling face. Maybe it's better not to answer. We haven't talked once since the breakup, not even, "I still have your sweater" or, "Do you want your mail?" Why would he call me now? Do I want to know?

I do.

"Hey, Amy," Tom says. "Sorry about that. I was in a meeting. You're at the ER, right? You okay?"

Shit. He's still my emergency contact. I didn't even think of that.

"I just passed the security doors. Wait a sec."

Shit. Shitshitshitshitshit. "You don't need to come back here," I stammer. "I'm fine, I sw—"

Tom stands in the doorway, phone to his ear. We stare at each other. He brings his phone down in slow motion.

"Amy. What happened?" He glances at my neck.

"I made myself a new man," I say, pulling up my blouse. "All it cost was a rib. Pretty good deal, right?"

Tom greets this joke with an exasperated pause. "I wanted to make sure—"

"Well, you've made sure. See you later."

"It's not, um, self-inflicted?"

"Tom."

"It was your sister, wasn't it?"

"It wasn't my sister."

"Amy."

I cross my arms. Pain sings up my side in bright white lines. *You wanna know the story, Tom? After what you did? I came home to a half-empty apartment and a wad of cash on the table. Like I was a whore you'd grown tired of. My life is closed to you.*

"Let me take you home."

"No."

"Don't you live in El Cerrito now? That's way too far to—"

"It's fine. Mina will lend me money for the—"

"Don't be ridiculous."

"I'm not being ridiculous. Leah took my wallet, my cash, my credit cards…"

"Leah, huh?"

Tom smiles his infuriating, victorious smile. Dull heartache returns, transfigured into venom.

"How did you feel when Holly didn't run off with you?" I ask, before I can stop myself. "Now you have to hold your peace. Forever."

Tom falls into a sulk. We stay like this for a moment, trapped in a mutual silence. Holly is Tom's "one that got away," a girl he's been more or less in love with since high school. I thought it was less, the tiny ember of an old flame, until the day he left me. Ten days before her wedding.

"I'm sorry about your sister," he says. "I found some of her drawings in one of my boxes. I'll mail them to you."

"Why? They're worthless." The laugh hurts as it leaves my chest.

"They belong to you." He pauses, wipes the corners of his mouth, his eyes passing over my face. "If she took your wallet, you'll need money for—"

"Stop. You can't make every problem disappear by throwing money at it."

Tom walks into the room, pulling out his wallet. "This is

your problem, not mine," he says, dropping a few bills on the bedside table. "And 'throwing money at it' will get you home. You can figure it out from there."

Our eyes meet. For a moment, I see the Tom I loved. He's the man who texted me Latin poems at work, who read me his stories, who sang with my family on Christmas Eve. And then the moment passes. I look away.

This is the last time I'll ever see him. There's no emotion attached to this thought: I might have thought *the sink needs cleaning* or *the pharmacy closes at seven.* Six weeks ago, Tom Templeton and I were destined to leave this awful theme park of a city, get married, make babies, live together forever in love. In my head, I'd planned everything, from our wedding invitations to the plants in our front yard. None of that will happen.

"I'm sorry I left you like that," Tom says. "It was spineless. If I could turn back time, I'd...I'd be a man about it."

This, it turns out, is the one thing I don't want him to say. I don't want you to be sorry, Tom. I want you to not be the kind of person who'd do that to me. "Too late now," I say instead. "It's done. *Temporus edax rerum.*"

"Tempus *edax rerum,*" he says gently. "Time, the devourer of all things."

"Even love," I murmur to myself.

Tom's footsteps grow fainter and fainter down the hallway.

Zuckerberg San Francisco General is three miles from my job. Too far to walk. I wait at the northbound tram station. The next one arrives in thirty minutes. When I call her, Mina tells me to take the day off. "I already told you to, an hour ago. You don't remember?"

"Not specifically."

"Everything's a disaster here. That new video from Hell-star, the one he's been promising to drop off for six weeks? Ten minutes after you called, he came. They're in some file format that won't convert, even in VLC. Oh, get this—all the lights exploded in the gray room, *again*. Thank God no one was in there. I swear, there's some crazy bad juju in the air today. You feel it, too, right?"

"Did that guy from Modus ever call back?"

"If he did, I don't know about it. Anyway, honey, don't come in. I'm not having you bleed out on the floor. If you do, though, make sure to write an artist's statement first."

"I love you too."

I work as an assistant manager at Orpheline, an art gallery south of Market. It's part sales, part crisis management, part body English, part schmoozing. I'm trying to "build my skillset" to get a job as a grant writer. This skill-building mostly involves standing in front of the mirror, saying "I'm very detail-oriented," and trying to look like I'm not lying.

Cars glide down Potrero. The midday sun shines on my face. A low breeze ruffles my skirt, sending a thick lock of hair across my eyes. My crown braid must look a fright; I don't dare check it in the glass. My purse dangles from my hand. I try shouldering it. Bad idea.

I look around the station. Someone's pasted stickers all over it, all of the same image: a circle of thick black rays, all converging in the center, surrounded by a snake eating its own tail. Not Leah's artwork.

"We could use that," I murmur, thinking of my employer. Our gallery's name comes from *L'Âme d'une Orpheline* (The Soul of a Girl Orphan), a nineteenth-century novella about a girl's sexual awakening. It's a rude awakening, starting with her rape at thirteen and getting more grotesque from there. Orpheline takes many lovers, including an English Duke, a Russian anarchist, a consumptive poet, a sexual psychotic, and many other charming gentlemen. At the end of the book, the writer shows us Orpheline in an all-night café, alone, her shaking hands bringing a cup of coffee to her mouth.

Whether it's the name or the attitude, our gallery draws in depraved artwork, even by San Francisco standards: oil paintings of porno stills, fake snuff films, mannequins splattered with blood and semen. Despite all this, the office culture is easygoing, even with Trump's campaign putting everyone on edge. I hate the art, but I'm barely qualified for anything else and I need the health insurance. That's what I tell myself, anyways.

I look at my phone, count down from twenty, then hit the green button. *Dialing Mom*, the screen reads. The picture shows Mom smiling in the backyard, the forest dark behind her.

Here we go.

"Hi, you've reached Jacqueline De Paul Snowberger. Please leave your name and number and I'll call you back as soon as I can. Thank you." *Beep.*

The story tumbles out of me in fits and starts. I pace as I talk. I'm still talking when the line beeps off. I hang up.

I walk back to the tram stop and check the display above the station map. Twenty-two minutes until the next tram. Should I bite the bullet and take an Uber? Today wouldn't be complete without a dollop of sexual harassment, would it? I glance at my phone. One text from Cassidy Clark, my best and oldest friend: *WAIT*. Wait, what? I didn't text or call her today, according to the phone's call history. Maybe someone (and I think I know who) called her on my behalf. In any event, I'll tell her about it later. First, I need to get home.

I zone out, walk back and forth along the platform, watch cars and people pass. The sky is blue and cloudless. Sunlight glints off the tram rails. Two girls, maybe sixteen, run shrieking down the sidewalk. I check the clock again. Seven minutes until the next tram. There it is, rolling out of the shimmering haze at the end of Potrero. I watch it come closer, try not to think.

My phone vibrates in my purse. *Mom calling.* My heart flops. "Are you okay?" Mom's voice is a string ready to snap.

"I'm fine," I say in a near-whisper, my hand over my mouth. A man in scrubs glances at me. I walk away from the tram station. "She wanted money. You know how she thinks I stole from—"

"Yes."

Leah's a Voldemort figure between the two of us, someone to be hinted at, never invoked. I always call Mom on Leah's birthday. Beyond that convention, my sister's a ghost. This is the closest we've come to discussing her in at least a year.

"It couldn't come at a worse time, could it?" Mom says, laughing without humor. Worse time?

"I can come by," I say, brushing off her cryptic comment.

"How? You're an hour away." I can hear in her voice that she wants me to.

"You had this commute for years, Mom. I can handle it for one day."

"It's a terrible commute. I don't know why I did it for so long. Didn't Tom take the car, though?"

"I can take the bus to San Rafael, meet you at Greenhall," I say, hurrying past the mention of Tom. Greenhall Holdings is Mom's long-time employer, a commercial real estate firm with branches all over the bay. "What do you want for dinner? I'll make you something."

Confused pause. "What was that dish you told me about?" Mom says doubtfully. "Vandelay something?"

"You mean vindaloo? Sure. We can make it with lamb, pork, chicken—"

"Is it spicy?"

"Everything I eat is spicy, Mom. You want something else?"

The tram judders to a stop in front of us.

"Where are you, sweetie, I—"

"Mom, the tram's here. I gotta go."

"Honey, let me—"

"Mom, I'll talk to you—"

"Yo, Amazing Amy! Get off the phone!"

I look behind me and see Cassidy Clark, my best friend in the world, grinning out the window of her car.

CHAPTER TWO
STORY OF THE HUMAN RACE

Cassidy waits for me to buckle my seatbelt. She doesn't say, and I don't ask, but I'm pretty sure Tom called her.

"You were getting on the *tram*? Didn't you get my text?"

"'Wait'? Seriously? You couldn't be more specific?"

Cassidy rolls her eyes as she eases into traffic.

"I thought you'd be at work," I say.

"Election flu. I forced them to give me my own PTO. Half the department's been sick for months."

"This fucking election."

"I know. Every conversation, it's Trump this, Trump that, the polls, the tax returns, the emails, blah blah blah blah *blah*."

"Only three—no, two and a half months left. Then the nightmare's over."

"Hopefully."

"Cass. He *can't* win."

Cassidy shakes her head.

"I'm not being a Pollyanna, the math—"

"Hey! Election flu, remember? Don't turn it into election pneumonia."

"Okay. Jeez."

Cassidy looks at me when we come to a traffic light. Her eyes snag on my neck. She points to her own neck, eyebrows raised. "You wanna talk about it?"

I give her the story in snapshots: the church doorway, the long walk down Mission Street, the car bumper, the ambulance. Tom's appearance lies on the cutting room floor. She doesn't mention him, either.

After a moment of deliberation, Cassidy hands me her scarf. I loop it around my neck, moving slowly to stave off the pain. Cassidy surveys my handiwork at the next stoplight. "It's funny," she says. "I picked that out this morning, even though it looks horrible on me. On you, though, it's perfect. Must be fate."

"Or luck."

"No, fate. Why else would I wear cerise-colored—anything? That's a star-crossed scarf, for real."

"What's wrong with cerise?" I look at the scarf, which is a dark, cherry pink. I don't know cerise from chartreuse, or what skirt length goes with what heel height, despite Cassidy's patient and persistent tutoring.

Cassidy shakes her head. "Cerise overpowers me. It's perfect for your complexion, though. You don't even look like you got stabbed."

"Thanks a lot."

We drive under the shadow of an enormous building. A man in dirty black sweatpants sits on the sidewalk, next to a shopping cart filled with trash bags. His eyes meet mine as we pass. A moment later, the car's in sunlight again.

"Traffic's gonna be awful going back," Cassidy says. "If I stayed the night, would that be awkward?"

"I don't think so. I'll call her."

Cassidy leans back in her seat, blows a stray blonde bang out of her face.

"Cass, you don't have to—"

Cassidy silences me with a look. "Your sister tried to kill you. For all we know, she's trailing you right now."

I look back reflexively and see the back seat, full of tissue-topped shopping bags.

"What about Nate?"

"Nate can look after himself for one night. No one's trying to kill *him*. Except me."

Cassidy and I wouldn't be friends if we met today. She's blunt, even when she shouldn't be. She's cynical to the point of perpetual gloom. Her interest in culture begins and ends with fashion magazines—hence the gloom. She's still the best friend I've ever had. We're there for each other in a way no one else is. That's what counts, not the music she listens to or the books she doesn't read.

"Thank you so much, Cass," I say, and give her a one-armed hug. White-bright pain bolts up my side. I pull away, blink away the tears. A perfunctory smile flickers across her face.

The San Francisco Bay gleams in the late afternoon light. Tiny white sailboats dot the water below. I lean back in my seat, watching the beams of the Golden Gate Bridge fly past my window. The fence's bars turn into a blurred red haze over the water.

Mom, it turns out, is over the moon at the thought of a sleepover, "Just like when you were girls." Cassidy lived with us for the last year of high school. She reminds Mom of the good times, before Dad died and Leah vanished into the drug life.

Cassidy gazes intently at the traffic ahead. "What were you doing at church?" she asks. I tell her. "Are you Catholic now?"

"I don't know what I am."

"Is he cute?"

"Who, Jesus?"

"No! The, you know, the new guy. The one who reawakened your love for the Lord? Is he Mexican or something?"

"There is no guy this time."

"That's a shame."

Cassidy's referring to an old college crush of mine, who led one of UC Davis's Christian groups. I went to church twice a week, for about six months, just to be near him. Yes, he was that cute. Church was nice, a bit bland: lots of platitudes about Doing the Right Thing and Loving One's Neighbor. The music was old, staid, not that Jesus-is-my-boyfriend crap you hear on the radio. When my crush picked a different girl, I faded away from church, from Christianity, and never went back. Until today.

Sunlight sparkles on the water below. The sky is a cloudless pure blue, fading to white along the horizon. The Farallon Islands stand, tiny and hazy-gray, above the water. A seagull hovers parallel to the fence, floating on a breeze.

Cassidy sighs and leans back in her seat.

"What?" I say.

"It's weird, you being religious again."

"I lit a candle in a church. I'm hardly an up-and-coming saint."

"What would your dad say?"

"I don't know." And I don't. When Dad was a kid, his mom got sucked into a cult. They lived in a commune for a while. Dad refused to discuss it. If I pressed him, he'd say, "That's in the past." At some point, they left. That was it for Dad and religion.

"Would he be mad?"

"No, he…He never talked about that stuff. Good and evil, life after death, is there a God…it wasn't on his radar. Maybe he thought you die and that's it. No mystery involved." An image rises from the depths: Dad's coffin, lowering into the earth.

We pass into the Rainbow Tunnel. I love everything about

tunnels: the cylindrical roar of the air, the tube lights strobing overhead, the glowing red taillights in front of us. We leave the tunnel, soaring high above Sausalito, past highway lights, bushes, and golden-green pines.

Cassidy laughs.

"What?"

"Your sister, my brother, they both tried to kill us. We could start a club."

"With badges."

"Of course. A couch badge, for every hundred hours of therapy. I'd have a dozen of those. Paper bag badges for panic attacks. Flashbulbs for flashbacks."

"A building block for every time you block a number or—"

"Yes—*yes*. I'd have *so* many block badges." Cassidy's laugh is bright and sharp, like mirror shards under a spotlight. The smile oozes off her face. She sighs, runs a hand through her hair.

"He hasn't tried to call you again, has he?" I ask.

Cassidy shakes her head. "Téa said he looks homeless now. Long beard, long fingernails, broken teeth. Mom wants to go to Mongolia, hand him off to the shamans there."

"They're going to Mongolia? When?"

"Who cares."

Cassidy's brother, Jack Paradise "Slice" Clark, is a paranoid schizophrenic. We think so, anyways; he's never been officially diagnosed. When their parents weren't on vacation, which was rare, they "treated" Slice with new age moonshine: essential oils, reflexology, crystals, herbs. None of it worked.

When Cassidy was sixteen, her brother tried to kill her by drowning her in the toilet. If her sister, Téa, hadn't stopped him, Cassidy might have died. Today, Slice still lives with his parents, still goes by his high school nickname. Cassidy doesn't talk to them.

"He's a sensitive soul, Cassie," I say.

"He's a sensitive soul, and we have to *love* him," Cass says, taking on her mother's ethereal voice. "If we could only *see* and *appreciate* your brother's unique perspective, he wouldn't have these little issues."

Richardson Bay glints through a break in the trees. I close my eyes against the sun.

"How old is Slice? He must be, what, late thirties, early forties? Good God. *Tempus*—"

"He turns thirty-nine…tomorrow, actually. You guys have the same birthday, remember?"

"What do you mean, tomorrow—oh." I check my phone screen, look for the first time at the date: *Thursday, August 25.*

"Shit. It is tomorrow, isn't it?"

"Your golden birthday. Twenty-six on the twenty-sixth. And we both have the day off. It's fate."

"Or luck." I rest my forehead against the glass. A small hill, covered in dry grass and green fennel, zooms past my window.

"Shit," Cassidy says.

"What?" I say, right as I see it. A field of red brake lights stretches from the bottom of the hill to the overpass. Gridlock. Cassidy eases the car to a stop. The car next to us blasts some bass-heavy song.

"I think it's the Backstreet Boys," Cassidy giggles. "Listen." She rolls down her window. Sure enough, the driver of the car— invisible behind tinted windows—is playing "Larger Than Life." We sing along until the car pulls ahead. I look out my window. A white-haired man in neon spandex zooms down the bike path. A speedboat skims across Richardson Bay.

Cassidy pulls the emergency brake. She half stands in her seat and reaches into the back, rifling through her bags. At length she sits back down, hands me a little red box. I open the top. It's a cupcake.

"Early birthday present. Strawberry's okay, right?"

I cry, red-faced ugly baboon crying, hiding my face in my hands. The car lurches forward. Cassidy rubs my back. My fit dies down as the traffic clears.

"Don't worry. Tomorrow will be better."

"It better be." I blink away the tears. "After Leah left rehab, I went to a recovery group. Not NA, maybe...I dunno, Women for Sobriety? Anyway. The group leader said, 'Whenever you want to do something you know you shouldn't, play the tape to the end.'"

"The tape?"

"The movie of your life. Say you want to do drugs. Ignore the craving. Think about what happens after. You'll run through your money, start stealing again, sooner or later you'll get kicked out of your apartment, maybe live in your car, strip clubs, craigslist, skeezy old guys, drug hovels—over and over, till you die."

"Now *that's* depressing."

"That's the point. Don't stop at the good times. If you keep doing drugs, you won't ever leave a mark on the world, not even as a tragic figure. Just an obituary in a database, a journal in a shed somewhere. The end."

A close silence fills the car.

"Would that stop you?" Cassidy says.

"What, playing the tape? I think so."

"I don't. Look at me—I *need* to lose fifteen pounds, I *want* to lose fifteen pounds, but I can't not eat the doughnuts in the break room. They're not even good."

"You're not fat."

"Not yet. I've tried MyFitnessPal, keto, paleo, ankle weights, even nicotine gum. But if I let my mind wander for a second— bam. Chow time."

"If you can't do it, nobody can."

Cassidy shoots me the evil eye. "Almost everyone who loses weight gains it back within two years," she says. "Talk about playing the tape to the end. All that does is tell you who you are. What you're going to do, whether you want to or not. Knowing the outcome doesn't make any difference."

"That's awful."

"It's realistic. Even divine intervention only goes so far. Remember that Bible verse you showed me once, 'I don't do the good I want to do, and I do the evil that I don't want,' something like that? Story of the human race."

"No," I say, fighting the sinking feeling in my gut. "It's not easy to change, but you can do it. People don't because they're sleepwalking with their eyes open. That's why every AA, therapy, all these programs, make you acknowledge your problem before you try to change. If you wake up, you have a chance."

Cassidy smiles. The sun bursts through the clouds.

"What?" I say, pulling down the visor.

"That's such an Amazing Amy answer. If only people could think like *I* think, do what *I* know is right—'"

"Yeah, me and only me. I'm the only person in the world who—"

"That's not what I mean. As long as I've known you, you've pushed people to do what you want, 'for their own good.' Remember Tom's stories about Rome? You can't force him to publish those, but you tried."

"I only said—"

Cassidy smiles.

"You haven't read those stories," I protest. "He's got enough material for a whole series. If he'd only talk to a—what?"

Cassidy shakes her head, smiling. I glare at her for a moment before turning to the window.

Cassidy and I talk about other things—old classmates, ex-boyfriends, the latest dramas at our workplaces—but her words gnaw a hole in my head all the way up Highway 101. Cassidy asks me what I've been watching. Nothing, really, since I moved to El Cerrito. She's shocked that I removed myself from Tom's Netflix account. "Voluntarily? You really are an up-and-coming saint."

Cassidy turns onto Railroad Avenue, the main thoroughfare through Woodacre. Dappled sunlight covers the road. The tires crunch over gravel and twigs. We drive by the same houses I've passed thousands of times, the same redwoods and willow trees and Monterey pines, the same passion flower vines, rock gardens, and high wooden fences.

I roll down the window, letting the afternoon air pass over my face. It's always strange to come back here, to a familiar place that doesn't remember us. We might have been gone twenty years, or twenty minutes.

"This is so weird," Cassidy says. "It's like the past has been waiting for me all this time. I still have nightmares about going back."

"To Woodacre, or the past?"

"Both."

A few kids, middle school age, run along the street's edge, giggling.

"Baxter, wait up!" one of them calls out. The kid at the head of the group, a ginger in a Burger King crown, turns back. His dark brown eyes meet mine as we pass.

"Let's go for a drive tomorrow," I say to Cassidy. "We could go down to Stinson, see my grandma. I haven't seen her in forever. We'll blast some Wolfmother, drink beer on the beach. I'll flirt with some cute surfer boys, pretend I'm still seventeen. If I wear this scarf, they might flirt back."

"If you want."

The car ascends steep and narrow streets, higher and higher into the hills. Cassidy swings the car onto Blackwood Drive, a one-lane road winding through the forest. A police cruiser is parked in front of Mom's house. Cassidy pulls up alongside it, rolls down her window.

"Have they caught her yet?" she says. The policeman's unfocused eyes meet hers.

"Leah Snowberger. My sister," I call out. I pull down the scarf, point to the bandage on my neck.

The officer stares at the bandage, then stumbles out of the car. He checks our IDs, says something into his walkie talkie, does another survey of the road.

"Nobody's seen her," he says when he's finished, shuffling from foot to foot. "Sorry. Nobody's been by here all day."

Cassidy pulls into the driveway, rolls up the windows, shuts off the car. We sit there, listening to the engine click and cool, hearing a breeze rustling over our heads.

Redwood trees loom over the car. I look out into the cool darkness of the forest, at the shrubs and shoots growing dense between the trees.

"Let's pretend that everything's normal," I say. "Let's pretend that my Dad's still alive, that Donald Trump isn't running for President, that my sister's not a junkie. Let's pretend that we're not just killing the planet, that our lives mean something. Let's pretend we're not part of some big cosmic joke."

Cassidy looks over at me, reaches out, readjusts my scarf. "If you want," she says. She doesn't look at me as she gets out of the car.

CHAPTER THREE
117 BLACKWOOD DRIVE

"OH, SWEETIE, HOW *are* you?"

Mom envelops me in a hug. My ribs almost crack with pain, but I don't dare move. I breathe in the close house air, all cotton and Glade. Macchiato, Mom's tiny, brown-and-white Pomchi, trots into the front room, his collar jingling. Wolf Blitzer intones something on the living room TV. Cassidy helps me take off my jacket as Macchiato jumps at our legs.

"Cassidy," Mom says, reaching out. Cassidy returns the hug with one arm, awkwardly patting her back.

"It's nice to see you again, Mrs. Snowberger."

"Call me Jackie, *please*." Mom smiles at us, eyes soft and wet. "Look at you two. I remember when you were girls, and now…" The smile drops from her face. She's staring at my neck. The scarf's slipped down. I hastily readjust it.

Mom kneels down to dandle Macchiato. Cassidy and I side-step her, exchanging a glance. Mom's redone the kitchen. The cabinets are golden-hued wood, the counters black stone. Ingredients are laid out neatly by the stove: bay leaves, onions, chili peppers, spice bottles, a ginger root.

"I'll show you how to tie a French twist," Cass murmurs, jutting her chin toward my scarf. "Stays in place."

"The pork's in the fridge," Mom says behind us. Macchiato trots behind her, worry in his eyes. She walks up beside me, picks up a jar of mecalef. "I couldn't find any garam masala, but I have this. Is it alright?"

"It's fine."

"You won't make it *too* spicy, will you, honey?"

"We can make something else."

"No, no, no. It's your birthday, L—Amy. What is it with you and spicy food, anyway? You never liked it as a kid."

"I told you. The lunch thief at my old job only stopped when I had spicy food. Then she tried to get me in trouble. Some people, right?"

"Your blouse is torn."

I look down. Sure enough, there's a giant gash in my blouse where Leah's knife cut through it. Of course there is. Why didn't I see it before? I hug Mom. A few sobs rack her bird-like body. Macchiato jumps up our legs, barks. Mom, sniffling, looks away with an embarrassed smile.

The kitchen fills with the smell of peppers, onions, coriander, and bubbling pork. Macchiato peers up at me, begging for scraps. Cassidy shows Mom how to connect her phone to the Bluetooth speaker, again.

"You can run a board meeting but you can't figure out Bluetooth?" I chide.

"It's my only weakness. Officially, that is."

Bossa nova jazz fills the kitchen: muted trumpets, saxophones, lilting Portuguese, soft drums and cymbals. Mom relaxes, opens a bottle of wine, drinks, laughs. Vindaloo cooks fast, so I stand over the stove while Mom and Cassidy putter around. After spirited begging, Macchiato grunts and curls up in the corner of the kitchen, his soulful eyes boring into mine.

Cassidy tells Mom about her wedding. "Nate arranged everything. He called in every favor to fast-track our reservation. That *never* happens. The only thing I had to worry about was my outfit, hair, and makeup."

"And you called me."

"And I called you. My maid of honor."

"You could have planned a little further in advance," Mom grumbles. "How was City Hall?"

"Insane. People everywhere. This huge crowd of tourists took pictures of us. Even the mayor was there for a second. He liked my dress."

"Your dress?"

Cassidy closes her eyes, preparing herself for the revelation. "Vintage Valentino. Cool-toned red, tea length, off-the-shoulder with cap sleeves. Matching lipstick, matching nails. Shoes dyed to match—thank *God* they came out right, I was terrified they'd be amaranth or burgundy or something. And this pearl necklace Nate gave me—I swear, he knows nothing about jewelry, but it *fit*."

"Why not white?"

"We've been together since college. Who'd believe...um."

"I wore a gray dress," I say, rushing past the awkward moment. "It was about, um, knee length—"

"—it was adorable. Pewter with black polka dots, gathered knee-length—wait, was it box pleated? No, it was gathered, right?"

"Yes," I say, mock-serious.

"And you brought—Amy made us this wonderful apricot jam."

"You made apricot jam?" Mom says, her eyes shining. "We used to make that when the girls were little. As a family."

"Could we make some this weekend? Nate and I tried, but it tasted off. If you showed me how, I'd be in your debt forever."

I look at Mom, her face framed by expensively gray hair. The wine in her glass catches the light. She's so different from the harried woman I knew growing up. Which one is the real Jackie Snowberger? *Even divine intervention only goes so far.* How far, exactly?

Mom tells us her wedding story: New Year's Day, the hungover groomsmen, Grandma Mimi throwing a tantrum, Aunt Zelda lighting off fireworks. Cassidy and I pretend it's a new story.

"Richard didn't want to get married," Mom says, which *is* new. "He thought you 'don't have to tell the state that you're in love.' You can thank his mother for that brilliant idea."

"How did you change Dad's mind?"

Mom scoffs. "*I* didn't do anything. The only person who could change Rich's mind was Rich himself. Even that was touch and go sometimes."

"Like Grandma Rose."

Mom nods, pointing to me while swallowing. "Exactly like Rose. You know she still owns this house? I made her an offer years ago—a very fair, very generous offer, even. She smiled, shook her head."

"At least you're saving on the property tax."

"That's what keeps me tethered to this place. That and, well, being broke. Rehab isn't cheap. Or effective..." She pours herself another glass. I turn back to the stove.

"How did Rich change his mind?" Cassidy says.

"One day, he looked at me—he had his hands on his hips,

like a gunslinger—and he said, 'Jackie, how'd you like to stop being a De Paul and become a—'"

"What's that?"

"My maiden name, hon. I was—"

"No, that sound."

We strain our ears, past the jazz, the kitchen fan, the bubbling pork. Mom turns down the speaker.

"Forget it," Cassidy says. "It's gone."

Cassidy brings the speaker, now playing a slow, sleepy rendition of "Ev'ry Time We Say Goodbye," onto the back porch. Mom's already out there, lighting tea candles. Macchiato sits on Mom's lap, watching the food with enormous, hopeful eyes. The evening air carries the scent of wood smoke, redwoods, and flowers.

"A toast," Mom says, raising her glass. Cassidy and I share a puzzled look.

"To growing up. Thank God you only have to do it once, right?"

"Amen."

We clink glasses. The conversation flows, from cooking shows to our worst coworkers. Macchiato explores the backyard, sniffing at the tree line. Mom hisses at "election flu."

"I can't talk about *him*," Mom says emphatically. "Somehow, though, every single conversation, he worms his way—"

"I know!"

"It's terrible."

"I have to force myself to turn the TV off. It's a car crash—"

"Look!"

Cassidy points to the woods behind our house. A bright light shines through the trees, casting long rays into the backyard. Macchiato's collar jingles as he bolts through the backyard, away from the forest.

"Oh, they're back," Mom says. "There's some church choir that practices out there, late at night. I hear them singing sometimes. Strange, beautiful music. I can never make out the words."

Macchiato's claws scrabble against the porch wood. He scratches at the back door, whining.

"What's that light, though?" Cassidy says.

"Lanterns, maybe? I don't know. Oh! I almost forgot." Mom gets up and walks into the house. Macchiato runs in after her. We watch the forest, straining to hear any music. The song on the speaker fades out, leaving only silence. No wind rustles the trees. No birds sing. The light swings wildly through the woods, casting shadows and beams into the backyard.

"She's sad," Cassidy says. The light touches her face, making her glow like one of Fra Angelico's holy women.

"Of course she's sad. Her husband's dead, one daughter's a drug addict, the other's still single—"

"Still? You're twenty-five."

"You're married. And I'm only twenty-five for one more day. Tick, tock."

Mom returns, holding a small box wrapped in silver paper. An envelope, with *Amy* written across it, is taped to its top. "Happy birthday," she says.

I swallow the sob. The light from the woods flashes red through my eyelids. A strong floral scent wafts out of the forest. Mom rubs my back.

"You're turning into such a lovely young woman," she says. "Your father would be so proud."

"Thanks, Mom." I put the present on the table.

"Aren't you going to open it?"

"It's not my birthday yet."

The light passes over Mom's face. A few voices, high and sexless, sing out deep in the forest, swaying around some minor chord. When I look to the woods, they stop. The light's gone. So is the sun.

Then I hear the song playing on the speaker. It's a jazzy cover of "The Circle Game," one of the songs our family sang together every Christmas. The singer even sounds like Leah, if Leah could sing and didn't smoke drugs. Mom sighs and refills her glass.

"It's so weird," Cassidy says. We're washing the dishes while Mom brushes her teeth.

"What's weird?"

"There's not one photo of Leah. Anywhere."

She nods to the photo collage on the far wall. There's me at six, dressed as Heidi for Halloween. There are Mom and Dad, kissing at their wedding, both wearing party hats. There's Dad at seventeen, running track with the wind in his hair. There are four photos of Misty, the beagle Mom adopted after Dad died. There's the ocean, stretching out blue into the horizon. There are no photos of Leah.

I walk to the mantle in the living room. It's cluttered with framed pictures: Mom and Dad on their anniversary, me as a baby, Mom's grandfather squinting against the sun. There's a blue-glazed urn, pawprints painted on the lid. No photos of Leah. Not even the photo of Mom, pregnant with Leah, in all her eighties career-woman glory. I can see it if I close my eyes: Mom's giant hair, the phone cradled between her shoulder and ear, her belly straining against the buttons on her coat. It's not here.

I know this is Mom's way of coping. Putting away the pain. Moving on, as much as she can. I understood it in the abstract. It's scary in person.

When I come back to the kitchen, Cassidy's holding a cup. She hands it to me without a word. It's a photo cup of Leah and me, one teenage Halloween. I'm dressed as a French girl, scowling beneath a black beret.

"Is that a French twist?" I say, pointing to the scarf around my teenage self's neck. "Maybe we..." The sentence dies, unfinished. Leah's dressed as a gothic Lolita, complete with a poufy black skirt, but she's missing a face. Someone scratched it out, leaving a jagged white nothing in its place. A few fitful scratches run down the length of her dress.

"Bathroom's free," Mom says from the doorway, Macchiato under her arm. My hands fumble the cup onto the drying rack.

"Everything alright?"

"Everything's fine, Mrs.—Jackie. We'll be done soon."

"Don't worry about me, hon. I could sleep through the end of the world."

Mom hugs us both. She smells like toothpaste and hand cream. What if she sees the cup on the drying rack? If she does, her eyes gloss over it. When she leaves, we look at each other, waiting for her bedroom door to close. Cassidy takes the cup and looks at it again.

"That looks like a French twist," she says, pointing to my picture on the cup. "Do you remember how to tie it?"

"Not anymore."

Cassidy shows me how to tie a French twist in the bathroom mirror. "Now show me," she says, untying the scarf. I try three times, then make a show of measuring out my pain pills. She doesn't press the issue. We lie on the living room couches, try to fall asleep. I undo the scarf.

"You don't have to stick around tomorrow. If you and Nate have anything planned..."

"You're kidding. This is the first time in years I've felt like I had a family."

"Mom would adopt you if you asked her to. Just don't do drugs, and you're golden."

Cass falls asleep. I don't. My mind spins seven thousand times a second. I close my eyes.

Dad's family moved here after they left the cult. It was his home for the rest of his life. He came here every weekend through college and grad school. His parents gave him this house after he married Mom. He raised Leah and me under this roof. He died here.

Growing up, I always thought home was fixed. Home was 117 Blackwood Drive, breakfast in the kitchen, parties on the back porch, fussing with the shower knob, reading in bed. Home was finding remnants of the past everywhere: Richie and Zelda's height chart behind the wallpaper; old flyers for "Paradise Voyages," my grandfather's old travel agency; Dad's old yearbooks in the bottom of a box. Home was constant, eternal.

Now I see the truth. Dad's dead. He'll never again paw through the fridge, chase us through the yard, or putter around in the garage. Leah and I are grown and gone. 117 Blackwood Drive is Mom's home now, where she sits up watching the news, browses Facebook on her phone, mutters to herself as she folds the laundry. Someday she'll be gone.

I open my eyes again. The ceiling transforms under my gaze, revealing swirling patterns and phantoms. What will this house be like in fifty years? Sold off, remodeled, demolished? All that life, all those memories, dreams, and stories—all bubbles floating on a river.

If I keep the house, and raise my own family here...then what? Will my children—not Snowbergers, but Smiths or Hartegens or something else, maybe (some shameful part of me hopes) even Templetons—will they keep the house to start their own families? Where will they go when it's over?

After I left for college, Mom knocked down the wall between Leah's bedroom and mine. She ripped out the carpet, repainted, moved in an Aeron chair and a giant desk. The new room is both eerie and familiar. There's the window that used to be mine, the windows that used to be Leah's. There's a dim outline on the wall where Leah's door used to be. Other than this, everything is different. The floor is wood instead of carpet. The walls are painted a soothing, medical shade of white. *You are stronger and more powerful than you know*, a pink-and-gold poster says behind Mom's desk.

I walk to the place where my bed used to be. There's a box on the floor marked *MEMENTOS*. My rib smarts with pain as I bend down. Still, I have to know. Did Mom really destroy every trace of Leah?

She didn't. Here, in a leather-bound photo album, is toddler Leah grinning up at the camera. Leah, on the first day of kindergarten. Leah, hugging Mom's baby bump. And there's me, a baby, gazing into my sister's eyes.

Sobs pulse through my body, smarting at the crack in my rib. I remember Leah and me singing at Christmas, Leah teaching me how to skip a stone, Leah running ahead while I ran after her. We were innocent once, innocent and happy. Why did it turn out like this?

Everything changes, nothing disappears. Tom said that to me once, I don't remember when. But this *will* disappear. Even now, the Leah and Amy in these photos are gone, never to return. Who will take their places?

The sobs ebb away, leaving me hollow. There's a silver notebook at the bottom of the box. It's blank, save for indentations on a few pages. Maybe I used it to bear on while writing something. I consider rubbing a pencil across a page when exhaustion washes over me.

I lie on the floor. For the first time in hours, my rib doesn't hurt. I stare at the ceiling. Glow-in-the-dark stars shine down on me. Maybe they're real. Either way, I'm too tired to care.

"Happy birthday," I murmur, and close my eyes.

My alarm clock beeps at 6:00 a.m. Never mind that I haven't used a real alarm clock in a decade. Never mind that I fell asleep in Mom's office, with my phone in the other room. I set it on snooze without thinking. Its big red digital numbers barely register. I turn over and go to sleep, until it beeps again at 6:05. I sigh and get out of bed.

I brush my teeth in the bathroom. A red-and-blue toothbrush, just like my old one, sits in the same blue cup. Those painkillers must be stronger than I thought, because the sink seems taller than it was last night. I don't look in the mirror. I can't feel the bandage on my neck, or the stitches. Maybe they dissolved. Lucky break.

It's only when I'm back in my room that I realize something's wrong. It's my room, for one, not the office I fell asleep in. The wall between my room and Leah's is back. It's a museum piece, perfectly preserved. There's a Styrofoam mannequin head on my bookshelf, lips filled in with silver sharpie, bucket hat pulled over its eyes. I threw that head out a long, long, *long* time ago—unless Mom saved it. There are glow-in-the-dark stars pasted above my bed. And there, on the wall that shouldn't exist, is a photo of me dressed as Heidi, the colors more vivid than they were yesterday.

Here's my old dresser—the one I gave to Goodwill, circa 2008. What's it doing *here*? The second drawer sticks, same as I remember. I didn't know I remembered. Every drawer's full of kid clothes: jeans with elastic bands, pastel shorts, dinosaur shirts, overalls. Nothing I've worn for years. Nothing that would fit.

Not to mention that I'm wearing Paul Frank pajamas. I haven't worn Paul Frank anything since Bush was President. I look down the front of my top and—no. That's not possible, either.

I'm wide awake now. Something is very wrong. I'm skinnier and—and *shorter*. My hair's shorter, too. Did Cassidy cut my hair in the middle of the night? Did she put magic mushrooms in the vindaloo? What the fuck is this?

My hands reach for my neck. There's no sign of a cut there, not even a scab. My rib doesn't hurt, even when I press on it. It's as if yesterday—a whole lot of yesterdays—didn't happen. I check the clock again. 6:10. This alarm clock broke back in high school. *It* shouldn't exist, either.

I peek out of the bedroom door. No futons. No Cassidy. It smells different, with none of the faint doggy musk that Macchiato brought into the house. The couches look fuller and dirtier than they did yesterday. The TV set's different, too.

Icy fear pours down my spine. I can't find my purse, my wallet, my clothes, my phone, *anything* from my current life. Here's my old backpack, a colored pencil, a yearbook: Forest Knolls Middle School, 2002-2003. I flip to the sixth-grade class portraits. That's me, big teeth and short hair, baby fat face. The face I saw in the mirror.

I take a deep breath and re-enter the living room, hoping to see *something* from yesterday. Why would my adult things be in my room, anyway? Didn't I put my purse in the front hall? It must be there.

But there's nothing of mine anywhere. Not in the front hall, not on the couch, not in the bathroom. I'm about to do another sweep when something stops me cold.

It takes me a moment to identify it. There, on the mantle,

is a picture I know well: Mom, heavily pregnant, in an eighties power suit. It wasn't here yesterday. Neither was that picture of teenaged Leah, smiling on the beach.

Mom's in the kitchen, rustling papers. I can hear the coffee maker bubbling. The speaker's playing soft rock. *She's mastered Bluetooth, at last. Miracles do exist.*

"Mom," I call out as I walk toward the kitchen. "Do you have my clothes?"

I pause at the kitchen door. The song swells on the other side. *Suppose this is all in your head. What are you gonna say? She already lost one daughter. Don't make her lose another.*

"Mom, please don't panic," I say as I open the door. "I think I'm…"

My father sits at the kitchen table, reading a newspaper and eating a sandwich. He looks up at me. I scream.

It's my father, and he's *alive*.

CHAPTER FOUR
GHOSTS OF ADOLESCENCE PAST

My father died when I was nineteen. Sudden heart attack over breakfast. He was gone by the time his head hit the table.

"Like turning off a light switch," the coroner said, and snapped his fingers. "That quick."

At the funeral, Dad's boss cornered me to say that he told Richard to watch his diet, he told him to exercise, but Richard never listened, so here we are. I chased him out of the church and into the parking lot. "What the fuck does it matter now?" I screamed in his face. Before he closed his car door, he asked me to "be rational for once in your life." In the snottiest tone. Who says that to someone whose dad just died?

But Dad isn't dead. He's sitting right here. He meets my stare with a perplexed smile.

"Happy birthday," he says, and moves to stand. "How does it feel to be—whoa, easy!"

Dad stumbles backward as I glomp onto him. He smells like

cotton and camphor, the same as I remember. I didn't know I remembered. He strokes my hair. I can hear his heartbeat.

"Sweetie, what's the matter?" he says. "Did you have a bad dream?" Yes, Dad. I had a hideous nightmare where you were dead and you were never coming back and I didn't know if you went to hell or heaven or anywhere at all. But you're not in heaven or hell or the void anymore. You're here.

A feeling beyond happiness lifts me out of myself. If Richard Snowberger is alive, how can there be sorrow or fear or pain? Tears stream down my face.

"What's going on?" Mom says from the doorway.

"You tell me," Dad says over my head. His voice! It's really him. Have *I* died? Am I in heaven? Maybe one of my cuts opened overnight. Maybe everything since the car hit me has been a dying hallucination. Hot tears turn the kitchen into an avocado blur.

"Did you say anything?" Mom says.

"I was reading the paper."

"She's really upset."

"It's a big day today."

A big day? Must code for…wait, why is Mom here? Is she dead, too? What about Cassidy?

"It's okay," Dad says, stroking my hair. "It's not the end of the world."

I ball up his shirt in my fists. Is *this* my birthday present? Every bargain I offered to God and the devil, every wish on a dandelion or 11:11 or a lucky penny, every secret prayer I ever uttered since he died—they've all come true. And I don't know why.

The microwave roars to life. Leah's standing in front of it, shoulders slumped, black hair wild. My blood freezes. Leah turns, and—she's not the Leah from yesterday. She's *young*, with baby fat cheeks, acne constellation on her chin, an insouciant glare burning in her kohl-rimmed eyes.

And her outfit: purple velvet dress, fishnets, vinyl boots. Glossy dark lipstick, black ribbon necklace. Talk about the ghost of adolescence past. She even has chipped black nail polish and a mood ring. Did she die, too? Is this her fate, to live forever as teenage wildlife?

Mom's different, too. Gone are the dangly necklaces, the long silver bob, the deep lines around her eyes. This is the Mom I used to know: bottle-brown Rachel haircut, loose charcoal suit, coral lipstick. This is the Mom who's never quite there, even when she's hovering over you. She's wearing her old perfume, the one that smells like gardenias and champagne.

"Cheer up, kiddo," Dad says, handing me a tissue. "Summer vacation has to end sometime."

Summer vacation? That's a throwback. I haven't had a real summer vacation since middle school. Not since—

A cupcake, with chocolate frosting and star-shaped sprinkles, sits on the counter. There's a candle in it, waiting to be lit.

The world clicks into place. This is my thirteenth birthday, which fell on the first day of seventh grade. Which means this isn't real—not this house, not my room, not the cupcake, not Dad. I'm going to wake up and he'll be dead again. Forever.

Dream-Dad smiles at me and pats me on the back. He got up this morning, took a shower, grabbed the paper from the driveway, and started eating breakfast, not knowing that he doesn't exist.

I stagger into the living room. Something should give at this point: the TV, our wallpaper, maybe a mirror. I should disappear behind a curtain and reemerge in a forest, a classroom, a theater. Only I'm not disappearing. Nothing in the living room looks out of place. I stare into the mirror over the mantle. A child looks back at me. Her enormous gray eyes gaze into mine.

I pinch my inner elbow, as hard as I can. It hurts. Nothing changes.

"Amy, what's going on?" Mom's standing by the kitchen door, holding her purse. "You have to get going," she says, looking at her watch. "It's almost…"

I brush past her into the kitchen. I turn to Leah, now drinking from a mug by the counter. She raises her eyebrows at me.

"I'm older than you," I say. My voice sounds helium-squeaky, but it's true. Leah must be seventeen, almost ten years younger than me. I stifle a laugh. This *has* to be a dream. Get ready for another ride on the grief roller coaster, without seatbelts, safety restraints, or speed limits. A toast to growing up. Thank God you only have to do it once, right?

The front door slams. Mom's heels clack against the outside steps. I check the clock: six twenty-five, on the dot. Mom always left for work at six twenty-five. How did I forget that?

Everything, from the refrigerator hum to the color of the cabinets, strikes me as an obscene, magnificent joke. A laugh racks my body. Dad watches me, chewing his muffin. Leah looks at me like I've grown a third head.

As I get dressed, vague memories swim to the surface of my mind: kid after kid looking me up and down with scorn. Girls bumping me in the hallway as they passed. Boys asking lewd questions with stinker smiles. My gut hitches.

"Let's get going, Amy," Dad calls out from the kitchen. I empty my piggy bank, put most of the change in my backpack, a little more in my jeans' front pocket. There's a five and a twenty-dollar bill in my top dresser drawer. I'm putting them in my pocket when the connecting door opens. Leah's behind it, her eyes wide.

"You okay?" she says.

For a second, I see her future face, gaunt and vacant, overlaid on her teenage one. *You tried to kill me.* I flash her a grim smile. "I don't think so."

Leah looks me up and down as I empty my backpack. "You'll need those books."

"Not on the first day." *Why am I arguing with a dream-person?* "It's all syllabi, permission slips, that sort of thing."

Leah looks doubtfully at the books on my bed. "You know it's not gonna work, right?"

"What's not?"

"Playing crazy won't get you out of school. Even on your birthday. They'll put you on Prozac, and you'll *still* have to go. Ask me how I know."

I look through the bedside table drawers for something, anything, that will help me escape. In Marvel movies it's always The Glowing Thing: a space rock or magic stone or radioactive MacGuffin that shines with unearthly light. Where's my Glowing Thing? Where's my portal to the real world?

"You are playing crazy, right?" Leah's eyes dart from my face to my hands. "You didn't take any...you're not on anything, are you?"

"What did we do yesterday?"

"You mean Monday?" she says, laughing nervously. "I went to school. You were with Grandma, I think?"

"Why didn't I go to school?"

"Your school didn't start 'til today. Teacher development or something. You really don't remember?"

"We didn't meet at a church. You didn't see me lighting a candle..."

The smile falls from Leah's face. She pulls away. She's about to speak when Dad knocks on my door.

"Amy, let's go!" he yells. Leah walks backward into her room, still staring at me. Behind her is a canvas filled with graphite rays converging on a center point.

"What?" I say. Leah shakes her head, her eyes locked on mine.

"I dunno," she says. Dad pounds on the door again. Leah shakes her head, as if startled from a trance, and closes the door.

I feel the tip of Leah's knife pressing into my throat, hot blood dribbling down my neck, the car hitting me, my head knocking against the pavement. But there's no cut on my neck, no pain in my ribs. I feel my own hair, now chin-length and layered, with choppy bangs. This better be a fucking dream.

What was that expression on Leah's face? Does she have a shadow memory of things to come? Déjà vu—or would that be après vu? Maybe the future makes an impression on the past. Maybe that's the key that unlocks the door of this world.

Dad left his keys on the front hall table. I palm them and slip them into my pocket. Dad walks past me, musses my hair. It's wonderful to see him again, even if he's not real.

No one looks at me as I walk out the front door. I walk down the driveway, feeling the gravel crunching under my shoes, hearing the coins clink in my backpack. I don't glance back at the house. If I glance back, dream logic dictates that someone will see me and thwart my plan. The car door opens with a dull click.

"Sorry," I say, to no one in particular.

Tears blind me before I can sit down. Dad's car smells so familiar: cloth seats, wintergreen gum, old French fries and cheeseburgers, plus that ineffable Dad smell. I blink my tears away and adjust the seat. I can barely see over the dashboard. I stuff all the crud in the passenger seat, the jackets and fast food bags and cups, under my butt. A little better. I can reach the pedals if I stretch.

The engine trundles to life. I back out of the driveway inch by lurching inch. *Play the tape to the end,* I tell myself. I have to get out of here before I go completely crazy. That's how these dreams work, isn't it?

Dad runs down the driveway—as much as he can run—as the car lurches onto Blackwood Drive. He lumbers after me, shouting something I refuse to hear. I turn on the radio. A car commercial drowns out his voice.

He'll call 911 in a minute. Let him; he doesn't know he's an illusion. The real him is long gone.

Sir Francis Drake is the only road out of Woodacre. Sooner or later I'll have to take it. If Dad is on the phone with the police, then they'll stop me long before I get to the city. I won't be able to escape, let alone figure out what this dream is trying to teach me.

I need a different car.

The streets in Woodacre loop and wind into each other. If the police are near, it's only a matter of time before I meet them. Especially if this is a dream. I survey the cars parked along each street.

Sirens wail in the middle distance. I park the car by the side of the road. The sirens draw closer, from no obvious direction. I run up the road and around the corner. With mad faith, I test the back door of an old BMW. It opens, revealing a pile of blankets. I slam the door shut behind me, wrap myself inside them. The movement shifts some empty bottles, which cascade to the floor with deafening clanks. Why is it, whenever you're trying to be quiet, every noise you make is louder than a foghorn?

A long silence, punctuated by sirens. A car passes feet from my head, then stops around the corner. Footsteps crunch and scud along the gravel, getting closer. I wonder if my hair pokes out, if my silhouette is obvious beneath the blanket's folds.

Footsteps stop next to the car. I hold my breath. Static, scratchy voices, blips from a nearby walkie talkie. A man says something, his words muffled by the car windows.

"Morning," a voice, male, older, calls out from the opposite side of the car.

"Morning."

"Something I can help you with, Officer?"

"We're looking for a girl who, uh, stole her dad's car. She 'parked' it right around the corner."

"What's she look like?"

"Uh, white girl, thirteen, brown hair, gray eyes, about five-foot-three."

"Haven't seen anything."

"Thanks."

"Of course."

The policeman's footsteps continue down the street. The other man trudges through the gravel to the driver's side door. I hold my breath.

The driver's side door opens. The seat creaks in front of me. I suppress a sudden, overwhelming urge to cough. A key slides into the lock up front. The engine sputters to life. The car dips and rolls as it pulls off the gravel and onto the asphalt. I scrabble at the seatbelt buckle to keep from falling.

The man drives in silence. No radio, no music, no monologue, no cell phone conversation. I listen to the rumble of the engine, air streaming overhead, the swoosh of passing cars. I try to guess, based on the traffic and the number of stops, where we are. Everything in me wants to cough, to scratch an itch on my back. I bite my knuckle until it bleeds. The car speeds up, makes no more stops or turns. We must be on Sir Francis Drake.

I count down from ten, twenty, sixty, one hundred, then one hundred again. We're still driving. Bloody drool drips down my cheek. The roar of traffic surrounds us. A highway, maybe 101, maybe 580. I shut my eyes. *If he gets into an accident now, you will die. You might kill him as well.* I grab the seatbelt buckle.

We're passing through a tunnel. Has to be—the cylindrical roar of the air, the rhythms of shadow and light. Most likely the Rainbow Tunnel, but I can't be sure. I don't dare look.

More time passes. The front window rolls down, lets in a blast of cool air. The blanket flaps around my legs. Fear saps all strength from my body. The driver's seat creaks under him. The car slows nearly to a stop. A moment later I hear him say "Thanks." "Thank you," a woman replies outside the window. The car speeds up again.

The tollbooth. We must be in San Francisco. The driver hums.

After a small eternity of steep hills and sudden stops, after pitching forward and back and gripping the seatbelt buckle for dear life, the car slows and comes to a stop. I strain my ears, hear nothing but urban silence. The driver isn't getting out. He's not shifting in his seat. What is he *doing*? Part of me wants to pull the covers back. The superseding part forbids it.

"You wanna explain yourself?"

For a moment, I think the driver's talking to someone, maybe on the phone, maybe outside. And then it hits me like a blast of cold air.

"I know you're back there," he says. He's smiling with his voice. "Why don't you take those blankets off, so we can talk?"

I wish, on a cellular level, that the policeman found me in the backseat. If only Mom was reaming me out right now—instead of the literal reaming I'll endure in a few minutes. So much for dream logic.

I kick off the blanket, or try to, and lunge for where the door handle should be. Empty air. I scream. Any minute now, he'll grab me. One hand closes around the handle and wrenches the door open.

My head hits the concrete as I fall out. A tire passes by, feet away. My feet are still tangled in the blanket. My head's still on the pavement, ready to be shorn from my shoulders by the next passing car. I scream again.

This still doesn't feel like a dream.

When I fall out of the car, when I stumble around it and onto the sidewalk, I run, as fast as I can, up a series of steps—and through the doors of Saint Patrick's Church. I stop at the atrium, exactly where Leah stood yesterday. The scene of the crime.

It looks a little different. The atrium is in disrepair, the windows dirtier, the doors more scuffed. But there's no mistaking where I am. I push through the second doors. The stained-glass windows are dirtier than yesterday, the pews less well-varnished, the lights above the reredos dingier. I walk to the candles, watch their flames burn in the semi-darkness.

It's dream logic. That's why you're here. This is when you got mugged—down to the minute. Right on cue, the bell tolls overhead. *Dah duhh dah-duhhh...duh-dah da-duhhh.* I'm counting off the eighth bell when a voice startles me at my ear. A familiar voice.

"Let's talk," he says. Low, calm. Definitely not a suggestion.

CHAPTER FIVE
CREEP MAGNET

A MASS BEGINS at the front of the church. A gray-haired priest stands in front of the altar, speaking to a dozen scattered parishioners. I drop a coin in the offering box, light a candle, say a wordless prayer, cross myself the way I've seen in movies. Maybe, if I act normal, everything strange will disappear.

I watch the driver out of the corner of my eye. He's not a monster—not at first glance, anyway. He's in his fifties or early sixties, with receding white hair, a ponytail, a close-cropped beard. His eyes are calm and intelligent. He's wearing linen slacks, a white peasant shirt, leather moccasins. He could be the meditation leader at a Buddhist retreat, a jewelry teacher at a community college, an old session musician who gives guitar lessons to students. I've seen this Mr. Patchouli type at Farmer's Markets, concerts, gallery openings, fundraisers. He smells of smoke and fresh-cut flowers.

"What are you running from?" he says.

"You tell me. You're clearly in the know."

"Am I?" He meets my look with an ironic smile. I feel suddenly, intensely thirteen. A walking target, a creep magnet. Any lingering dreamlike feelings die in this moment. Whatever this is, it's real enough.

"Let's start with something simple," he says. "My name's Claude Belissan. What's yours?"

"Rosemary," I hear myself say. My middle name.

"It's a pleasure to meet you, Rosemary. Who are you named after?"

"My grandmothers."

"Both Rosemarys?"

"Something like that."

Claude smiles, takes a step closer. I step back, jostling the table full of candles. Claude holds up his hands. "What brought you here, Rosemary?"

"You did, genius. You were driving."

"Really."

I try to meet the eyes of someone, anyone, who can intervene. There's no one in the back pews. The priest stares down at the altar, doing something with his hands.

"You can tell me the truth," Claude says.

"Sure, Claude." I take another step back. The priest's voice pops in the microphone, dragging Claude's attention away. I bolt past him, fly through the doors. When I get to the bottom of the steps, I run—I can run *fast*, faster than I ever remember running—and venture a look back. He's not behind me.

I jog down Mission Street, my heart thumping in my chest. No payphone in sight. A sunburned woman on the opposite sidewalk pushes a shopping cart containing a pit bull. A man in a suit, talking on a tiny silver phone, side-eyes me as I reach the crosswalk. I can't see Claude anywhere. That doesn't mean he's gone.

Knots of men in dirty clothes sprawl on the sidewalk. I notice one with a scraggly beard and grayish dreadlocks, crouching on a skateboard, blankets piled around his waist. The blankets fall away. The stumps where his legs should be are covered by cut-offs, their frayed ends trailing along the ground. As he pushes himself along the street, shame floods through me. Wouldn't he trade places with me in half a second, if he could?

"Sir? Sir! Hang on—"

The man stops, looks up. I come level with him, stoop down. I reach into my pocket and fish out a crumpled bill. Hopefully it's the five instead of the twenty. I want to go to heaven, but not too soon.

The man's face breaks open in a smile. "Thanks, sweetie," he says as he takes the money. "You have a good day now."

Orpheline is a few blocks away, on Hawthorne. I could go there, or—a silver car juts into the crosswalk.

"Hey pigtails!" the driver barks. I jump back and run toward the nearest bodega. The driver lapses into a guttural moan before speeding off. I head to the back of the store, eyeing the convex mirror in the corner. Sometimes these guys drive around five or six times before they quit.

Two men enter the store, dressed like Barksdale's soldiers from *The Wire*. They amble toward the back, toward me. One of them meets my eyes with a dull, shark-like stare. Worst-case scenarios unspool through my mind. I speedwalk to the exit. They don't follow me. There are no silver cars in sight. I bolt up Seventh Street, heading toward Market.

A hand grabs my wrist, pulls me back. I look up into the pink, peeling face of a boy with greenish dreadlocks. He smiles, showing a mouthful of sparkling white teeth. Twenty, maybe younger. His eyes burn up and down my body as I fight against his grip. He's stronger than he should be.

"Leave me alone!" I shout.

"Be nice," he says, pulling me toward him. He reaches for my other arm.

"She's a kid, man."

"Let me go!" My scream comes out tiny, shrill. He's got both of my arms now. I can't break free.

"You're gonna get us in trouble, dude."

"What? It's fine. We're just talking."

"Cop. There's a cop, man."

"Where?" As my captor turns, someone yanks me backward. An icy fist clenches my heart. Here it comes, whatever it is. My arms break free of the captor's grip. Whoever's holding me spins me around, shoves me away.

"Go," a voice, not my captor's, bellows behind me. I stumble, then sprint away. When I reach Market, I glance back. A few kids hold my captor, talking to him, while he stares after me, eyes on fire.

There are a few payphones in the Metreon, right by the bathrooms. I call my own cell phone first. I massage my wrist, try to rub away the street kid's touch. The fake street kid, judging by the state of his teeth.

As the phone rings, I stare at a sticker pasted by the coin slot. It's the same as the ones I saw yesterday: black lines, converging in a center point, surrounded by a snake eating its tail. What is that called, that snake symbol? There's a word for it, Greek or Greek-sounding. The ringing stops.

"Hi, you've reached Rob and Sarah. Leave us a message and we'll call you back." *Beep.*

I count the remaining coins on my palm. Almost six dollars. Enough for a few calls, or one long one.

Cassidy's cell phone number has been the same since high

school. She made me memorize it, "in case something happens." Thanks, Cass. The phone rings twice.

"Humboldt Acquisitions," a sleepy voice answers. Not Nate's.

"Hey, is Cassidy there?"

"Cassidy...oh." Groaning, shifting on the other end of the line. "Sure, we got, uh, Cassidy. You want any kind in particular, or...?"

I hang up.

I don't remember Tom's number, but I remember his parents'. It's my home phone number with a 928 area code. I once thought that was an auspicious sign. Now it turns my stomach.

I shove almost every quarter I have into the slot. The phone rings three times.

"Hello?" a familiar voice answers.

"Tom?"

"Uh-huh."

"Tom Templeton, from Prescott, Arizona?"

"Yee-up."

"Were you in San Francisco yesterday, by any chance?"

He laughs. "What's the rumor this time?" He sounds relaxed, happy, the way he used to sound after a beer or two.

"Why aren't you in school?"

"I'm sick."

"You're a...junior in high school, is that right?"

"I'm a senior, actual...wait, what?"

"My name is Amy. Amy Rosemary Snowberger. Do you remember me?" I put in four more quarters before he speaks again.

"I don't...how do I know you?"

"Please keep writing your Roman stories," I say. "Show them

to someone at UA. You're already taking classes there, right? If you keep—"

"Did Holly tell you to do this?"

"No, Tom. Holly was not in any way involved—"

"What did she say about me?"

"You're already obsessed with her? Fucking really, Tom? She doesn't even notice you!"

"I'm not obsessed with her! This is—"

"She's not into you, Tom. She doesn't love you. You can't force someone to love you by doing them favors."

Numb silence on the other end. I remember these silences. It's our old pattern of argument, seen through the wrong end of a telescope. I squeeze the remaining quarters in my palm. *What's wrong with you? He's not the man who broke your heart. He's a kid.* I want to say something, anything, but the words stop in my throat.

A flash of white catches my eye. Claude Belissan approaches from across the courtyard, his peasant top flapping in the wind. He smiles at me, stretches out his arms.

"I gotta go," I say into the phone. "Take care, Tom."

"Who are you?" he says as I hang up. The payphone swallows the quarters with a mechanical belch. I turn and walk away.

"You running off again?" Claude says behind me.

"I gotta talk to somebody. Not you."

The bells chime overhead: *Dah duhh dah-duhhh...duh-dah da-duhhh.* I say nothing as I walk toward the church. Claude follows me inside.

"I have something to tell you."

Silence. I look through the little screen. A man sits on the other side, eyes forward. Smooth skin shines through the hair on his scalp.

"You're not gonna believe it," I venture. I know this ritual from films and TV shows. You can say anything in here, even that you killed somebody, and the priest can't tell a soul. He can't lock you up, he can't put you in a mental ward. All he can do is listen and forgive.

So why is saying it so hard?

"You all right?" the priest says.

I've already fucked up. I didn't say "Bless me father, for I have sinned," or tell him how many weeks since my last confession—because there was no last confession. Leah and I were baptized Catholic, mostly to appease my grandmother, Mimi De Paul. But Mimi died when I was a toddler, and my college crush was a Calvinist.

"You can probably tell from my voice that I'm a kid," I blurt out. "And apparently, it's 2003. Right?"

"As far as I know."

"What if I told you that, for me, yesterday wasn't 2003, but 2016. I was twenty-five. I had a job, health insurance, my own apartment—well, a room in an apartment. Now, I've stepped through a doorway into my past, and I don't know how to walk back through it."

The priest clears his throat.

"That's a new one," he says, with a light chuckle. "You don't think it was a dream?"

I think of Leah's knife at my throat, the car slamming into me, the pain pulsating in my ribs. "I doubt it."

"I hope this isn't a dream of yours, either. I'd hate to think what happens to me if you wake up."

I look down at my inner arms. Even in the half-light of the confessional, the bruise is obvious: two little egg-shaped rings, surrounded by green splotches. Pinch bruise.

The priest doesn't speak. I count down from twenty, then

twenty again. Has he fallen asleep? Did he press a secret button, like a bank teller? Is he angry? Is he dead?

I tell him everything, starting with Leah's knife and ending with Claude. When I'm done, I sigh and lean back on my heels.

"God walks with all of us, even when we can't feel him beside us," the priest says. "He feels your confusion, your terror, your pain. There's nothing you can hide from him."

"I wish he would drop me a clue, then."

"Have you asked him to?"

The priest tells me to pray and to seek forgiveness, which I do in a faltering confession. It feels fake, to tell this stranger everything I ever remember doing wrong. Still, what doesn't feel fake today? What's one more thing?

"I don't think you're crazy," he says at the end. "And I don't know what happened to you. But you should tell someone you can trust. Otherwise, you really will go crazy. And then where will you be?"

"I don't know where I am right *now*."

"Then ask. Seven Our Fathers, seven Hail Marys, and pray the rosary every night for guidance." He makes the sign of the cross. "Peace be with you, my child."

"Okay, have a great day," I say as I get up. A flush spreads across my face. *Have a great day?* Outside, the noises of the city return. Shafts of colored light fall through the dust. The confessional door creaks shut behind me.

The church is silent, save for the outside flow of traffic. Claude isn't here. I drop my last nickel in the donation bin, then light a candle.

"Our Father," I say, seven times, under my breath, then "hail Mary" seven more—more or less. Wait, shouldn't I be praying or something? I clasp my hands under my chin. Something in my shirt pocket brushes against my arm. It's a business card with nothing written on it, just that now-familiar image of a snake eating its own tail with lines converging in its center.

A cold finger traces my spine. I turn the card over and read these words:

Claude Belissan - 415.555.3055

"Those numbers only work in movies. What a fucking joke." A woman glares at me from the doorway. "*Sorry,*" I mouth. The door swings shut behind her. I look through its window. Yesterday, Leah held her knife to my throat, right there. Only it wasn't yesterday, was it? That yesterday won't come for a long, long time.

I put Claude's card back in my shirt pocket. There will be no escape until I know where I am and why I'm here. Whatever this world is—and it's not a dream, or not only that—the best way to understand it is to join it. How can you outrun a monster, let alone defeat it, if you don't even know what it is?

The Virgin Mary gazes down at me from a painting above the candles.

Here we go.

CHAPTER SIX
TOTALLY DU JOUR

MOM'S WAITING IN the hallway, her face set to murder. I don't hear what the doctor tells her, or what she says as she leads me through the building. I barely hear the radio in the car. White noise fills my head. *This isn't a dream. You're really here.*

"Are you even listening?"

"I'm sorry."

"I don't want you to be sorry. I want you to be the kind of person who doesn't *do* things like this. Honest to God, Amy, what were you thinking?"

"Didn't the doctor tell you that?"

Mom laughs her "oh, you're in trou-ble" laugh. I brace for impact.

"You know you could have killed someone? Or been killed? The cops said they found you in the Tenderloin."

"It was the Metreon. There's—"

"You could be in the back of some guy's van right now, tied up like a turkey. Do you realize that?"

What can I say? *I'm sorry, Mom. I needed to know if I was in a dream world or not.* No. Saying that will get me the real crazy pills, the ones that make you drool into your Grape Nuts. Besides, Mom's right. Thirteen, no phone, the Tenderloin. What was I thinking?

I told the cops, and the doctor, that I hid in the backseat of a car. No, I don't remember which one. No, I don't remember which street. Someone—I think it was a woman—drove from Woodacre to the city. No, I don't think she saw me back there. She parked in a garage right by MoMA. I went to the Metreon, hung out until the cops found me.

Mom smolders in silence. A panhandler stands on the median strip at Lombard and Buchanan, holding a cardboard sign. It's Leah, has to be. She's here to break the spell, bring back reality. When we get closer, I see it's a man. His sign, written in unsteady capital letters, says something about Dick Cheney and Vietnam.

"I have half a mind to cancel your birthday party," Mom says. "You can forget about an iPod, now and forever. Okay?"

"Okay."

"Why am I not giving you an iPod? Am I mean?"

"You're not mean. You're worried."

Mom opens her mouth, but her voice hitches. Her knuckles pop white on the steering wheel. She's so different from yesterday, stress crackling off her like sparks off a Tesla coil.

We drive onto the Golden Gate Bridge. Another seagull floats on a breeze above the rails. The green-blue bay shimmers in the sunlight. From up here, everything looks the same as it did yesterday. What a lie. It couldn't be more different.

"I talked to Dad while you were with the doctor," Mom says. "If school is too much for you to handle, we could send you somewhere with a more structured environment."

"Like Grandma's house?" Grandma Rose, Dad's mom, lives in a nice little house overlooking Stinson Beach. Leah and I practically lived there when we were little, while Mom and Dad worked super-long hours. Not exactly a structured environment, but a peaceful one. Grandma taught us how to play the guitar, how to sing in harmony, how to make necklaces out of shells we found on the beach. I wouldn't mind living there again.

Mom shakes her head.

"No. There's this behavioral center in Colorado for kids with problems. They have therapy, hiking, camping in the wilderness. You have to work, too—lots of construction work, digging holes, hiking with huge backpacks. It's not a vacation."

Glacier water floods my veins. I've read about those camps. Some of them had "struggle sessions" straight out of Chairman Mao's playbook, where students would hurl abuse at one kid until he cracked. Others locked their students in cages, beat them, made them work for hours without a sip of water. Kids die at those camps. No, thanks.

"That's not necessary," I say. "I can do better. I promise." Mom taps the steering wheel off-rhythm with the radio song. Her mind's whirring like a computer with an overworked fan.

We pass into the Rainbow Tunnel. The lights are yellower and dimmer than yesterday. The roar of traffic reminds me of the ocean. I close my eyes.

"Go to your room," Mom orders once we're in the house. "I'll get you the student directory. You will call your classmates until one of them gives you the homework. Don't come out until you've finished it. Okay?"

Maybe my room is Mom's study again, with the IKEA desk, the papers piled high, the mementos box open on the floor. It isn't. It's my old room, more or less as I left it this morning—as I left it thirteen years ago.

A moment later, Mom opens the door and throws a small book, along with a cordless phone, onto my bed. I flinch as the door slams shut. Her footsteps recede down the hallway, into the kitchen. She's picking up the kitchen phone so she can listen in. I remember that. I didn't know I remembered.

It takes me a moment to realize that my class is the sixth grade class. Memories return to me as I run my finger down the names.

ALVAREZ, Marina

Never knew her that well. She started selling candy, erasers, Pokémon cards, etc. in fifth grade. Or was it fourth grade? She switched to a "pimp my Myspace" business in high school. She might have moved away before graduation. No idea what happened to her.

ANDERSON, Lindsay

One of the popular girls at Forest Knolls. Semi-popular in high school. Not a mean girl, not a saint either. Went to UC San Diego, married a Marine Corps officer. Had—will have—two daughters and a son. Once tried to sell me essential oils through Facebook.

CARDUCCI-RITTER, Natalie

The queen bee of Forest Knolls Middle School. More feared than loved. Once told me my shirt would look "pretty on a pretty person." Went to Marin Academy for high school. Business major at Rutgers, then an accounts manager at Disney World. Tons of Facebook posts about CrossFit, green smoothies, her three dogs. Or is it four dogs?

CLARK, Cassidy

Ran away from home, lived with me for the last year of high school. Went to Davis, same as me. Got a bookkeeping job at a mortgage broker in Emeryville. Lives in El Cerrito with her husband. Still reads British *Vogue* religiously. Still my best friend.

A wave of reality crashes over me. *You have school tomorrow. Your life is gone. You have no idea how to get it back again.* When I've finished crying, I pick up the phone.

I call Cassidy's house first. The phone rings once, barely, when the line picks up. Airy silence, one, two, three seconds long.

"Hello?" I say.

"Hello?" a deep male voice echoes back. It's Slice. His voice sounds wrong: slow, careful, without feeling. I gulp and paste on a smile.

"Hiiii Slice. Is Cassidy there?"

Slice laughs. "Cassie's been gone a long time, but she's back. Téa, too. Nothing else changed. Nothing but the trees." He laughs. Indistinct yelling behind him.

"Slice, uh, do you think I could—"

"Hold on!" he yells into the phone. "I'm talking to someone." More yelling, shuffling against the receiver.

"Hello?" a young woman says on the other end. Softer, gentler than Cassidy.

"Téa, hi," I say, "It's Amy. Is Cassidy there?"

"She's out with her friends, sweetie. Did you try her cell?"

Slice says something in the background.

"What's her cell number?" I say. 415, 834…or was it 843? I can't remember. Slice mutters in the background, louder now.

"Sorry, hon, you'll need to call back. It's not a good time." The phone clatters into the receiver. The line goes dead.

I look at the phone in my hand. This is Cassidy's nightmare made real: living in her parent's house with a dangerously unstable brother. There has to be a way to help her before he tries to kill her. I dial quickly.

"411. City and state, please," a woman says on the other end.

"San Rafael, California."

"Thank you, what listing?"

"Um, Child Pro—"

"What are you doing?" Mom says, bursting in on the line. "You've got the numbers right there."

"Hello?" the operator says.

"Mom, I—"

"Do your homework, Amy. Nothing comes before homework."

I hang up. Shit. I'll call when Mom goes to bed.

So many names sound familiar, names attached to vague faces and half-forgotten memories. My finger stops at *HILLIS, Sean*. My high school boyfriend. Last time I talked to him, he was selling cell phones in Idaho, living with some Mormon girl he met on the internet. Not an observant Mormon, since she was pregnant with his kid.

"I've got sixty thousand dollars in student loans. That's not even counting the interest," he told me. "I can't join the military. Starbucks turned me down. My current job doesn't have health insurance. Now I have a baby on the way. What the fuck do I do, Amy?"

I didn't know then. I don't know now. If this world is real, then Sean's a kid again, those worries as distant as Xanadu. Maybe *he* sent us back in time. If anyone needs a do-over, it's him.

"Hey," Sean says when he picks up the phone. His voice is higher than I remember, but still his.

"Hi Sean. It's Amy Snowberger. Do you have the homework for today?"

"Yeah." Long pause. Background sound of a TV, somebody yelling, maybe Jon Stewart. "Hey, can I ask you something?"

"Sure."

"Did you really hotwire a car?"

"When?"

"Well, ever, but…I heard you stole a car and drove it into the city."

"I didn't do any of that. I commandeered a tank, *Fast & Furious*-style."

"I don't think that movie had a tank, but…if you say so."

"I do say so. What, you don't believe me?"

It's our old pattern of teasing, one I'd forgotten until now. What does Mom think as she listens to this, one finger pressed over the speaker? I pick up a pen, roll it along the desk. My skin crawls.

"Can I ask you something else?" Sean says.

"Uh-huh." My pen rolls away and falls behind my desk. Shit. I get down on my knees to grab it.

"Do you really smoke meth?"

A clear tone fills my mind. The pen evades my grasp. I stretch my fingers as far as I can. "I'm sorry, what?" My fingertips touch the pen. I roll it through the carpet into my hand. If Mom's listening right now, I'm fucked.

"Hector's brother saw you smoking meth at Stinson."

"Hector who?"

"Hector Villanueva."

I clamber onto my chair. I remember Hector a little. Didn't Cassidy bump into him once, maybe 2014? She told me he sold Audis at a dealership in Palo Alto. Don't remember his brother.

"So," I say. "Hector Villanueva's brother said he saw me. And he told Hector, who told you. Maybe he saw Elvis, too." I spin around on my desk chair, watching the ceiling revolve above me.

"Is it true, though?"

"No."

"Your sister's kind of a junkie, though, right?"

I imagine teenage Leah leaning over a piece of foil, lighter in hand. Sharp pain blooms in the center of my head. The old excuses return. "Leah gets good grades. She's sold a bunch of paintings. She's not some kind of…even if she was, that's her. Not me."

"I mean, it sounded bogus," Sean says. "But I wanted to make sure."

"Well, you've made sure."

My eyes fall on a silver notebook sitting on the edge of my desk. The same silver notebook I saw in Mom's office yesterday. Was it on the desk before I reached for the pen? Must have been, but I don't remember. I pick it up, feel its weight. Its pages are blank, smooth. I write my name inside the front cover. My handwriting looks the same as it did yesterday: cramped, slanted cursive. I take comfort in that.

Sean gives me the homework, repeating every assignment to make sure I get it right. He'll fax me all the handouts I missed. I try to remember our fax number. He points out that it's in the directory.

"Thank you, Sean. I owe you one."

"One what?"

"One, ah, rotten eggplant. Or a candy bar. What's your preference?"

"Mmm, tough choice. I'll think about it."

After I hang up, I turn to the back of the student directory. There's my name, between *SHARKEY, Lisa*, who grows up to sell handmade dolls online, and *SPAR-DESMOND, James*, whom I don't remember at all. I open last year's yearbook. James isn't there. Bretlyn Sunhouse, the third-string popular girl, smiles in the photograph next to mine.

I run my finger down the homework list, wishing none of it was real.

MATH

Pages 82-6: Problems 4, 5-8, 12-18, 20-26, 28, 30, 42, 47

HISTORY

Read Introduction and Chapter 1

Answer study questions on page 17. Answer in COMPLETE sentences only.

Essay due Thursday: "My Favorite Person in History." Write essay on historical figure of your choice. Three double-spaced pages, typed.

ENGLISH

Read guide to citing sources & library call letters (fax)

Sentence diagram homework due Weds (fax)

BIOLOGY

Bring in science binder with dividers for: notes, assignments, experiments, group projects, presentations, science fair (next semester). Must have CLEAR SLEEVE at front and back.

Fill out ecosystem and bio-sphere handouts (fax)

"Health and the human body" permission slip (fax)

SOCIAL STUDIES

Read pages 11-29 in textbook

Fill out "The Three Branches of Government" handout (fax)
Due Friday: "What is the purpose of government?" Two
double-spaced pages.

I get up and walk to the fax machine in the living room. Mom comes out a few minutes later, watching the papers judder and fall into the receiving tray.

"Do we have any binders?"

We do. They even have clear sleeves. I insert the dividers while Mom watches. The fax machine shakes and whines behind us.

"What's going on, Amy?"

"I don't know," I say.

Mom grimaces and sits on the couch. When the faxes are done, I retreat to my room.

First comes the math. It's not as hard as I feared. *Find the greatest common factor of 65 and 91. Identify the prime and composite numbers in this set. Calculate the mean, median, and mode...*It's easy, once you warm up to it.

The TV blares in the living room. I scrounge up some dirty earplugs from my nightstand, but the sound still filters through. Especially the commercials. "Introducing Alberghini Country-Fresh Soups." "A great start to every day, the Inspyrathon Way." "Ask your doctor if Seranta is right for you."

I'm now plodding through the history questions. *What were the preconditions for the American Revolutionary War? Name three.* When it's done, I start on the sentence diagram homework. Subject, verb, and object go above the line; modifiers and prepositional phrases go below it. What's a prepositional phrase, again? You'd think an English major would know.

I turn to my bookshelf, looking for a dictionary. My eyes

sweep over the titles: *The Dark is Rising, The Wisdom of Dolphins*, the first two *Harry Potter* books, every *Dear America* diary known to man. A few of Grandma Mimi's old cookbooks sit on the top shelf. The bottom shelf's full of spiral-bound, be-stickered notebooks.

I kneel down, flip through them one after another. Most are a quarter full, at best—a few class notes, magazine cut-outs, recipes. They're written in a stranger's handwriting, a bubbly mix of print and cursive, little hearts drawn over the i's. This stranger was me, but the distance between us is too great to bridge. We'll never meet.

I'm skimming through one book when a fear jolts up my spine. I reread the page, trying to ignore the drawing next to the words:

MY PERFECT GUY

-Brown hair, blue-blue eyes

-Muscles but not TOO big

-Smart. Can hold a real conversation

-Sings, plays guitar

-Not a MAN-HO

-Eyes for ME only—no other girl (or BOY!!!)

Next to this description is a crude but jarring likeness of Tom Templeton. Same smile, same haircut, same outfit, even, as the day I met him: white dress shirt, blue jeans, brown belt, brown leather shoes. At least the description's off-base. Tom sang like a deaf sea lion. I never knew him to play guitar. He only had eyes for one girl, and it wasn't me.

Mom's frayed voice, muffled by the wall and the TV, pulls

my attention away. Dad answers, his voice low and intense. Mom responds. That's right—they always fought in their room, where they thought we couldn't hear them.

"—see that this is a problem?" Mom says. Dad mutters something in response. I can't make out what Mom says in return, save the words "can't believe you."

"What can you not believe, Jackie?" Dad says. "You saw her this morning. She was crying out for help—"

"—crying out for *guidance*, Rich!" Mom says, followed by a flurry of muffled invective. I turn back to the notebook, flipping to the end.

The last page is filled with doodles of snakes: slithering down the page, eating their own tails, in silhouette, as skeletons. Another snake, mouth open, tries to swallow a black circle—or is that an ink blotch? I look through the notebook, trying to find a rough date for the sketches. The phones ring throughout the house, braiding with Mom's muffled yelling and the TV. I examine the drawings again. Why did I draw them?

"Phone call for you," Mom says behind me. My shoulders jump around my ears. When I turn around, her eyes are boring into mine. I jump up, hold my hand out for the phone.

"You were zoned out," she says, giving it to me. "Have you finished your homework?"

I hold the phone to my ear.

"Happy birthday, dear Amy," Grandma Rose sings on the other end. Mom stares at me, unmoving, in the doorway. I turn to the window.

"Thanks, Grandma."

"You're very welcome. Are you excited for your party on Saturday?"

"There's not going to be a party."

Confused pause. Another current of air opens on the line. I glance at the doorway. Mom's not there anymore.

"Why not, sweetheart?"

"Because I ran away."

"Oh. Yes." Awkward pause. "What happened today, honey?"

"Nothing. I was stressed out, that's all."

"I'll bet." Grandma Rose laughs gently. "If I was in your shoes...my God, if I was in middle school again, I'd run away too."

"Yeah?" A frozen talon traces the back of my neck. "There's a second time for everything, huh?"

"No, thank God."

"Grandma—" my breath catches. Mom's listening. What can I say that won't get me the extra-strength zombie pills? "Grandma, I've had the strangest day of my life today. I still can't believe what's happened."

"Did anybody hurt you, sweetheart?"

"No. It's something else."

"Amy, you know you can tell me anything, right?"

In the silence between us, I can almost hear the ocean roaring on her end of the line. What I wouldn't give to be in the Stinson house right now, drinking hot chocolate next to the fireplace, listening to some Bach or Joni Mitchell. I'd give up true love for an evening like that.

"I know, Grandma," I say.

"I know you're under tremendous pressure. But honey—running away, getting into a stranger's car, that's dangerous. We were all terrified."

"I'm sorry, Grandma."

"Oh, honey, don't apologize. The way they keep you locked up in that house...Even still, times have changed. Do you remember Polly Klaas?"

When I was barely out of diapers, a career criminal abducted Polly Klaas, a twelve-year-old from nearby Petaluma. The case sent shockwaves throughout the Bay Area, if not the country. I grew up with Polly's ghost hovering over me, forbidding me to open the window, play in the front yard, or walk down the street alone. Her sad eyes haunted me in dreams. *Don't,* she'd say when I tried to escape. *There are monsters out there.*

"Polly Klaas was abducted at home," I whine. "If you're not safe in your home—"

"You're even less safe in a stranger's car."

In my mind's eye, I see Mom holding a cordless phone to her ear, finger pressed over the speaker. "You're right," I say. "I'm sorry. I won't do it again."

"The world's changing, Amy. I believe things will get better, but…it might take time. It might take a miracle."

"I know."

"Now. Onto more pleasant subjects. What else would you like for your birthday? Any last-minute gifts you want me to get?"

"How about a miracle, for starters."

Grandma Rose laughs.

"All right. One miracle, coming right up."

I'm finishing my social studies essay when a voice startles me out of my reverie. I turn in my chair, anticipating Mom's wrath. It's Leah, standing in the open doorway between our rooms.

"Did you use my shampoo?" She's holding a half-empty bottle of Herbal Essences. My heart beats double time.

"No," I say, though I feel a twinge of guilt when I say it. Leah's eyes narrow. My pulse throbs in my neck. "How was school?"

"It's *Tuesday.*"

"Oh."

Leah goes—went—*goes* to a high school that meets once a week. Every Monday, she meets with her advisor, turns in last week's assignments, and picks up the new ones. There are study halls during the week, a few P.E. classes, but for the most part, Leah's time is her own.

"This was almost full last week," she says, waggling the bottle. "What do you think happened to it?"

"You used it."

Leah raises her eyebrows.

"What? You have long hair, I have short hair. Who would use more, you or me?"

"So you *did* use some."

"I didn't touch your gross orgasm shampoo," I hear myself say. Leah rolls her eyes. I've turned back to my desk when her voice jolts me again.

"What really happened today?" She's leaning in the connecting doorway, arms folded.

I tell Leah what I've told no one else. I tell her about the street kid with perfect teeth, the legless man on a skateboard, the man moaning at me from his car. I don't tell her about Claude. Leah bites her nails as she listens, worry and anger passing over her face.

"Nothing happened. Nobody got to me."

"They could have, though."

"Yeah. They could have."

"What were you even trying to do?"

"I told you. I got lost."

"That's not what I mean." Leah studies me for a moment, shifting from foot to foot. "Did they put you on drugs?"

"Who, the creeps?"

"The *doctors*. You went to the hospital, right?"

"Yeah. Yeah, they put me on one called…Sarah Quill?"

"Seroquel. Have you taken it yet?"

"No."

"Good. Don't. When you're on it, you're moving through molasses. Remember when I couldn't sit down without nodding off? That was Seroquel."

"I wasn't gonna take it anyway."

"Really." Leah raises her eyebrows in unspoken question.

I look away. Yesterday, Leah pulled a knife on me, and now she's standing here, full of life—annoying, angsty, hormonal life, but life all the same. She's not the same person. There's no way she's from the future.

"They'll watch you," she says, with a glance at the door. "Mom especially. She used to wake me up at five to take those drugs. If she does that, put the pills in your cheek or under your tongue and pretend to swallow, like this...I did that every day for six weeks. But she trusts me now."

I remember all the orange pill bottles in our medicine cabinet, full of pills in all colors, shapes, and sizes. It never crossed my mind she wasn't taking them. "What do you do once you fake swallow it, or..."

Leah gives me an are-you-kidding look. "*Whoosh*," she says. Her finger, pointed down, spins in a descending spiral.

"Don't do that. Those drugs get into the water supply. They fuck up the fish's brains."

Leah laughs.

"It's true. I read it somewhere."

"Where? *Crackpot Weekly*?"

"*National Geographic*, maybe. I dunno. Somewhere respectable."

Leah looks at me for a moment, then laughs. "Look at you. You've been thirteen for one day and you're already a little rebel girl. I bet you'll have a studded belt and a lip ring by the end of the year. It'll be hella cute."

"That's never been my style."

Leah covers her mouth with her hand. "You've never *had* a style!"

"Yeah I have."

"What, Snoopy shirts and kid jeans?"

"Snoopy shirts are totally du jour."

Leah laughs. The curtains billow with the wind. Outside, the trees rustle, restless in their sleep.

"Mom threatened me with a 'troubled teen' camp," I say. "Out in the wilderness."

Leah's smile evaporates. She darts a look at the main door, then crosses the distance between us. "No bullshit," she murmurs. I shake my head. Leah looks at the doorway again. "I'm gonna give you a can of bear mace. Don't go anywhere without it, even the bathroom. Even when you're asleep. Wear real clothes to bed—shoes, too. Sleep over the covers. You'll get used to it. If somebody wakes you up with a flashlight, use the mace and run. Don't let them take you without a fight. And yell for me, okay?"

"Then what?"

"Get the fuck out. *Don't* wander around the forest. You could get lost like—" she snaps her fingers in front of my eyes. I flinch. "Go to one of the side streets, hide, and wait. Ray can pick you up and take you to her house. You can stay there until it's safe."

"What about her parents?"

"Old-school hippies. Don't worry about them."

Leah walks into her room, leaving the door open behind her. A drawer rasps as she opens it. A minute later, she returns with her friend Fay Ray's number, written on a magazine tear-off, and a wad of cash. I unfold the bills. Three crisp hundreds, five ratty twenties.

"Don't spend this," she says, "Not unless it's life-or-death. Do you understand?"

I nod.

"Where's that travel belt Mom got you?"

"I don't know," I say, but my body gets up and walks to the dresser. It's there in the top drawer: a slim, canvas pack with a snap clasp. I put the money inside the pouch, put it on, enter Ray's number in my phone. "What if Mom doesn't change her mind?"

"We'll work on Dad. He can grow a backbone when he wants to."

It's a stupid plan, but at least it's a plan. I nod solemnly to match her mood. "Has Mom threatened to send you to camp?"

Leah shakes her head. "I'm a good girl. Good grades, good extracurriculars, good prospects. Good at lying." She laughs. "Ever notice how a word stops meaning something when you say it over and over? 'Good-good-good-good-good.'" Her eyes fall on the lamp on my nightstand. "I'm glad you're not taking those drugs. I still don't have them out of my system."

I remember Leah staring empty-eyed at her plate. I remember her waking up at eleven and going to sleep at five. I remember her staring at the same page in a book for hours at a time. I remember her trying to mount a bicycle, her arms and legs moving in slow motion. I thought she was pretending to be stupid. I guess not.

I think of Leah in the hospital, about ten years from today, picking at the tape holding her IV in place. I don't like psych meds either, but maybe she needs them. If not them, then something.

"Why'd they put you on those pills?"

Leah stands up, beckons me into her room. I follow. She

pulls a sketchbook down from her bookshelf, rifles through the pages until she finds something. I avoid looking at the painting on her easel.

"Here," she says, handing me the sketchbook. It's opened to a pen sketch of a baby, perfect ink-black circle in front of its face. Its right hand holds a knife as big as itself. The knife looks familiar.

"Mom thought this was a 'cry for help.' I showed her some Japanese comics, *Like a Velvet Glove Cast in Iron*—just to show her that art can be weird. You can imagine how that went.."

"Is this an eclipse?" I say, pointing to the black circle.

"I guess. I see it in my dreams sometimes."

"What dreams?"

Leah shrugs. Did she ever really look this young? There's hardly a line on her face. Oil shines on her forehead. There's a flush to her skin that wasn't there in church. For a second, I can see how she might have looked, in another lifetime, if she wasn't homeless and on drugs.

"Just dreams. Gordon says it's a symbol of nirvana." Something changes in her eyes as she looks at me. "Why'd you say we met in church yesterday? I had a dream about that. Did you...?"

"I don't think that wasn't a dream."

"What was it, then?"

"I'll let you know when I figure it out."

1:57 AM. Sleep is galaxies away. I get up, turn on the light. More homework passes in an agony of boredom, saved only by a *Brandenburg Concertos* CD. There's a plastic spinning top at the back of one desk drawer. I spin it as fast as I can. It wobbles, reels to a stop, falls on the floor.

I open my silver notebook to a new page. Time passes

quickly; when I finish writing, it's nearly four. I reread it, hoping to see the hidden pattern or purpose that eludes me now.

WHAT YOU KNOW

1. *Everything (so far) looks like it did in 2003*
2. *Everyone (so far) acts like they did in 2003*
3. *It's not clear if this is real*
4. *It's not going away*

POSSIBLE EXPLANATIONS

1. DREAM

You're stuck in a lucid dream. Maybe you'll wake up, maybe you won't. Maybe this is your brain's way of dealing with death.

HOW TO TEST: *The top stopped spinning, didn't it? Look for other tells. If this is a dream, it's a tenacious one.*

2. VIRTUAL REALITY

You're a glitch in the matrix. Maybe the timeline's gone bad. Maybe you're an android, reliving false memories in order to become human. Or you're being tested, to see if your past, and therefore you, are real. Is this the world's most advanced Voight-Kampff test? Who can say for sure? (You, hopefully.)

HOW TO TEST: *Find anyone who has memories of the future. Look for anything, no matter how small, that seems out of place. Seek out like-minded people who can "see through" the illusion. DON'T take pills from strange men.*

3. PSYCHOTIC BREAK

You've snapped under the strain and are living in your own world. You're trapped in an illusion, with little—if any— real world input.

HOW TO TEST: *Can you control airplanes with your mind? If you feel like the President is talking to you through the radiator, go to the hospital and ask for help. Don't do anything stupid. Remember: humans can't fly.*

4. COMA

It's serious. You'll be here until your brain recovers. That's if your brain recovers. Hopefully, you'll wake up in a hospital bed with Mom and Dad crying over you. SHIT!

HOW TO TEST: *See #1. Don't walk into the light. Pray for your salvation, in case the light comes looking for you.*

5. CAPGRAS DIMENSION

The people surrounding you are NOT your real Mom, Dad, sister, etc. They're robots, ghosts, memories, simulations— facsimiles sent to wheedle information out of you. (Part of the Voight-Kampff test? See #2) What do you know that nobody else does?

HOW TO TEST: *Ask questions only the real Mom/Dad/ sis/etc. would know how to answer. Do all conversations lead to the same topic, no matter who you talk to? Look for bolts, ID tags, horns, shimmering edges, any clues to their true natures.*

6. ALTERNATE UNIVERSE

Parallel timelines, multidimensional portals, tangent uni-

verses—take your pick. This is a real place, just not your place. Which begs the question: what happened to the other Amy? Did she wake up in your 2016 life? Can you contact her? Can she contact you? If you're not there, who is she?

HOW TO TEST: *Research time travel. Study quantum physics. Realistically, talk to someone who understands quantum physics. If a machine got you here, could a machine bring you back? If yes, find that machine!*

7. LOOP UNIVERSE

Time is a flat circle. Everything that's happened has happened before, and will happen again. You're doomed to repeat ages thirteen through twenty-five, forever and ever. Lucky you.

HOW TO TEST: *Try to remember any other lives. Don't make the same mistakes, in case this is a...*

8. "GROUNDHOG DAY" UNIVERSE

A loop universe with an escape hatch. You have to make things right before you return to reality. After you figure it out, you'll have a better life than you'd ever imagined. This could mean a repeat of one day, week, month, year, even several years. You may have to:

-Stop Leah doing drugs

-Stop Dad overeating

-Stop Donald Trump running for President

-Save Cassidy from her family home

-Live a less selfish life

HOW TO TEST: *Do the right thing, no matter what. If*

you keep waking up in the past, experiment. You'll have plenty of time to get it right.

9. BASIC TIME TRAVEL

This is the real world. The future is unwritten or erased. Everything from the past thirteen years winked out of existence sometime last night. Maybe some mad scientist bears the blame. Maybe this is another bizarre phenomenon, like ball lightning or petrified wood. It wouldn't be the craziest thing you ever heard, would it?

HOW TO TEST: ~~It's just a jump to the left...~~ *Seek out all possible explanations. Look for people with similar experiences. Don't fuck Tim Curry, tempting though it may be.*

10. 2016 WAS THE DREAM

What you think of as adult life was an epic fever dream, a prophetic warning, both. Now it's over. You're either the harbinger of doom, or crazy.

HOW TO TEST: *Look for any precedents: medical case studies, psychology, memoirs, etc. Read more about dreams (academic and amateur). Get an MRI.*

11. HELL

You're dead, you're damned, and you're doomed to live forever as a seventh-grader. Great job, asshole!

HOW TO TEST: *Test your immunity to holy water, crosses, garlic, et cetera. Church didn't hurt at all, though, so maybe you're in purgatory. Who knows? Hell pretty much looks like seventh grade anyway.*

I get up, stretch, look in the mirror. A child's face glares back at me. *I must be dead. I couldn't dream this. This is death and nothing else.*

I shut off the light, pull the covers over my head, will the cold away. No matter what the explanation is, I need to sleep. I'll still be dead tomorrow.

CHAPTER SEVEN
FKMS

"WHERE WILL YOU go after school?"

"The school library."

Mom watches me fake-swallow the pill and chase it with water. I close the bathroom door behind her. The pill's only in my mouth for thirty seconds, but a bitter, chemical aftertaste remains. I roll the pill in toilet paper, then shove it in my front pocket. It would be easier to flush it, but I can't do that to the fish. They never did anything to me.

Mom drives me to school, early. Leah sits in the front seat, which she leans all the way back. I watch her fiddle with the cuff of her hoodie.

"Ray can pick Amy up," Leah says.

"Who's Ray?"

"Um, Fay Ray Duckworth? The girl who—"

"No."

"Why? Ray's mom is totally cool with guests. We can—"

"What did I say?"

Leah woofles and slumps down even further. "What about Grandma Rose? Ray could drive us—"

"Enough." Mom fiddles with the dashboard. The radio switches from soft rock to a news segment.

"—leen Vandergraf, who disappeared from her home in Forest Knolls yesterday afternoon," the newscaster announces. "Police said—"

"That's Gordon's mom. No one saw *anything*."

"Who's Gordon?"

"Ray's boyfriend."

"—briefly seen at a gas station in Fairfax, but did not speak to anyone," the reporter continues. The radio fills with an indoor silence: humming equipment, jostling glass. Then a woman speaks.

"She seemed out of it," she says. Thirties, maybe, slight Latin accent. "She'd take a magazine off the shelf and stare at the cover, then take another one and stare at that one. I thought—"

"Ray says she's not surprised," Leah blurts. "Kathleen has major, major problems. When Gordon got up yesterday, he walked downstairs and—as soon as his mom saw him, she turned *white*. Didn't say one word, just threw up right there."

"Is she on drugs?"

"No, Mom. *God*. Everything's drugs with you."

I crack open my window. Cool air streams in, bringing in the scents of pine trees and flowers. It's cooler than it was last night. Mom turns off Sir Francis Drake, her eyes fixed forward.

"It's shocking, really," a middle-aged, adenoidal woman intones on the radio. "You don't think it could happen here, until it—"

"You know she had Gordon when she was nineteen? Her husband basically bought her from her parents. Isn't that fucked up?"

"*Language*."

"Sorry." Leah turns in her seat and grins at me. "You know

she has the same birthday as you? She went missing a few hours after you ran off. Maybe you did it."

My veins flood with ice.

"Ray said she was tripping about turning thirty-nine. Her life's half over, and—"

"Ray's boyfriend is over eighteen?"

"No, he's…"

It takes Leah a moment to realize her mistake. She slumps down further in her seat, studies the cuff of her sweatshirt.

Forest Knolls Middle School looms up ahead. It looks like an enormous barn, with white clapboard siding, a black gabled roof, bay windows on the first and second stories, rows of dormers on the third. There's the sports field, the cracked basketball court, the traffic island, now full of cars. *WELCOME BACK*, the signboard says.

I feel the outline of the bear mace through my front pocket. Could I run away, maybe crawl into a nearby wormhole? Is it too late to make that jump to the left, then step to the right? The car pulls into the pickup circle, then stops. A roaring ocean sound drowns out the world.

Here we go.

My backpack must weigh as much as I do. I feel the textbooks straining at its seams. Did I remember all my homework? *Two days ago, you had an apartment, a job, a credit score.* Despair passes over me like a cloud's shadow.

"Behave," Mom calls from the car. I turn back.

Good luck, Leah mouths at me, or maybe, *You suck.* She waves as the car pulls away. I wave back.

I don't look at the school as I stumble forward. This can't be happening. How heavy is this backpack, anyway? Two girls, who I vaguely recognize, stare down at me from the doors, hands covering their mouths. A wicked smile plays over their eyes.

"Yo, Jess-i-kuh!" someone yells, right in my ear. I turn and see Mark Watkins, all ruddy, freckled cheeks and blue braces.

"Hey, do you have some tissues I can borr—" His face twists in disgust. "Oh, it's *you*," he says. "Hey, are you on drugs now, or what?"

I jog up the stairway, eyes forward.

The halls of the school swell with children: running, walking, talking in clusters, locker doors opening and slamming, laughing, shouting, high-fiving, fighting, arm wrestling, thumb wrestling, even singing. Two kids stare at an iPod, one earbud in each of their ears. One boy does the robot for his friends. "I. Am. Dah Gov-ah-nuh," he says in a bad Austrian accent.

The smells hit me in waves: Axe Body Spray, fruity perfumes, Simple Green cleaner, Starbursts, mint gum, corn syrup sodas, chalk. Girls whisper to their friends, hands cupped over their mouths. A girl walks by with a pink plastic lanyard swinging from her backpack.

The sixth graders look like preschoolers. *Everyone* looks like preschoolers, including me. I felt incredibly short yesterday, but that feeling ebbs away in the crowd. Most of the boys are even shorter than I am. Only a few unfortunates, mostly other girls, tower over the rest of us, arms hugging their chests.

A hand jams something crumpled and scratchy into the collar of my shirt. I look up. The hand belongs to Natalie Carducci-Ritter, now smiling with the foretaste of pleasure. The crumpled paper falls down my shirt and onto the floor. I pick it up. It's a dollar bill.

"That's for a hairbrush," she smirks. A few kids laugh. Natalie flounces away, hiding her smile.

This must be hell.

My first class of the day is biology. My teacher, Mr. Weathers ("Not your meteorology teacher?" Dad used to quip), looks the same: pale, elongated, a handle of salt-and-pepper hair around the back of his head, fine fluted fingers with well-tended nails. I take a seat toward the back of the class.

Names and faces return to me as I look around. There's Andrew Jacobs, suburban punk, sitting near the front. There's Emily Padovano, slouching under a pink newsboy cap, pulling and releasing a bead on her bracelet, over and over again: *tak, tak, tak.* There's a kid I vaguely remember, fiddling with an iPod under his desk, ash blond hair untucked to hide his earbuds.

What happened to them? Andrew Jacobs worked for Hewlett Packard. Emily was a bartender, last I heard. No clue what happened to the blondish boy. And there's Lisa Sharkey, future doll entrepreneur, now a baby emo wearing a necklace of Barbie doll heads. Fitting.

Marina Alvarez sits in the middle of the room, her long black hair bound in a braid. She's resting her cheek on her palm, tapping a pen on the desk. Everybody called her Maria, except for—

"Hey, Marinara," Scott Garson says, pulling Marina's ponytail.

"Stop!"

Scott pulls so hard she lifts out of her seat.

"What the fuck!" I shout. The class falls silent. Scott's beady eyes swivel to my face.

"What's that, Amy?" he says, still holding Marina's ponytail. I gulp. Scott's one of the few seventh-graders who's already got his height. He walks toward me, hand still clasped around Marina's ponytail. In the corner of my eye, I see Natalie turn to Lindsay. She might as well have used a bullhorn, because I can hear her whisper from across the room.

"You know she gives blowjobs for drugs? Just like her sister."
Eyes swivel to my face. Scott chuckles. My cheeks burn.
What the fuck does Natalie know about my sister? I grip the
edge of my desk, murder in my mind, but the thought of troubled teen camp stops me cold. *They're not worth it. They're kids.*

"Okay, everyone, let's get started," Mr. Weathers says, with a
pointed look to Scott. Scott drops Marina's ponytail and takes a
seat with the knot of boys huddled around a desk. Right there,
inside the knot, is Sean Hillis, my future boyfriend. Right now,
we're only classmates, thank God. His baby fat makes him look
like a chipmunk; there's barely any hint of the man he'll become.
His eyes meet mine for a moment. *Thank you*, I mouth. Blood
rises to his face.

"Let's take attendance. Anderson, Lindsay."

"Here."

"Carducci, Natalie."

"Carducci-*Ritter*. Here."

I skim the time travel list I wrote yesterday. Dream, virtual
reality, psychotic break, coma, Capgras Dimension…definitely
not a Capgras Dimension. Everything fits, from the smell of the
classroom to the A.C. unit rumbling in the corner. (It's not even
nine. Why is the A.C. on?) Dad's cough, Mom's walk, the size
and shape of my bio textbook…Nobody could duplicate all this.
Not without getting something wrong.

"You better hit the nuclear bomb," Scott says. I look over.
Sean, Scott, and the other boys are staring at a notebook open
on Sean's desk. Their game comes back to me: holding a pencil
by the eraser, you flick it from the bottom to the top of a page.
The pencil makes a line, hitting or not hitting various bombs,
mines, powder kegs, and other drawn-on explosives. The more
distant the obstacle, the bigger the explosion.

"Gimme a second," Sean says. There's a short pause, then a disappointed groan.

"You weren't even close. You weren't aiming for it."

"I *was* aiming for it!"

"Are you blind? Your line's all the way over there! You didn't even hit the—"

"Boys," Mr. Weathers warns.

"Sorry, sorry," the boys say, and start whispering to each other.

"*No, not TNT! We need more—*"

"*—dude, hit the grenade—*"

"*—no, not that pencil!*"

Mr. Weathers watches them for a moment, then sighs, before turning back to the attendance sheet. His eyes meet mine. "Snowberger, Amy."

"Here."

"*Boooooom!*" the boys shout with one voice. Mr. Weathers strides over to where they're sitting.

"Dude, I can't believe he hit it! I can't—"

"Oh my God, dude, oh my—"

"Out," Mr. Weathers says.

"You can't touch us! That's a lawsuit! That's a—"

"Now." The class holds its breath. Lisa, eyes fixed on Mr. Weathers, continues to fold a fortune teller. The boys look up sheepishly for a moment before getting up and, with a collective huff, walking to the door.

"We weren't doing anything," Sean gripes.

I close my eyes. For a moment, it's summertime. I'm driving with Cassidy to Stinson Beach, windows down, Wolfmother blasting. The wind streams over my face. The sun kisses my skin. I thump the steering wheel in time to the beat. It's obvious that nothing will ever go wrong.

Maybe, when I open my eyes, I'll be somewhere else, some-

when else. I can almost feel "White Unicorn" thumping against my ribs. I bet I'm already there, alive and stupid and totally happy.

My eyes open. I'm still in room 238 at Forest Knolls Middle School, sitting underneath a rattling air conditioner. Mr. Weathers is writing *ECOSYSTEM* on the board.

"Hey," a voice says near my ear. I turn. Lisa Sharkey's looking at me, holding her fortune teller. "You want to know the future?"

"Would I."

Pick a number, one through four. I pick three. With a glance to the front of the room, Lisa murmurs the numbers as she moves the fortune teller: *one, two, three. One, two, three. One, two, three.*

Mr. Weathers' eyes snag on mine. I hold my breath, but he passes on, calling on Andrew Jacobs instead. I pick another number, this time from inside the fortune teller. Lisa opens the flap.

"'Agonizing death.' That means horrible pain." She shakes her head in sympathy. "You should have picked four. You could have married Johnny Depp."

Beneath the word "death" is a small snake eating its own tail.

"What's that from?" I ask her, pointing to it.

"I don't know. I think it's a skateboarding thing."

"I guess that's one way to do a three-sixty."

Lisa rolls her eyes and turns back to her sketchbook.

Someone will see how absurd this is. Someone will look in my eyes and *know* that I'm not thirteen. They'll contact whoever you contact in this situation and set everything right. Again. How could this not happen?

I review my time travel list several times. Alternate universe, loop universe, *Groundhog Day*, hell…

Mid-morning break finally comes. Eighth graders sit outside, at the tables by the vending machines. These tables were—are—for eighth graders only, by unwritten rule. I didn't know I remembered that.

"Yo, Jessica!"

It's Ryan Morrison, sitting next to Becca Osborne, staring directly at me. Ryan was—is—the captain of the eighth-grade basketball team. He's King Shit right now, though he fades away in high school. I don't know what happens to him. Becca goes to UCLA, works as a model, then starts a fitness studio with a college friend. The studio gets profiled in *The Wall Street Journal*. They make great kale shakes, apparently.

"I'm not Jessica," I say, moving away.

"No, you're…" Ryan's face opens in a smile. "You're Amy, right? C'mere."

Tables fall silent around us. The air hums with anticipation. Becca and I meet eyes. Ryan shifts in his seat.

"Do you want some coke?" Ryan asks me. I look toward the vending machine, kitty corner from us. A suppressed laugh ripples across the courtyard.

"That's not *funny*, Ryan," Becca hisses.

"I'm good," I say.

"You sure?" Ryan says, leaning back. "How about later? If you're nice to me…"

A banana pokes out of his fly. Blood rushes to my face. Their laughter cuts me as I run away. Tears turn the courtyard into a beige-green blur. Becca yells something behind me. I rush into the hallway, determined not to hear it.

Why does it hurt, when it's so stupid?

I slam into someone. We both fall. Books spill across the floor. "Sorry," I mumble. Cassidy, gathering her books, glares at me as she stands up. *Cassidy!* She's positively babyish, even with that flinty gaze. Her face pinches with disgust.

"Don't touch me," she spits, and walks away.

Of course. Cassidy started hating me in fifth grade. We barely talked until sophomore year of high school, when we met at the County Fair. We moved from AIM conversations to hanging out at lunch. She apologized for being a bitch, but by then I didn't care.

I care a little now.

"Hey. You okay?" a voice says behind me. I turn. It's Becca Osbourne.

"Fine," I say. She smiles down at me. I take a step back.

"Ryan's an asshole. He thinks he's better than everyone because he plays basketball and his dad's a lawyer. Just ignore him."

"I will. Thanks."

Becca surveys my outfit with an appraising frown. Here comes the gut shot.

"I'm not on drugs," I blurt out. "I ran away 'cause…I don't want to be here. That's all."

"Tell me about it." Becca looks behind her, waves to someone outside the glass door. "I gotta go. Take care, Amy."

"You, too."

Not exactly Mother Teresa, but not the Marquis de Sade either.

I'm on the landing between the second and third floors when someone taps my shoulder. I flinch as I turn. Marina Alvarez stands there, backpack slung over one shoulder.

"Hey," she says.

"Hey, Marina."

She smiles. "Thanks for saying my name. I promised my mom I wouldn't get in trouble, but if one more person calls me Maria…" She squeezes her fist.

"Duly noted."

A sixth grader comes up to us, asks to borrow a pencil. Marina sells him a mechanical pencil ("This is stainless steel, not that plastic shit") for five dollars. He doesn't say her name, thankfully.

"What about you?" she says, showing me the inside of her backpack. It's stuffed with pencils, erasers, lanyards, candy bars, tiny cereal boxes, all neatly organized in mesh pouches. Not one book. It must weigh a ton.

"I don't have any…" I start to say, but I remember the dollar bill in my pocket. *That's for a hairbrush.* Fuck you, Natalie.

"Do you have any, uh…Twix?"

"Everyone wants Twix today. Normally it's seventy-five, but…" She holds up one finger. Behind me, a group of eighth-grade boys barrel down the stairs. When they've passed, I give Marina my dollar. She takes it, then hands me a Twix. She pulls out another one, holds it up. "I'm only giving this to you because I know you won't tell, okay?"

"I won't," I say, taking the second Twix. Marina flashes me a retail-friendly smile.

"You better not."

My sister got me hooked on heroin and crack. I'm a drug dealer's girlfriend. I'm a street prostitute in the Tenderloin. I do strip-teases on the internet. I wear foundation on my arms to cover my track marks.

"That's *ridiculous.* Who does that?"

Jessica Truesdale, sitting sideways in her seat, glances at my arms. "Models do it," she says, with a look that says, *And you're no model, sweetie.*

"So what?" I say, but she's turned away. It hurts worse to hear this from Jessica, my near-doppelgänger. The two of us have the same chestnut brown hair, the same gray eyes, the same oval faces. We got mistaken for one another all the way through high school. The yearbook mixed up our pictures at least once.

There's one big difference between us: Jessica's better at almost everything. She's taller, thinner, more elegant. She placed first county-wide in track and field, while I failed to make the team. She taught herself German "for fun," while I can barely ask where the beer garden is. She graduated high school with a 4.4 GPA; I barely cracked 3.6. She went to Amherst and Harvard Business School, all on her parent's dime; I left UC Davis with twenty grand in loans. She worked for UBS; I worked for peanuts. At twenty-four, Jessica married a guy on the Forbes 400. Not a gross old man, a startup founder who caught lightning in a bottle. Just looking at her raises my blood pressure.

I sit next to the window, half-listen to Mrs. Rice's monologue on the revolutionary war. In front of me, Mark Watkins draws interlocking Celtic knots in his notebook. Bretlyn Sunhouse and Cassidy whisper and giggle on the other side of the room. In the window reflection, I see them looking at me. I cover my ears.

This must be what fame feels like, minus the cash and screaming fans. When you're famous, everyone spreads rumors about you: the more outlandish, the more people talk about them. Everywhere you go, someone's watching, waiting for any lapse in dress or behavior. Embarrass yourself? Get ready to relive that moment for years to come. No matter how popular you are, no matter how loved or talented or beautiful, you're always at risk of dropping down that ladder. And so many people want to see you fall.

No wonder famous people go insane.

Something hits me hard behind the ear. I turn. Something small and shiny flies toward me. Before I can duck, it hits me right above the eyebrow, then clatters to the floor. It's a penny, dull and dirty from use. Another one hits the window behind me. Scott Garson, sitting in the back, laughs. He's holding up a rubber band slingshot.

Déjà vu hits me between the eyes. I remember this moment, this *exact* moment, complete with my confusion. I'm not confused this time.

"Fuck off," I mouth, and flip him the bird. My ears steam as I turn around. *Play the tape to the end,* I remind myself, my nails biting into my palms. *Zero tolerance, remember? If you make a scene, you'll get in trouble. Which means detention. Which means troubled teen camp. What if he denies it, and they believe him instead of you? For God's sake, you're not even Jewish.*

Like David Letterman or Dr. Seuss, I have a Jewish-sounding name despite not being to the manner born. Things like this don't happen often, but they do happen. Mom once said that, if she knew what she knows now, she would have picked different names for us, names like Hazel or Fiona or Christine.

Another coin zings past my head. It hits Mark Watkins on the neck. Mark turns, his face twisted in anger. "Who did that?" he bellows. The class falls silent. Scott Garson fear-grins, the rubber band frozen in his hand.

Mrs. Rice looks from Mark to Scott and back to Mark again. "Out," she says. "Both of you." Her arm extends, finger pointed, to the door. With a fearful glance at Mark, Scott stands up and shuffles to the front. Mark follows. The door clicks shut behind them.

The trees outside bend and sway. A finch swoops through the air, buffeted by the breeze. Time trickles along. Scott glares at me when they return from the office. I review the time travel possibilities again. *Dream, virtual reality, psychotic break—*

"Amy!" Mrs. Rice shouts. I look up. "Are you with us?"

"Yes."

"Wonderful. Since you've been paying such close attention—" the class titters "—please answer my question."

I clear my throat. I spent two years in the art world. You think I can't bullshit, Mrs. Rice? Watch this.

"History teaches us that we're part of a long continuity far greater than our individual lives. It gives us a common foundation and language to understand the world, and ourselves. And it's fascinating—think of all the people who lived before us, people who were once just as alive as we are. Learning about them is the closest we can come to time travel."

"My question was, who was the King of England during the American Revolution," Mrs. Rice says, after a stunned pause. "Nice try."

Another titter ripples through the classroom. Andrew turns and looks at me, puzzled. Cassidy and Bretlyn roll their eyes. I examine the marks on my desk: an anarchy symbol, *S.H. + L.S.* inside a heart, *ERIC SUX* carved into the wood, a few spurting dicks. I rest my head on my palm. Two more years of this, four years of high school, then college, and then…

And then? Years—decades—of waking up early, staring up at the ceiling, searching for any excuse not to go into work. Maybe marriage, maybe children, maybe not. Money problems, flaky friends, time rushing on faster and faster until the very end. Is that my future? For God's sake, what is it for?

I rewrite my list on a blank page.

Dream

Virtual Reality

Psychotic Break

Coma

~~*Capgras Dimension*~~

Alternate Universe

Loop Universe

"Groundhog Day" Universe

Basic Time Travel

2016 Was the Dream

Hell

Computer class. Two girls, sitting side-by-side, confer over Neopets. A few boys huddle around a screen, laughing at a video of human-mouthed rodents. Lisa Sharkey's looking at a Dollz webpage, full of pixelated, Barbie-like avatars. Mr. Dutrain, our long-suffering computer teacher, has written *Today's Task* on the board: *Make a pie chart, a bar graph, and a line graph based on the Excel spreadsheet "7g_week1.exe" in the folder marked "Class Files."*

Everyone ignores the assignment, except for Jessica Truesdale, Andrew Jacobs, and me. I finish it in about five minutes, print it out, and hand it to Mr. Dutrain. He goggles at the paper for a moment, then at me.

"Already?" he says.

"I'm an expert in Excel," I lie. Not for the first time.

"Expert? You make a lot of spreadsheets in your spare time?"

"You have no idea."

Two girls giggle behind me. My cheeks flush. They might not be laughing at me, but it feels like they are.

I search every term I can, looking for a clue or a sign: "2016," "August 25 2016," "8/25/16." I search a few random terms, looking for any hit: "Rihanna," "Spotify," "ISIS," "Make America Great Again." Nothing relevant appears on Google, Yahoo,

Dogpile, anywhere. After combing through several angst-filled blogs, a new idea takes possession of me.

If there's nothing out there yet, it's my job to put it out there. Time to go anonymously public, à la Deep Throat. My "pitch," if you could call it that, will be short and to the point, repeated everywhere:

> *August 25, 2016. Sound familiar? If so, get in touch immediately. Tell me something about the U.S. elections, or tell me what "ISIS" means to you.*

There's no wordpress.com yet, and I can't buy my own self-hosted website. I could start a free blog, join a few forums, leave some comments in somebody's guestbook. There must be ways to promote yourself online. Doubt overtakes me. What if it doesn't work? What if nothing works?

What if you never try, and you never get out of here? What then?

Twenty minutes pass in a blur of mind-numbing activity. I register accounts at Blogger and Livejournal, both under the same username. I make my profiles as generic as possible, filled with keywords some lost soul might google in a frantic attempt to make a connection. When I'm done, I survey my Livejournal profile. Let's hope this leads somewhere.

oracledoll

Name: *Oracle Doll*

Location: *Northern California, California, United States*

Birthdate: *08-26*

E-mail: *oracledoll at hotmail dot com*

About me: *August 25, 2016. Sound familiar? If so, get in touch immediately. Tell me something about the U.S. elections, or tell me what "ISIS" means to you.*

Interests: *2016, 2016 presidential elections, 50 shades of grey, <u>aleppo</u>, barack obama, <u>bernie sanders</u>, black lives matter, breaking bad, bruno mars, chris pine, florence and the machine, <u>game of thrones</u>, <u>grimes</u>, <u>h.g. wells</u>, <u>hope</u>, justin bieber, kit harington, lana del rey, lorde, marvel movies, nicki minaj, <u>nostradamus</u>, pokémon go, rihanna, <u>science fiction</u>, <u>supernatural</u>, syrian civil war, syrian refugee crisis, taylor swift, the hunger games, <u>time machines</u>, <u>time travel</u>.*

Interests are only underlined if more than one person has listed them. I browse through a few, looking for anything relevant or at least suggestive. Grimes is the name of a small city in Iowa. Who knew.

"Dude," Andrew says. "Look at—hey James, put *this* as your background." He points to his own computer screen, now filled with pictures of sweaty, shirtless men. The other boy, James presumably, turns away. A flush spreads across his cheeks.

"James, James—yo, James!"

"That's enough," Mr. Dutrain says, not looking up from his monitor. "Let's get back to work. No talking."

An uneasy silence descends on the class. I look at the blinking line on my screen. The keyboard clatters under my fingertips.

8/25/16

[mood | apprehensive]

[music | Jethro Tull: Living in the Past]

The center cannot hold. Terror in the Middle East (but that's no surprise). The Golden Dawn descends from his tower and slouches toward the seat of power. A woman fights him for her husband's place, spilling secrets with every step.

Unease fills my mind as I reread my post. Will the Dawn/Don connection make sense to non-native English speakers? What if no one understands it? What if it attracts the wrong kind of attention? I still don't know why I'm here, or what here is exactly. I could wake up in a holding cell, on a spaceship, or in some interdimensional rift. It's a risk I have to take.

Andrew stands up and lumbers to the printer. I sneak a look at James. He's on MS Paint, writing our school's initials, "FKMS," over and over in a text box.

My feelings exactly.

CHAPTER EIGHT
THE DOOMSDAY GARDEN

Kids stare as I pass their tables. A few girls whisper to their friends behind their hands, eyes swiveled to my face. I'm ready to bolt when Sean waves me over to his table. Sean sits, as always, with the out crowd: Lisa Sharkey, Andrew Jacobs, Hector Villanueva, and a few others, all wearing band T-shirts and studded belts.

"Catch," I say, throwing a Twix to Sean. He fumbles it, then fishes it off the floor. He looks at me in confusion.

"For faxing me the homework. I owe you one, right?"

"Those sit on the shelves for months," Lisa says.

"They're partially hydrogenated," Andrew says through a mouthful of mashed carrots. "It could sit there for twenty years and it wouldn't make a difference."

"Partially what?"

"I didn't tell you what I wanted," Sean says, tearing open the package. "That rotten eggplant sounded mighty tempting."

"Too bad."

Voices echo and bounce throughout the cafeteria, drowning out all thought. I don't mind. Andrew and Hector improvise a game of hackey sack with a crumpled-up piece of paper. Lisa shows Sean how to make a fortune teller; he feigns interest, noisily slurping the dregs of his milk.

"Didn't you get suspended?" Hector asks me.

"For what?"

"For ditching on the first day."

"I didn't get suspended. I didn't even meet with the principal."

"Seriously?"

"No detention? Nothing?"

I nod, amazed. I got in so much trouble at home, I didn't think about school. Not until now.

"I told you, girls never get in trouble," Hector says to Sean.

"Do you have ADD?" Lisa says. "You can't get detention if you have ADD. That's why Scott never gets in trouble."

"I don't have ADD."

"Maybe 'cause it didn't happen at school," Sean says.

"Maybe."

"Why'd you do it?" Andrew says.

"It was my birthday."

"So? I got a root canal on my birthday."

I can't tell them the truth. At best, it'll spread more rumors. At worst, I'll get a one-way ticket to troubled teen camp, where they fix trauma with more trauma. If I look past Sean's shoulder, I can see one sixth-grade boy staring at me, whispering something to his friend. I look down, take another bite of apple.

"Did the cops really find you in a crack den?" Hector says. Sean glares at him. I shake my head, struggle to swallow.

"I was at the Metreon," I say. I retell the story I told everyone: the stolen car, hiding in the backseat, the parking lot near MoMA. I finish with a whopper about watching *Pirates of the Caribbean*, in IMAX, while the cops prowled the theater.

"Luke knows these guys who did hella worse than that,"

Sean says. "They broke into their old school and wrote *Sick T-Rex*—no, *Sick Tyrannosaurus* over the principal's door—"

"Sick what?"

"I dunno. It means 'kill dictators' or something."

"How does 'sick T-Rex' mean—"

"*Sic Semper Tyrannus*," I say. "'Thus always to tyrants.' It's Latin. Brutus said it when he stabbed Julius Caesar."

"Nice," Andrew says, shoving a tater tot in his mouth.

"They got arrested?" Lisa says.

"They had to do some community service, I think. I met one of the guys once, so I don't think they went to jail."

"That's fucked *up*," Andrew says, admiration suffusing his voice.

The rest of the day passes in a daze of anxiety, boredom, and petty humiliation. I sleepwalk through the afternoon, doodle in my notebook, watch the clock's minute hand. Unlike work meetings, you know roughly when each one is going to end. You usually leave with a clear task (do problems x through y, finish chapter z), instead of a vague notion of "what's next on the agenda." I'd still rather be in meetings, though. You can't leave the classroom without a pass, and you're not paid to be there. I imagine Mina Sirota standing at our office door, bellowing "The bell doesn't dismiss you—*I* dismiss you." Mrs. Haverfield asks me why I'm laughing. I shake my head.

I wait to be picked up in the school library. Cassidy, sitting a few tables down, turns her back to me. A snatch of some old song plays over and over in my mind: a ticking clock, counterpointed by an eerie music box melody. Humming "All Star" doesn't dispel it. Every sound wears at me: the squeaking sneakers and basketball on the court outside, the coach's whistles and yells, the A.C., Mrs. Petrelli clearing her throat. The song fragment plays over in my mind.

I get up and browse the bookshelves. Here's *Parenting for the 90s, The Fullerton Guide to Buying a Second Home*, Scarsdale and macrobiotic diet guides. Donations from parents, given covers and call numbers by someone who isn't paid enough to care. My eyes meet Cassidy's as I walk down the last aisle. She turns away, noisily flips through the magazine in front of her.

I reach into my pocket—the one that doesn't contain the bear mace—looking for a pen. Instead I pull out Claude Belissan's card. The symbol on the back magnetizes my attention. The inner music stops.

"Mrs. Petrelli," I say softly when I reach her desk. Mrs. Petrelli blinks at me over her book. She frowns, a little puzzled, and adjusts her glasses. I show her the card.

"Have you ever seen this symbol before?"

Mrs. Petrelli looks down her glasses, takes the card from me, squints. Something works deep behind her eyes. "You know, I have. Hold on," she says, hoisting herself out of her chair.

I follow her to the bookshelves near the back. "I know it's in this section," she says, glancing at one book after another. Cassidy sneaks a look at us. When my eyes meet hers, she turns away.

"Here, hon," she says, handing me a large hardcover. *The Calhoun Encyclopedia of New Religions*. And there's the symbol—a snake eating its tail, surrounding rays converging in the center—right between a spaceship and a meditating man. Mrs. Petrelli holds up the business card: the symbols are identical. "Where'd you find this?" she says, waggling the card.

"On the ground," I say, pulling it from her hand. She frowns down her glasses at me.

"You know that 555 numbers don't work, right? Someone's playing a trick on you."

"I bet."

My phone rings in my pocket. Mrs. Petrelli gives me a sharp look. I walk dutifully out to the hall.

"Where are you?" Mom says when I answer.

"The library, where you told me—"

"I'm outside. Get your stuff."

"I have to check out a book. I'll be—"

"You had all afternoon to check out a book!"

"It'll take two seconds."

"Unbelievable." A high, cutting laugh. "The day after you run away—the day *after*, Amy—you can't even come out when I ask you to. I should make you walk home."

"You'd never do that. Not after Polly Klaas. I *know* you."

My feet barely touch the floor as I walk into the library. How can this be happening, even in a dream? Cassidy's slumped over her table, head resting on her backpack. Guilt gnaws at me. I had all afternoon to call CPS, and I didn't. Why not? Téa will pick her up soon, drive her home. And then?

I walk over to her, my heartbeat thumping in my ears. *She's a little girl. What are you afraid of?* She doesn't even look like herself; giant gobs of baby fat obscure her future face. Only her eyes are the same.

"You can come over to my house, if you wanna wait there," I say. "We can get you a snack. Téa can pick you up, if you…"

Cassidy returns her attention to a magazine. My face flushes with rage. *Why the fuck was I ever your friend?* I walk to the circulation desk. Mrs. Petrelli's face is soft with pity, which makes it ten times worse. She hands me the encyclopedia.

"You take care, hon," she says.

I imagine the Clark family living room: white sloped ceiling, wooden floors, big bay windows overlooking the forest. Slice stands on the balcony, mumbling something I can't hear. He turns. His black eyes bore through my skull.

Mom's sitting in the car, clenching the steering wheel. She watches me walk over, her face pinched with tension.

"How was school?" she says when I've closed the door behind me. I can hear in her voice that she's forcing herself to be nice.

"School was fine. How was work?"

Mom pulls out of the pickup circle. I repeat the question. She shakes her head. Mom doesn't decompress by talking about her day. She doesn't decompress, period, for another decade. I reach in my pocket for some gum, and find a small bundle of tissue paper, wrapped around something small and hard. The Seroquel pill. I had all day to throw it out, and I didn't. Shit.

"I'm gonna take a nap when we get home," I say.

"We have to go to Safeway first. Dad wants sandwiches for dinner."

"What kind?"

"He wants the number seven."

"The fried chicken?"

"Crispy chicken."

Of course. Eight ounces of breaded and fried cutlet, slathered in cheese, ketchup, and mayo, encased in a slab of white bread as big as the Rock's forearm. About as "healthy" as a fried Snickers bar.

"I know this amazing grilled chicken recipe. It takes five minutes to make, max," I say. "It's cheaper than the sandwich."

Mom glances at me as she steers around a curve. "Where'd you learn that?"

"I have my ways."

A smile plays across her mouth.

"I don't understand Dad sometimes," I say, pressing my advantage. "He's a P.A. He works for a doctor. He goes to the doctor. Healthy eating isn't a hermetic mystery to him."

"Hermetic mystery. What's that from, *Harry Potter*?"

"Mom."

Mom sighs. "Dad's struggled with his weight ever since he quit smoking."

"He quit thirty years ago."

"It hasn't been thirty years." Mom laughs. "It was right before I had Leah."

"Leah's...okay, it's been *twenty* years. Nearly."

"It hasn't been..." Mom's face falls.

"What does Dad weigh, anyway? He's two-fifty if he's a mosquito. The car squeaks when he gets in. He's gonna die if he doesn't—"

"He's not gonna die."

"Did he bathe in the Styx? His heart won't last the next ten years. You know that. *He* knows that."

"Don't be dramatic."

"I'm not being dramatic. If you're gonna help him kill himself—"

"You are out of line," Mom says, her voice deathly calm. "I do everything for this family, while you sit in your room, just, 'La di da, I won't do my homework. La di da, I'll run away to the Tenderloin. La di da, I'll call my mother a murderer while she pays for everything I own.'"

I think of Dad's casket lowering into the earth.

"What would you have me do?" Mom says. The car swings wildly around a curve. "How can I make him get healthy? Go ahead. Tell me what Amy Snowberger, the world's smartest teenager, would do in my situation."

"You could, I dunno, not buy him a fried chicken sandwich."

"Crispy chicken."

It's the same damn thing, Mom.

I slide further down my seat. The car speeds past a telephone pole covered with flyers. *MISSING*, they all say in big red letters, above a grainy photo of a woman's face.

Mom sends me to get the milk while she waits for the sandwiches. Once I'm out of sight, I let out a huge sigh. For the next few minutes I can be by myself, not "on" for anyone or anything. The tension falls away from me with every step.

There has to be a trash can somewhere in here. By the free samples—but there are no free samples. Look—oranges for $1.50 a pound. Apples for $1.25. Five pounds of potatoes—five!—for $2.30. A dozen eggs for $1.20. Here's the milk: one gallon for a wallet-busting $1.99. What are gas prices? Maybe $2.50 a gallon, maybe less.

I drop the pill into the small trash can by the restrooms. Andy Williams croons "Holly" on the overhead speakers. I remember Tom in our kitchen, humming along while I set the table. I see myself at a payphone, destroying teenage Tom's dreams. *She doesn't love you*—why did I say that? So what if it's true?

The basket, now heavy with a milk carton, thumps against my shins. I walk down the spices aisle, humming to blot out the song. Two forty-something women, all turquoise pins and iridescent scarves, talk in the middle of the aisle. I scoot behind the one with henna-red hair. She barely notices me.

"Her husband hasn't returned one phone call," Henna Lady says. "If he wasn't in Korea, I'd say he did it." I slow down, survey the spices. Ground cayenne pepper, peppercorns, paprika, cinnamon. I stand on my tiptoes to grab a jar of cayenne pepper.

"Mike thinks someone's not talking," her friend replies. "Nobody vanishes into the air—"

"She lives right by the forest. Maybe she wanted to end it quietly, you know?"

"With a daughter in kindergarten?"

Henna Lady shakes her head. "You know he wouldn't even talk to her on the phone? Married twenty years, she had to call his—"

"What are you doing?" Mom barks behind me. "I told you, get the milk and come back. If you can't do what I ask, you can wait in the car."

"I'm sorry."

"I don't want you to be sorry. I want you to not be the kind of person who doesn't follow directions. Why is it so hard?"

Adolescent anger simmers inside me. Mom purses her lips, reaches into my basket, takes out the bottle of cayenne pepper. I watch her put it back on the shelf. Henna Lady and her friend are now staring at Mom, mouths agape. Mom walks past them without a glance, pushing her overladen cart. Henna Lady gives me a sympathetic shake of her head. I trail behind Mom, my empty basket thwacking at my shins.

Mom wasn't always like this. When we were kids, she was kind, fun, way higher-energy than our friends' boomer parents. On her days off, she took us boogie-boarding and canoeing, made jam with us, read to us at bedtime. It can't have been easy, but we didn't know.

Something snapped when Leah started middle school. The combined pressures of her job, her commute, and the college application process (which starts around sixth grade, if not earlier, in Marin) awakened some inner monster that lay sleeping for years. Dad once joked, when Mom was well out of earshot, that "the ghost of Mimi De Paul" had taken over her body.

After Leah spiraled out of control, an exhausted version of Mom's old self emerged from the ruins, resigned and sad. Not that she's happy now. I wonder if she ever was.

We're at the checkout when my body turns cold. I look up in slow motion. Leah's ex-sponsor and ex-pimp stands behind us, looking over the magazines. He must be in his twenties, but he's wearing an eternal teenager uniform: tent-like hoodie, sweatpants, ratty sneakers, sparse goatee. For all I know, he has another girl locked in his house right now. Maybe he's prowling for fresh meat. Maybe he's not that bad, yet.

Our eyes meet. I feel clammy and dirty, like someone poured sewage into my soul. His eyes flit to Mom. He turns and walks back into the store.

What is his name?

Mom's busy with her purse. I hide the crispy chicken sandwich in between two copies of *The Moon*, a black-and-white tabloid. *GARDEN OF EDEN FOUND—ON THE INTERNET!* the headline shouts. A woodcut paradise fills the screen of an old desktop monitor. A snake leers at me from a tree in the center.

Dad's waiting for us when we get home. He hugs me and everything disappears. And then he lets go.

We unload groceries together while Mom disappears into the bathroom.

"How was school?" he asks.

"Fine."

"Anything interesting happen?"

"Some boys acted up in Mr. Weathers' class."

"Who's Mr. Weathers, again?"

"My bio teacher. He's nice, but—"

"Not your meteorology teacher?"

I groan, hiding my smile. *Dad's alive.* A supernova of joy explodes inside me. I wipe my eyes. *Isn't all this bullshit worth it, just to see him again?*

"Where's Leah?" Mom barks as she reenters the kitchen.

Dad's looking in the grocery bag, lost in thought. "Richard, where is—"

"Where's my sandwich?" Dad says. He's holding one of the sandwiches in its white tube, waggling it back and forth.

"It's in there. Where's—"

"The crispy chicken?"

"Uh-huh."

More susurration of plastic bags.

"Here's your BLT. This is Leah's veggie sandwich. Amy's…" More susurration. "Why'd you get Leah a sandwich? She's at her friend's house."

"Which friend?" Mom says, very quiet.

"Farrah."

"Fay *Ray?*"

"Could be. The one that looks like…whatsername. Angelina Jolie."

Flames ignite in Mom's eyes. She takes up the entire doorway; I couldn't pass her if I was invisible. Dad throws up his hands.

"I have told you many, *many* times that she can't leave the house—"

"Who decided—"

"Let me—let me *finish*, Richard—that she is *not* allowed out of the house until—"

"—really think you're being too—"

"—un-*til* she finishes all of her applications to—"

"—still so early—"

"—I'm sorry, did you not understand what I—"

"Where do you get off, telling me what to do?" Dad bellows. I shrink into the corner. "Leah filled out the Common Application two weeks ag—"

"They don't all *take* the common application, Richard, which you would know if—"

"It's August, Jackie. The applications are due in—"

"—isn't the point, Richard, the point is—"

"She's a straight-A student! She got fourteen-twenty on the SATs. And yet—let me finish, *Jackie*—she can't leave the house because she's only applied to five colleges? Listen to yourself! What the hell is wrong with you?"

I cross my arms, try to roll up like a millipede. Mom turns back to the table.

"Where's my sandwich?" Dad asks again. Now *his* voice is dangerous, or trying to be.

"Maybe I forgot it." Mom sighs. "I know I ordered four sandwiches, though."

"It's fine." Dad turns to me, his eyes still smoldering. "Amy, do you want your sister's sandwich?"

"Not really."

Dad laughs. "Take it anyway," he says, and pats his stomach. "I need something hearty to feed this beast."

"I don't want Leah's sandwich."

A shadow passes over his face. He laughs in warning. Mom looks from him to me.

"You don't need to feed the beast," I say. What was it the interventionist said? Come from a place of love—love, and "I" statements. Always use I statements. "I get so sad when I see you eating junk food. I don't want you to die of a heart attack like Grandpa Doug."

Dad stares through me, his face fixed in stony objection.

"I can make you some grilled chicken. I know this recipe, it takes five minutes. I'll show you how to make it."

"Amy, you will—"

"Give her the sandwich, Richard."

Mom's looking at me with new eyes. For one moment, I'm sure that Mom knows everything. Maybe this really *is* a Capgras

Dimension, where everyone's in on the cosmic joke except for yours truly. Then the moment passes. Mom grabs the sandwich out of Dad's hand and hands it to me.

"Come on," Dad whines. "Leah's sandwich is lettuce and olives. Don't push that on me. This is *your* fault."

"You'll live." Mom's eyes meet mine. Something passes between us. She knows—about the sandwich, at least. And she's not punishing me. Why not?

Dad watches helplessly as I unwrap it, then sighs like a moody kid. Mom meets my eyes again. This time she smiles.

I eat my remaining Twix alone, in my room, with the lights off and the curtains drawn. I mentally read off my list, one more time:

Dream

Virtual Reality

Psychotic Break

Coma

~~*Capgras Dimension*~~

Alternate Universe

Loop Universe

"Groundhog Day" Universe

Basic Time Travel

~~*2016 Was the Dream*~~ *(I wish!)*

Hell

Adolescent loneliness washes over me. It's half sexual

hunger—maybe more than half. I raise a hand over my face, look at the ceiling through the spaces between my fingers. What clues have I found? What research have I done? Claude Belissan and his symbol creep me out, but there's nothing explicit to tie him to time travel. Right now, though, it's my only lead.

I flip through the book until I find Claude's ouroboros at the top of page 143. The caption is short and to the point:

Top: The Doomsday Garden's "logos logo," showing the union of "chronos" (time, represented by the snake) with "kairos" (eternity, represented by the converging rays).

I stifle a laugh. It, sounds like something dreamed up by an exceptionally pompous Tool fanboy. I read on.

DOOMSDAY GARDEN, The. One of several apocalyptic cults that arose in mid-1960s American counterculture. After a fire destroyed its main center of activity, a Victorian mansion in San Francisco's Haight-Ashbury district, the group fell apart, though its art and philosophy influenced New Age culture and spirituality for decades to come.

The Doomsday Garden traces its origin to Sebastian Spar (1885-1949), an obscure Franco-German doctor and mystic. The youngest of thirteen children, Spar was born in Kehl, a German village just across the border from Strasbourg. He spoke both French and German from childhood, and may have picked up Alsatian from a nanny. Spar trained as a doctor at the University of Bonn before finding a job as a surgeon in Offenburg.

During the First World War, Spar worked at a military

hospital on the Western Front. This experience haunted him all his life. "Never did I imagine such cruelty lurked in the hearts of men," he wrote in his diary, "nor that civilization could be swept away like leaves in a gust of wind." Spar was struck by the horror of a war that pitted his own family against itself, sending nephews and cousins to die fighting each other in the trenches.

One night, after a grueling three-day shift, Spar was walking to his quarters when a white light opened in the air in front of him. Stunned, the doctor walked through it and into a forest. The forest was dark and forbidding, but "a great force impressed itself upon me and drew me in further." Spar walked through the forest to a small circular glade filled with flowers. Two interlocking trees stood in the clearing's center, ascending into nothingness above. Both had "varied large fruits, streaked with many different colors, translucent and filled with radiant light, hanging from every branch."

Spar could not enter the clearing, no matter how hard he tried. He looked down. An enormous snake, its tail in its mouth, encircled the clearing, and would not let him pass.

"[The snake's] bright eye stared deeply into mine," Spar wrote. "It spoke to me in a language beyond language, telling me things impossible and true."

When Spar looked up again, the glade was desolate. The trees in its center were dead. The snake was gone. Spar entered the clearing, where "a feeling of appalling gloom" overtook him. He looked up and saw a black sphere "falling upward, growing smaller and smaller, until it was but a tiny point in the darkness."

The scene vanished, leaving Spar shaken and cold in the street. He stumbled home, strange music filling his ears. He wrote down his vision in a medical notebook, then fell asleep for thirteen hours.

"When I woke up," Spar wrote, "I knew that I had glimpsed the true Garden of Eden. I felt in my soul that mankind must return to it at once, before we destroy ourselves and even God Himself in an orgy of violence and hatred."

Spar moved to California in 1921, where he married and fathered three children. For nearly thirty years, he lived and worked as an orthopedic surgeon in Pasadena. In his spare time, he wrote and self-published books on spirituality, philosophy, and the future of the human race.

Spar believed that the story of Adam and Eve was a mystical metaphor for an "eternal world" that mankind had once inhabited. Many religious and political movements, Spar noted, aimed for a "heavenly-earthly existence at their end, free of pain and strife. Eden is in the strongest race-memory, and the most universal: it is not a dream but a place waiting to be found, like Columbus and the Americas."

How to find it? Simple. Destroy time—or rather, ordinary time, the "chronos" we all live in. "Kairos," the "appointed time outside of time—the connection between time and eternity," provides a doorway between the eternal world and the fallen one. These terms, borrowed from Ancient Greece by way of Orthodox Christianity, gave Spar's writings a mystical force that belied their insubstantial character. Spar never explained how kairos could be found or made, preferring woolly mysticism and sentences as complex as they were meaningless.

Spar was neither charismatic nor publicity-minded. "I refuse to prostitute my words before that wicked harlot, the press," he wrote in a letter to his wife. "I should rather die than let this tender creature uncoil itself where the world can squash it underfoot." At the time of his death, his followers had dwindled down to his widow, a daughter, and a few Los Angeles eccentrics.

Sebastian Spar would have faded into obscurity if not for his daughter, Beatrice. Beatrice had what her father lacked: limitless energy, missionary zeal, and charisma that could "charm the horns off a goat," as one follower put it. While an undergraduate at UC Berkeley, she began re-publishing her father's works, reframing them as a "transcendent philosophy" for a new, enlightened age. Contemporaries remembered her holding court in Berkeley's many coffee shops, sometimes late into the evening, surrounded by an "admiring coterie" of students and beatnik types.

Most dismissed the younger Spar as a crank. One article described her as "a glorified huckster, on the same level as the gypsy women who read the palms of bored housewives." Others damned her with faint praise, calling her an "intelligent, dangerous woman" and an "adventuress of the first order." Despite this, Sparism (as it was initially called) attracted a small but devoted following throughout the 1950s. One of these followers, William Redeker, married Spar, changed his last name to hers, and cared for their children during her many lecture tours. His devotion was by no means unusual: many members gave up life savings, private incomes, and houses to Spar's movement.

Beatrice Spar moved to San Francisco in 1964, after a follower donated a house in the city's Haight-Ashbury neighborhood. Spar repainted the house entirely in white and installed large gardens in the front and back yards. This house was the locus of the Sparist movement: every day of the week, Beatrice (or one of her followers) held conferences, concerts, symposiums, lectures, and rituals. One former attendee remembers "young people in Edwardian dress, mod costumes, military jackets, big platform shoes—sometimes all of the above—gathered on the steps of a modest white-washed Victorian, wanting to see and to be seen."

It's unclear how the group became "The Doomsday Garden." The name probably comes from a line in an essay by Sebastian Spar: "The prophet preaches the end of the world while he tends to the flowers in his garden." Locals were less kind. They called Beatrice Spar and her acolytes "Doomsdayers" or "Snake Charmers," after the large ouroboros, with thirteen black lines converging in its center, that one follower painted above the doorway. This became an identifying symbol for Doomsdayers and fellow travelers, and the butt of many jokes. One comic from the time shows a blue-collar guy asking a white-clad hippie girl, "Man, what snake crossed your ass today?"

The Doomsday Garden went everywhere that was anywhere. They handed out thousands of flyers at the first "Human Be-In." They showed up regularly to anti-war protests, community meetings, acid tests, street performances, lectures, even bridal fairs. The movement published provocative mini-magazines on local topics of interest: Vietnam, atomic science, the revolution, the nature of time. A reporter might drop by to ask about their latest missive, just in time to catch a "symbolic play" featuring girls in bikinis. So the wheel turned, bringing the group increased publicity, scrutiny, and police attention.

Rumors swirled about Spar, each more outrageous than the next: she was the only woman ever admitted to Bohemian Grove; she published a monograph on the Lister-LeNormand Hypothesis under an assumed name; she could enlighten anyone by looking in their eyes. In public, she was often seen with professors and graduate students in physics, astrophysics, neuroscience, and chemistry. The Doomsday Garden, Spar asserted, had "mastered the art and science of psycho-temporalism" and could "create reality at will." Cartoons depicted Spar juggling planets, brains, and potted plants while meditating, sometimes on a bed of nails or some blissed-out Poindexter's lap.

Spar's powers of persuasion were legendary. She convinced a few of her wealthier followers that they had returned to their past selves, making her vicariously responsible for all of their worldly success. It wasn't unusual for a member of Spar's cult to credit her "temporal intervention" in changing their lives, years or even decades before they met her.

I reread the last paragraph. The phrase "returned to their past selves" chimes over and over in my mind. I copy the paragraph into my notebook. Who are these people? Are they still alive? If they aren't, they must have talked to a journalist, a researcher, somebody. I have to find out what they said.

The Doomsday Garden had many hallmarks of a destructive cult. Daily "chronos encounters," like Mao's struggle sessions, pitted one person against a vicious mob, sometimes for hours at a time. The person in the hot seat would not be permitted to speak, react, or respond in any way to the torrents of criticism aimed at him or her. Several people reached complete breakdown during and after the experience. Members were required to work for at least sixteen hours a day, often more. Ex-members report an oppressive atmosphere of "eternal overwork, stress, and self-doubt."

By the spring of 1967, San Francisco was bursting with runaways. The tiny Haight-Ashbury neighborhood could not handle the 300 new arrivals that streamed in every day. Malnutrition and disease spread across the city. Drug dealers, bikers, and other lowlifes moved in. Speed, heroin, and harder drugs circulated freely. Rape was "as common as bullshit on Haight St.," according to Chester Anderson, a local poet. Many young people left San Francisco damaged and disillusioned.

The chaos of the neighborhood mirrored the prophecies of doom that increasingly filled the Doomsday Garden's magazines. Issues featured long lists of news stories that proved the apocalypse was coming, soon: riots, assassinations, explosions, earthquakes. As the atmosphere grew more menacing, the movement's educated followers drifted away, leaving Spar to feed, clothe, and shelter those who remained.

The movement all but ended on August 26, 1967, when a fire engulfed the group's San Francisco headquarters, killing Beatrice Spar and twelve others. An electrical fuse had blown in the basement, setting the frame ablaze. Spar was found at the back of the house, where she'd succumbed to smoke inhalation. She was holding a picture of her father.

Without Beatrice to guide them, the movement collapsed. A few small groups are rumored to persist in Northern California, though this could not be confirmed. The extent of their activities is unknown.

I read through the entry again, writing down every proper noun and unfamiliar term. I'll google them tomorrow in computer class. There's one more illustration, this one without a caption: a thin man in rags, an *END IS NIGH* poster slung over his shoulder. His other hand holds a watering can. Broken lines fall from its spout to a small flower, its face turned up to meet them.

CHAPTER NINE
LIP GLOSS AND AGONY

THE WORLD OUTSIDE fades from deep blue to black. I get up and stretch. I lie on the floor, make carpet angels, climb a pretend staircase with my hands. My back gradually loosens. I have to call…who do I have to call? I don't remember, I only know it's important. The TV blares in the living room: hard rock, unctuous voiceover, the all new Chevy something-something.

The air's too close. I get up, open the window. The burglar alarm blats in the front hall.

Mom opens the door as I slam the window shut. "What are you doing?" she bellows over the alarm

"I opened the window," I shout.

"You're not dressed for bed!"

"It's eight o'clock—ow!"

Mom drags me, by the arm, into the hallway. "Turn around," she barks as we come to the alarm panel. I hesitate. She spins me away. My shoulder slams into the far wall. The bell rings ceaselessly above my head. I press my palms to my ears. Dad, sitting in the living room, goggles at us. The alarm shuts off.

"Visine for contacts does more than re-wet your lenses," a voice on the TV says. "It really, *really* refreshes your eyes."

Mom's feet thump against the floorboards.

I can't even open the window in my own room. Fuck. I'd rather pay rent.

"Name your favorite person in history. Three pages. Double-spaced."

I stare at the blank piece of paper in front of me. Do I have a favorite person in history? The obvious candidates present themselves: Sophie Scholl, Louis Pasteur, Nelson Mandela—wait. Are you a person "in history" if you're still alive? Great topic for a dorm room bull session. Not so great for a middle-school paper.

I pick Rhea Silvia, mother of Romulus and Remus. She's not my favorite person in history, but she's one I can write about without looking anything up. A passage from Tom's notebooks returns to me, unbidden:

Rhea approached the fire with dread. The goddess must have seen Mars overtake her in the forest; she would know Rhea's offense, and her deception. What would Vesta do if the girl tended to her sacred fire, clad in robes she had no right to wear? The fire might go out, or consume Rhea on the spot. But to fail in her duties would be just as unthinkable. That failure would raise questions, suspicions, and then...

And then? Only images: Rhea's eyes, the horror of the flame, relief as the fire accepted the branch, Rhea's singed hemline trailing behind her.

Some automatic part of me writes this essay while my mind wanders to the future past.

"This is incredible," I'd said to Tom, holding up his notebook. We were in Golden Gate Park, lying under the shade of a large tree, half watching a pick-up game down the field. My head rested on his stomach.

"Please," he said, taking the notebook back. "It's decent, at best."

"You dirty liar. That's better than two-thirds—no, three-quarters of all bestsellers."

"Only three-quarters?"

"I'm serious, Tom. I emailed that girl who works at Random House. She said—"

"Is this your new hobby?"

"Is what my new hobby?"

"This," he said, waving his notebook. "First it was teaching me how to cook. Now you want me to publish—"

"Tom. I'm gonna get carpal tunnel if I have to give you another deep tissue massage. I want you to be happy. It's completely selfish, trust me."

Tom lolled his head back in the grass.

"No bullshit, Tom. This book could change the world."

"It's not a cure for cancer."

"You're a portfolio manager. You're not curing cancer anyway."

"Touché."

"Before I read your stories," I said, tapping the cover for emphasis, "I thought of history as dust and dates. It never dawned on me that people from the past actually lived and breathed. They talked to their neighbors, they got drunk, they got bored, they laughed at stupid jokes…And if you could do that for me, make me see history as a living thing, why not other people? Doesn't that mean anything to you?"

Tom pinched the bridge of his nose. "Holly used to say the same thing," he said. "Said I could 'make statues come alive—'"

"Give yourself a chance," I pleaded, ignoring yet another mention of Holly. "Give Rhea Silvia a chance. Don't you think she deserves it?"

"You make it sound so simple. Maybe I should go on vacation, let you take up the strings. You could live my life for me, solve all my problems—shower me with your wisdom and benevolence."

"I thought you'd never ask."

Tom looked down at me and mussed my hair, but his thoughts were elsewhere. They always were.

I lean back, spin in my chair. The door connecting Leah's room to mine is locked. If I jiggle it right, it should open. It does.

Leah's stapled Christmas lights around the edge of the ceiling, filling the room with underwater green-blue light. Her walls are covered in artwork: sketches, paintings, xeroxed illustrations, a few portraits of Viggo Mortensen. Not all of it is hers: Arthur Rackham's Alice, assailed by playing cards; Ai Yazawa's long-limbed eyelash-girls; panels from *Ghost World* and *Sandman*. There's a photo collage above her bed: Leah and Fay Ray as schoolgirls from *The Craft*; Leah, smiling, in full Siouxsie makeup; a dozen black-clad white kids scowling at the camera. There's an overcrowded bookshelf, a half-empty jar of Manic Panic, a baseball bat, a SoBe bottle full of rainbow sand.

An easel stands in the far corner of the room. I stop short when I realize what's on it: a painting of a snake, looped thrice around a black sphere, over a background of black lines converging on some invisible center. I sidestep the easel and walk to her desk, jiggle the mouse of her blueberry iMac. The aurora vanishes, replaced by a login page. No other user accounts. No guest account. I try a few passwords before the computer locks. *Shit.* Hopefully she doesn't notice that.

I examine the Mary-Kate and Ashley calendar hanging over her desk. Leah's drawn over their pictures with Sharpie, whiteout, and metallic paint, turning the twins into gothed-out mopers.

"Only two things make us truly alive to ourselves: lip gloss and agony," Mary-Kate, or possibly Ashley, says via speech bubble. My mouth fills with a sour taste. I remember Leah in her hospital bed. That was the first time she really looked dead. And I can't remember the name of the man who put her there. I *saw* him and I still can't remember.

I feel Leah's knife against my neck. What strange line connects that woman to the girl who made this? How can they be the same person?

I shudder and turn to the huge stack of books on Leah's nightstand: an Aubrey Beardsley retrospective, several issues of *Gothic & Lolita Bible, Geek Love*. There's an Altoids tin, half buried between overlapping stacks of books. I pick it up. A rank, smoky scent wafts from inside.

You're already in deep shit. Don't dig any deeper.

I open the lid.

A small, glassine envelope of weed sits next to a lighter and a pipe. A noise outside startles me. The tin falls out of my hands and under the desk, spilling open on the carpet. *Shit.* I'm looking for the pipe when my head hits something metallic and hollow.

There's another tin duct-taped to the underside of her desk. I hesitate. I remember her knife against my throat. The tape gives way with a dull rip.

They could be candies. They're half-orange, half-white, roughly the same size as Mike and Ikes. So what if they're in a glassine envelope? Then I see the words printed on them: *ADDERALL, 20mg*. Not candy.

There are other envelopes below this one, full of pills in different colors and sizes, embossed with letters, numbers, robot heads, smiley faces. I close the lid.

I comb through the room. There's not much more: a few bags of weed, some nicotine gum, a half-full bottle of Adderall. I grab the trash bin from my room, throw everything inside. The connecting door closes behind me with a soft click. I sigh and slump against it. I remember Leah in the vestibule of the church. When I open my eyes, I see Mom, standing in front of me in the near darkness.

"Hey, sweetie. I wanted to say—what's that smell?" Her eyes laser in on the bin in my hands. She crosses the space between us in one step.

"No—*no*," I say, too late. The Altoids tins clink as Mom pulls the bin away. Pot fumes billow from its open mouth. Mom's eyes widen, then narrow in outrage.

"It's not what it looks like!" I blurt.

I look past Mom, her face now slack with shock. There's something on my bed that wasn't there before. It's a small box, wrapped in silver wrapping paper. There's a card, with *AMY* written across it in Mom's handwriting.

I know this present, and this card. Mom gave it to me for my twenty-sixth birthday. Why is it *here*?

"We're not mad at you, sweetie, but we are disappointed."

"You're not mad. I'm mad," Mom says, pacing in front of the TV.

"You shouldn't be doing drugs at your age. Your brain is still growing—"

"She shouldn't do drugs at any age." Mom fixes Dad with a warning look.

"I'm not doing drugs, I swear. Get one of those pee sticks,

test me right now. I'll bet you five hundred dollars it'll come up clean."

"You don't have five hundred dollars."

I'm about to snap back, when I think of the cash in the travel purse under my shirt. I slump back. The bin's contents are spilled all over the coffee table. A skunky odor fills the air.

"If the cops caught you with this, you'd go to jail for—I don't know, ten years. Twenty. Maybe more," Mom says. "Do you understand that? Your life would be over. No college, no job, nothing but prison cells and trailer parks for the rest of your life."

"I already told you—"

"You 'found' them at school. And instead of telling a teacher, or throwing them away, you took them home."

"I thought they were Altoids! I didn't look till I came home. They were gonna be a treat."

Mom laughs dangerously. I cross my arms. My lie is lamer than lame, but I can't narc on Leah. Not with troubled teen camp hanging over us.

Mom stops pacing and glares at me. The adolescent part of me hates her, but I see this tableau through adult eyes now. Yesterday I ran away, then got picked up on the outskirts of the Tenderloin. Today Mom catches me with a pile of illegal drugs and a nonsensical explanation. I must act very differently now, which doesn't help at all. There might be something else, something putting her and me and everyone on edge. There's an eerie feeling in the air here, a subtle wrongness that I can't ignore. I don't think it's my imagination.

"Mom," I say softly. "I will take a test right now—"

"How do you know about drug tests?"

"The news?"

"What story on the news?"

"I don't know."

"If you can't be honest with me, Amy—"

"Jackie."

"What?" Mom wheels on Dad. "What do you have to say that is so important, Richard?"

"Let her talk."

"You believe her?" Outraged laughter fills the air. "You actually think this is no big deal, even when—"

"I didn't say that. I said—"

"—your thirteen-year-old daughter is a drug dealer."

"I'm not dealing drugs!"

Steely displeasure lines Dad's face. Mom turns away.

"If I was dealing drugs, why would I put them in the trash? With all the Kleenex and old gum and shit—sorry, *stuff*, all the old *stuff*. Why would I do that?"

Mom shakes her head more and more violently.

"Jackie, maybe—"

"Don't you start," Mom snarls. Dad holds up his hands. Mom's eyes, glowing with anger, bore into mine. "No birthday presents," she says. "No computer access, period. No more books, no movies—no doors."

"Jackie—"

"I am canceling your birthday party—actually, no, *you* get to cancel it. Call everyone in your class right now—and you will pay me the reservation fee if it takes you ten y—"

"Jackie!"

"What?"

"That's enough."

They lock eyes. Mom's rage swells. Dad gets up, walks to her. "Who do you sound like?" he says.

Mom screams a response, wags her finger in Dad's face. He looks down at her, unmoving. Mom's face is nearly purple now.

A vein throbs at her temple. My heart slams against my ribs like it's trying to break through them. I scan the room for exits, shift on the couch until my path is clear to the door.

Mom's rage crests and ebbs, slowly, against Dad's unyielding gaze. She sags onto the couch. Dad sits next to her. Air floods back in the room.

"That is not fair," Mom says.

Dad puts a hand on her shoulder. "Take a break. Nothing good happens when you're like this."

"This is my *house*, Richard."

Dad murmurs something into Mom's ear. She looks at him with wounded, angry eyes.

"Calm down, or leave. Up to you."

Mom stands up and trudges into the hallway. The master bedroom door closes behind her. *The ghost of Mimi loses this round.* Dad looks at me and whistles, eyebrows raised. He's just stood up when the front door opens.

"Hi Dad," Leah says as she tromps into the living room. "Sorry I'm late. Ray and I had to study for our physics…"

She slows to a stop, taking in the table, the drug pile, the knocked-over bin. Her eyes dart from Dad's face to mine. Her mouth falls open.

"Later," Dad says, shepherding her away.

Leah shoots me a confused look. A wedge of blue-green light appears as she slips into her room. Dad sits down next to me. The couch creaks under his weight.

"Amy," Dad says, "I love you very, very much. Even if you've been running drugs for the Hell's Angels, I promise I won't get mad. See?" He holds up his pinkie. Hot tears spring to my eyes. I close them as we pinkie swear.

The priest's words come back to me: *You should tell someone you can trust. Otherwise, you really will go crazy.* I open my mouth, but the words won't come. They never do when it counts.

"I'm not on drugs," I say instead. "I'll take a test—Mom can watch me take it. Please, Dad."

Dad pats my back. Leah shuffles around in her room, opening and closing drawers. Muffled and not-so-muffled swears. Her closet door slams.

"Why don't we get some pizza?" Dad says. "What do you think? Four cheese, some breadsticks—"

"Dad, you gotta stop. The pizza, the ice cream, the crispy chicken—you're gonna die."

"I'm not going anywhere—"

"Stop!" I push him away. "Let's make something together. Some grilled chicken. It's super-easy, I promise." A bubble of snot grows in my left nostril. *Why are you doing this now? He was on your side. Don't fuck it up.*

Dad strokes my hair. Hopelessly naïve, self-indulgent Dad. He's sleepwalking with his eyes open. If there's some magic incantation that will wake him up, I don't know it. I sink against the couch.

"Don't worry about me, okay? Worry about you." He nods to the master bedroom door. "I think you're gonna have to."

Dad disappears into the master bedroom. No one comes out. After five minutes, I return to my bedroom. Mom and Dad are talking, low, on the other side of the wall. I put my present on the nightstand, then collapse on the bed. The connecting door opens with a squeak.

Leah charges me. She's holding something. I realize what it is when she presses it against my face. A pillow. I claw blindly at her, fighting for air.

"Do you promise not to scream?" Leah murmurs. I nod

beneath the pillow. She pulls it away. I gasp, blinking away the white points bursting in my eyes. Leah sits over me, her gaze burning through me. For a moment, I see the woman she'll become, the dark stars opening in her eyes.

"What the fuck?" she whispers.

"I had to."

"Had to what? Had to steal my fucking property? You *had to* do that?"

"Leah—"

Leah shoves her hand over my mouth. Her eyes search the wall behind me. Mom and Dad have stopped talking in their room. Leah looks at me, holds her finger to her lips. A long minute passes with no sound. Leah leans in close.

"I stuck up for you. I *gave* you that bear mace to protect yourself. I would never stab you in the back."

Blood burns in my cheeks. "I didn't rat you out. I told them the drugs were m—"

Leah pushes the pillow over my face. I kick with my legs. My hands grab and find her hair. My fingernails dig into her arms. The pillow falls away.

We glower at each other for a moment. Leah gets up, snatches away the pillow. I turn to the side, bring my knees to my chest.

"In case you haven't noticed, *I'm* not the fuckup in this family. I—" Leah glances above my head, leans in closer. Her voice returns to a low murmur. "Yes, I smoke pot. You know what else I do? I take college classes. I'm building a website. My portfolio won first prize at the Marin County Fair. What the fuck have you done? Ever?"

"Leah—"

"God help you if you ever do drugs. You'll be such a loser." Leah looks me over with disgust. She walks away, her body still tight with rage. The connecting door slams behind her.

Leah throws something at the door. It lands with a loud crack. I turn to the nightstand, pick up my present from the future. I turn it over in my hands. Maybe this is the key. It's at least a clue. I open the notecard first.

Amy,

How can it be twenty-six years since your father and I brought you home from the hospital? Now here you are, an accomplished young woman with a life of her own. It has been incredible to watch you blossom into adulthood.

I hope you are not too grown-up to remember when we made jam together, when we sang Christmas carols at Grandma Rose's house, when you used to run down the beach or build castles in the sand. When I look at you I still see that little girl, and I marvel at how she grew into such a wonderful woman.

This present was a gift from my grandfather, a kind and thoughtful man. Please take this to remind you that you are beloved (the meaning of your name) and irreplaceable.

Love forever and always,

Mom

I read the note several times. How can this note, or this present, exist? Is Mom's psycho persona just kayfabe? Did she travel through time, too? Unbelievable, nearly impossible—then again, so is time travel itself. I try to imagine the mom who wrote this letter acting like the mom I saw today. No. I can't square that circle.

What was the noise I heard in Leah's room? Did it come from outside, from my room, or somewhere else? I test my hazy memory against a dozen possibilities: a glass breaking, a brush rustling, a cough, a tapping finger. No joy. My attention was elsewhere; I simply can't remember.

I reread the card. I've seen Mom's grandfather in photos: reading to Mom in her crib; sitting beside her at her confirmation dinner; hugging her at her high school graduation. I don't know his name.

The wrapping paper unfolds, revealing a small white box. Inside the box is a silver, circular locket on a chain. Etched rays radiate from the raised symbol in its center: a heart shape, encircled by barbed wire, surmounted by a cross in the center of a flame.

The locket has the instant familiarity of something from early childhood. How, then, to explain the symbol? This can't be barbed wire, not if Mom's grandfather gave it to her. I hold the locket up to the light. What I thought was a nick in the metal is actually a part of the design: a cut across the bottom of the heart, eternally weeping silver blood.

"What the fuck," I say aloud. *Maybe this isn't from Mom at all,* an inner voice says. *Maybe it's another cult symbol.*

I pry open the locket. The left-hand side has a blank piece of paper, with the outline of a man's head drawn on it. "Future Mr. Right," Mom's written where his face should be. The other side is a picture of me, taken at Tom's Fourth of July party in 2016. In the picture, I'm smiling, squinting against the sun. My hair's pinned up in a crown braid. There are lines around my mouth I never noticed, crow's feet lengthening under my eyes. I look older than I've ever felt. I close the locket.

Play the tape to the end. There must be an explanation.

If this is real, there's a reason why this locket is here. The woman in that picture will be me soon enough. This world will become the world I remember. Too bad.

CHAPTER TEN
SPACE VACUUM FROM OUTER SPACE

LOCKER DOORS SLAM and shudder around me. A few girls walk by, wearing their P.E. uniforms: red shirts, green shorts. I don't have my uniform. I have no idea where it is. I fool with my backpack for a while, pretending like I have something in there, maybe under a trap door. Maybe there's a bin somewhere with an extra uniform. There isn't. There's nothing.

The locker room empties out. A piece of pink paper floats from the wall to the floor. I pick it up and read it.

Vote JESSICA TRUESDALE for 7th Grade Rep!!!

Beneath the headline is a picture of my near-doppelgänger. Someone's drawn a piece of tissue paper poking out of her tank top. *I MUST, I MUST, I MUST INCREASE MY BUST!* a drawn-on speech bubble adds, to draw the point home. There's another paper stuck to it: a missing persons poster for Kathleen Vandergraf (*Last Seen: Fairfax, 8/26/03*), defaced with devil horns, black eyes, and a gaping mouth.

The chemical aftertaste of Seroquel lingers in my mouth. I could leave again, run away to…where, exactly? I clasp the locket hanging around my neck. The metal feels cool under my palm. I take a breath and walk to the door.

Miss Barnett's standing in the middle of the field, squinting against the sun. I remember her clearly, looking as she looks now: severe blonde bangs, pinched face, too-tan legs under salmon-colored shorts. Her eyes bore holes through my head. "Amy," she says, and crooks her finger at me. "Come here."

Even the birds in the trees fall silent. A heavy ball of dread sits in my stomach. I walk forward.

"What are you wearing?" Miss Barnett says. No feeling in her voice, save a tinge of impatience.

"Jeans, Miss Barnett." The class titters. Blood rushes to the tips of my ears.

"Where are your gym clothes?"

"I don't know."

"What about your shoes?"

"I'm wearing shoes."

"Not your gym shoes. See everyone standing behind me? Notice anything?"

Kids shift in place as I look at them. They're all wearing puffy white sneakers. I'm not.

"You need approved gym shoes to participate in gym class," Miss Barnett continues. "Didn't you read the syllabus?"

"What syllabus?"

Miss Barnett gestures to the students behind her. "Somehow, they all got it. Even Scott."

Kids chuckle. Scott's friend elbows him. Seconds pass like

kidney stones. *Say something. You're twenty-six, for God's sake!* Absolutely nothing comes to mind.

"This is unacceptable," Miss Barnett says, scribbling on her clipboard. "If this happens again, you'll get detention. Do you understand?"

"Yes."

"Are we going to have this problem again?"

"No."

"You'll have to run around the field ten times after school. Do you take the bus?"

"Sorry?"

"Do you take the *bus*," Miss Barnett repeats, slowly. Out of the corner of my eye, I see one girl cup her hand around her friend's ear, lean in to tell a secret.

"No," I say.

"Who picks you up after school?"

"My Dad."

"Can you tell your dad that you have to run ten laps before he picks you up?"

"Yes."

"Yes, what?"

"Yes, I will."

"I want you to say it back to me."

I blink against the sun casting her face in shadow. "Yes, I will tell my Dad that I have to run ten laps around the school."

"*After* school. Not around the school—around the field. Go sit on the bleachers." She turns back to the class and raises her voice. "Okay everyone, let's start with burpees. MOVE!"

The class groans. Miss Barnett's whistle pierces the air. Kids hurl themselves into burpee after burpee to the sound of "One, two, three, four—HUP, HUP! Three, four—keep-it-moving-keep-it-moving—hustle, hustle, hustle, hustle, hustle—HUP!"

A boy, sitting by a window on the third floor, waves at me as I walk to the bleachers. I wave back.

Hills of golden dry grass, dotted with dark clusters of redwoods, rise above the school. A bird coos somewhere in the distance. Uniforms, grades, tests—all seem meaningless compared to the grandeur of the redwood trees and the birds' wordless love songs.

Cassidy runs next to Mark Watkins. She laughs, tucks her hair behind her ears. Looking at her, you'd never know about her home life. Running up the stairs to her room, dragging her dresser in front of her door, praying that Slice doesn't flip out again. Phone calls from her parents, off in Monaco or Montreal, asking what souvenir they should bring her this time. I was supposed to call CPS yesterday, tell them what I knew about Cassidy's home life, try to put a stop to it the way I didn't as a kid.

There's a payphone on the first floor, just visible from the bleachers. I'll call after school, after everyone leaves. After I run laps. I promise.

"Wanna get high?"

Everyone asks me that, in the Towelie voice, as I walk through the hallways. I pretend not to hear, even when Scott yells it in my ear.

English class. I sit toward the back, leafing through my silver notebook. Sean Hillis takes the seat to my right. He turns to me. I clench my fists.

"Did you do the homework?"

It takes me a moment to realize it's a genuine question, not another Towelie impression. "Yeah."

"How do you put 'after the game' in the diagram? Is it a straight line, or…?"

I show him.

"Thanks," he says, smiling shyly. He's impossibly young, a child wearing my ex's face. *We used to make out in the back of your dad's Volvo.* No, that's not true. We didn't used to, because it hasn't happened yet.

Mark Watkins whistles at us. Sean blushes. I flip Mark the bird.

"Hey, Amy, that's not very nice! Why'd you flip me off, Amy? Hey Snotbooger, I'm talking to—"

"Settle down, Mark," Ms. Steffensen warns.

"She started it!"

Mrs. Steffensen stares him down. Mark woofles, slumps in his seat. "Girls get away with *everything*," he grumbles.

Class starts. I doodle in my notebook, wonder again if this is better or worse than work. You're paid to work, you can quit, you can find a better job. If you're skilled, companies will compete to hire you—so I've been told, anyway. And many jobs let you leave your work at the office door. Who would stay in a job where you took work home, on five to eight different projects, every single night?

I lean my head against my palm. What's good about school? Summers, of course. Only seasonal and educational jobs give you three months off every year. Your pathway to success is clear: get good grades, take extracurriculars, make friends, don't get pregnant or do drugs. Do this, and the world should open for you like the eye of a serpent. In school, your future begins at some nebulous endpoint, which you can hardly imagine at thirteen or even nineteen. You can tell yourself things won't always be this way. It takes a while to learn the truth.

"What music do you like?" Sean hisses in my ear. My shoulders shoot up in surprise.

"Keep your voice down," I whisper back.

A moment later, Sean passes me a note—blank, save a stylized eighth-note and a question mark. My pen hovers over the page. What music did grown-up Sean enjoy? If I ever knew, I can't remember now. What would he have heard of? Let's make an educated guess.

ADELE

RIHANNA

JUSTIN BIEBER

LORDE

Sean frowns at the paper. "Who's Ah-della?" he says. Heads turn. Ms. Steffensen warns us with a glance. After she's turned, Sean hands me back the sheet.

"You've never heard of her? Never ever?" Sean shakes his head. I wait a few seconds. No flash of recognition.

"Are they German?" he says, pointing to Justin Bieber's name.

"Swiss."

"That's cool. Do you speak Swiss?"

"Poorly."

I entertain a bad idea. "I already know your favorite bands," I say to Sean. Lisa Sharkey turns in her seat, glares at me. Sean shakes his head.

I turn the paper over. What was on the mix CDs Sean used to make me? I write the names I remember.

AGNOSTIC FRONT

FLOGGING MOLLY

MINOR THREAT

CRASS

Sean's eyes widen in astonishment as he reads. "Are you psychic?" he murmurs. "My brother loves all of these bands. Maybe you picked up his signal instead of mine."

Sean's brother. How did I forget him? His face is clear in my memory: meaty, self-serious, framed by a buzz cut. What was his name?

"Have you ever been to Gilman?" Sean asks.

You took me once, I want to say. *We saw a band called Space Vacuum from Outer Space. You threw up on my lap.*

"Mom won't let me go," Sean continues, not waiting for an answer. "My brother got in one stupid fight at the Pound—"

"Sean," Ms. Steffensen says.

"Sorry. I'll be quiet."

Ms. Steffensen eyes us both, then turns back to the blackboard.

Sean waits for a moment before whispering, "Luke's starting a band. He said I can't be in it, though."

Memories wash over me. Luke Hillis, bassist for Fat Hammer, Don't Call Me Stupid, Synthysys, a dozen other bands. How could I forget him? Last I heard, he sewed up his earlobes and became a paramedic. I'm about to lose myself in memories when I see Sean's eyes. They're soft with devotion, even wonder.

Oh honey, no. You're a child. Go pick on someone your own age. I feel nothing for him save nostalgic goodwill.

"Hey," Sean whispers, and puts a hand on my shoulder. It feels like the hand of Frankenstein. At least he's trying to be nice. No one else is.

"I know you don't do drugs," he says. "Natalie spreads rumors about every pretty girl in school. Don't listen to her."

I hide my smile. It's a nice compliment. It might even be true.

CHAPTER ELEVEN
TIME TO BLINK

ANOTHER DAY, ANOTHER Excel file. This time, computer class is all business: calculate Mondocorp's gross and net profits, profit margin, and the return on investment for an advertising campaign. Make a chart. I've had worse projects, but between kids talking, the printer whining in the corner, and Miss Barnett's whistle blowing outside, my concentration is shot.

After two minutes, I give up. Everyone else has. Even Jessica Truesdale's taking an online quiz. I pull out my silver notebook, run down all the things I have to look up. I start with my locket.

The symbol on my locket is "The Sacred Heart of Jesus." I've seen it on Mexican candles, but I didn't make the connection until now. It represents Jesus's great love for humanity, despite the way we treated him on Earth. Despite the way we treat each other, and everything else for that matter. I think of Mom's grandfather giving her this locket. Maybe he meant it as an amulet against Mimi's abuses. Maybe it worked.

The Lister-LeNormand Hypothesis yields a few results, though they might as well be in Voynich. Put plainly, this hypothesis concerns a branch of physics that's utterly beyond my ken.

It's based on some notes found in a police archive, a few cryptic letters, telegrams—it's hard to tell amidst the jargon. An ancient university webpage yields one paragraph that I do understand:

> *We have so little to go on, and what we do have leaves so much for interpretation, that the few who could understand it choose not to try. The superstition, rarely stated aloud, is that studying this hypothesis invites misfortune. "I can't possibly research [Lister-LeNormand]," one colleague told me. "Not with my wife pregnant." This sentiment, so out of place in the hard sciences, reveals the eldritch aura surrounding the idea, apparent even to those who know little about it.*

I look up Claude Belissan. Nothing, save a listing for "BELISSAN REALTY" in Berkeley, California. A reverse search of his 555 number turns up nothing. My mind wanders from the task at hand. I visit the *New York Times* website. The Iraq War, IED blasts, Arnold's gubernatorial campaign. What a relief to see an entire front page without Trump's name on it.

Then I see it, right at the bottom.

ALLEGED TRUMP ATTACKER DIES AT SCENE

Cold sweat breaks out across my body. My chest tightens, as if someone shoved me in an ice corset and yanked the laces. I click on the headline.

> *NEW YORK, NY: Donald J. Trump survived a possible attempt on his life yesterday, according to several eyewitnesses.*

On Wednesday night, Mr. Trump was dining at The Arthur Club, a steakhouse in Midtown Manhattan, with friends and family. Around 8:30 P.M., a man identified as Henry Lasko, a 26-year-old project manager from Oakland, California, walked through the restaurant, evading the maître d' and other restaurant personnel. Mr. Lasko approached Mr. Trump's table and allegedly took a firearm out of his coat. He was restrained by another patron, Jeremy Dale, a Vice Admiral in the Marine Corps.

According to several eyewitnesses, Mr. Dale disarmed the young man and wrestled him to the floor. In the ensuing altercation, Dale allegedly cut off circulation to Lasko's carotid artery, killing him. No shots were fired.

"Whoever's running security at [The Arthur Club] should be fired immediately," Mr. Trump said when reached by phone. "I know they can't afford it, but they should hire [Vice] Admiral Dale instead. He was very tough, very brave, very smart last night. He grabbed the kid before anyone else saw the gun."

Calls to Mr. Dale's home and cell phones were not returned.

Raymond W. Kelly, Commissioner for the New York Police Department, declined to comment on the incident. Several sources within the NYPD, speaking anonymously because they were not authorized to comment, doubted the department would bring charges against Mr. Dale.

"He was in a life-or-death situation," said one source familiar with the case. "He protected Trump and everyone else in that restaurant. I mean, what did [Lasko] think was

going to happen? If you pull a gun on a billionaire, don't be shocked if you get choked out."

"Our security is very tight," The Arthur Club's manager, Raphael Sanseverino, insisted. "We have never, ever had an incident like this before." The restaurant was closed on Thursday for extra training, including reviews of security camera footage. "I want everyone to know that they have nothing to fear at The Arthur Club," Mr. Sanseverino said.

Mr. Trump denied knowing or having any association with Mr. Lasko, whom he described as "some nut." He declined to address rumors that he'd paid off the mortgage on Mr. Dale's house in Arlington, Virginia. "We're going to make sure the Dales are very happy and very well taken care of," he said.

I read the story three times. Maybe I missed this the first time around. Who was Trump, to me, in 2003? A name, a hairstyle, a punchline? There's an article about Henry Lasko in the *San Francisco Chronicle*, complete with a picture. He doesn't look crazy, but many crazy people don't. I read the article, skimming the redundant parts.

ALLEGED TRUMP ATTACKER'S MOTIVES STILL UNCLEAR
Friends, Colleagues Left with Unanswered Questions

…It was not immediately clear how Henry got from Lagunitas, California, where he was staying with family on Monday night, to Midtown Manhattan on Wednesday evening. Reports that he booked a last-minute flight, from

San Francisco to JFK International Airport, could not be confirmed at press time.

Lee Simon, Henry Lasko's employer at The Moon Publications LLC, denied the story entirely when reached at his office. "That's impossible," he said. "Henry? No [expletive] way. If you think that, I've got a bridge to sell you in Sausalito."

Max Duckworth, a 25-year-old property manager in Brisbane, California, painted a different picture of his longtime friend.

Wait a minute. Fay Ray Duckworth is Leah's friend. Max could be Fay Ray's brother, stepbrother, uncle, cousin. I write *Max + Fay Ray?* down in my notebook.

"If I had to put words to it, I'd say [Henry] was looking for the meaning of life—at least his life," Max said. Henry attended events at numerous churches, synagogues, monasteries, temples, and other spiritual groups starting in high school. He talked about fasting, becoming a monk, taking up the sitar, meditating on a mountaintop. Little, if any, of this talk translated into action. He took vows of celibacy, then rescinded them on a whim. He was never violent. He rarely raised his voice.

Still, there were moments that seem more sinister in hindsight. Duckworth described one incident where Henry, then about sixteen, described an "invisible snake" that followed him around.

"He'd talk to this snake," Max recalled, "and the snake would talk back, and he'd tell me what it said. When I

mentioned it the next day, he had no memory of it." These incidents weren't common, so Max dismissed them as "Henry being Henry." He'd never been concerned about his friend until the morning of August 26th—the last time the two spoke.

"Honestly, he didn't sound like himself," Max said. "He kept asking me what day it was. He told me all this strange [expletive] about the end of the world. He said his mom's funeral was yesterday, when I saw her three days ago. He wouldn't tell me where he was, so I couldn't call the cops. Next thing I knew, his face was all over the TV."

The "invisible snake" reminds me of the Doomsday Garden. Same with the apocalyptic rant. I can't assume they're connected, though. Unless he left a note, and the police publish it, I can't assume anything about his mental state.

Henry himself has no online footprint. No blog, no website, no Hot or Not profile. If he had a pseudonymous blog, I can't find it. Neither can anyone else. there are no links to one, no quotes in any articles. *The Moon*'s website already removed him from the staff page.

Max Duckworth has a website, though. There's not much there: a few photos, a résumé, links to other sites. The link to "Sister Ray" leads to the Livejournal of "fayrayrunaway." That answers that question. I send Max an email:

I think something happened to Henry. I think the same thing happened to me. This isn't a joke. Please let me know if anything I say sounds familiar to you.

-Did Henry mention something called "ISIS"? He

might have also mentioned Aleppo, Syria, or refugees from the Middle East.

-Did he mention any slogan or catchphrase with the word "America" in it?

-What exactly did he say about Trump?

-He might have also mentioned Hillary Clinton. Did he say anything about her, especially in relation to a certain medium of communication?

-He may have also mentioned at least one Democratic Senator or Representative from Delaware, Illinois, or Vermont. No one that's currently in the news.

This isn't a joke, Max. I'm not a reporter or a look-ie-loo. Please read my journals. I couldn't be more sincere.

Oracle Doll

oracledoll.blogspot.com

livejournal.com/users/oracledoll

Fay Ray's journal sucks me in with its compelling mixture of angst and ephemera. There are song lyrics, AIM conversations, quiz results. Ray rants about her job at Borders, writes her name out in band names (**F**aith No More, **A**poptygma Berzerk, **Y**ves Montand…). I add her to my friends list. Maybe she'll add me back. Her last entry is one sentence long:

what's the most fucked-up dream you've ever had?

I read the comments with bated breath, looking for a sign. I don't have to look far.

the dream I had last night

leahafterdark

2003-08-26 22:24

it didn't feel like a dream. i was walking around downtown sf. everything was tinged this awful greenish-gray color, like a bruise. i felt dead. there was a giant void in the center of my soul, and i was looking for the missing piece, even though I knew that piece was gone forever. you could throw the universe inside me and it wouldn't make a difference. the void would still be hungry.

then i saw my sister walk past me and up the steps of a church. she didn't look at me and that made me mad. it was strange, because i wasn't allowed to be angry for a long time—i remember that clearly. i followed her in there, watched her light a candle, and the void reached up and swallowed me too. after that, i remember sitting in an alleyway, late at night. when I looked up, the sky was breaking apart.

I close my ears, listen to my own heartbeat. I never knew Leah had a Livejournal. I can't bring myself to read it now. I add her and Ray to my friends list. Maybe they can help.

Lee Simon, Henry's last boss, is an SF State graduate, a professional illustrator, a long-time editor at *The Moon*. An old hippie, with his Bob Ross hair, his close-cut beard, his brightly patterned dress shirt. On page three of the search results, I see the words "Doomsday Garden." My stomach drops. The page loads slowly. Black text on a white page, no columns or headers. Nice and simple.

The Doomsday Garden and Me:
A Short History of the End of the World

"You gotta hear this!"

I was at Lee Simon's pad, smoking dope and pontificating about life, per usual. Lee showed me an album cover: a willowy blonde wearing a long white smock, backlit so you could see every curve and crevice. "THE DOOMSDAY GARDEN" was written in drippy letters along the top.

"Friend of yours?" I asked, raising an eyebrow. Lee laughed.

"No talk. Only listen," he ordered. I knew better than to argue. In the past year, Lee had introduced me to Gurdjieff, Louis Wain, Anna Kavan, Dziga Vertov— all sorts of far-out stuff that wasn't easy to get ahold of in 1967. Lee hung out with Owsley, Kesey, Cassady, even Bill Graham. He'd taken me to my first dances at the Family Dog and dropped acid with me on Mount Tamalpais. When Lee Simon told you that you gotta hear something, read something, or do something, you did it.

When the needle hit the groove, the sound blew me all the way back to the Pleistocene. Here were strange choral harmonies that sounded like the Beach Boys' score to a horror film. Here were ten thousand voices, more, continuously darning one note into infinity. I went out of my body, out of the room, out of my mind, off the planet. For a little eternity, there was no "I" to speak of. Then the record stopped. The needle lifted. I looked at Lee and he shook his head.

"That's nothing," he said. "You need to hear them

live. Makes that," he pointed to the record, "sound like a
radio jingle."

The next day we skipped school, smoked a jay, and
hitched a ride to the city. It was the spring before the
Summer of Love. The Haight was full of signs of the
impending apocalypse: men with long hair, longer than the
girls'; braless girls in gypsy dresses; paintings and psychedelic
posters and posted poems and protests for peace; God's Eyes
leering from apartment windows; mimeographed mani-
festos; record shops, head shops, thread shops, deadheads,
dead-eyed dope dealers, starry-eyed innocents. The air was
heavy with the smells of grass, joss sticks, frying food, sweat,
young bodies in motion. Kids streamed in from all over
the country. They begged on Haight Street, slept rough in
the park, scrounged for food, dropped acid, played guitar,
crashed with the Hare Krishnas, the Diggers, or whoever
would have them.

Lee and I reached Doomsday H.Q. At the time, the
house was painted all white, with the snake symbol over
the door, and a lush garden out front. Outside, there were
white folks, black folks, Spanish, Chinese, hippies, plastic
hippies, speed freaks, Jesus freaks, about a million teenybop-
per runaways, drug dealers, old ladies, college kids, even a
few businessmen, all looking at the house, waiting.

The windows flew open. Inside the house, voices erupted
in song, ringing in the air like a church bell. It was as if the
house itself was singing. Cars stopped in the middle of the
street. A policeman stood entranced at the corner, gawping
with the rest of us.

As I listened, my chattering ego turned tail and ran.

The flowers in the garden unfurled their glory; every petal, every vein, stood out in clear light. I felt a boundless peace and an impulse to take swift action, to bring this peace into the world. Such a thing seems possible, even easy, at seventeen. Lee and I embraced, tears in our eyes...

The author runs on for a few paragraphs about his father ("an old man for an old world"). I skim until he starts discussing the cult again:

I started spending all my free time at Doomsday H.Q. Lee and I worked for the Doomsday Express, *the movement's magazine. Lee drew pictures, while I learned to use the printing press. I told my old man I got an after-school job at a paper, so he let me borrow the car. Never asked for a pay stub. If he'd known!*

Grace Slick, Bob Weir, Chester Anderson, R. Crumb, everyone who was anyone came by once or twice. Charles Manson visited with his girls, tried to pick up a few more at our lectures. At one point, he wanted to teach some classes for us, but he wandered off after Beatrice asked him to pull some weeds. We gave flyers to anyone who'd take them. And anyone did!

Our most devoted followers tended to be the strangest. You could feel something off about them from seven blocks away. One man in particular gave me the creeps, and not just because he was old and square. This man was despair in human form, always crying about his son Billy, whom he said had "vanished" when he "went back in time." The guy insisted that Beatrice had sent him back in time to "beat the stock market" and "earn money to prepare for doomsday." He didn't look rich to me. Maybe he took something he couldn't handle and it twisted his mind. There were a few people like that—people who insisted they'd gone back in time somehow, some way. They all died in the fire, every single one...more on that later.

We were so young. We were changing the world! Nothing would be the same after we got through with it. The house's garage, only open to Beatrice and a few eggheads, was felt to be the focal point of the movement, the neighborhood, perhaps the entire world. Whatever they did there often shorted out the electricity, and there were occasional whirrs, hums, and whines from beneath the floorboards, sustained for hours or even days.

Toward the end of the summer, when the streets got wild, Beatrice started to lose control. So many kids were coming in, we couldn't possibly feed everyone, even if we did nothing else. Hustlers and charm artists moved in, trying to carve out a piece of our pie. Manson was not the only flower-power psychopath in the district, not by a long shot. The magazine staff fought over everything: layouts, titles, font sizes, gerunds. Kids wandered, stole pictures off the walls, threw up on the chairs, stripped the rooms of anything that could be pawned or sold. We got static from the FBI and the IRS, harassment from the local police, a constant pressure to sell more courses, magazines, books, pendants—a tall order, selling things to kids with no money. My drug-addled teenage brain only observed, never interpreted. I had a girlfriend, a job, a vital role in the revolution. What more did I need?

I went back to school in the fall, exhilarated and exhausted from my Summer of Love. Everything in me *wanted to drop out and join them, but it didn't happen that way.*

I was on Haight Street, selling magazines, when I heard an enormous boom. A few seconds later, smoke billowed up into the sky. Lee met my eyes. A horrible feeling passed over both of us. We forgot our quotas, forgot everything as we ran back to base.

Smoke billowed out of the first-floor windows. Orange flames licked at the wood. The snake painting bubbled and cracked. Rose MacLeod stood in a second-story window, a child under each arm. Someone grabbed a ladder from a neighboring garage, tried to reach her. The ladder fell, as did the man, right into the belly of the house. Rose screamed.

A few moments later, the fire brigade showed up. Two big men hoisted Rose and her kids out of the house. I watched a fireman put a mask over her children's faces while Rose sobbed, and my dream of a better world broke like a soap bubble.

"It was the garage," Lee insisted. "Whatever they were doing down there—they must have blown a fuse. I thought this might happen."

I held the atmosphere of the neighborhood responsible. All that fear and anger and frantic vice, all the prophecies and pronouncements, had all taken form and exploded in that basement. It was only luck that I survived.

I lean back in my chair. Rose MacLeod is my grandmother's name. Both Dad and Aunt Zelda were alive by 1967 (*a child under each arm...*). If she and her kids almost died, of course they wouldn't want to talk about it.

If they almost died...the clause hits me like a hammer to the third eye. If that fire truck had come two minutes later, I wouldn't be here. Richard Snowberger would be a grave in a cemetery. No one would bring him flowers.

I jolt again when I read the link at the bottom: *Return to Claude's Webpage-O-Wonders.* I click on it. There's Claude Belissan, smiling invitingly at the top of the home page. Maybe you're not surprised, but I am. I rarely see these things coming.

There's a bit more on the webpage-o-wonders, none of it helpful: descriptions of the flora and fauna in the San Geronimo Valley, an essay on seeing Jimi Hendrix live ("wild star pulsating in the center of my head, orgiastic joyous inferno, rivers of sound boiling, melting, bubbling, rainbow steam rising through the air..."), a few photos of Haight-Ashbury in the sixties. One picture commands my attention: a white Victorian with an ouroboros painted above the doorway, black rays emanating from its center. I count them. Thirteen.

Class ends. Kids flow out into the hallway, carrying backpacks, shouting, laughing, talking, shuffling. I float outside myself, thinking of Grandma Rose standing in a second-story window, holding her children close to her, smoke rising through the cracks in the floorboards.

CHAPTER TWELVE
DÉJÀ VU

QUESTIONS RUN THROUGH my mind all morning. Did Henry Lasko, the failed Trump attacker, know the future? Did he know Claude Belissan? If one, or both of them, went back in time, was it an accident, or on purpose? I'm still mulling this over at lunch, when Sean waves me over to his table. I feel out of place in my flared jeans and pink blouse, an outfit so bland it might have been chosen by corporate committee.

The table's embroiled in a deadly serious discussion: who is the fakest celebrity?

"Avril Lavigne is so fake. She is not punk rock at all," Lisa Sharkey says, with a pointed look to me.

"That's a persona," Andrew says. "All great entertainers have personas. Even Madonna—"

"Madonna's the queen of the fakes. She's goth, then new age, now she's hip hop—"

"That's not her, though, that's her outfit! What about David Bowie, is he fake?"

"Who's David Bowie?"

Andrew gawps. "Seriously? Did you grow up in a mine shaft?"

Lisa rolls her eyes.

"Marilyn Manson's kinda fake," Hector ventures. "All that makeup—"

"No, no, no. Manson is the real deal." Andrew leans forward, lowers his voice. "You heard what he did to his ribs, right?"

Lisa, grimacing, puts her glass back on the table.

The cafeteria din swells until it drowns out all thought. Hector cups his hands around his mouth to be heard. Mrs. Steffensen, at the front of the room, raps on the wall. The noise lowers to a restless murmur.

"You guys want to hear something crazy?" Lisa whispers. A look of utter boredom passes over Sean's face.

"What?" Andrew says.

"You know that lady who just went missing? Kathleen, um—"

"Vandergraf."

"Yeah! My sister and I were talking about her yesterday—"

"That's not crazy."

"No, no, no, wait. Last night, my sister and I had a phone call *about Kathleen* while we were dreaming. We both remember it. We had pocket video screens—"

"Wow, that really is crazy," Sean says. "You're not kidding—hey, when's your bar mitzvah?" It takes me a moment to realize that he's talking to me.

"*Bat* mitzvah," Andrew says, before I can respond.

"What?"

"*Bat* mitzvah. When it's for a girl, it's called a—it's spelled B-A-T, but you say it like 'bot.'" Andrew rolls his eyes at me knowingly.

"Uh-huh," Sean says, turning back to me. "It's after you turn thirteen, right? How soon after do you—"

"Wait, did you go to religious school over the summer?" Andrew winces in sympathy. Lisa looks me over, eyebrows raised.

"I'm not—"

"Don't you guys go to the same church?" Sean says.

"I told you. They're not called churches, they're—"

A loud *whap* draws our attention to the front of the cafeteria. All sound ceases. Time stops. There's a dead body, a black hole, or some other space-time anomaly just waiting for me to turn my head. My head turns anyway, slowly, of its own accord. A boy's stooped over, unmoving, in front of our table. Then he picks up his overturned tray, to boisterous applause.

Déjà vu overcomes me, so strong I taste it like iron on my tongue. The whole world sings with electricity, because I remember this moment. I didn't even know I remembered. It's as if I can see the memory imposed on the present, a double exposure where the pictures are slightly off.

"Amy?" Lisa says. I turn my attention back to her. "You want me to tell your fortune again? I made a new one."

She's holding a small fortune teller, made out of binder paper, its numbers written in sparkly green ink.

"Sure," I say. My déjà vu dissipates. I pick the number three, three times. Lisa opens the flap.

"'You will change the world,'" she reads, her voice dripping with contempt. A green star sparkles beneath this pronouncement.

"I knew it," I say.

Sean's laugh echoes through the room. Half-chewed tater tots sit in the back of his mouth.

CHAPTER THIRTEEN
FATHER'S PREROGATIVE

I RUN TEN laps around the field. Sounds fill the air: car doors slamming, the hydraulic jounce of the school bus brakes, kids laughing and shouting, adult voices straining over the din. Running is so easy now, almost easier than walking. I get high on the wind against my face, the track disappearing underfoot, the fused rhythms of moving and breathing. The boys on the basketball team, stretching before practice, watch me run, faces slack with boredom. A sixth grader walks outside the fence, holding a book close to her chest. I wave. She waves back.

I wash my face in the bathroom sink, drop the Seroquel in the trash. It's quiet here, save the distant sounds of a basketball skirmish. Muscles knot and twist under along my shoulders and spine. Backpack pains. I stretch in place. No wonder my posture sucks.

Kathleen's missing persons poster hangs in the hallway.

Kathleen Vandergraf

Have you seen this woman?

Age: 39

Race: Caucasian/white

Height: 5'5"

Weight: 125 lbs.

Hair: Black

Eyes: Brown

*Last seen 8/26/03 in Fairfax, California, wearing a
white blouse, khakis, and dark blue shoes. May have been
wearing pearl stud earrings.*

I study her picture. Jet-black hair, enormous dark eyes, a
rictus of pain on her face.

I walk down the hallway toward the payphone. I have to
call CPS, before I forget. I've put it off too long. My shoes
squeak against the linoleum. A giggle cuts through the air. Becca
Osborne's already in the phone booth, leaning against the wall.

"She's so pretentious," Becca says. Her eyes pass through me.
"Wow, you know the capital of Syria. You probably looked it up
in—no, go ahead."

"How long?" I mouth to Becca.

She looks at me hazily, then covers the receiver. "What?"

"How long are you gonna be on the phone?"

Becca holds up two fingers. "You're in the library, right? I'll
come find you when I'm done."

"Thanks."

"You're welcome—no, just another student. Uh-huh.
Uh-huh. No *way*."

I'm at the library door when Dad yells my name. He's ten feet away, smiling innocently. *If your father is alive, how can there be sorrow or fear or pain?* And yet there is: just ask Cassidy. I'll call CPS when I get home. If Mom asks, I'll tell her the truth.

There's a Burger King bag on the passenger seat.

"Happy birthday. You're not a vegetarian too, are you?"

"No."

Inside the bag is a box of chicken tenders and French fries. Two enormous milkshakes fill the cupholders in the center console.

"Your old favorite. I didn't forget."

"Dad."

"I might have stolen a few of your fries, though. Father's prerogative."

Traffic slows to a crawl on Sir Francis Drake. Dad fishes another handful of fries out of the bag. I look out at the tall fennel shoots growing along the road's edge.

"I meant what I said last night," I say. "Sometimes it's hard to do the right thing, even if you want to. I mean, we both need to eat healthier, right?"

"You worry too much," Dad says, talking through a mouthful of mashed fries. "Yes, I'm a little—I'm aware of the spare tire situation."

"We could make—"

"Spinach paste and rhubarb salad? Please."

"No paste. There are soups, stir fries, chilis, entrées…"

Dad sucks deeply from his milkshake. The car inches forward. "Tell you what," he says. "If you tell me why you ran away, we'll have anything you want for dinner. Okay? Even spinach paste." He holds up his hand, pinkie extended. "Deal?"

I swallow the lump in my throat. I picture Dad telling Mom

everything I've said, with a few flourishes and exaggerations. Can I trust him with information? Can I trust anyone?

Dad's gravestone rises up in my memory. I wrap my pinkie around his. He smiles. When I let go, he pats my head. I take a deep breath.

"I had a…kind of waking dream of growing up. In this dream, I was twenty-five years old. I'd lived through all the time between now and then. It was 2016—"

"What's twenty-sixteen?"

"Thirteen years from now?"

"Oh," Dad says after a pause. "Oh, two thousand sixteen. I get it." He slurps noisily at the dregs of his milkshake. "So, you had a dream about growing up, and when you woke up, you…" Something shifts in his face. He puts the milkshake back in the center console. The traffic breaks. Dad turns onto Railroad Avenue, but he parks on the side of the road. He turns the car off, looks at me. His face is pure white. "You're telling the truth," he says with a stranger's voice.

"Yes."

"It's okay if you're not. You won't get in trouble."

"I'm not lying, Dad."

"Okay." Dad blinks. "Okay." He reaches out for the milkshake, then pulls back, his hands shaking too badly to hold it. "Tell me more about this dream."

I tell him, in broad strokes, about my adult life: UC Davis, the rented room in El Cerrito, Orpheline, vague plans for a better job. "No boyfriend?" "No one." I don't tell him about Leah mugging me in the church vestibule, or Claude Belissan's disquieting presence. If Dad knows about Claude, he'll try to confront him, and something tells me Dad would be hurt more than I'd be helped.

Dad sighs, runs his hand over his face. "Reminds me of the

Doomsday Garden." His voice trembles. The name hangs in the
air between us. He's never said it out loud. Not to me. "A couple
people there said the same thing about waking up in the past.
They said it wasn't a dream."

"Can I talk to them?"

"They died."

Of course they did. *They all died in the fire, every single one…*
Wasn't that in Claude's essay? Maybe it's true.

Dad turns the car around, heading back out of Woodacre.
Nets of shadow and sunlight dance on the asphalt in front of us.
We turn left on Sir Francis Drake, headed toward the coast. The
silence grows between us. Trees fly by my window, casting the
car in mottled shadow.

"How much do you know about the Doomsday Garden?"
Dad says.

"I know Sebastian Spar, his vision of Eden, Beatrice—"

"I mean…our part in it. Grandma and Zelda and me."

The sun hangs low over the hills, suffusing them with an
orange-gold glow. I lean my seat back.

"I know you were born while Grandma was at Cal. She
never married Grandpa, even though they were together forever.
I know you joined a—joined the Doomsday Garden when you
and Zelda were little, and then you left, and you don't like to
talk about it. I don't know any more than that."

"Grandpa didn't join. He tried to get us out. If not for the
fire, I don't think…"

A Peregrine falcon swoops above the road, slowly flapping
its wings.

"It wasn't a good time," Dad says. "They'd put you in the
center of a circle and yell at you for hours. They even did that
to Zelda. She must have been, what, three, three and a half…"

"That's terri—"

"You had a sense that you were always on stage. Even in your room, when you wanted to sleep. There was always noise—people shouting, singing, clapping, weird humming in the basement. You couldn't ever close the door to your room. You couldn't say no, either."

"You mentioned a few other people who, um, had 'waking dreams,'" I venture. Dad says nothing for a long time. When I look over, I see tears rolling down his face. "Are you okay?"

"I'm sorry," he says, his voice small. "You tell yourself you'll put it away, you won't think about it, but it always comes back."

"I didn't mean to—"

"It's not your fault." He grabs my hand. "Oh, honey, it's not your fault."

"Dad, you don't—"

"They had these ceremonies," he says, blinking away the tears. "I don't remember them well, but...whatever they did, they changed things." He swallows. "Sometimes they changed in the silence or the feel of the air. Other times it was as if an atom bomb exploded in your face. And when you came out of the room, everything was different."

"Different how?"

Dad shakes his head. "Sometimes it was just a feeling. Like the world moved while you stood still. Other times...you'd see posters for a band you'd never heard of, or someone would go missing and no one else noticed."

"No one? Are you sure?"

"I can't be sure of anything from that time. If you asked what was going on, they'd say, 'You're eating your own tail, man.' I never found out what that meant."

"What about the people who said they went back in time? Did you ever—"

"They were strange. One guy was always crying about his

son. We'd be trying to sleep while he rolled around on his cot, yelling, 'Billy, Billy, Billy.' There was something wrong with his eyes…they…"

The car drifts onto the shoulder, toward the trunk of a huge redwood tree. I grab the steering wheel and turn it back. Fear fills my mouth with an oily, old-metal taste. Dad starts out of his trance, wrests the wheel away from me. The car fishtails, screeches, then wobbles back onto the right side of the road.

Sweat beads on Dad's forehead in huge, hemispherical drops. We say nothing until the turn off for Shoreline Highway. When Dad stops the car, he looks at me. His eyes are pink and tiny in his face.

"Ask Grandma," he says. "She can answer more questions than I can." His look turns stern. "Don't tell her about your waking dream, okay? Let me handle that."

I lean my head against the window. It's cool, for late August. The wind blows and tangles my hair. If I close my eyes, I can almost hear "White Unicorn" blasting from the speakers.

The front room of the Stinson House looks like something out of an architecture magazine. The walls are well-varnished cherry wood, carved into gently sloping planes. Bookshelves line the walls, their protective covers glinting in the light. There's even a record player in the corner. The big bay window overlooks the bluff, the beach, and the ocean beyond. Leah and I used to sit bundled-up on the back porch, drinking hot chocolate and watching the waves.

"You're getting so *big*," Grandma Rose says. Her bracelets jangle as she reaches out. Her familiar scent, all cinnamon, clover, and apple shampoo, washes over me. "What have you been feeding her, Richard, magic beans?"

"Only the best for my girl."

"I remember when you were a tiny baby," she says. "Two weeks later and here you are, starting—what, fourth grade?"

"Seventh."

"Seventh! You think it's bad now, Richard, wait 'til you're my age. It goes so quickly, and there's nothing you can do about it. 'Time, devourer of all things.'"

"Is that Shakespeare?" Dad asks, hanging his coat in the hallway.

"It's Ovid," I say. "From the *Metamorphoses*. *Tempus edax rerum*."

Grandma goggles at me, then turns to Dad. "Now she's a genius, too. Of course, we already knew that..." She pauses, turns slowly, then walks past me to the door. "Where's Leah? Jackie?"

"Just us, Ma."

"Oh. Why?"

Dad beckons Grandma over to him. She smooths my hair as she passes me. I walk to the bay window. The sun's already set, the sky fading through deeper and deeper shades of blue. I can see Grandma looking at me in the reflection of the room.

A few minutes pass. Grandma starts a fire, makes us cups of hot chocolate. I get the mug with red begonias painted on the outside. I didn't know I remembered it.

"Do you want honey in yours, hon?" Grandma asks me. Her words, and the honey bear in her hand, pierce through me. How many hundreds of times has she asked me that? I nod, blinking away my tears.

"I finally got a ticket to MoMA," she says, turning to Dad. "Saturday morning. I haven't been to the city in six months. Of course, I'll be there for Amy's party, but...what?"

Dad drinks deeply from his mug.

"Mom canceled it. I told you over the phone, remember?"

"You're kidding. She wouldn't—"

"Amy, can you go set the table?" Dad says to me.

Grandma whispers to him furiously, as I walk away.

Over dinner, Grandma Rose asks me the usual questions: How is school? How are your classes? Any cute boys in your grade? No, or maybe? We circle back to my birthday party, or lack thereof.

"It's preposterous. You can't cancel a party over…" She turns to Dad, searching for support. His face hardens. Hers falls. "I'm just saying, Richard. If you didn't keep them cooped up every waking moment—"

"Grandma."

"Yes, sweetie?"

"It's okay. I'm not mad."

Grandma's anger melts into pity. She shakes her head and looks down at the food. I excuse myself.

I pause in the main hallway. There's Grandma's picture on the wall. She looks about thirty, closer to my true age than I am now. She stares at me, face resolute beneath a messy poodle cut, holding up a placard with some numbers and letters on it. It's a mugshot. How did I never see that?

"Richard tells me you asked about the Doomsday Garden," Grandma says when I come back.

"Yes."

Her laugh sounds bright and hollow. I push the couscous around on my plate. I should ask about the mugshot, but I don't know how.

"It's so strange," she says. "I know that it's real, but…what do you think, Richard? Do you feel like it really happened, or like it was a long, waking dream?"

Dad grimaces.

"I used to call it 'time outside of time,'" she continues. "I had a normal life, and then I joined the group, and I went outside of time for a while. Then I came back, and normal life resumed."

Dad stares absently at his plate. His shoulders are tight around his ears, his face dark with blood.

"Did you know Beatrice Spar?" I ask.

Grandma nods, chewing. "Everyone knew her. We used to call her Lady Keane, on account of her big blue saucer eyes. There was this artist, Keane something, who painted..."

"Margaret Keane. The 'big eye' painter. Her husband took the credit for years."

Grandma holds her hand out, palm up, in my direction. "You see, Richard? I told you she was a genius. You—"

"Dad mentioned there were some Doomsdayers who, ah, said they traveled back in time. Do you think they were telling the truth?"

She studies my face, gears turning behind her eyes. "Not really. I didn't think much of them, to be honest. We also had followers who said they were Jesus. I took all that with a giant grain of salt."

"Beatrice believed them," Dad says. "She said we were all scientists, discovering a new—"

"Mmm. Yes. And there was the garage project. Very mysterious. The young men who worked down there were sworn to secrecy..." She covers a smile. *Is she tipsy?* "Sometimes the whole house shook like rocket ship, or hummed like a power plant. Do you remember that?"

Dad empties his glass of wine. The ocean roars on the other side of the bluff. The water's black in the near-darkness. A few stars shine above the waves.

The phone rings.

"One sec, hon." Grandma Rose gets up and walks into the house.

There's something wrong with Dad's eyes. It takes me a moment to realize what it is: the color's gone. His normally hazel eyes are black. I say "Dad" a few times, then "Richard." He doesn't answer. He doesn't even look at me.

"Yeah, they're here," Grandma says inside. "Well, I'm sorry, Jackie, but I didn't...Yes, yes, I'm sure that—he's *eating*, but if you...all right, hold on." She sashays into the dining room, dragging the phone until the cord straightens, two fingers pressed over the speaker. "It's your wife, Richard," she announces, with the same tone of voice you'd use to say *The dog puked on the couch again*. Dad takes the phone and walks into the living room.

"Hello? Yes, we're...uh-huh—uh-huh—uh-huh—yes..."

Grandma Rose scootches her chair closer to mine. "What got you interested in the Doomsday Garden?" she says.

"I wanted to know if time travel is real or not. If it's possible—"

"Oh, hon. The time travelers, the reborn Jesuses, the street-side prophets—they weren't bad or crazy, just...lost. And Beatrice found them. You have to understand—she could tell you that there were two moons in the sky, and you'd see both of them. If she wanted them to believe that they'd gone back in time...they didn't have a chance."

"She brainwashed people."

"Oh, of course not. They weren't tortured. They were telling the truth as they knew it." She shrugs. "Maybe it was the truth. 'There are more things in Heaven and Earth than are dreamt of in our philosophy.'"

"That *is* Shakespeare. *Hamlet.*"

"Very good." She takes a drink, frowns. "How do you know all this? You're not learning it in school."

"Do you remember Claude Belissan?"

Her gaze retreats inward. "Describe him to me."

"He was in high school when he joined. Lee Simon's friend—"

"I remember Lee. He drew cartoons for the Express. But Claude...mmm. Vaguely." She pours another glass of wine. "What does he look like?"

"White hair, white beard. Wears peasant shirts with linen pants."

"That narrows it down." Her laugh turns into a cough. Inside, Dad paces, running his hand down his face. A seagull flies up from the bluff, kicking up sand.

I look down at Grandma Rose's hands. On one of her wrists is a golden bracelet depicting a snake, its mouth open wide, swallowing its own tail.

CHAPTER FOURTEEN
HATED ART THOU AMONGST WOMEN

DAD SNORES ON the other side of the wall. Blue-green light leaks from under the connecting doorway. I wear earplugs, use a sock as a sleep mask. I drift off for a few minutes, then startle awake. I'm now standing, facing the window. Great, now I'm sleepwalking. I lie down over the covers.

Tomorrow's Friday. The thought brings me no joy. Who cares? I can't drive. Even if I had a bike, I can't. If I get caught with drugs or booze, even wine, I'm finished. Forget sex. I'd never sleep with any man who'd have me—not in my current state, anyway. I can't even open the window without sounding an alarm. I have to sleep in my clothes and shoes, pepper spray tucked into my front pocket, because Mom might pay some fake rehab to kidnap me.

A bad idea blooms in my mind. There are a few loose beer cans in the pantry. I could drink one, put it in the recycling when I'm done. No one would ever notice. Mom might not wander in at the wrong moment. The universe could, in theory, cut me a break. I wouldn't object.

I'm walking through the living room (*you moron, you'll get caught, she'll send you to camp*) when something catches my eye. It's shiny, concave, undulating softly in a nonexistent wind. It's an animal in agony, mouth open in a silent scream. Fear hums down my nerves. The animal falls onto the floor with a metallic rustle. It's an empty chip bag, its reflective insides turned toward me.

Rage swells inside me, rage and hatred for this bag and what it represents: Dad's gravestone; Grandma Rose with her thousand-yard stare; Aunt Zelda wailing in Mom's arms; Leah, silent, arms hugging her chest. I think of Dad lying on the couch, emptying this bag into his gullet. The bag crinkles in my hands.

Who cares if you throw away empty bags?

I open every cabinet in the kitchen. Crackers, chips, cookies—so, so many cookies—cereals, candy bars, cupcakes. I place them all in the trash can, letting them down gently so they don't make a sound.

You moron. Play this tape to the end. The very end. Dad's food doesn't belong to you. You didn't pay for it. He's going to eat himself to death, no matter what you do. Mom is this close to sending you away. Is this really your hill to die on?

I see Dad's gravestone, his oversized coffin lowering into the earth. Some inner force pushes me forward. When I'm finished, the pantry is nearly empty, save for spices, mac and cheese boxes, a few bags of rice, jars of apricot jam.

Only when I get to the front door do I realize my folly. The burglar alarm is on, blinking red in the quiet of the front hallway. Mom never told me the code. Leah will never tell me now.

I slump against the wall, slide down until I'm sitting between the trash bags. Half of me wants to fling open the door, have it out with Mom, with Dad, with Leah. I'll tell them everything, *show* them their futures, open the locket and reveal the horrible truth. The other half wants to give up, put all the food back, succumb to the tide of despair rising around me.

A memory bubbles up from the depths: Leah, dressed in black vinyl, putting her finger to her lips. Leah, standing at the alarm panel, punching in the code. Leah, giggling, probably high, teetering over to me, bending down and whispering:

One one eight three.

Of course. Mom and Dad married on New Year's Day, 1983, so Dad could never forget the date. They were so young, barely out of their teens. All the groomsmen were hung over, I think as I key in the code. The maid of honor didn't even show.

The light on the alarm turns from red to green.

The air outside is cool and quiet. The redwoods around me sigh in the passing breeze. The trash bags thunk into the neighbor's bin with a satisfying finality.

Someone is watching.

I scan the street. Nothing's out of place. A neighbor's blue-white security light casts a dismal glare over the scene. Long shadows stretch across the road. Dark redwoods rise far above the houses. I smell the damp forest earth, the redwoods and pine trees, the smoke from someone's fireplace, the scents of many flowers.

I cross myself as I run up the driveway.

"It's now six twenty-seven on this beautiful Friday morning," the radio announcer chirps. I flash back to my days at the call center, putting on my "empathy voice" while customers poured their rage into my ear. My pill's chalky aftertaste lingers in my mouth. The car rumbles onto Blackwood Drive.

"Run this by me again," Mom says. "You were sleepwalking." She laughs. It's not quite a dangerous laugh—there's a note of confusion in there—but my hair still stands on end. "You 'misplaced'…maybe a hundred dollars in groceries? A hundred and fifty? Where'd you put it, anyway?"

"How should I know? Maybe dad ate it. It was all candy and chips, right?"

Mom looks to the side, sighs, and runs her hand over my hair. "Amy, you don't need to worry about your father. He's fine."

"Grandpa Doug died when he was, what, sixty-five? And he was skinny as a shoelace! You think Dad's got twenty more years? Even ten?"

The radio cuts to a car lot ad. Mom pulls her hair away from her face. "What's going on, Amy?"

"Dad's—"

"I mean with you."

The pill's still wrapped in my front pocket, underneath the mace. I consider telling her. Maybe she already knows. If she does, she'll have to tell me herself. She doesn't.

Dressing for school is an art in itself. In the morning, before the night air dissipates, your breath fogs and your hands hurt if you stay outside too long. Even inside the school, you'll need to wear your jacket. You can take it off around 9:00, although you might want an outer shirt or a sweater. Everything should look nice, but not too nice. Nothing too slutty or too dorky, nothing with rips, holes, or stains. Nothing that anyone could comment on. It's not as easy as it sounds.

The weather's nice until about 10:30. By the end of lunch, the school's a heat trap. You'll need a breathable shirt, light pants, shorts, or a skirt (don't forget the bicycle shorts). Avoid tight jeans, short skirts, plaid skirts, tank tops, rhinestones, anything with cutesy names or sayings. Mrs. Rice sent Emily

Padovano to the office because her shirt had Daisy Duck on it. Too suggestive.

We're not supposed to wear high heels to school, or makeup, but girls have found ways around that: flared jeans to hide their shoes, jellies with kitten heels, low wedges. If you can't get away with those, puffy white sneakers are a good alternative. Just don't get them dirty.

I re-learn the habits and personalities of the teachers. Mrs. Rice, our history teacher, humiliates any student who zones out. Ms. Steffensen, in English, makes the worst students participate and (worst of all) read aloud. Mr. Weathers hates disruptions, but if you don't bother anyone, he'll leave you alone. Mrs. Haverfield, our Social Studies teacher, constantly pulls the class out of their seats and into small group discussions, games, a mock recall election, and other "interactive learning" modules. Our Pre-algebra teacher, Mr. O'Brian, can't stop kids from goofing off. And then there's Mr. Dutrain, Computer Science teacher, who doesn't care what his students do, so long as they leave him alone with his computer.

The Pure Heart of Alexandria will wreak havoc through the ninth ward. The water will rise and swallow the living and the dead, and

I stare at the blinking cursor. And what? And FEMA will leave thousands without water or food? And people will die in the Houston Coliseum? And Kanye West will…no. I delete the whole thing.

I'm in Computer Science class, first period. A few boys crowd around one monitor, watching the Britney-Madonna and

Madonna-Christina kisses over and over again. Boys alternate between Beavis-chuckles and retching sounds.

I turn back to my computer.

Real Bad News

[mood | pensive]

[music | The Smiths: How Soon is Now?]

A hurricane next year will break the levies in New Orleans. Hundreds of thousands, if not millions, will be turned out of house and home. The Louisiana government and FEMA will handle it poorly. People that didn't need to die will die.

Bankers are playing a game of musical chairs with stepped-on mortgages. When the music stops, it will trash the world economy and lead to a global recession. Don't believe me? Check the numbers. How does a dental assistant afford a 700K house in Covina? Get smart.

I publish the entry on Blogger and Livejournal. No comments on either platform, yet. Ray and Leah both added me as friends. I still can't bear to look at Leah's journal, but at least she's seen mine. Maybe, when I tell her everything that's happened, she'll actually believe me.

"What are you reading?" a voice says by my ear. I turn. Lisa Sharkey's sitting next to me, reading from my monitor. She mouths a few words as she reads, her eyebrows furrowed in confusion. On her screen, there's a Dollz creation page. A pixelated blonde, dressed in flared jeans and a rainbow tube top, smiles coquettishly within the "Build Doll Here" window. Lisa grabs my mouse, scrolls up to the top of my journal. Her brow furrows.

"Are these horoscopes?"

"I think they're prophecies. Dreams about the future."

Lisa's eyes pop. She looks around, leans toward me. "You have them, too?" she whispers. "Aren't they weird? Last night, I dreamed I was taking photos of some weird-looking doll. I had lights and a fake background and everything. At first I thought I was shooting a movie."

"It didn't feel like a dream."

"Nuh-uh," Lisa says, shaking her head emphatically. "It felt like a memory. A boring memory." She looks at my computer screen. "You think someone dreamed about this...what is it, flood?"

"Hurricane."

"Oracle Doll," she says. "Huh. Cool."

A girl, several seats down, stares blankly at us. *She heard everything*, I think with insane certainty. My stomach clenches. I turn back to my computer.

Two professors have emailed me back. "There's nothing to that hypothesis whatsoever," one says. The other says that it's "not worth pursuing." Max Duckworth's reply is more promising:

Hey Oracle. You can call me anytime. My phone number is in my signature. I really can't speak to the questions you've asked me.

What do you think happened to Max?

Laughter erupts from the boys watching the kissing videos. Mr. Dutrain doesn't look up.

"Why didn't they put Britney and Christina…" one boy says, leaning over the binder on his lap. I turn back to my computer.

Hi, Max. Thanks for reaching out.

I'd rather discuss this over the phone or, if possible, in person. I'll call you when I can.

Yours sincerely,

Oracle Doll

In the hallway, Scott Garson and friends circle a boy with ash-blond hair. I don't know the boy's name, but I know him by sight. He's in seventh grade, but he looks about five.

"Do you have a crush on me? Do you want to kiiiiiss me?" Scott sucks in his cheeks, makes kissy-fish noises. The small boy stares at his shoes.

"Four against one. Very brave," I call out. Scott looks at me, his mouth working without making a sound. I turn to my locker and start on the combination.

"Hey, Amy," he says. The attention of the group shifts to me. My locker pops open. I turn.

"What, Scott?" I take a few steps toward him. Scott's eyes glitter with malice. The lock weighs heavy in my hand.

Scott grabs my hair and yanks me away from the locker. He's too far away to hit. My hair rips away from my scalp, strand by strand.

A few hands grab at me. I'm floating above my body now. The blond boy watches, an overeager smile spreading across his face. He yells something out, I don't know what.

I'm falling. My head slams on the linoleum. Little white spots glitter in my eyes. A few kids yell "*Ohhh!*" above me.

I look up and see Scott towering over me. He leans down. My arm swings up and connects with something solid. Scott bends down, holding his side. I swing again. The lock cracks against his head. Scott stumbles away.

I get up, my hand clenched around the lock. My free hand feels the bear mace in my front pocket. Scott's entourage stare at me, momentarily stunned.

"Donadio!" one boy shouts. The call echoes up and down the hallway. Two boys grab Scott and drag him away. His eyes meet mine for a second, wounded, angry. Then he's gone.

James, laughing uncertainly, runs after them. Maybe he thinks they're friends. He's wearing a backpack with his initials embroidered on it. *JSD.*

What does that stand for? I don't know of any seventh graders whose last names start with D. There weren't any in last year's directory, but maybe he's new. John Daniels, Jason Dean, Jeremy Spencer Donahue…or James Spar-Desmond. *Spar-*Desmond— as in, possibly, a descendent of Sebastian and Beatrice.

Someone grabs my hand. I rear back, ready to fight. It's Cassidy, wearing about a pound of Skippy-colored foundation, sparkly lip gloss, and a pink velour zip-up with matching pants. She holds out a small bottle of beige fluid.

"In case you get a bruise. Blend it in circles, then pat." She mimes with her other hand. I take the bottle.

"Thank you…" I say, but she speed-walks away before the words are out of my mouth. Lindsay and Bretlyn are coming up the stairs. Cassidy runs up to them.

"Oh my *Gawd*, you guys. You will not believe…" Lindsay and Bretlyn stop walking, listen to her with looks of much-tested forbearance. I look down at the bottle in my hand. Neutrogena oil-free makeup. It's sealed.

You haven't called CPS yet. Some friend you are.

I wait for Principal Donadio to summon me into his office. The rumor's all over the school. Emily asked me if I really punched Scott in the balls. Yet nothing happens. I get a bathroom pass, inspect my face in the mirror. No bruises yet.

Amy Slutburger sux DICK for CRACK!!!

There's even a heart over the "I" in "DICK." The girls' bathrooms are the school's main gossip hub. Every rumors, rants, and confession is written on the stall walls: *whoever reads this is a HO, Megan Song cut off her eyelids, Jessica Truesdale stuffs her bra, i saw Kathleen Vandergraf in the woods.* That last bit invited many comments: *really?, liar, u r seriously disturbed—GET THERAPY, me too.* There are a dozen-odd hearts with initials in them, eyes, Stussy Ss, nonsensical tags: *qtpicrew loves u, cowgrrrls ROCK, runnnnn jimla, only angels go 2 haeven.* There's even an ouroboros behind the stall, drawn directly on the porcelain.

The door opens. Heels clack against tiles, sending out cubic echoes through the bathroom.

"Their agents make them do everything," one girl says. "They can't even choose their nail polish color. For real." It's Becca Osborne, future gym impresario.

"It was on the news," the other girl says. I know her, too: Erin Roscoe, Becca's best friend, plainer and meaner. The clacking heels stop. Their voices come from the sinks by the mirrors.

"Bush is blowing up little kids in Iraq, but they only care about—"

"Exactly. No one wants to hear about the war. They'd rather stick their heads—"

"I know!"

A long silence follows, punctuated by the plastic rasp of an opening lid.

"I can't wait to go back to the city," Becca says. "There's so much going on there, you know? Not like this fucking cow town."

"Haha. Yeah."

"Even L.A.—and I *hate* L.A., don't get me wrong—but at least there are things to do there. What can you *do* in Forest Knolls?"

"Probably why that girl ran away."

"Her older sister is a complete speed freak. It's super sad. My stepbrother says—"

"Whose sister is this?"

"Amy's. The girl who ran away?"

I sink into the toilet seat. I'd rather stay in here all day than let them know I know they know about my sister. I lean back, press my feet against the stall door. The door creaks. The silence changes.

"What was that?" Becca calls out. "Who's in here? Go check."

Erin's footsteps echo through the bathroom. Her feet pass by the stall. She stops, pauses, turns. I hold my breath.

"Probably you-know-who," Erin says.

"Who's you-know-who?"

Erin whispers or mouths something. Dull plastic clinks against the rim of the sink.

"Come on," Erin says. "Just for a second."

"You have to walk over there, turn off the light, then find your way back—we don't even have a candle!"

"We don't need a candle. If you're in absolute darkness, you just spin around three times and say it." Footsteps move toward the far wall. I can almost see Erin by the far wall, her finger suspended over the light switch.

"So...what, she comes out of the mirror if you say—"

"*Shhh!*"

I hold my breath as Becca deliberates.

"Fine," Becca says. "If she comes out, I'm sacrificing you first. Not kidding."

The light disappears. Muffled giggling fills the room. Heels clack against the tiles.

"Where are you?"

"I'm over here. Hurry up."

More footsteps, more giggles. After a brief pause, Becca and Erin's voices echo in unison throughout the room.

"Bloody Mary, full of guts, the devil's with thee. Hated art thou amongst women, and hated is the fruit of thy empty womb. Unholy Mary, daughter of—"

Their chant cuts off mid-word. No one screams, giggles, breathes. The silence swells in the darkness. My heart flutters in my chest like a trapped moth.

Time passes, don't ask me how much. I don't move; I barely breathe. The darkness swells with the scent of fresh flowers. Something is in here with me, something that isn't Becca or Erin. I won't say someone—it's not quite a someone. I can feel its gaze moving over my body.

It's a trick, I tell myself. *The moment you scream, they'll laugh. You'll see.*

A taut and muscled coil brushes against my shoe. The coil rises along one calf, shushing against my jeans.

Oh God, I pray, *I know I haven't believed in You for a long time, but I promise You if You get me out of this I'll go to church every week and I won't ask questions. I'll read the Bible every day, I'll think whatever You want me to think, I'll even sing Christian rock, just please, please, please, please, please—*

There's something behind the door.

It's glowing white, putting the door into black relief. Maybe it's a fire, but I don't see flames. A tiny tongue flicks against my knee. I look down.

A snake is coiling around my leg. Its bones glow through transparent, shimmering scales. Its eye looks into mine. Its cold flesh presses against my thigh.

I reach for the mace in my front pocket. No good: the snake's coiled too tightly around it. Half-remembered prayers stream through my mind: *The Lord is my shepherd, I shall not want, star of wonder, star of light, Jesus wants me to lie in green sunbeams, oh shit oh shit oh shit oh shit—*

A hand of pale fire passes through the bathroom door. A hand, then a wrist, then a forearm. A perfect circle of nothing opens in its palm, growing wider and wider the longer I stare at it. The snake tightens, lowers its head between my legs. A scream erupts from my throat.

Something burns my chest. It's my locket, glowing white-hot. My skin sizzles underneath. The hand vanishes. The pressure of the snake's body gives way. The heat from my locket ebbs, returning me to darkness.

It takes me a long time to stand. My hands won't hold still. I can't button my jeans, no matter how many times I try. Kids shriek, bellow, and laugh in the hallway. Second period must be over, or nearly over. The latch for the stall door evades my grasp for minutes that pass like centuries. At last, it gives way beneath my shaking fingers. My footsteps echo in the silence. My hands grasp empty air, then the wall, then finally a light switch.

Fluorescent beams flicker on, revealing toothpaste-green tiles and dull gray bathroom stalls. My stall door stands halfway open. There's nothing to mark the spot where Becca and Erin just stood, save a little pink compact, balanced precariously on the lip of the sink. The bathroom's unchanged, and empty—

except for me. I cross myself, remember my ridiculous promises to God, and turn away, ashamed. I would never sing Christian rock.

Natalie and Cassidy stare at me from the doorway, hands over their mouths, eyes sparkling with malicious delight. I smile back. They're not going to kill me, are they? The air's still redolent with the scent of flowers.

The red mark on my chest chafes under my locket. By fourth period, it's an angry blister. I zip up my jacket, despite the heat. If no one can see the burn, it didn't happen. I must have dreamed it. When I overhear Ryan Morrison ask if anyone's seen Becca, I force myself to ignore it. They'll turn up.

They don't.

Rumors fly in the cafeteria line. Becca and Erin are *gone*. Gone where?

"They're out sick. Food poisoning."

"Nuh-uh. They ditched. Becca's boyfriend picked them up."

"I just saw Ryan—"

"Um, no, her real boyfriend? She has this talent agent—"

"I heard they're smoking weed in that stoner spot. Mark Watkins said he saw them out there."

"They're probably eating each other out in the boiler room. They are such lesbos."

"Ew."

The cafeteria quiets. A heavyset policeman, with thinning black hair, walks into the room. Officer Rampling, also wearing a uniform, follows him. She's plumper, younger, her hair more red than gold, her eyes a bit brighter.

"Why are there cops here?" Andrew Jacobs says.

"Becca and Erin," Lisa says. "They're missing." My ears ring in the silence.

"Can I have everyone's attention?" Rampling's partner says. "Thanks. Ah, who here has seen Erin Roscoe or Rebecca Osborne after about ten o'clock?"

I raise my hand. Two hundred heads swivel to look at me. I stand up, make my way through a sea of eyes. Rampling and her partner lead me to the science classroom. They introduce themselves as Karen and Victor.

"Who did you see?" Karen asks. "Was it Rebecca, or Erin, or both?" I look into her eyes, waiting for a flicker of recognition. It doesn't come.

"It was both of them," I say. "I was in the second-floor bathroom, in a stall. I heard them talking."

"What about?"

My sister's drug problem. Children dying in Iraq. Summoning Bloody Mary, demon queen. You know, the usual.

"Amy," Karen says, leaning across the table. "It's important that you tell us everything you remember. Even the tiniest detail could help us more than you know."

A knot of muscle tightens between my shoulder blades. I give them a lightly edited version of the conversation, ending with the Bloody Mary chant. I omit the snake, the heart-shaped burn now itching on my chest.

"Is it possible they left and you didn't hear them?"

"If they took their shoes off. I didn't see any light from the doorway, though."

Victor and Karen exchange a glance.

"I know it sounds nuts, Officer Rampling," I plead, "But I can only tell you what…" I trail off as her eyes shade over with suspicion.

Victor bursts into laughter. "Man, you guys move fast," he says to Karen, still laughing.

I look down at Karen's left hand. I don't remember if she wore a wedding band in 2016, but she doesn't now.

Karen cuts her eyes to her partner, then returns to look at me. "It's Officer Franklin," she says quietly. There it is, at last—the puzzled second look, the shadow memory returning.

Paranoia spreads. Rumors swirl of drug gangs, mafiosi, serial killers. Kids pester me for information. I just heard them talking in the bathroom, I say. About what? Stuff. After lunch, concerned parents arrive en masse to collect their children. By sixth period bio, only a few students remain. Mr. Weathers puts on *Gattaca*. Marina Alvarez sells me a red gel pen. I make a fortune teller out of binder paper, half watching the movie.

My mind's eye shows me a paparazzi photo of Becca, circa 2014. She's pushing a double stroller with two sleeping children inside. She wears a light-brown coat and a diaphanous white blouse, in the shabby chic style that was so popular that year.

If anything happens, the Becca Osborne in that picture won't ever come to be. Her daughters will never grow in her womb, never take their first breaths, never smile. Thus a tree branch is pruned forever, turning into a scar.

"Amy," Marina whispers.

"Yeah?"

"What happened?" she mouths, with a cautious look at Mr. Weathers.

"Bloody Mary."

Marina's eyes pop. "For real? You saw Bloody Mary?"

"I saw something. I didn't ask for a calling card."

"What'd she look like?"

Mr. Weathers glances back at us. Marina leans forward in her seat.

"I didn't see a face." I show her the burn on my chest, explain about the locket.

"You're lucky. If not for that, she coulda killed you."

Onscreen, two boys swim in the ocean. The music swells. I feel the snake coiling around my thigh, see the hand with the void spinning from its palm.

"You think it's connected to those dreams?" Marina says, right when I'm on the cusp of reentering the movie.

"You've had them, too?"

"Yeah, tons. Last night, I dreamed that I was in this long, dark room, giving some presentation about 'B2B' and 'CRM.' I don't even know what that stands for, but I understood it perfectly in the dream."

"Lisa Sharkey has those dreams. Not about B2B, but—"

"You don't get them?"

"Not everyone gets them," I say, guessing. Marina nods.

"That's true. My brother had no idea what I was talking about." She laughs. "I heard this lady in Safeway who dreamed about sitting in a chemo lounge. She booked a doctor's appointment the second she woke up."

"Did this all start on Tuesday?"

Marina thinks about it, for a minute, then nods. "I think so. Why?"

The lights flick on. Mr. Weathers walks to the TV. Ethan Hawke's face vanishes in an instant.

"If you're not going to watch the movie, you can study. In silence." He crosses his arms.

Marina rolls her eyes in sympathy with me, and pulls out a Harry Potter book. Mr. Weathers pulls up the shades.

CHAPTER FIFTEEN
NO INCOMING CALLS

THE SCHOOL CANCELS every after-school activity, including detention. A cop car idles in the parking lot. A security guard patrols outside. The few students left gather in the library, where they disappear into the stacks, slouch in front of the computers, or lie on the carpet. A book sits, open and unread, on Mrs. Petrelli's desk.

I look at my cell phone. I could call Max Duckworth, CPS, Lee Simon, even Claude. These calls would show up on the phone bill, and I'd have to explain them all to Mom. I check my wallet; the change is bulging out of its pocket. Why didn't I take this to SF? Oh well.

Mrs. Petrelli eyes me as I walk to her desk.

"I have to make a personal call," I say. "To my priest."

She eyes me dubiously. "Your 'priest.' Can it wait?"

"If I call him at home, Mom will listen. It's…private."

Mrs. Petrelli leans back in her chair, looks at me through the glasses on the tip of her nose. "We're not supposed to let students out of the library."

"You can watch me from the door. It won't take long, I promise."

The payphone sits in an alcove off the hallways. Mrs. Petrelli watches me from the library door, arms crossed. I run my finger down all the numbers written in the back of my silver notebook. I'll start with the most important call.

"Marin County CPS," a woman answers.

"I need to report a case of neglect—"

"Speak up, hon."

I tell her what I know about Slice's rages and delusions. I tell her about Mr. And Mrs. Clark's extreme hands-off parenting—un-parenting, Cass called it. The payphone eats quarter after quarter. I tell her their address. She sounds sympathetic, concerned, but not upset. I'm sure she's heard worse.

"Thanks, sweetie. If you hear anything else, call us back, okay?"

Mrs. Petrelli shifts her weight from foot to foot. I turn to the next number on my list. The phone rings four times before someone answers.

"Hello?" says a young man's voice.

"Max Duckworth? It's, uh, Oracle Doll."

"Oh. Hi," Max says, his voice thick with sleep. "So, um… what's your deal, exactly?"

"I think I know what happened to Henry," I blurt out. Mrs. Petrelli probably didn't hear that. Probably. I lower my voice. "He went back in time—or his mind did. One minute, he was living in 2016, then he woke up—"

"Woah-woah-woah-woah. He did what?"

I breathe deep. "Before Henry…went off, was he hanging out with anybody new? Did he pick up any hobbies, join any groups, talk about anything strange?"

Max groans. The bed, or couch, or whatever it is, creaks underneath him. "I don't think so."

"Did he ever mention—"

"*Please insert more coins.*"

The line beeps. Max says something lost in the noise. I shove in two more quarters. The beeping stops.

"Did he ever talk about the Doomsday Garden? It's this spiritual group, from the sixties—"

"Not to me. Henry gave up 'organized spirituality' about a year ago. He was trying to figure things out for himself. Clearly it didn't go well."

I let the pause linger.

"When you say he traveled through time," Max says, "are you saying he had a vision of the future and—what, decided he had to kill some random rich guy?" He laughs.

"I think his future self may have…superimposed itself on his body, so to speak."

"What?"

I put a dime in the slot. I should have called collect.

"I said, his future self—"

"Wait," Max says. Recognition dawns in his voice. "This sounds so familiar. Henry said something about…Listerine? No—ugh, what was it called?"

"The Lister-LeNormand Hypothesis."

"Yeah. He said—how did he put it? He said there was this way to make a mind 'travel' through time and space, until it found a receptive vessel. I thought it was more satori chakra mumbo jumbo. He was always—"

"*Please insert more coins.*"

"You wanna call back?" Max shouts. My coin purse is about half-full now. I put in dimes until the beeping stops.

"What did Henry say about Lister-LeNormand?"

"I'm not sure. He had this friend, an old hippie guy he met through his boss. They'd smoke weed together and talk astrophysics and shit. He—" Max cuts off mid-breath. The silence stretches between us. He's not breathing.

"He mentioned something he was gonna do Monday night, near his mom's house."

"In Lagunitas?"

"Uh-huh. He was really excited, but he wouldn't tell me anything. He…" Another breathless pause. "You know what the weirdest thing is?"

"No."

"When he called me on Tuesday, he said a lot of weird shit. But he kept saying, over and over again, 'It's cooler now, it's cooler now, the weather's really different.' What's that about?"

My answer sticks in my throat. A young female voice mumbles something in the background.

"You still there?" Max says.

"Uh-huh."

"I gotta go, sorry. Can you call me later?"

"I'll try."

The line clicks off. *Beep, beep, beep.* The payphone swallows my money. I look at Claude's card. No, not yet. I scan through the numbers again, then pick one. The payphone eats six more quarters. It's only to the East Bay, but it's still long distance.

"Hello?" a man answers.

"Is this Lee Simon?"

"Yes, it is. Who might this be?"

"I'm a friend of Claude Belissan's. You two go way back, right?"

"You're his *friend*," Lee says, breaking a long, uncertain silence.

"Not a close friend."

"Not a close—you're not a long-lost daughter of his, are you?"

"I hope not."

Big, booming laugh on the other end. "So. You're not his daughter, but you're—I'm sorry, what was your name?"

"Rosemary."

"Rosemary. That's a strange name for someone your age, isn't it?"

"I guess."

"It's a lovely name, don't get me wrong. My mother used to play bridge—"

"*Please insert more coins.*" The line beeps as I shove more quarters into the slot. Little more than a dollar left. No wonder payphones went the way of the dodo.

"Run this by me again," Lee says when the line stops beeping. "You know Claude, and you want to talk to me because?"

"I want to know about the Doomsday Garden."

Lee says nothing for a long time. I shove my last four quarters in the slot. A cop walks by outside, looks through the window. Mrs. Petrelli points to her watch.

"The Doomsday Garden," Lee says, tapping something on his desk. "Is this for a school project or…what? Your own interest?"

"Claude's up to something. Something he learned—"

"Okay. I see how it is. Claude sees himself as an ascended sorcerer, directing the music of the spheres—all that mystic horseshit. He's…what has he told you about himself, specifically?"

"Nothing," I say, realizing it as I say it. "He hasn't—"

"He was the smartest kid in our school. Way smarter than I was—and that is saying something, *believe* me. He was learning Einstein manifolds while I was stuck on trains leaving stations. He started publishing academic papers really young, maybe nineteen."

"He's a…professor?"

"He was headed in that direction for a while. He went to Stanford, nearly got a PhD., then quit. Some arcane dispute with the Physics department. That was that."

"What does he do, then?"

"Claude's old man bought a few commercial properties in Oakland and Berkeley. When he died..." Lee sighs.

Only a dime left. I send it clattering into the belly of the payphone.

"What kind of stories was he telling you, sweetheart?"

"Not stories. Two girls disappeared today, and a woman went missing this week, and I think—"

"What missing girls?" Lee says, his voice clouded with suspicion. "Is this about, ah, whatsername, Kath—"

"*Please insert more coins.*"

There are no more coins, not even pennies, not even in my jeans or my backpack's front pocket. I swear and hang up. The payphone swallows my money with a mechanical belch. I sigh.

The phone rings.

I look at the sign on the payphone. *No incoming calls.* My hand trembles as it reaches for the receiver. "Hello, Claude," I say.

"Hello to you, too, Rosemary. How's your Friday?"

"How do you think?"

"I wouldn't know. I can't read your mind."

I lean against the wall, fighting the coldness creeping up my limbs. Mrs. Petrelli's glaring at me now. Bars of golden light touch the lockers. I close my eyes and see the hand of pale fire, a void expanding in its palm.

I cradle the phone between my ear and shoulder. Five seconds pass, ten seconds, maybe more. Claude says nothing. I'm not sure if he's breathing.

"What happened to Henry Lasko?" I say. No answer. "What

happened to me? Is thirteen-year-old me in my grown-up body, trying to figure out the world?"

Claude chuckles. "Now wouldn't that be something. Can you imagine? No, I don't know what that future is. It's not relevant."

"Billions of people's lives are 'not relevant'—"

"Did you like your old life?"

"Not really."

"Why not?"

"It was pointless. Jobs come and go, friends come and go. No community, no future. No escape."

"What would your perfect life look like?"

There's an offer hidden in that statement. I wait for him to make it explicit.

"What if I told you that you have a once-in-a-lifetime opportunity to change the fate of the planet?"

I hang up.

Mrs. Petrelli raises an eyebrow as I walk down the hall. "Are you unburdened?" she asks. The blister on my chest smarts.

There's James Spar-Desmond, sitting by himself. He's hunched over his homework, his head almost touching the desk. I walk over to him, holding out my fortune teller with a shaking hand.

"Hey," I say.

He looks up, blanches.

"Pick a number."

CHAPTER SIXTEEN
THE TRUTH

"'Your memories will change the world.' That's my *fortune*?"

"It's the wisdom of the universe, James."

James looks at me skeptically.

"Now you pick one for me," I say, handing him the fortune-teller. "Here—put your fingers…"

My fortune, we learn, is to die violently inside a machine. "Maybe a fax machine," I say, and mime getting sucked into the input slot. That breaks the ice. James, I learn, lives most of the time in San Geronimo with his mom. On the weekends, he stays with his dad up in Guerneville.

"They're divorced?"

"Separated. It's only been six months."

Guerneville is the North Bay's version of the Castro District or Greenwich Village. If your dad moves out to live in Guerneville, it can only mean one thing, at least to other middle school boys.

"What a pain," I say.

James shrugs with one shoulder. "At least they're not fighting. I can sleep."

"Which one's Spar and which one's Desmond?"

"Mom's Spar. I *hate* having a hyphenated name. When I grow up, I'm gonna change it."

"To Desmond?"

"I dunno. I could be 'James Spar.'"

"It's a cool name. Is it German, or French?"

James looks sharply at me. "Why'd you say that? It doesn't sound French."

I say 'Spar' in a French accent. James thaws a few degrees.

"It's German. My great-grandfather was half-German, half-French, though. When World War One started—you know, the one before Hitler—he worked as a doctor on the front lines. He saw *hella* awful things—guys choking on poison gas, guys with their limbs blown off, dead guys flailing around like fish. So he started looking for answers for how people could do this to one another. One night, he…" James looks at Mrs. Petrelli, then the sixth grader across the library, leans in close.

"Promise you're not gonna tell," he murmurs, his face the picture of earnestness. In that look I read his life story, the same trust broken again and again. *Promise you're not gonna tell*—the burnt fool's bandaged finger goes wabbling back to the fire.

"I won't tell," I say.

"He learned how to send people through time. Not their bodies, but their minds. It's hard, though. There's usually some kind of…colloquial damage."

"Colloquial damage?"

"That's what they used to call friendly fire. When my great-grandfather went back in time, he tried to stop World War One, but he couldn't do it. His neighbor went back with him by accident. It broke him. Totally normal before, totally insane after. Great-Grandpa never forgave himself for that."

"Really," I say, trying to sound casual.

"I know, it sounds crazy, but…I'm not supposed to tell, but I've been to one of their rituals. That's where they send someone through time."

"How do they do it?"

James clears his throat, looks around. Mrs. Petrelli's paging through a magazine. He leans toward me.

"They have this machine out in the woods. I haven't seen it, but…it made this enormous sound, like a thousand voices in one. We held hands in a circle, with this guy in the center. I was right in front of him. I saw it in his eyes when he changed. And then…okay, you're *really* gonna think I'm crazy, but—when we went back home, this cut on my foot was gone."

"What do you mean?"

"I mean, it was gone. No mark. It didn't even hurt."

I touch my neck.

"Things changed. Mostly little things. My sea turtle poster, that I've had in my room since second grade—gone. Mom didn't even remember it. Or that one guy running for governor, not Arnold, um…Cruz Belafonte? I could have sworn he was somebody else. Sometimes I'll mention something that happened, and…it never happened."

A Burger King crown flashes in my mind's eye. "Who was the guy from the future?" I say, trying to dispel the out-of-place image.

James's face shadows over. "I'm not supposed to tell."

"Why not? Would he be in danger?"

"No."

"Why'd he come back?"

"To 'save the world.' They all say that."

"They *all* say that?" I try to laugh. "How many of these things have you seen, anyway?"

James looks around again. He reaches into his backpack and takes out a well-worn paperback, encased in a plastic cover.

"This talks about everything…mostly in code, or poetry. This is where I learned about this stuff." *The Major Writings of the Doomsday Garden*, the cover reads, *by Sebastian and Beatrice Spar.* White text on black. Under the title is a familiar symbol: a circular ouroboros, black rays issuing from its center. James turns to a bookmarked page. "See that? This illustration used to show the snake as a skeleton. Now it has scales. Mom says it's my imagination, but I *know* it's different."

The snake's eye stares into mine. The burn on my chest stings. I reach out and touch the drawing.

"Could I borrow this?"

Uncertainty flits across James's face. He pulls the book back. "Why?"

I consider telling him everything. It might end up in the rumor mill tomorrow. It might lead to a new nickname. It might get back to the wrong people, and I don't know what happens then.

"You know Henry Lasko? The guy that tried to kill Donald Trump?"

All color drains from his face.

"You think it broke him, too?"

"Amy," Mom barks from the doorway. I look at James pleadingly. James considers for a moment, then hands me the book. His face is still white.

"It'll be okay," I say, handing him the fortune teller. He swallows as he takes it.

Mom's heels clack against the asphalt. She's walking fast and out of rhythm, like a drumbeat that's got away from itself. I half run to keep up.

"Traffic *all the way* up Sir Francis Drake," Mom says, her voice a frayed cable ready to snap. "I couldn't get through to your father. He was in surgery, he was in a meeting—and your sister is not answering her phone. The home phone rings and rings. The police *laughed* at me—" She yanks her car door open so hard that it bounces in its socket. I barely get my seatbelt on before she's pulling out of the parking lot.

"You gave a statement to the police," she says, her eyes too big and unfocused to meet mine. For a moment, she looks exactly like Leah in the church vestibule. Ice water floods through my veins.

"I told them what I…well, heard."

"Did you tell them the truth?"

A gulp prevents me from answering. Mom stares through me.

"Of course," I lie. Mom's eyes hover over my face for a moment before she pulls onto the road. I turn on the radio.

"—continues on Thursday for Kathleen Vandergraf of Forest Knolls, who went—"

I turn it off again.

"You wanna go to school somewhere else?" Mom says.

"It might be nice to go to Stinson," I venture. "I could stay with Grandma Rose, see you on the weekends—"

"Not Stinson," Mom says, tapping the steering wheel. "Farther away." A bird, standing on the road, flies up, missing our windshield by inches.

Farther away? Aunt Zelda lives by Clearlake. Mom has family in Massachusetts. I have distant cousins in Switzerland. That might be nice. Fairytale villages, Alpine vistas, chocolates and cheeses, better (and cheaper) healthcare. I could practice my abysmal German, meet some cute blond boys who speak better English than I do. I could see snow…

"There's this wilderness retreat for teenagers who—"

A cold hand closes around my heart. I feel for the bear mace canister in my front pocket. "No."

"You'd be safe."

"I would *not* be safe. Do you know what they do at those camps? What kind of kids go there?"

Mom taps the steering wheel again. "There's something wrong," she says. She's right. It's as if reality went half a degree askew, and is just now tilting and whirling out of balance.

Dad arrives five minutes after us, still in scrubs. Mom walks to him with the same lopsided gait. Dad meets her eyes and blanches.

"Where's Leah?" she says.

Dad's eyes bug out. "She's not here?"

"You're going to leave and bring her back *right now*. You've ignored my calls all day."

"I haven't been ignoring your—"

"Yes, you have, Richard, I must have paged you fifty times—"

"Calm d—"

"I will *not* calm down, not with my daughter—"

It's cool and murky in my room, smelling faintly of rain-soaked earth. The Styrofoam head looks at me impassively. I pull the bucket hat over its eyes.

"—don't know why you're being so unreasonable!" Dad yells, his voice a muffled roar. *Good, sweat,* I think. *Burn some calories for once in your life.* Mom says something back, low and poisonous.

CHAPTER SEVENTEEN
MISTER PSYCHO KILLER

Leah comes home after dinner. Mom corners her in the kitchen. Sharp words fly over the din of the television. A song fragment fills my head: ticking clock, music box melody. I press my palms against my ears.

The argument drags on and on. "It's the top art school in the country," Leah shouts. "It's not some…" An ad on the TV drowns out the rest. I pull James's book out of my backpack, open it to the beginning.

"AOL now has an exciting, fun service just for kids," the TV blares. Leah shouts indistinctly over the din. There are no earplugs in my desk, dresser, or nightstand. I make ersatz ones out of paper napkins. *Try to focus.* I force my brain to read.

Be not trapped in this dead world of passing illusions. The Garden is yours in unity, consuming and creating itself anew, forevermore…

"—I'll just go to *Com*!" Leah bellows. Her footsteps thump

across the floorboards. Her bedroom door slams, rattling the cups on my desk. I try again and again to focus on the book, but my attention slides away. It's Žižek, if Žižek was a monk that dropped binders full of acid. The song fragment ticks over and over in my head. I stare at the page.

Time and Eternity yearn for kairos—the moment of transformation—when they will be united by a drop of blood. Therefore, we wait patiently for the newborn blood of a soul mid-transformation, taken by a scarlet virgin, to open the portal to the Garden…

There are photos: Sebastian Spar as a young doctor; Beatrice, smiling in her cap and gown; the San Francisco house; my grandmother, holding Richey and Zelda on her lap. There are illustrations, too: the aforementioned snake; a dark forest; me, or a sixties pop art version of me, complete with a flipped bob and winged eyeliner. *The scarlet virgin*, according to the caption.

"You know what this means, right?" Leah says, startling me out of my trance. She's standing in the connecting doorway, black eyeshadow smudged across one cheek. Anger radiates off her like heat off white metal.

"What does what mean?"

"Those girls going missing? It means we're grounded for the rest of our lives. This is *Polly Klaas II: Dead and Deader*."

"We don't know they're dead."

"Uh-huh."

Leah's right. Not about them being dead—at least I hope not—but about being grounded. It's surprising Mom's not in here right now, making sure we haven't dematerialized.

"At least you have your driver's license," I say.

Leah scoffs. Her eyes wander around my room. "Good thing you threw out my drugs," she says, bitterness tingeing her laugh. "If Mom goes looking now…"

Outside, the world's turned deep blue. A branch taps against the glass.

"You still have the mace I gave you, right?" Leah asks.

I pull it halfway out of my front pocket.

"Did you have to use it?"

"When?"

"When…you know." She fixes me with a pointed, questioning stare.

I tell Leah about the Bloody Mary incident, including the apparitions. Her expression changes from anger, to shock, to puzzlement. When I've finished, she leans against the doorframe, one foot swinging back and forth.

"You know you can tell me if something's going on, right?"

"I know."

Leah sits on my bed, kicks her feet off the edge. She studies my face. "You're different now. You didn't get your period, did you?"

"I don't think so."

"Are you pregnant?"

"No!" I stand up and walk to the window. The silence thickens between us.

"What did you and Grandma Rose talk about?" she asks.

I turn to look at her. "The Doomsday Garden."

Leah's eyes fly open. "She talked about the cult? Why?"

"It just came up."

"Bullshit, it just came up. You know how many times I've asked about that? No one will talk about it—ever."

Tell her, an inner voice says. The words crumble in my mouth.

"I read about it in a book," I say instead. "When Dad saw it, he must have—"

"You are such a fucking liar, Amy. There's something you're not telling me. I can feel it."

I look at the floor. The connecting door slams shut behind her. A moment later I hear her screams, muffled by a pillow. I press my palms into my eyes.

I finish my math and biology homework before collapsing in defeat. Thank God it's Friday. I read through my silver note-book, looking for clues. If only I could call Max without arousing Mom's ire.

Wait. I knock on the connecting door. The Super Mario knock—*dud-dud-dunh dud-duh dah*—our code for "We need to talk, now." The door flies open. Leah glowers at me.

"This better be important."

"You know Max Duckworth, right?"

"Yeah, he's Ray's brother. Why?"

"Did you ever meet Henry Lasko?"

Suspicion casts a shadow over her face. "Ray told me about him. He was kind of strange, but not…" Her eyes meet mine for a second. "He's got the same birthday as you."

"Who does?"

"Henry Lasko. Mister Psycho Killer. I don't know what it is, but everyone born on your birthday is a total fucking lunatic. Ray says it's 'cause you're all virgins."

"We're what?"

"'Virgo.' Your Zodiac sign. It's Latin for 'virgin,' or Greek, or something. So, Henry Lasko's a virgin, Kathleen Vandergraf's a virgin, you're a virgin—you *are* a virgin, right?"

My brain screams in a language I don't understand.

"Right?" Leah says, urgency underlining her words. "Amy, you're—"

"Shut up."

Leah's face pinches into a scowl. She reaches up to hit me. I block her without thinking. Slice's eerie voice echoes in my mind: *Cassidy's been gone a long time, but she's here now.* And Cassidy's voice, back in 2016: *You guys have the same birthday. Remember?*

Thud. There's your connection. Every possible time traveler has the same birthday. Slice, Kathleen, Henry Lasko, me. All missing, dead, or crazy. Except for me.

"Henry was twenty-six, right?"

"Yeah, for two days. He—"

"How old was Kathleen, again?"

"Thirty…nine?"

My eyes meet Leah's. "Thirteen," I say, and laugh. Leah frowns, takes a step back. "We all turned multiples of—wait, how old is Slice?"

"Who the fuck is Slice? Amy—hey!" Leah grabs my arm as I turn away. "Answer me!"

"It's complicated." I wrench my arm free. My silver notebook gleams on my desk. I need to see the connections written down. *August 26th. San Geronimo Valley. Doomsday Garden. Thirteen.*

Leah wrestles me for the notebook. "'It's complicated?' The fuck does that mean? I know you're hiding something. Just *tell* me."

"No!"

"I swear to God, Amy—"

"Girls!"

Mom's standing in the hall doorway, arms folded. "What are you doing?"

We break apart.

"Nothing," we say in unison.

"Your father's tired," Mom sighs. "Can you keep it down?"

"Sorry."

"We'll be quiet."

Mom searches our faces. I grab the notebook back. After a moment, Mom closes the door.

Leah looks at the Bic pen in her hand. Our eyes meet for a perilous second. We burst out laughing, leaning on the desk and on each other. When our laughter dies down, Leah's looking at me, concern in her eyes.

"Why don't you tell me what's going on?"

"I can't explain it in one sentence."

Leah's face closes. "Oh, fuck you, Amy."

The door shudders when she slams it.

CHAPTER EIGHTEEN
THE LIGHT IN THE WOODS

My EYES SNAP open. It's dark. The air is too cold, too fresh. I'm standing, I don't know where.

Something crunches underfoot. A million tiny points prickle the soles of my feet. The smell of damp earth and redwood trees. I hear crickets chirping in the distance, feel the cold night air against my face.

A silvery edge of moonlight gilds the world around me. I'm standing in a tiny hollow, hemmed in on all sides by enormous redwoods. There's enough room to turn around, to sit, but not much else. I'm wearing what I wore to bed: a long-sleeved shirt, a hoodie, jeans, thick socks. The mace canister is still in my front pocket.

I look around me. There's a path, not too wide, leading over a ridge. There's some strange unevenness in the darkness, right off the path. It doesn't move. My imagination paints it as a mountain lion, waiting to pounce.

When you get lost in the forest, you have to stay where you are. Don't move, unless you're about to get eaten. I sit on a root, tear apart a loose piece of tree bark.

A pale light moves across the tree in front of me. I turn, look through a gap between two trunks. A light bobs and moves above the ridge, casting huge shadows through the forest.

"Hey!" I scream. "Over here!"

The trees are so close together, even thirteen-year-old me can barely squeeze through. The light returns, stronger this time. Voices murmur on the other side of the ridge.

"Hello?" I call out. I squeeze between two trees, spurred on by the promise of discovery. "I'm over here!" I yell, waving my arms as I run along the path. The light's growing brighter, closer. My foot snags on something. I freewheel through the air. My hands scrape against the ground. One knee bangs against a root.

Darkness closes around me. Pain shoots up from my knee. There's a new smell nearby—perfume and rancid meat. I cover my mouth.

My free hand touches something cold. It's firm, with a yielding, cushiony surface. Long, cylindrical protrusions issue from its center. Perhaps it's a type of mushroom. I touch a thin, cool band around one protrusion. The penny drops.

It's a hand.

I stand up, back away. My eyes readjust to the moonlight, giving the darkness shape and form. Strange shadows resolve into a tangle of fish-pale limbs and a spray of dark hair, surrounded and half-buried under leaves.

It's Kathleen Vandergraf. She's wearing the outfit described on the missing person's poster: dark fleece jacket, khakis, dark slip-ons. Pearl studs glint on her earlobes. The way she's fallen, she looks like she's doing some complicated yoga pose, her arms and legs bent at awkward angles. Her lips are gone, exposing her teeth almost to the roots. There's no light in her eyes. There are no eyes.

A white square peeks out from her pants pocket. Maybe it's

a suicide note, a ransom letter, something meant for her children. Or maybe it's a map of the forest, a note for yours truly. *Hello, Amy. I want to play a game.*

"Sorry about this," I say, as I maneuver the paper out of her pocket and tuck it into mine.

"Hey!"

Whose voice was that? I look to Kathleen, expecting her mouth to move. My hand freezes in mid-air.

"Hey!"

I look up. Flashlights swing wildly through the branches past the ridge.

"Luke, wait up, dude!"

"Over here!" I scream. I stand up, wave my arms. "I'm over here! Please!"

A beam of light swings through the trees, over Kathleen's body, then up to my face. I hold my free hand over my eyes.

"What the fuck," a male voice says. The beam falls away. Feet crunch through the dirt and leaves. I look up, blinking past the red splotches in my vision. Two men approach. They're wearing masks and holding guns. I fall backward, over Kathleen. A scream rips from my throat.

"It's Airsoft!" one of the men yells. "Look—" the flashlight beam swings wildly, lands on the tip of his gun "—orange tips, see? Chill out!"

The beam returns to my face, then to Kathleen's.

"Shit," the other one says. They sound sixteen, maybe younger. I rise to my feet.

"Dave, you gotta come see this," Orange Tips says into his walkie talkie. "Over." *Bleep.* The three of us look at each other.

The other boy retches and staggers away. Orange Tips looks from Kathleen to me. He has a buzz cut, a squarish jaw, a serious expression. It's a face that I *know.*

"Did you find her like this?" he says.

"I did." I look at him again. "You're Luke Hillis." Luke nods. "I'm Amy Snowberger. I go to school with Sean."

Luke nods, still expressionless.

"I'm gonna lose it," Luke's friend says, leaning against a tree.

"You are not gonna lose it. Ian—look at me. We're going back together."

"What about her?" he says, gesturing vaguely toward Kathleen. Luke and I look down at her, still motionless in the leaves.

"We'll tell the cops where to find her."

Ian and I follow Luke up the ridge, away from Kathleen's body. Their flashlights make loose figure eights on the path ahead.

"What were you doing out here?" Luke says.

"Sleepwalking."

"In your clothes?"

I explain about troubled teen camp.

"My cousin went to one of those," Ian says. "He had to rat on one person every single day. He got in trouble for making stuff up."

"What kind of trouble?"

"Solitary confinement…they'd put him in this tiny closet for, like a whole day, sometimes longer."

We walk in silence, punctuated by our footsteps crunching over pine needles.

"Sean says you're psychic," Luke says.

"I'm not psychic. I probably heard the search party out here. There was this light over the ridge—"

Ian whips around, his face slack. Luke stops walking and stares at me. A garbled voice crackles on their walkie talkies.

"Did you hear voices?" Luke says.

"Yeah, but—"

"What did they say?"

"They were too far away. There were lots of them, though. I'm surprised you didn't see them."

Ian's eyes bulge.

"Listen to me," Luke says. "Do not ever, *ever* go towards that light. You understand?…If you go into it, you come out different. *If* you come out. Even looking at it can change you."

"Change you how?"

"Luke. Let's go."

We follow Ian along the path. "It makes you crazy," Luke says. "One kid walked into it one time, and—" he snaps his fingers "—dude is *mental* now. He's twenty-six or something and still lives at home. He can't even take a shower by himself."

"Slice Clark."

"You know him?"

"A little."

Ian leads us through a maze of paths and trails. We barely speak. A few pinecones and brambles cut into my feet. The walkie talkies chirp on Luke and Ian's shoulders. A garbled voice says something I can't understand.

"No, Dave, we can't do another round. There's a fucking dead body in the woods. Over," Ian says into his walkie talkie.

A thousand voices, male and female, rise around us in polyphonic chant. A bright light casts our shadows long in front of us. Luke takes my hand. We run. Branches, thorns, and nettles sting my legs. The light casts everything into harsh relief.

Luke stops, picks me up, hoists me over his shoulder. The singing continues, amplifies. More voices. Luke runs. Branches thwack me as we pass through the trees. I don't look up.

We burst into a clearing behind a house, dark save one amber light in a window. Another boy, presumably Dave, stares at us, clutching his Airsoft gun to his chest.

Luke sets me on the ground. "You all right?" he says.

"Fine." The singing's now distant. Long strips of light pass over the yard, touching the edge of the house. Dave shades his eyes.

"We found Kathleen Vandergraf," I say. "She's dead."

Cops fill the Hillis house. They take my shoes. Ian and I wait for our parents in the kitchen. Luke, with his father, speaks to a cop on the back porch. I can just make out their voices over the hum of the refrigerator.

Debbie Hillis hands us mugs of peppermint tea. Her eyes flit from me, to Ian, to the back porch. I bounce on the balls of my feet, trying not to blink. Every time I close my eyes, I see Kathleen.

"Hi, Amy," Sean says from the kitchen doorway. He's wearing an Operation Ivy T-shirt and plaid pajama pants. How many hundreds of times have I seen that shirt? It doesn't yet have that rip on the sleeve.

"Hi, Sean."

"I looked up those Swiss bands you told me about. I couldn't find anything."

It takes me a moment to connect the dots. The bands from the future I showed him in class. Another loose end. "Did you look in German? Or French?"

"Why German or French?"

"That's what they speak over there."

"I thought they spoke Swiss."

"Sean, honey, go back to sleep," Debbie says, ushering him out of the room. "You can talk to Amy tomorrow."

In the bathroom, I pull Kathleen's paper out of my front pocket, smooth it out on my leg. For a moment I think it's printed in a neat cursive font. The ink, which darkens at the end of each word, shows otherwise. Where do people learn to write this well? By the time I finish the first line, I no longer care.

Lucas is gone. His mother, my daughter, sleeps in his bed. High school, work, boyfriends, childbirth—all these things are years away. Lucas's father is God knows where.

Say my daughter and her boyfriend meet again. If they have a child, will it be Lucas? The odds are astronomically against it. If it doesn't happen, Lucas will die without ever being born.

But you're not really dead, are you, Cricket? I can feel you here with me, as close as my own heartbeat. I've heard your cries in the forest. I'll find you, no matter what.

To anyone who reads this: my grandson's name is Lucas Jonathan Vandergraf. Please help me find him.

Kathleen Vandergraf

26 August, "2003"

I read the letter again. Leah's words return to me: *Gordon walked downstairs and—as soon as his mom saw him, she turned* white. Kathleen must have known right then, in one moment of horror.

I fold the letter back up. If I give this to the police, I'll have to explain why I took it. Why did I wait to hand it over? Do I know what it means?

Someone knocks on the door. "You okay in there?" Debbie Hillis says from the other side.

"Be right out." If I flush this letter, I lose one of my few connections to the world I lost. It's not proof, but it's suggestive. I put it on the back of the toilet, on top of the magazines.

Another, more abrasive knock on the door.

"One second!"

"I'm here, sweetie," Mom says. "Are you—"

"I'm *fine!*"

I look from the note to the toilet. It would be so easy to flush it, pretend that it's all make-believe, from the hand of pale fire to the light in the forest. But I'd always know the truth.

Here we go.

Officer Franklin reads the note several times. "You removed this from the body?" she says. Her eyes pierce through me. I nod.

"Where was it?"

I explain. "I thought I was gonna die out there," I plead. "I thought it might be a map or instructions. Like something out of *Saw.*"

"Like what?"

"Like, uh, in a horror movie, where the killer leaves clues for his victims on how to escape."

"You thought Kathleen was murdered?"

"I didn't exactly do an autopsy."

I go over my story three times, repeating the same points: waking up in the woods, the lights, the body, the boys who found me.

"And they told you—"

"Don't go into the light. There's this guy we know—" I see my opportunity, and take it "—Slice, who's completely—"

"Slice?"

"That's his nickname. His real name's Jack Clark. He's probably schizophrenic, but his parents won't take him to a doctor.

They give him crystals, herbal teas, foot massages." I swallow, sit forward on the couch.

"He has two younger sisters. One's about twenty-three, the other's twelve. The twenty-three-year-old basically takes care of them both."

"You saw Jack out in the woods?"

"No. While we were walking out, Luke said that Slice—that Jack—went into the light."

"What light, hon?"

I try to explain.

It's almost morning when the police let me go. The outside world is infused with blue-gray light. Officer Franklin talks with Mom on the porch while I wait in the car. When Mom comes back, she looks worn out, a marionette on frayed strings.

"What's really going on Amy?"

"I don't know."

Mom nods a few times, swallows, then turns the keys. The car engine roars to life. The radio blares. Michelle Branch, mid-chorus, asks me if I'm happy now.

I don't know, Michelle. What do you think?

CHAPTER NINETEEN
HUNTER AND HALO

THERE'S NO MEDIA scrum outside our house. No clutch of news vans at the end of Blackwood Drive. Helicopters circle over the forest, near the Hillises. Dad ushers us into the car, his head on swivel.

"Don't talk to anyone who comes up to you," he says, fumbling the key into the ignition. "If anyone bothers you, page me right away. 'Kay?"

"Is it really on the news?" I ask.

Leah nods at me from the front seat, eyebrows up. "It was on CNN this morning."

Dad starts the car.

"—not said whether the disappearances are connected—" an unctuous NPR woman says. Dad switches the radio off.

Dad drives through Woodacre in silence. He's taking us to the library, ostensibly to study, mostly to decompress. Mom spent the last few hours pacing the kitchen, slamming cabinet doors, fiddling with the radio. After Dad gets home from work, we'll pick up a couple pizzas, stop by Video Droid. We can rent whatever movies we want. Dad promised.

A dark green Honda follows us down Blackwood Drive. I know, without knowing how, that it isn't one of our neighbor's cars. Dad doesn't seem to notice. I catch Leah's eye, jerk my head toward the back window. She looks outside, puzzled. *The car*, I mouth. She rolls her eyes. *Relax*.

The green Honda follows us out of Woodacre, down Sir Francis Drake, and into Fairfax. It continues driving straight when we turn into the library parking lot. Maybe Leah's right. I hold on to my locket as we park.

Then I see it. It's parked on the curb, near the front. I gasp. Leah follows my line of sight, then pales.

"What?" Dad says. I explain. Dad gets out, marches up to the green Honda. I bite my lower lip so hard it bleeds. Dad examines the car, walks around it, turns to us. He gestures us over.

I get out and approach the car, against every instinct screaming in my brain. Pine needles, green and brown, coat the hood. I look up. Sure enough, there's a Monterey pine overhead, swaying in the mid-morning breeze.

"See?" Dad says. "It's been here forever."

I back away. There's something wrong. Dad walks to me, envelops me in a hug.

"It's gonna be fine," he says. "I promise." A car door slams behind us. Leah walks toward us, holding her backpack. Dad pulls her into the hug. I look at the car once more, trying to calm the unease growing inside me.

That's when I see it. It's parked on a red curb. A fire lane. Even in sleepy Fairfax, it would have been towed ages ago, long before all those pine needles could have fallen.

Inside the library is all grays and browns: slate-colored carpet, plywood tables, metal bookshelves, cheap oak chairs. Fay Ray

Duckworth sits by the magazines, feet propped on a low table. She's reading a battered copy of *The Wind-Up Bird Chronicle*, frowning in concentration. Her boots are scuffed and deeply creased; chipped red polish shines on her fingernails.

Fay Ray's pretty in a gothed-out jezebel way, her face all rounded curves and soft peach fuzz, her eyes dark and intense. Even here, reading a book in a hoodie and jeans, she exudes quicksilver, vampish intensity. She looks up and beams at us. Who wouldn't want to be her friend?

"Snow mountain and sister. What's up, Amy?"

"'Sup Gay Ray," Leah says, stepping in front of me. "Where's Gordon?"

Worry transforms Fay Ray's face. "He's not here?"

Gordon stands in the 700s aisle, skimming through a joke book. He has his mother's cheekbones, her straight black hair, her pale, almost waxy skin. He goggles at us, his face taking on the same haunted expression from Kathleen's "Missing" picture. "Hey Amy," he says to me. "They haven't, uh, found Mom yet."

I float in place. "I'm sorry to hear that, Gordon."

Fay Ray pulls Gordon into a hug. Gordon stares at me. I wave.

Gordon's car, a blue Datsun with the paint flaking off, sits in the parking lot. I avoid looking at the green Honda, still parked in fire lane. Gordon and Fay Ray walk in front of us.

"Fucking paparazzi camped outside his house last night. They screamed at his sister when Gordon drove her to school. 'How do you feel about your mom disappearing?' She's in second grade."

"Where is she now?"

"Her friend's house," Fay Ray answers.

"Always good to have a friend."

"I guess," Fay Ray says, digging the keys out of her jean's front pocket. "Unless your friend's psycho—here we go."

The car smells of cigarettes, weed, cloth seats, Old Spice. Gordon slumps in the front passenger seat. Fay Ray pauses, her hand on the ignition.

"Your grandma's really gone?" Fay Ray says to Leah. "You're sure?"

"She's an old hippie, Ray. If she's home, it's not the end of the world."

The car judders to life.

We pass through San Geronimo Valley. On the tape deck, Lux Interior moans over jangly guitars and a caveman drumbeat. A CD player sits on the dashboard, connected to the tape player by a thin black cord.

We drive past skinny redwoods and ivy thickets. Ray rolls down the windows halfway, letting in the cool morning air. A finch flies off the road and into the trees. The CD skips on one of Lux's more demonstrative grunts. Ray swears and pounds the dashboard. The song hiccups, then restarts.

Leah gasps. I know what it is before I've turned to look. There, ten feet behind us, is the dark green Honda.

"What's up?" Ray says. Leah explains. Ray swears again. "You had a car *following* you and you didn't fucking tell me?" Leah explains about the pine needles. Ray scoffs. "You know the police are watching you, right? Even if you can't see them. And they've got nothing on the fucking press. At least ten news vans followed Gordon to Borders last night. The parking lot was a seizure disco—flashbulbs popping, people screaming, this huge crowd swarming us. I had to escort *him* for once."

Leah and I look through the back window, watching the Honda pass through patches of light and shade. The car pulls back, disappears behind the next curve. The driver is a dark blur, vaguely male.

"Could be anybody," I say.

Gordon's watching me from the front seat.

"Are you okay?" he asks.

"I'm fine. Are you?"

"I talked to Luke Hillis. He said you were very…self-possessed, when you found her."

"I didn't feel self-possessed. I woke up alone in the woods, near a dead body…sorry. I don't think she suffered, though. Whatever happened, it didn't seem violent."

"Luke said the same thing." An awkward silence fills the car.

"I can't believe the police haven't found her yet," Fay Ray says. "Luke knows the woods like his own face, right? I bet he could lead them back to that exact spot."

"He did. There was nothing there. A cougar might have dragged her off."

We all gasp. Fay Ray reaches for Gordon's hand.

"I'm fine," Gordon says, pulling his hand away. "It's the natural order. 'In the midst of death, we are in life.'"

Ray frowns at Gordon, runs her hand over his hair. He stares out the window, arms crossed.

"Something's wrong," Leah blurts out. "I can't put my finger on it, but I feel it."

"What, you mean apart from three women going missing and strange lights in the woods? Apart from that fucking chanting and wailing at all hours? Yeah, I can't put a finger on it either."

"That's not what I mean. Remember that dream I wrote about, where I went to that church? Amy had the same dream."

"For real?" Ray says, meeting my eyes in the rearview mirror.

I nod. "Exactly the same? Or was it from your perspective, with you lighting the candles?"

"From my perspective."

"Collective unconscious," Gordon says. "There are lots of things we share, as a species, that go deeper than culture or language. Symbols, archetypes, feelings, instincts…and dreams."

"Maybe the collective unconscious is having a collective psychotic episode," Leah says testily.

We turn onto the Pacific Coast Highway, heading south. Wind buffets us as we drive, sending our hair flying. Ray sticks her hand out the window, yells something I can't hear.

The Honda follows us along the PCH. I still can't see the driver. I can't read the license plate, either, not even with my awesome thirteen-year-old eyes. I look out the side window. If I pretend hard enough, I'm sixteen again, sitting in Cassidy's car, drinking cool beer, listening to a song that doesn't yet exist.

The mid-morning sun fills the world with clear light. The Green Honda disappears and reappears around each bend in the road. Gordon lights Ray's cigarette. The smoke, which she blows out the window, flies in my face. Leah stretches her arm through the open window, spreads her hand out in the wind. No one stares at a screen, unless you count the CD player display.

Fay Ray rants about work.

"Sometimes these creepy guys follow me around the store for hours, or *stare* at me. One guy just stood next to me while I sorted the political science section. Then he tried to follow me into the storage area. He had the creepiest stare…" She shivers.

"You still got that mace I gave you?" Leah says. Ray nods, takes a deep drag from her cigarette.

"Brian won't kick them out. I should sue him, seriously. I've told him a zillion times, I have class at Com on Tuesdays and

Wednesdays from five to seven. Guess when he schedules me. Then I have to run around calling people to take my shift. I might quit."

"The class, or the job?"

"The job, duh. What am I gonna do, work retail the rest of my life?" Ray laughs. "That class cost almost three hundred bucks. I'm not flushing that down the drain."

What happened to Fay Ray Duckworth? I looked her up once. She lived in Boulder, managed a CVS, wrote a blog about learning to sew. Relationship status: "It's Complicated" with some weather-worn hippie dude. She had a son. No, two sons. What were their names?

"Oh! I have to tell you about Tiger. This dude comes in every week. He's forty-five if he crawled out of the womb yesterday. He's got beef jerky skin, Chiclet teeth, his hair's frosted like a fucking Backstreet Boy. He wears super-baggy jeans with Ecko and Spitfire shirts. He even wears a puka shell necklace."

"His name's Tiger?"

"No, that's what we call him. He only buys teen beat magazines, so we call him 'Tiger,' short for 'Tiger Beat-Off'... What? I had to ring him up once. He asked me," she affects a chain-smoking Liberace voice, "'Which boy is your favorite?'"

"Ewww! What'd you say?"

"Nothing! He kept needling me, you know, 'Do you like Stevie Brock? What about Aaron Carter, he's pretty cute, right?'"

"Aaron Carter's, like, fourteen."

"I know! If I ever see him talking to a kid, I'm calling the cops. He's on a watchlist somewhere, for sure."

"He should get a subscription," Gordon says.

"He's a perv. Doing it in public's how he gets off."

"Doing what?"

"Buying the—" Fay Ray bops Gordon on the back of

the head, "—buying the magazine! You are such a fag. Get your mind…"

Gordon laughs tepidly, shields himself with his forearm.

The green Honda grows closer. "Maybe it's one of my stalkers," Fay Ray says. "This ESP bomb must have made them crazier."

"What ESP bomb?" I say.

"Ray," Leah says, shading her eyes.

"Leah. You saw those lights in the forest, right?"

"Those were kids."

"Doing what, testing klieg lights?"

"*Ray.*"

"The day after that—the *day* after—Henry Lasko went insane, Kathleen ran into the woods—oh, and get this. Half the books we sold on Tuesday—that's five-zero fucking percent—were about physics, paranormal shit, or religion. That *never* happens."

"ESP bombs aren't real."

"I know you think that, but you're wrong. Too many things don't add up. Why would Henry try to kill Donald Trump? Why would Kathleen—"

"Same birthday," Gordon interjects.

"I know, right? Thirteen years apart. Henry turned twenty-six, Kathleen turned thirty-nine." She reaches for Gordon's hand. "That's gotta be ten million to one."

"Not really. Tons of people are born in late August," Leah says. "Amy has the same—" her voice catches. Her gaze turns to me.

"No shit. How old are you, Amy?" Ray says, meeting my eyes in the rearview mirror.

Tom once told me that if you have twenty-three people in a room, there's a fifty percent chance—a fully fifty fucking percent chance, even—that two of them share a birthday. Don't ask me how it works—he tried to explain, and my brain dribbled out of my ears. How many people in Woodacre were born on August 26th? How many people in the San Geronimo Valley, in West Marin, in all of California?

"I'm thirteen," I say. Leah's staring at me, a question in her eyes. Ray laughs.

"No shit. And you ran away the next day, right? I told you. ESP bomb."

I sink into my seat, lean my forehead against the window. What do Kathleen, Henry Lasko, Slice Clark, and I have in common? We're all born on August 26th. We all turned some multiple of thirteen in 2003. We were all in the San Geronimo Valley on the night of August 25-26, 2003. We all ran away from our daily lives on August 26th. Two out of four of us are dead.

Still—why us? There must be more than four people in the area who meet some or all of those criteria. Did they all travel through time? Maybe they're not all going crazy. Maybe they are, just not in a newsworthy way.

"I think I know what happened to Henry and Kathleen," I blurt out. My eyes meet Gordon's. We both know I'm talking about the note. "Becca and Erin, too. I think they're all connected."

"Connected how?" Gordon says.

"I called Ray's brother, and he said—"

"You called Max?" Ray says, her face a picture of confusion. Her puzzlement dissolves into a wide smile.

"Wait, *you're* Oracle Doll?" She laughs. "I thought she was this emo girl we know. Leah, did you know about this?"

"No."

"What do you think happened?" Gordon says to me. Ray's laugh ebbs away.

"I think Henry and Kathleen saw the future. Or their own futures. There's some force that—"

"Do you have those dreams, too?" Ray says. Leah's stare pierces through me. The same question's written in her eyes. I shrug instead of answering.

"I had a fucked-up one last night," Ray says. "I was ice skating and holding this guy's hand, and wondering if I'd lose the baby if I fell down. They were playing a techno remix of 'White Christmas.' I was *sure* I was pregnant, even after taking three tests…"

We stop for gas in Bolinas. "Two twenty-six a gallon? Fucking really?" Ray says as she pulls in. She and Gordon disappear into the convenience store. The dark green Honda drives into the station, parks at the next pump. No one gets out. I avoid Leah's eyes.

Hunter and Halo. Those are the names of Ray's future sons: Hunter and Halo Duckworth. In the store, Ray's laughing, one hand on Gordon's arm. Gordon stares vacantly ahead.

"What'd you say?" Leah asks me.

"Nothing."

"No, you said something."

I shake my head. Poor Hunter and Halo Duckworth, floating in oblivion with Kathleen's grandson, the class of 2028, about a billion other souls. Leah asks me something.

"I'm sorry?" I say.

Leah doesn't answer. Her eyes follow Gordon and Ray, now walking back to the car. Leah pulls her hand away from her mouth. She's bitten a bloody strip of skin off her ring finger.

"Check this out," Ray says as she bounces into the driver's seat. She shoves a black-and-white magazine at Leah, who takes it gingerly. It's an issue of *The Moon*, Lee Simon's tabloid.

"*Abominable Snowmobile Terrorizes Beach Party*," Leah reads. "You *bought* this?"

"I couldn't steal it with the clerk right there."

Gordon fiddles with the gas pump outside. Leah pages through the magazine.

"*My Dog Can Read: Prodigy Pooch Plows through* War and— seriously? This is retarded."

"Don't be so fucking pretentious." Ray leans over the seat. "They have horoscopes. You're a Scorpio, right?"

"Sagittarius."

"Oh, God. That explains *everything*."

Leah scowls. "Horoscopes are meaningless. 'Watch out on Tuesday for malign influences. A secret admirer will make his presence known.' Anyone could make that up."

"They're not made up. *The Moon* is *never* wrong."

Leah rolls her eyes.

"It's true." Ray leans over the seat, taps the open page. "You know Scott Peterson? Six months before he killed his wife, *The Moon* ran a story: *Twisted Fisherman Uses Wife's Body as Bait*. They got everything right: the mistress, the pregnant wife, the 'fishing trip.' Even the bleached hair."

Leah flips through the pages, one story following another: *Untreatable Superbugs Confound Doctors*; *Aliens: Earth a 'Flyover Planet'*; *Al Gore Statue Cries Real Tears*—

All the blood in my body drains to my feet.

"Give me that," I say, in a voice not my own. Ray looks at me in confusion. Leah reads the headline. Her eyes meet mine. Something passes between us.

CHAPTER TWENTY
THE KEY

TIME-TRAVELING TEEN SAYS: THE
FUTURE SUCKS!

HONOLULU, Hawaii—One teenage boy says he's come back from the future—without aging a day!

Justin Kealoha, 18, claims that he's jumped back in time from 2029. One night, he went to sleep as a middle-aged claims adjuster, and then woke up in his college bedroom, in his old body, with a full head of hair!

"At first I thought I was dreaming," Kealoha said. "But as the day wore on, I started to meet people I'd completely forgotten. They all looked so young—I looked so young. And I saw on TV that George W. Bush was the President. That's when I knew this was real."

Kealoha has been seen by neurologists, psychologists, and other physicians. Despite a full brain scan and blood panel, no one can detect anything wrong with him.

"One doctor told me that my old life was a dream,"

Kealoha says. "I'd imagined graduating college, marrying my wife, and my entire career. But I don't think so. My memories are so detailed—I couldn't dream this stuff if I tried."

Dr. Eugene Stafford, professor of the paranormal at the University of Honolulu—where Kealoha is currently a student—says that time travel is not unheard of, but there's no precedent for the teenager's case.

"Usually, when people time travel, they keep their original bodies," he says. "You don't go back into your body from the past. Perhaps he somehow willed himself back. Perhaps there are forces at work here, far greater and more powerful than anything we could imagine."

But this clock-jumping coed isn't fazed. Although Kealoha is enjoying being a college freshman again, he's taking life one day at a time. Regrets? Only one, he says.

"I wish I'd gone back six months earlier, before I took out my student loans. I have no idea how I'm gonna pay them off!"

Next to this story is a gray sidebar with several predictions:

A GLIMPSE OF THE FUTURE

We asked Justin Kealoha for some snapshots of life in 2029. Here's what he said:

CONTACT WITH ALIENS: *Aliens will appear on every American TV screen—but not for the reason you might think. "Aliens are huge fans of Survivor," says Kealoha. "When the show was almost canceled, the aliens jammed* *the airwaves, saying they would blow up the planet if it happened." Not surprisingly, Fox reversed their decision in a hurry!*

DIGITAL DRUGS: *The drugs of the future are all electronic, all digital, and always there! "Lots of people carry around digital cigarettes, that give them a 'hit' of nicotine whenever they want," Justin says. If that's not your thing, there are digital versions of alcohol, marijuana, cocaine, even heroin. "You press a button, and you get high—whenever you want, wherever you want." Is it as good as the real thing? Nope, but it is legal!*

TOUCHABLE COMPUTER SCREENS: *No more buttons or mice. In the future, screens will respond to touches and gestures, leaving the world wide web literally at your fingertips. Be careful, though: "A lot of people smudge their screens, especially after they eat greasy food. If you want to keep your screen clean, either buy some screen cleaner, or wear gloves!"*

PRESIDENT OPRAH: *Move over, Hillary Clinton! In 2008, the American people will elect Oprah as the first black and female President! Oprah will balance the budget, fix the school system, and send Osama bin Laden to the great big bunker in the sky. She'll even bring peace to the Middle East. "Oprah is very popular," Justin says. "That's probably why we gave her six terms."*

IT'S NOT THE END OF THE WORLD (YET): *Despite all the predictions of gloom and doom, the world hasn't ended by 2029. "I'm not so sure, though," Kealoha says. "I'm not even sure about 2003 anymore. Let's just say there are big, big changes ahead."*

I put the magazine down, my hands shaking. *Anyone* could predict touch screens or e-cigarettes. Besides, the article was wrong about aliens, peace in the Middle East, President Oprah…

And yet.

Leah reads the article after I do. She looks at me a few times, but says nothing. On the stereo, Nick Cave laments the sun's aimless revolution. Clumps of fennel grow at the road's edge. On the hillside, small bushes shoot up amongst the dry grass. We pass a small eucalyptus grove. A kite surfer on the marsh leaps into the air. I lean my head against the window frame, feel the wind in my hair.

Maybe this magazine is a limited hangout. If they—whoever 'they' are—put the real story in a tabloid, who's going to believe it's really happening? What if Lee knows more than he's saying?

Something flat taps the back of my hand. It's Leah, holding a small piece of paper. I unfold it. *Did this happen to you?* she has written. When I look up, she's pointing at the magazine. Something in my face gives it away, before I can nod. *How?* Leah mouths. I look away. How, indeed?

"Why are we here?" I ask. We're standing in front of Grandma Rose's house, looking up at the front door.

"To avoid all my adoring fans," Ray says, stamping out a cigarette underfoot. "Besides, Gordon hasn't been to the beach in, what, a year?"

"Three years."

"Three years! I rest my case. Come on."

Ray runs up the front steps. We follow. Leah takes my hand and squeezes. "Does Grandma Rose know we're here?" I ask her. She shakes her head. I look over my shoulder: the green Honda's parked across the street. Still empty, now coated with a fine layer of sand.

The house is unlocked. Ray barges in. We shuffle in after, pause at the door, take in the cherrywood darkness of the living room. The mingled scent of cloves, cinnamon, camphor, and old books fills the air. Gordon sits on the couch, stares absently at the empty fireplace. I pull the blinds down on all the windows. A late morning fog rolls in off the ocean.

"This place is nice," Ray says, running her hand along a wall. "It feels old. Solid."

"My grandpa bought it back in the fifties."

"For his wife, or your grandma?"

"Ray!" Leah jerks her head in my direction, then stops abruptly. She turns and looks at me as if seeing me for the first time.

"What?" I say.

Leah's mouth falls open.

"Oh my God, Leah. Just *tell* her."

"Grandpa Doug married some girl right after high school," Leah says. "They never got divorced."

"Do his other kids know about us?" Visions of half-siblings, with half-familiar faces, fill my mind.

"There were no other kids. Mrs. Snowberger was...what's that word? Barren."

"Oh." The vision dissipates. "Who was she?"

"I don't know. I couldn't find her on the internet. She's not in any of Dad's papers. Believe me, I checked."

"So how do you know about her?"

"Aunt Zelda told me."

A wispy memory returns to me from early childhood: Mom, phone sandwiched between her ear and shoulder, talking about "Doug's wife." *Why isn't she saying Grandma's name?* I thought at the time. Later, when I learned they weren't married, I was even more confused. I'd forgotten that until now.

"Why are we Snowbergers, then? Why aren't we Amy and Leah MacLeod?"

"*That's* how you say it?" Ray says, turning from the stereo. "I thought it was 'mack-lee-odd' this whole—wait, how do you get 'mah-cloud' from M-A-C-L-E-O-D?"

"It's Gaelic. You know how Enya's real name is spelled 'Eyeth-nee?' Same convention."

Ray shakes her head, turns back to the stereo. "Fucking Gaelic, man. Fuck me."

"To answer your question," Leah says, side-eyeing Ray, "I think Grandma pretended they were married. You could do that back then." She smiles. "You never thought about that before?"

A loud *tick, tock, tick, tock* blasts from the speakers. An eerie music box counterpoints the percussion. The hair stands up on the back of my neck. This is Heather MacRae's "Hands of the Clock," the song that's been playing in my head for the last week.

"I haven't heard this in forever," Leah says. "Grandma used to play it all time, remember?"

"Not all the time. It freaked me out as a kid."

"That's right. You used to hide under the bed."

"Your grandma listens to this? She's a lot cooler than my grandma is." Ray stands and hands me *The Moon*, now open to the *Mysteries of the Zodiac*, and walks to Gordon, still sitting on the couch. She murmurs something I can't hear. Gordon grumbles a response. Ray hugs him. His arms hang limp at his sides.

The Virgo horoscope is short, to the point:

You will soon endure a great trial. Remember: no good deed goes unpunished. No bad deed, either.

"Come on." Leah takes my arm, pulling me down the hallway, past Grandma's mugshot, into our old bedroom, with its twin beds and toybox. She shuts the door, stands in front of it. "Well?" Her eyes dart to the magazine in my hand.

"I don't know where to start."

"So start anywhere. Pick a place."

Outside, the gray ocean stretches out to the horizon. In the silvery, fog-muted light, the sand looks dark brown. Mom and Dad married there twenty years ago, just beyond the bluff. What are those twenty years made of, that separate this moment from that one? I can walk to the exact spot where they got married. Could I walk to that exact moment, too?

"What do you see in your dreams, anyway?" Leah asks.

"Dreams?"

"Yeah, the dreams about the future. Lots of people have them, Amy. They don't make you a freak."

"What about sleepwalking into a dead body? What does that make me?"

Leah crosses her arms. A shrill tone in my left ear whines louder and louder before ebbing away.

"I know you've been shutting me out. That's why you stole the drugs, right? So I'd be too mad at you to notice."

"Leah!" Ray yells from the living room. Leah walks over to me, her eyes soft. For a moment, I hear the closed, fluorescent hum of a hospital room. I see the youth fall from Leah's face, the light die in her eyes. Prerecorded bells ring above our heads. *Dah duhh dah-duhhh…*

"You wouldn't believe me if I told you."

"So? Tell me anyway."

I consider it. I told Dad, didn't I? Maybe Leah is the key that opens this world. I turn away instead.

"You don't have to be scared of me," Leah says. She smells of freshly-washed cotton, jasmine, and smoke. No hint of the metal-ammonia stench that will follow her for years, that telltale smell that belies the most convincing show of sobriety. After Leah leaves, I sit on my old bed, watch through the window as seagulls fly into the fog.

Leah, Ray, and Gordon talk in the living room. The front door opens, then slams. Feet thump on the outside steps. I wipe my eyes, blink until the world returns to normal.

I reach in my front pocket for a tissue, finding instead a small rectangle. Here's Claude Belissan's card, with his name and number. I get up and pick up the phone in the hallway. Do 555 numbers really work outside of the movies? Ray, Leah, and Gordon are in the front yard, still talking earnestly. I dial the number, listen. The phone rings once, twice, three times…nine, ten, eleven, twelve…

"Hello, Rosemary," Claude says.

"Why are you following me?"

Claude chuckles. "I didn't know you were Rose MacLeod's granddaughter. You should have told me. Rose is a dear, dear friend of mine."

"She doesn't remember you."

"She doesn't?" He sounds disappointed. "Has she ever mentioned—"

"How are you doing that trick with the car?"

"Why do you think I'm following you, Rosemary? I'm sure many, many people want to take a look at you. You're the survivor, aren't you?"

"For God's sake, answer the question."

Silence lengthens between us. I bend and twist the phone cord in my free hand. A strange whistling sound fills the line.

Claude clears his throat. "You're a smart girl. Maybe the answers are closer than you think."

A sharp *thud* in the hall. Grandma's mugshot lies on the floor, picture side up. The line goes dead.

I stare at the picture for a moment, not moving. It's foreshortened by the angle of its fall, making Grandma look pugnacious. The phone's *blaaat* startles me out of my reverie. I hang up.

I bend down and pick up the photo, my hands shaking. There's something taped to its underside: a little brass key, the letters "D.G." written on it in Sharpie.

"Amy?" Leah says. Leah, Ray, and Gordon stand at the end of the hall. Leah stares at the key blankly for a moment. Her face opens in a childlike smile.

"It's been locked our entire lives," Leah explains to Ray, as we stand outside Grandma Rose's shed. "Maybe the Holy Grail's in there."

"Or a dozen of them. Choose wisely."

"You can't smoke in there, Ray. If Grandma smells it…"

Ray shrugs and lights her cigarette. Gordon, hugging himself, paces the yard.

The green Honda's not parked across the street anymore. I can feel Claude near, even though I can't see him. I cross myself reflexively. Leah laughs.

"I was kidding about the Holy Grail. It's probably just old files or something. Jesus, Amy. You're even more paranoid than I am."

Leah slides the key into the lock, then turns. It gives with a rasp. I hold my breath as the door swings open. A small patch of light penetrates the darkness, revealing an old wooden floor and the metal cord for a lightbulb. Leah and I enter; Ray and Gordon watch us, unmoving, from the grass.

"I told you. It's fine," Leah says, pulling the cord. The room fills with yellowish light. Metal shelves, covered with unsorted books, records, trinkets. The smell of the room hits me in waves: mildew, old paper, dried flowers, rotting wood.

"Come on," Leah says, pulling me in by the hand. "What'd I tell you? It's nothing to be scared of."

I peruse the shelves. There doesn't seem to be any sort of order or pattern: a plastic dinosaur, a box of pushpins, a *Pretty Little Liars* paperback, a Polaroid camera. No storage boxes, envelopes, or treasure chests.

"Maybe this was Grandpa Doug's stuff," Leah says doubtfully. "Or from when Dad was a kid."

"This is too recent. I don't think Grandpa read…"

My gut drops. I turn back to the shelf. The *Pretty Little Liars* paperback is still there. I'm floating in place as I pick it up.

"What's that?" Leah says.

I flip to the front matter. *Copyright 2006 by Alloy Entertainment and Sara Shepard.* This book shouldn't exist. I wheel around, fully expecting to see the snake behind me, coiled and ready to strike. But there's nothing, just a blank wall.

The door's gone.

Leah and I make our way to it slowly, feeling it with our hands. Nothing, just solid wood.

"Look for a crowbar, a hammer, a big metal rod. Anything to break through," I murmur to Leah. She stumbles away from the wall.

Something else is wrong. It takes me a moment to place it. There are no sounds, save the boards creaking under Leah's feet. Somebody's singing. The voice, neither male nor female, comes from far, far away. Leah's eyes, huge in her face, meet mine.

"What is that?" she whispers.

The smell of fresh flowers fills the room. The voice comes

closer. No, not voice, voices. They're all united in one breathless minor chord, rising in tone and volume.

There's a small hammer on a bottom shelf. I grab it, and am about to hand it to Leah, when a tongue of fire catches my eye. I look up.

Lines of fire glow on the wall, forming a familiar symbol: an ouroboros with black rays inside it, all converging on a center point.

Leah screams.

The boards give way under me. I fly forward, my hands scrabbling at the shelves. Leah runs to the wall. The light is too bright. The voices are too loud.

A prayer returns to my lips, out of hazy memory of youth groups past: "Our Father, who art in Heaven, Maker of Heaven and Earth, and of all things seen and unseen, deliver us from evil, now—"

I'm floating in pale light. Voices surround me. The song bends and dips. I try again to pray.

"The Lord is my shepherd, I shall not want," I try to say. The words leave my mouth as a strained gasp. The light pulsates. The voices grow louder, more insistent. The light blinds me, searing red through my eyelids. Something's coiling around me, squeezing me hard.

"He—" I say, and no more, because I can barely breathe. The light presses against my brain, the voices pound against my eardrums. *Breathe,* an inner voice instructs me, deadly calm. *You'll be okay if you breathe, but you need to breathe. You need to breathe. You need to—*

The locket sizzles on my chest. My flesh screams as it burns. The light grows even brighter. A hand caresses my face.

You need to breathe. You need to breathe. You'll be okay, but you need to—

The light dies. For a time outside of time, there is no me. Nothingness gives way, starting with sound.

"Amy!" someone screams overhead. *That's my name,* I think, returning to myself.

"—the paramedics, *now*," a young man barks overhead. "She's—"

"Amy!" Same voice, same scream. *That's my sister.* A palm thrusts rhythmically, painfully, against the center of my chest. Angry words clash in the background.

"—if they think we gave her something—"

"—dump it out, then, because—"

"Amy!"

Air floods into my lungs. My eyes open. Leah looks down on me, backlit by a cloudy sky. I cough until my lungs hurt. Leah, crying, pulls me close to her. I look up.

I'm in the backyard, lying on the ground. Ray and Gordon stand to the side. Gordon's holding his phone open; Ray's arms are crossed. All their faces are bone-white and drawn.

I look to the shed. A jagged piece of wood juts from the center of the door. It's half open. Inside the shed is completely black, save a small patch of light that falls on the floor. A vague floral scent wafts from the darkness.

"I'll tell your grandma I went in there to smoke, freaked out in the dark," Ray says, staring at the jutting piece of wood. Leah, still crying, doesn't respond.

Fog streaks through the air, almost low enough to touch. The ocean roars on the far side of the bluff.

"If I tell you guys something, will you promise not to laugh?"

"Of course," Leah says, smoothing the hair out of my face.

I clear my throat.

CHAPTER TWENTY-ONE
THE WEIRD CORE OF
THE UNIVERSE

NOBODY SPEAKS. LEAH crosses her arms, face slack. Ray rubs her mouth. I scratch the weeping burn on my chest. Gordon holds his head in his hands.

I didn't tell them everything. I didn't say one word about their futures. I didn't cover every detail of Trump's Presidential campaign—not that I could. I told them about Claude, the Doomsday Garden, my phone call with Slice Clark. I told them what I saw in the bathroom, in the woods, in the shed.

"At least we know Mom wasn't crazy," Gordon says. "If my sister had a kid—"

"She's seven."

"In the future. She'd be…2016, right?…she'd be twenty. A little young to have a kid, but not impossible. If Mom thought her grandson died, or ceased to exist…" He lapses into a gloomy silence.

"You are different," Leah says to me. "The way you carry

yourself, the way you speak…it's like some brilliant imitator's possessing your body."

"I'm not an imitator. I'm me."

"Maybe it was a Charles Darwin thing," Ray says.

"Darwin?"

"You know, Tiny Tim, the Ghost of Christmas Past—"

"That's Charles Dickens."

"Yeah, exactly. Maybe you had a super-long, super-vivid version of those dreams we've all had."

"I haven't had them," Gordon says.

I fumble with my locket. The cover gives way with a metallic rasp. "Here," I say, holding it open, facing them. Ray squints at the photo inside, then laughs.

"What?" I say, but she waves her hand, falling onto the grass.

"It's so…*you*," she giggles.

Leah's eyes dart from the locket to my face. Her mouth falls open. Gordon pales and turns away. Ray's laugh cuts off. She looks at me, eyes huge.

"What?"

"*The Moon*. They must have written that article weeks ago. Did they know this would happen? Did Henry know?"

Five minutes later, we're huddled around the magazine, now spread out on the living room coffee table. I tell them what's correct and what isn't.

"Any other stories ring a bell? Are there weeping Al Gore statues in the future?"

"Not that I know of. This is Lee Simon's magazine, though…"

"Who's Lee Simon?"

"Old friend of Claude Belissan's. They were in the Doomsday Garden together. He was Henry Lasko's boss…"

Two minutes later, we're huddled around the house phone, listening on speaker. A chintzy dial tone cuts through the air.

"Probably not at the office," Leah murmurs. "Saturday."

After a few rings, the tone gives way to open air. "Hello?" Lee Simon answers.

"Hi, Mr. Simon. It's, um, Rosemary. I spoke to you last—"

"Rosemary, yes. I'm very glad you called."

Rosemary? Leah mouths at me.

"I spoke to Claude. Honestly, hon, I don't think you have anything to worry about. Okay? I know it's scary, but statistically, you're more likely to get struck by lightning—twice—than get abducted."

"I'm actually calling about something else. That time-traveling story, in this week's issue? It's really…groovy." Leah rolls her eyes. "How'd you think of it?"

"We source our ideas wholesale from a man in Richmond. I think he imports them dirt-cheap from Laos. They come wrapped in these strange papers—"

"I was in the room when those girls went missing. I saw a snake, a hand made of light, with a void in the center of its—"

"It's not that I don't believe you, okay? But this is a matter for the police and maybe a psychiatrist. Not for me."

"Have you ever run a story about the Doomsday Garden?"

Stunned pause. "Never."

"Why not?"

"We've run related stories, sort of. *Army Harvests Hippie B.O. for Bioweapon*, all that shit. Nobody knows the Doomsday Garden, though. Some minor cult that lasted a few years? Too obscure."

"Maybe you've written about it the way you wrote about Scott Peterson."

"We've never written about Scott Peterson."

Ray jumps in to explain. Lee considers this for a few beats. Papers riffle in the background.

"Holy shit. I forgot all about that," Lee says, his voice quavering. "*Twisted Fisherman...*"

Silence dilates on the line. More riffling. When Lee speaks again, his voice is softer, his tone more conciliatory. "You know this recall business? With Schwarzenegger and everything? We've run stories about *Arnold for President* I don't know how many times. We ran a story where he summoned the ghost of Ronald Reagan." He inhales deeply, his seat squeaking beneath him. "I don't know how or why, but we have some taproot into the weird core of the universe. You still there?"

"Uh-huh."

"Run this by me again, would you, hon?"

I explain about the green Honda, the 555 number, the key to the shed. I remind him about "Billy's dad," the man from the Doomsday Garden in mourning for his lost son. I tell him about Kathleen's note, what Max said, the lights in the forest. He makes no noise as I talk. For a moment, I think the line's gone dead. Then he speaks.

"This is several tiers—several *lightyears* above my paygrade. You're not messing with me, are you?"

"No."

"You don't ever really know someone, I guess." He laughs. In the background, liquid pours into a glass.

After the phone call, we all look toward the shed. A rectangular patch of wood shines against the darkness.

"I'll go in," Gordon says.

"Don't be retarded."

"I'm not being retarded, Ray. I'm walking into a room."

"You saw what it did to Amy. You *saw*. What if it does that to y—"

"I'm doing you a favor, Ray. My Mom is dead. My Dad

won't talk to me on the phone. I left my *sister* so you could do spooky bullshit with your friends."

"It's not spooky bullshit! Amy could have died, Gordon. If you die, your sister will be all alone in the world. Please."

Gordon crosses his arms and glowers out the window.

Ray stands, smoothing her hands down the front of her pants. "Fine," she says, walking to the door. "The slut always dies first."

We follow Ray down the steps. She strides toward the shed, arms swinging, then disappears inside. I hold my breath.

"We shouldn't have let her go in," I say. No one answers me.

Nothing changes inside the shed. I grab my locket, take a few steps forward. A heavy *thud* comes from behind the door. My heart jumps into my throat. Blood, thick as chocolate syrup, oozes through my veins. There are footsteps inside now. They're heavier, slower than Ray's.

It's Kathleen. It's Henry Lasko. It's Becca, and Erin, and every-body who's died because of the time slip. The footsteps grow louder.

Ray appears in the doorway, holding a large flower-print satchel. She stumbles over the threshold. The door eases shut behind her.

"Why'd you take that?" Leah says.

"That's all there was." Ray frowns at the satchel. "It's way lighter now."

We walk together back to the house. The shed door's now smooth, the lock re-clasped.

I feel for the key in my pocket. It's not in there. There is a business card. I don't take it out.

"Are you okay?"

Gordon's looking down at me, worried. We're sitting in the living room, the flower-print satchel lying on the coffee table.

"I'm fine. Are you?"

"Under the circumstances…I guess."

"We have to open it," Ray says. "Right now."

"Ray—"

"If we take it with us, we'll get in a car crash! Come *on*—"

"—just put it back—"

"—not a movie, Ray—"

"After what Amy's gone through, I—"

"Amy's my sister—"

"Ray, please—"

"I'll open it," I say.

Inside, there's a spherical black paperweight, a leather-bound book, a manila folder, and an LP in a flat paper bag. I take out the paperweight first. It's heavy, cool, completely opaque. It rolls off the coffee table, no matter where I place it.

"Some paperweight," I say, handing it to Leah. "What do you think it's made of? Onyx? Glass?"

"Obsidian," Gordon suggests. Leah shrugs, turning the sphere over in her hands.

I take out the LP next. I already know what it is.

"Trippy," Ray says, staring at the cover. *The Doomsday Garden*, it reads in drip-wax font, above a photo of a thirty-something blonde in a white peasant dress. Her china-blue eyes stare soulfully at the viewer. Beatrice Spar.

"We've got to play this," Ray says, grabbing the record out of my hands.

The folder contains an old, faded copy of the *Doomsday Express*. The cover illustration shows a skeletal ouroboros, rays converging in its center, surrounded by human faces in every extreme of anger, fear, and ecstasy. I turn to the first page. "Proof of the End of the World," I read aloud. "No man knows the day, or the hour, but anyone can see the signs."

The needle falls on the record. Scratches punctuate the silence, which ends with a scream. An enormous choir fills the air with minor key madness. Higher fidelity than any old record has a right to be. A current passes over my skin. Gordon's face whitens, then turns an alarming shade of gray. He gets up, walks to the window, steadies himself on the sill.

Ray walks over to him. "You okay?" she murmurs. I don't hear his answer.

The song continues, voices ascending in a Shepard tone. Leah curls into herself, her arms hugging her chest. Gordon leaves. Ray follows him.

I read the first page of the magazine:

PROOF OF THE END OF THE WORLD

No man knows the day, or the hour, but anyone can SEE THE SIGNS.

The prophet preaches the end of the world while he tends to the flowers in his garden.

WHY?

Because those flowers will rise up and end the world. Their petals will transform into flames of destruction. Their seeds will be poison unto the earth. Their roots will reach to the center of the world, and their stems will become the new trees of Eden.

Flowers in flames, flames in flowers, stars in the ocean, ocean in the sky. Through this mystery, ETERNITY BECKONS.

Underneath this is an outline of a hand, a black circle in its palm. I turn the page.

SIGNS OF THE (END) TIMES

Flu epidemic hits Moscow on May Day, 1967…

Earthquake slams Mongolia—nine out of twelve on the Richter Scale—epicenter at the junction of two rivers, the Englin and the Selenge…

£30 million worth of gold stolen from armed car in London—ammonia used in the attack—guards found tied up and bloodied…

Forty armed delegates from the Black Panther Party barge into Sacramento State Capitol—protesting racism of Oakland police force—"worst invasion in the legislature's history"…

Bomb hits Yugoslav consulate in Sydney, Australia— Yugoslav nationals interviewed without result—no injuries reported…

Headline of an article on safety engineers: "Some People Always Look for Trouble"…

The song bends and swoops until it reaches an awful crescendo, then subsides. Ray, now back inside, walks to the record player. Silence fills the air. Ray fumbles with her cigarette pack.

"You can't smoke in here," Leah says. Ray doesn't listen.

"Where'd Gordon go?" I say. Ray nods toward the beach, cigarette pressed between her lips. A flame flicks up from her lighter. The end of her cigarette glows orange in the semi-darkness.

I take out the last item in the satchel: a black, leather-bound book. The first page is full of neatly written cursive. Grandma Rose's handwriting: I know it from birthday cards and grocery lists. I read the first lines:

January 4, 1967

Rain. Richie zoomed around the apartment—jumping jacks, cartwheels, handstands. "Who cares about a little water? I need AIR, Mom!" Zelda lay on the ground and kicked her feet up…

When I look up, nobody's there. The front door's swinging open. Then Ray's voice drifts through the open doorway, mingled with Leah's and Gordon's.

God, if you're there, please see me through this. Leah's left the paperweight on the couch. I feel its cold, smooth roundness underneath my palm.

"Livejournal is totally gay. You should make posters instead."

"I can't even open the window in my room. How am I gonna put up posters?"

Ray looks to Leah for confirmation. Leah nods. "Your parents fucking suck," Ray says, shaking her head. "No offense."

The fog's lifted, leaving a shimmery haze over the beach. Ray pulls something out of her back pocket and hands it to me. It's a worn Moleskine, a chewed pen clipped into the spine.

"Write your info in the back. Gordon and I can put up posters all over West Marin."

"What about the cops?" Leah says.

"What about them? It's freedom of speech."

"They're Marin County cops. They're bored."

"Then I'll deal with them when the fuck they show up, all right?"

I think of the homeless man skateboarding across Mission

Street, dreadlocks hanging around his face, leg stump bandaged in frayed jeans. Would he ever be this blithe about the police?

Ray watches me write in her notebook. A black dog runs down the beach, tongue lolling out of its mouth. Its owner, a DILF in wet swim trunks, waves at us as we pass. Gordon and I wave back. I turn to watch him run.

"So, are you into older guys now, or what?" Ray says, nodding toward the DILF. I shake my head.

"Not even him?"

"Well, not *now*. If he's still got his hair in ten years…"

"You'll be legal in five."

"Uh-uh. You do not date grown men who fuck teenagers. I can wait."

"Smart. I dated a twenty-two-year-old when I was fifteen. The guy worked at Petco and lived with his mom. If *I* went back in time, I'd kick his ass."

"He died?"

"No, he's…not worth it."

A seagull keens overhead. The sun burns white through a cloud. A plane, tiny and silver against the blue sky, flies south.

"Where'd you go to high school?" Leah asks. Ray and Gordon are a few steps ahead now, Ray's arm over Gordon's shoulders. Leah's next to me, hunched over, arms crossed.

"Drake," I say.

"How was it?"

I try to put words to my memories. High school feels like a movie I watched a long time ago, one I barely remember and feel nothing about. I shrug.

"College?"

"UC Davis. Double major in Psychology and English. Doubly useless."

"Then you got that job in the art gallery?"

"More or less."

"Did you like it?"

I waggle my hand.

"Was my art in the gallery?"

"It was a different type of gallery. More…modernist. Paint drips and yellow triangles." Lies. Leah's art would have been perfect, if she'd made enough of it.

"What do *I* do?" she says. In profile, she looks like a child—and then the sun emerges from behind the cloud, the light changes, and she turns to me, a shadow of her future self.

"Do you really want to know?" I say.

A breeze blows my hair in front of my face. When I pull it back, Leah's running ahead, calling out something to Ray and Gordon. They turn to look at her.

"Leah, wait up!"

Summer, 2003, maybe late July. Leah and I ran along the waterline, feet skimming across the firm wet sand. Foam bubbles hovered midair, borne up by the winds, before wheeling and bursting overhead. Leah ran two feet ahead, then five, then ten. We ran like that for miles just above the waves, then up through the soft sand, where a piece of driftwood sent me flying forward. I lay there, waited for my breathing to steady, for the white spots to disappear.

"You okay?"

Leah held out her hand. I took it. A moment later we were running, hand in hand, giggling as waves lapped at our feet.

"You want a piggy back ride?" Leah said. I rode on her back to the beach entrance, where she stumbled and staggered, groaning under my weight.

"Weakling!" I shouted. Leah threw me on the sand.

"You are such a brat. A heavy brat!"

We laughed.

The sun hovered centimeters above the horizon. Orange and purple light filled the clouds overhead. We walked in silence past the crowd at the beach entrance: surfers in wetsuits, kids eating ice cream cones, clusters of laughing, middle-aged couples. The parking lot was full of ambling bodies: families, yuppies, students, dog-walkers, hippies, off-duty chefs. A couple made out against a car. A toddler rode on her father's shoulders. A woman, with grimy hair and a sun-lined, unhappy face, herded three dogs into a van. We stepped into the park, making our way past picnic blankets and sleeping bodies.

"Are you gonna be famous when you grow up?" I asked Leah. She shrugged.

"I don't know."

"You could be. You have a little talent."

"A little?" We play-wrestled in the middle of the park. I ran ahead. Leah followed. Our laughter faded as we slowed to a walk.

"What about you?" Leah asked. "What do you want to do?"

I don't remember my answer.

We paused at the edge of Shoreline Highway. Across the road, a jazz band played on a restaurant terrace. The pealing of the guitar, the interplay of the bass and drums, mingled with the clinking silverware, the low murmur of conversation, the wind rolling off the ocean and into the trees, the seagulls crying overhead. People wandered across the highway in groups and pairs, laughing, talking, pulling each other close. In the fading light, I knew nothing bad could happen anywhere in the world. How could it, when there were moments like this?

When I open my eyes, I'm standing at the edge of Shoreline Highway, watching two girls run across the street, flip-flops flapping under their heels. Their voices sound familiar, but I can't place them. The smaller one turns to look at me. It's me. And that's Leah, holding her hand—my hand.

Not-me goggles at me for a second, then Leah pulls her forward. She stumbles across the street, casting a few worried glances over her shoulder.

"You can live this entire day over again, exactly the way you want," Claude says at my side.

"What are you doing? What is this?"

"I have to commend you. You've gotten farther than anyone else I know. Most people go," he brings his finger to his lips, "*bedebedebede*, or have a heart attack right then and there."

What's different about this world? We're in another time, or the illusion of one, but there's something wrong. Something else.

"It's not due to my excessive virtue," I say.

"It's still significant. And you've looked up the Lister-Le-Normand Hypothesis. You're doing well."

"Can you explain that to me? Lee said you're a genius—or you were."

The music sounds wrong—that's what it is. The guitar sounds like it's crying. I look to the terrace. The drummer's cymbal oscillates on its post, growing louder and louder, then goes still and silent when the drumstick taps it. A waitress, holding a full tray of food, walks backward through the doorway. A man puts an empty cup to his lips and fills it with wine. A woman's voice rises from a moan to a squeal. She floats to her feet, palms outstretched. And there's Leah and not-me, holding hands, walking backward, our voices rising and falling in nonsense inverted words, our flip-flops flying up to meet our feet. Not-me meets my eyes again, her confusion melting into happiness.

"The past is a vast ocean beneath us. It moves, and it moves us in turn. It's possible, under certain circumstances, to send an explorer or two into its depths. We can even change the tides. It's delicate work. Sometimes there are complications."

"Complications."

"Yes." Claude's mouth forms a grim line. "Tidal waves, rogue waves, maelstroms…there's no end to the ocean's power. It's hard enough not to drown."

I think of Kathleen's empty eye sockets, of her pearl earrings glinting in the moonlight, of her note, handwritten in graceful cursive. My hand closes around my locket. "You could stop any war," I say. "You could kill Hitler, Stalin, Lenin, Pol Pot. You could end world hunger, cure the Black Death, talk to Jesus or Confucius or the Man in the Iron Mask. Instead…what do you do instead?"

Claude's self-satisfied smile comes from behind his eyes. "We're bringing eternity to time, and time to eternity. Soon everyone will fly through the ocean and swim in the stars."

"You're insane."

"All geniuses are insane."

"That doesn't mean you're right."

"You don't want to fly through endless—"

"No."

"Why?"

"There are monsters down there."

I look both ways and step into the road. A car rockets forward, then stops, the bumper inches from my legs. I jump back.

Everything's still. The car's driver stares absently through me. Everything is frozen in place, from a man's open mouth to the leaves on the trees. I walk back to Claude. The noise starts slow, then speeds up to normal. The car drives past. The woman falls, palms out. She's laughing.

Someone's hand presses on my shoulder. I'm still at the edge of Shoreline Highway. Leah's looking down at me, saying something I can't understand. The sky's no longer on fire. All the world's bathed in the deep blue of twilight. Yellow-gold and amber lights glow in restaurant windows; diners talk and laugh on terraces across the way. There is no music.

Ray drives us to the corner store. "I need an iced tea, what about you guys? How about cigarettes? Not you, Amy, you're…well, your body's too young." The three of us wait in the car. Ray reappears in the doorway, holding a small plastic bag. She pauses to light her cigarette, which glows orange in the half-darkness.

"You should have chipped in," Leah scolds. Ray opens the door, thumps into the driver's seat.

"I thought Dad was taking us out."

"So? *Always* bring money with you. What if we got mugged?"

"You're not getting mugged in Stinson," Ray says. "Not unless some super-tweakers get you."

Leah's staring at me. I turn to face her, see her illuminated by the yellow glow of the convenience store windows.

"It's okay if you're kidding," she says. "We won't get mad."

"Why would you even say that? You saw her locket."

"That could be Photoshop."

"And the shed? That was Photoshop, too?"

"I'm serious, Amy. It's normal at your age to make shit up."

Ray mumbles something about "denial."

Leah rolls her eyes. "Case in fucking point, Ray. Remember when you thought you could start fires with your mind?"

"That was completely different." Ray stifles a laugh. "I completely forgot about that. I used to stare at dry leaves super-duper hard, say these Latin chants I made up—"

"Was this before or after we watched *The Craft*?"

"Duh. Then that grease fire started in the school kitchen and—"

"I still believe you did that."

"You're not the only one!" Ray and Leah share a laugh. Gordon looks through the front window, his eyes glazed.

"You're really not kidding," Leah says to me, the smile falling from her face.

I look inside the flower-print satchel. Beatrice Spar stares at me from the album cover, her eyes peeking out above Grandma Rose's diary. The black paperweight lies at the bottom of the bag, smooth and heavy in my lap.

It's almost sunset when we get home. Mom's not there. Dad's sitting in the living room, munching from a chip bag. The TV blares an ad for "Pirates of the Cara-Be-In." I turn the satchel until it's mostly hidden behind my back.

"Where'd you girls go after the library?"

"Ice cream."

"Nice," Dad says, because he trusts us. "What flavors did you get?"

"Chocolate," we both say.

"With sprinkles?"

"With gummy worms," I say, on top of Leah's "No." Leah disappears into her room. Dad looks up at me, smiles.

"How was your day?" I ask him.

"One patient came in with a grapefruit-sized tumor on his leg. Benign, but still. Wow."

"Amazing he let it get to that."

Dad shoves another chip into his mouth. "Present came for you today," he says, his mouth still full. "I think it's from Zelda—hold on." He rifles under the pillows, pulls something out, hands it to me. It's book-shaped, wrapped in newspaper.

"It came like this?"

"Uh-huh."

"Did Mom see it?"

I feel the weight of it, turn it over in my hands. Dad groans as he sits up. "Don't worry about your mother. I told her, Amy's gone through more in five days than some people go through in their lives. Now is not the time to crack the whip."

"Does she still want to send me to that camp?"

"That will not happen in my house." Dad pushes himself forward on the couch, pulls me into a hug. I swallow a sob. "You're not going anywhere," he says, patting my back. "You hear me? Anyone tries to take you, they're leaving feet first. I've seen every kung fu movie ever made. I'm prepared."

I laugh, blinking away tears. On the TV, a woman moans while lathering her hair. I press my ear into Dad's chest, try to block out at least half of the sound.

"I got a present for you, too," Dad says.

"What present?"

"I got a reservation at Chuck E. Cheese tomorrow. Short notice, but I made it work. I know a guy." He winks. I laugh, overcome by the absurdity. "I only sent out invitations by email today, so you might not get a lot of guests. Grandma and Zelda will be there, though."

I pull away.

"You wanna rent a couple movies, get a pizza?"

"Sure, Dad."

"Great." Dad ruffles my hair as he stands up. "I will make myself presentable, and then we'll get some horror movies."

"Workout videos," I call out after him.

"Ghaaa! Not *that* scary. Let's stick with monsters."

I glance over the newspaper wrapper. Here's a corner of a dish soap ad, a column on Schwarzenegger's run for governor, something about the Euro. In the center of the paper is a photo: a huge pile of flowers, bears, an imperious papier-mâché bust crowned in laurels. Two girls clutch each other in the fore-ground, one holding a bouquet limply in her hand.

ABOVE: Two students embrace in front of the West Wall at Prescott High School. An impromptu memorial to Thomas Templeton, 16, began after he

When I come back to myself, I'm sitting on my bed, hands shaking. The story, which starts on the inside of the wrapper, consumes all my attention.

CHAPTER TWENTY-TWO
THE LOVED ONE

PRESCOTT STUDENT MOURNED

BELOVED TEEN'S DEATH ROCKS COMMUNITY

PRESCOTT, Az. — Thomas James Templeton, a senior at Prescott High School, died Friday evening after a car accident left him in critical condition earlier in the week. He was sixteen.

At around 11:40 PM on Tuesday, Templeton was driving Southwest on Pioneer Parkway when his car veered off-road and struck a hillside just past Commerce Drive, authorities said. Templeton was airlifted to Yavapai Regional Medical Center West, where he remained in critical condition until his death. He never regained consciousness.

"The doctor said the impact was instantaneous. He didn't feel a thing," Allen Templeton, Tom's father, said. "I'm grateful for that."

The mood at Prescott High School was decidedly somber

this week. Students erected a memorial to Templeton at the front of the school, adding flowers, stuffed animals, cards, and a bust of Julius Caesar—a nod to Templeton's fascination with ancient Rome.

"It doesn't make sense," Holly Martineau, a Prescott High sophomore and Tom's longtime friend, told The Daily Courier. "One minute he's walking around, talking, laughing, then he's dead forever. How can he just be gone?

"Tom was one of the kindest and funniest people you could ever meet," Martineau continued. "My first day at Prescott [High School], Tom showed me how to get to all my classes. He was always there for me, no matter what."

Tom Templeton excelled from an early age. In second grade, he taught himself Latin and the Greek alphabet. He read Ovid's entire "Metamorphoses" in fourth and fifth grade. He took summer classes at the University of Arizona starting in middle school.

"I first taught Tom in an Ancient Religions seminar, maybe three years ago," said Stephen Arroyo, an Associate Professor of Ancient History at the University of Arizona. "On day one, he asked some detailed question about the Sabine gods. We joked that he'd write the history books one day.

"I can't believe that's it," Arroyo added. "It feels like he's supposed to still be here. If he walked through the door right now, I wouldn't blink."

This summer, the Templeton family visited Oxford, Cambridge, and the University of Glasgow, his father's alma mater. Tom was excited about college and the next chapter of his life.

"He was such a bright child," Allen Templeton said. "So much promise, destroyed in under a second. Our only consolation is seeing how he lives on through his friends."

For a moment, I'm gone. My mind isn't there to notice its own absence.

I slam back into my body, into the bedroom, into the world. Webs of pain spread across my scalp. I pick up the book, hands shaking.

The People and Their Gods: Sketches of Ancient Rome
By Thomas Templeton

I know the painting on the cover: four women, one of them dancing, in front of a deep pink background. It's from the Villa of the Mysteries in Pompeii, scene of a lost religious rite. One woman kneels, head resting in her nurse's lap, face twisted in agony.

I flip to the back cover. There's a small photo of grown-up Tom, smiling, alive. He's not the Tom I knew. His hair is longer, his smile more open. The Tom I knew would never wear a ratty T-shirt to a photoshoot. I read his biography.

Thomas Templeton's academic publications include papers in the Journal of Mediterranean Studies *and the* Roman Historical Review. *He has written essays for* Harper's, n+1, *and* National Geographic. *Templeton earned a Bachelor's Degree in History from the University of Arizona, and a Doctorate in History from Christ's College, Cambridge. He is currently a postgraduate fellow at the University of St. Andrews. The People and Their Gods is the first in his "Living History" series.*

I flip the book open.

Rhea turned her eyes to the ceiling. To whom could she pray for protection? Two other Vestals whispered in the corridor. A gust of wind roused the flame. Everything was the same as yesterday, and yet nothing was.

Rhea approached the fire with dread. Vesta must have seen Mars overtake her in the forest. What would the goddess do to a fallen woman who tended to her sacred fire, clad in robes she had no right to wear? The fire might go out, or devour Rhea on the spot. But to fail in her duties would be just as unthinkable. That failure would raise questions, suspicions, and then...

And then? Rhea steeled herself against the thought. She'd had the dream again, the one that woke her in horror months ago: blood, two crying faces, a small room with no windows. She shuddered and lifted the torch.

"Amy!" Leah yells. I look up. Leah's standing above me, her eyes bugged out of her head.

"What?"

"You okay?" Dad's standing behind her, wearing a fresh Hawaiian shirt. I nod toward him. Leah looks over her shoulder, then turns back.

"You ready for pizza?" she says, and mouths, *What is it?* I shake my head.

I read and reread the front matter in the car. *Copyright 2014, Thomas Templeton and Cambridge University Press. Copyright renewed, July 2016.* See? He's not dead. He has a future. You can't be dead if you have a future. Leah stares at me from the front seat.

As I page through the book—I can't focus enough to finish even one paragraph—memories return to me from Tom's stories: Silvestri, the tanner, shows his sons how to clean a pelt; an Illyrian pirate dreams of sea nymphs; Priscilla and Aquila sew a tent, minutes before learning of the order of expulsion.

Kathleen's not on the other side of my eyelids, for once. Tom's there instead, smiling beneath a mop of brown hair, eyes alight with some private joke. The world lay at his feet a few days ago. And then I called him.

She's not into you, Tom. She doesn't love you. You can't force someone to love you by doing them favors.

I wander through Video Droid, stare at the movie posters, barely see or hear a thing. On the TV screen, Jake Gyllenhaal talks to a teacher in a room full of blue chairs.

"Tell me what's going on," Leah says, low, by my ear. I hand her *The People and Their Gods.*

"Read the copyright."

She does, running her finger down the page. She pauses and looks back at the cover. A shallow line forms between her eyebrows. "Was this in Grandma's shed?"

"Our mailbox. Dad thought—"

"You girls find anything?" Dad's standing right next to us.

I paste on a smile. "I can't find the workout videos. If I find them first, though, you have to do every single workout on the tape. Deal?"

Dad laughs.

I lose time. When I come back to myself, I'm in my bedroom at 117 Blackwood Drive. My cell phone's dialing, close to my ear. Someone picks up.

"Hello?" says a male voice. Old, tired, more thickly Glaswegian than I remember. An image comes back to me: Allen Templeton, laughing, dull silver glinting in his molars.

"Allen, hi," I say. "This is Amy. I have history class with, ah, I was wondering if, um, if Tom..."

Heavy silence passes between us.

"Tom is gone," Allen says. His voice cracks on the last word. "He died yesterday eve—I'm sorry, what did you say your name was?"

I flip the phone shut.

Tom held me as we ascended the hill. The scent of roses wafted from my bouquet. I held it close to my body, watched the red blooms nodding in time with our steps.

"The Romans planted roses on their graves," Tom said.

"Why roses?"

"So the dead could live on as beautiful flowers. They could be young again."

Tears filled my eyes, turning the world to melting wax. Tom pulled me close.

"I haven't been here since the funeral," I said. "I thought if I came here I'd...I'd make it real, somehow."

Tom smoothed my hair.

"I almost convinced myself that he was working on some top-secret government project. One day, I'd get a postcard from Nowhere, Indiana, and I'd know...God, the stories, the *lies* I told myself."

Tom leaned over and kissed my hair. "*Omnia mutantur, nihil interit.* Everything changes, nothing disappears. Hence the roses."

"Hence the roses...even still. Why couldn't he change while

he was alive? We could have had the roses *and* Dad. Or just Dad. I'd make that trade."

The tombstone stood at the crest of a hill. I watched its dark granite face as we came closer. The rose stems shushed against each other as we walked. Tom's arm felt warm and solid across my shoulders.

I read the tombstone, a sob catching in my throat.

THOMAS JAMES TEMPLETON
November 2, 1986 - August 28, 2003

Tempus edax rerum
Time, devourer of all things

Above this, a familiar symbol: etched rays converging in a center point, surrounded by a snake eating its tail.

Leah knocks on the connecting door, jolting me out of my stupor. A Super Mario knock, soft but insistent: *dud-dud-dunh dud-duh dah*. I pull myself out of bed.

Leah's face is smudged with charcoal, her hair pulled back behind a sea-green kerchief. "Are you awake?"

"Yeah, *now*."

"How are you?" she says, studying my face. I bring her Tom's book, and death notice, as answer. Leah scans the article, then stares at the book, flips through it. Her lips move as she reads Tom's biography. Her eyes flit from his picture to the picture in the article.

"This doesn't make sense," she says. "If he died, how..."

I explain. Her eyebrows raise until her forehead's wrinkled all the way across.

"I think he killed himself because I told him that his crush was never gonna like him back, and he wasn't ready to hear it."

"When did you talk to him?"

I tell her about the payphone call. *She's not into you, Tom. She doesn't love you. You can't force someone to love you by doing them favors.* Was he thinking of those words—my words—when he plowed into that hillside? If he died of a broken heart, I broke it.

Leah pulls me into a hug that goes on and on. I bite my palm to keep from sobbing out loud. Leah smooths my hair.

I see Tom's face, laughing and drunk-loose, staring blankly at a screen, tired, kind, asleep, upset. There's Tom as he was one Christmas, singing "The Circle Game" with Mom and Grandma. Whenever Tom drifts from my mind, Kathleen's face comes in its stead, her pearl earrings glowing with unearthly light. *You killed him,* she whispers. *You killed him. You...*

"Shhh," Leah says, guiding me to her bed. I hide my head under her pillow. I see the light-hand reaching for me, feel the snake twisting across my thigh, hear the Doomsday Garden's hell-choir echo through my mind. *You killed him,* they sing in nine-part harmony.

An off-rhythm knock on Leah's door. Mom. I read the panic in Leah's eyes, but don't share it. Let her come in. Let her know everything. Let her ship me off to troubled teen camp, to a mental ward, to a hole in the middle of the earth. Whatever happens to me, it's better than I deserve.

Leah cracks the door open. Her toe presses the door wedge between the carpet and the bottom rail. "What is it, Mom?" she says.

"I heard crying."

"Uh-huh. I sent my personal essay to that counselor—"

"What's going on?" Mom says. The door rattles above the wedge.

"We're smoking crack. God, Mom. Get a grip."

The door rattles, harder this time. "Let me in, Leah."

"Or what? You won't pay for college?" Leah laughs. "That's the only reason I talk to you. That's the only reason anyone talks to you—money. You are not loved."

Dreadful pause. I take the pillow off my head. Leah slams the door shut. Mom screams. The door shudders under Mom's weight. Leah holds herself against it until it stops rattling. Mom whimpers on the other side. Leah rolls her eyes, twirls her finger by her ear.

There's a new sketch on Leah's wall: a hand, held out, thirteen black rays issuing from the center of its palm. There'll be hundreds more before she leaves for college, and hundreds after, and they'll all end up in some landfill or other. Someday she'll be a body in a cemetery—*I'll* be a body in a cemetery. Maybe not even that.

What is it all *for*?

CHAPTER TWENTY-THREE
SHIMMER

"No, I'm not—no, she can't come to the—no comment." The phone rings as Mom slams it into the socket.

"Same?" Dad says. Mom nods. An awkward atmosphere lingers after her late-night implosion. Mom herself looks waxen, her normally perfect Rachel haircut a disordered mop.

I pour myself a glass of water. The powder-chemical taste lingers at the back of my throat. I listen for the media scrum: mingled voices, bleeps, shutters, trucks rumbling up the drive. I hear nothing but the wind and a bird trill. My stomach churns with dread.

Dad turns on the radio.

"—declined to say whether the two girl's disappearances are related to Katheen's—" Mom slams a cabinet drawer. Dad turns the radio off.

"Fix your hair," Mom says, not looking at me. "You look like you just woke up."

"I did just wake up."

"Now, Amy."

The phone rings.

I shuffle toward my room. I want to go to Chuck E. Cheese like I want another toe. But I can't stay curled up in bed. I'd have to see all the pictures behind my eyes.

Leah's in the bathroom, taking a shower. I go to my room, squint at myself in a compact mirror as I brush my hair. In six months, I might be able to wear a crown braid again.

Six months!

In six months, I'll still be in seventh grade, Tom will still be dead, and so will Kathleen and Becca and Erin and God knows who else. Maybe we'll all get lucky and the world will end.

"Fuck you," I say to my reflection, and close the compact.

It's loud in here, full of shouting voices, whizzes, bangs, bleeps, poppy music, screaming children. Lights blink everywhere.

"Let's go, Dad," I whine, tugging on his sleeve. If he hears me, he doesn't show it. We pass a bay of Skee-Ball machines into a dimly lit row of overstuffed leather booths, all painted in bright yellows and reds. A beefy guy with a crew cut sits alone, three booths down. Two booths down, a mid-twenties woman with a long, lopsided face glances at me, then flips open her phone. The animatronic rat band's in mid-swing. "Round and Round We Go," the cheerleader sings.

I remember the woman in an alarming pink blazer who approached me in our driveway, of the way Mom twisted her arm as she hustled her off the property. If this becomes the next Missing White Woman National Freak-Out, then my face could end up on every tabloid cover and cable show. Nancy Grace will spit my name out like sour milk: *This lil' girl, this A-my Snow-berger—who we are led to be-lieve is a lost, innocent lamb—says she was the last person to see her classmates before they disappeared from school. Then, less than twenty-four hours later, she "sleepwalks" over to the body of Kathleen Vandergraf, still in her day-clothes.*

Folks, I have heard a lot of tall tales in my time, okay? I have heard a lot of stories, but this one takes. The. Cake.

Grandma Rose and Aunt Zelda are sitting in one of the booths. When they see me, the same smile breaks across both of their faces. Aunt Zelda stands up and pulls me into a hug. "I can't believe you're *thirteen*," she says. "How is that possible?" Zelda wears a full Ms. Frizzle outfit, from her star-print dress to her Saturn-shaped earrings. Only her hair, the same limp light brown as Dad's, spoils the effect.

"How are you, Aunt Zelda?"

"Oh, I'm fine. One of my old students is showing me how to make a website."

"Bet you wish it was still summer," Dad grins.

"I teach in the summer. The college runs year-round, Rich."

"Community college."

"Community *college*." She shakes her head. Dad laughs to himself.

"Awfully nice of you to pull this together," Grandma Rose says, her eyes boring into Mom's. Mom, still waxen, turns and walks away.

"All right, boys and girls, it's time to dance!" a rat robot says with a smarmy chuckle. A boy jumps on the stage and wheels his arms around, head shaking in time with the music. Crew Cut sucks on his soda.

"Come on, Amy," Dad says, grabbing my arms and pulling me toward the dance floor.

"Dad, no!"

"You heard the rat," Dad says, twisting back and forth. "You wanted to work out, we're gonna work out."

I dance with him, pretending to be more embarrassed than I am. Then I see it, out of the corner of my eye: Lopsided Girl's taking photos of me with a camera, hidden just under her table.

Dad laughs as I run through the blinking semi-darkness. Electronic blips and bloops drown out my thoughts. Yelling kids rush past me, alone, in pairs, in groups. I slam into someone. We both go down, hard, onto the floor. I'm already mid-apology before I get up. The person under me coughs, curls over on her side.

It's Cassidy, tiny twelve-year-old Cassidy, dishwater-blonde hair spilling out of her hoodie. The only halfway colorful thing about her is a dark red duffel bag lying next to her.

"Watch where you're going," she whines. An enormous cough racks her midsection. I offer my hand, but she pushes herself up on her elbows.

"Cassidy!" Dad calls out behind me. "How are you?"

"Great. Where's the bathroom?"

I sit in the booth, hands over my ears, staring at the half-eaten slice of pepperoni pizza in front of me. A video game next to me plays the same scale, over and over again, slightly out of sync with its flashing lights.

Cassidy's still in the bathroom when I walk in. She's standing at the mirror, brushing her hair, the duffel bag at her feet. A mom side-eyes us as she shepherds her toddler through the door. Cassidy pulls a hairbrush out of her kit, meets the mom's eyes with a defiant scowl.

"Have you ever worn makeup?" Cassidy asks me. Her hairbrush rips through her hair: *kffvvvvrrrk*.

"Yes. Lots of times."

Cassidy smiles at herself in the mirror. "I have this book, by Kevyn Aucoin," she pronounces it *oh-kwon*, in a swing and a miss at a French accent, "that shows you how to do your makeup like a celebrity. *This* look is called 'Shimmer.'"

Kkkkkkrrrrrvvrkkk. A knot of dark blonde hair floats to the floor. Cassidy meets my eyes in the mirror. "Were you really shooting up in the bathroom?"

"No."

"Oh." Cassidy looks my reflection up and down, then shrugs. "Natalie said your drug dealer buried them in the school basement."

"There was no drug dealer. There were no drugs."

Little girls barrel through the doors, shrieking, giggling, talking over each other. Cassidy glares at them, then returns to brushing her hair like she's trying to punish it. The little girl's voices bounce off the walls. I walk outside.

I wander through the arcade, play a round of whack-a-mole. Tickets spool out of the machine. I hand them to a nearby kid, who whoops with delight.

Aunt Zelda's beside me, her hand on my shoulder. "Tough week, huh?"

"You could say that."

Aunt Zelda pats me on the back. "Dad told me about your dreams." She smiles. "That's nothing to be scared of, honey. I get those dreams all the time."

"What dreams?"

"Dreams that feel real, even though they're not. Sometimes I dream about people I've never met before, but in the dream, I've known them all my life. I used to get these vivid, *vivid* dreams about being a hairstylist in Brentwood. I had coworkers, regular clients, friends—I knew all their names, their birthdays, their kids. And get this—one time, I went to Brentwood, and I found that salon. Well, I found the building—there was a shoe store where the salon was supposed to be. I went inside the shoe store, and the girl behind the counter looked *exactly* the same as one of my 'coworkers.' She even had the same name."

"Did you talk to her?"

"I couldn't get a word out. And when she looked at me, she crossed herself and ran into the back. I heard her voice…" Aunt Zelda stares into space, then shakes her head. "Moral of the story, don't worry so much. Even if those dreams are a portal into another dimension, there's nothing you can do about it. I'm sure that my 'coworkers' are doing just fine without me."

I play another arcade game, try to blot out Aunt Zelda's words. Someone's standing next to me. It's Cassidy, watching me play, dabbing clear lip gloss on her bottom lip. Skippy-colored foundation covers her face; her cheeks shine with chunky glitter. She's wearing a new outfit now: white newsboy cap, pink baby-doll shirt, low-rise cargo pants, white belt, crisp white sneakers.

"How are you, Cass?"

Cassidy scowls. "'Cass?' This isn't third grade. I'm not your friend anymore. You lost," she says, nodding to the game. I put in another ticket.

"How's Téa?"

"Still 'studying' at Com." Cassidy makes air quotes with her fingers. "Com" refers to College of Marin, our local, not-so-prestigious community college. "She's been 'studying' there for three years. I don't think she'll ever leave the house."

Yes, she will. Two weeks after you move in with me, Téa gets her own apartment. When your brother sticks your head in the toilet and holds you down, she's there to stop him. She's going to save your life, and you don't even know it yet.

Or does she? A dim memory returns to me from the past: Cassidy, shaken and pale, telling me that her sister "was sent home early because the restaurant was slow." What if the restaurant's swamped this time around? What if she has a different boss? What if Slice wigs out ten minutes earlier? What if Téa comes home to Cassidy's body slumped over the toilet, water dripping down her hair? What if it happens *today*?

Heavy guilt descends on my shoulders. I called CPS. I talked to Officer Franklin. Cassidy—grown-up Cassidy—would do much, much more. She'd kidnap me if she had to.

"How's Slice?" I say. Cassidy screws in the top of her lip gloss applicator, puts it in a zebra-striped purse. What happened to the duffel bag?

"Slice tore up every single book in his room last night. Every single one. Said he was gonna jump off the Golden Gate Bridge. I wish, right?"

We slip into silence. Kids mill about, cast wary glances at us. I lose again. Cassidy pulls out her makeup mirror, the one I remember from high school. It's black plastic, embossed with a fake cushion pattern. I didn't even know I remembered it.

"Mom's new thing is to expose him to nature. He has to meditate in the woods every day. And he *does* it! He wanders out there for hours sometimes. Maybe he'll get lost…"

Luke Hillis's words come back to me, his eyes burning in the wooded darkness: *If you go into it, you come out different. If you come out. Even looking at it can change you.*

"Does Slice have any new obsessions?"

"Oh, yeah. He says that he's back from"—she makes air quotes with her fingers—"'twenty-sixteen,' and so was Henry Lasko, and together they're going to save the world from the apocalypse. He thinks Henry's coming back from the dead." She covers her mouth as she laughs.

My heart hammers in my chest. So it is true: Slice, of all people, traveled through time. Cassidy takes a deep breath, fans herself, puts the mirror away.

"You want to sleep over?" I say. "We rented a few movies—"

"I'm going to the mall later."

"How about after?"

"How about never."

Cassidy's staring at herself in the glass of the arcade. For half a second she looks like a scared kid wearing too much makeup. And then her face hardens.

"You don't have to go home if you don't want to," I say. Cassidy scoffs. God help me, but it hurts.

This isn't the Cassidy you remember, I remind myself. *She won't be back for a very long time.*

Dad, Aunt Zelda, and Grandma Rose are talking, laughing, eating. I don't know where Mom is. Lopsided Girl fiddles with her flip phone, turning its camera my way. I run to the front door. Outside, a few kids mill around, one in a Burger King crown. There's a payphone, just down the walkway.

I have to call again. I have to press the issue. But…my resolve melts against that "but." What if Cassidy winds up in a foster care hellhole? What if nothing happens? What if it gets worse?

There's a huge corkboard by the payphone, covered in flyers: a Tae-Bo class, the Mill Valley Film Festival, an "Everyday Heroes" photo contest, Kathleen Vandergraf's missing person poster. Someone's drawn Xs through her eyes. There's a picture of Jesus pointing to his exposed heart, encircled with thorns, surmounted by flames and a cross.

I call collect. The phone rings three times. Officer Franklin accepts the charges.

"How can I help you, Amy?" she says.

"You know that girl I told you about? Cassidy Clark?"

"Which girl?"

I take a deep breath, and then I'm far away, watching myself talk.

CHAPTER TWENTY-FOUR
DEAR DIARY

"I ALREADY SPOKE to the guidance counselor, Mom. He said…"

A bush outside taps rhythmically at my window. I open it. The alarm blares in the front hall.

"Sorry," I call out, hurrying through the house to the alarm panel. I enter the code without thinking: *1, 1, 8, 3.* *Beeeeep.* Silence reigns. Mom and Leah gape at me through the kitchen door.

"You're not supposed to know that code," Mom says.

"Your wedding anniversary? Seriously? It's not the Enigma Cipher."

Mom looks from me to the alarm panel, back to me, then laughs.

Back in my room, I look through the satchel. The paperweight feels cool in my hand. I open Grandma Rose's diary to the first page.

January 4, 1967

Rain. Richie zoomed around the apartment—jumping jacks, cartwheels, handstands. "Who cares about a little water? I need AIR, Mom!" Zelda lay on the ground and kicked her feet up. Got them suited up in rainy-day finery—macs, galoshes, umbrellas, the works. After five minutes: "Mom, it's WET!" A miracle they went to sleep.

Seen outside: two girls, plaid-green skirts and white blouses, sharing an umbrella and a heartthrob magazine. Osmonds or Monkees on the cover, as always. <u>Not</u> giggling—reverently <u>studying</u>, mouths forming the words as they read.

Found my high school graduation portrait. If that girl knew what she would become...mailed it to Doug. Don't care if his wife finds it. Let the world burn.

January 5, 1967

Put up new calendar at work on Monday. This year's theme: the women, beaches, and black pearls of Tahiti, in that order. Slow season for travel now, the gossip mill churns at double speed. And I am on that wheel...

A few of Paradise Voyage's younger associates are frostily polite to me; to everyone else, I'm the Homewrecking Whore. The black dresses, the veils, the anonymous young soldier's picture on my desk—who am I kidding? Doug isn't affected. He's the boss, and a family man, after a fashion...

Cora asked for a raise. She watches Zelda all day, takes Richie to and from school. Why shouldn't she get paid a whopping 25 cents more per hour? Doug says he'll handle it. He wants to push her out, force me into the home. "I've given you everything but a piece of paper, what more do you want?"

Children impossible. Sleep beckons.

January 8, 1967

Took kids to the park. Youth of America in their Saturday best: face paint, gypsy clothes, middle-class greaser jackets, earnest appeals for every flavor of revolution. Meet Julianne, runaway, maybe fourteen. "Where's home?" Carson City, Nevada. She came to San Francisco "to see what's going on." Showed us Polaroids she took along the way: diners, motel rooms, flat expanses of sand and brush. A band played bluesy rock music—Zelda spun in place, arms and dress describing great circles in the air.

Doug doesn't want us living so close to the Fillmore. When can we move to the Stinson house? "What about your wife, Doug?" Says he'll figure something out. He's been saying that for seven years.

Richie sits with Zelda and they go over all the colors: red, orange, yellow, "gween," blue, "puh-pul." He's a caring boy, especially with her.

Chronicle hasn't published my letter about last year's Nursing "Sickout." Not a current enough event, I'm sure. Did I mention I was a Berkeley grad? Do they see me as a homewrecking whore?

January 14, 1967

Today was the "Human Be-In" ("human being," geddit?) at Polo Fields. Park was bursting with charmed children

in awe of themselves, half naked, smelling of grass, smoke,
soda fountains, impossible dreams. Foolishly took the chil-
dren on a walk.

Another call from Doug. Have I paid the bills, or did
I buy myself a pretty dress? I could quit (this again)—he
sees how the others treat me. What if the kids start speaking
"jive?" (Should have said—yes, what if Cora bathes them
and the color spreads?) Don't I trust him? Hasn't he always
taken care of me? "Be patient"—the war-cry of the shift-
less man.

My skin crawls at the thought of what could be. Doug
could throw us over any moment, and then—? Best not to
think about it. One way or another, we'll survive.

I try to imagine Grandpa Doug—*my* grandpa, who used
to rock me to sleep after dinner—calling his mistress, my own
grandmother, while his wife stared into space in the other room.
And Rose MacLeod, great feminist crusader, living on the charity of a married man. Having his babies, keeping his secrets.
Who are these people?

The entries continue in this vein: work problems, money
problems, quarrels with Doug, Richie and Zelda discovering
the world. "Tombstone faces" follow Rose and the children
for blocks, acid heads scream on street corners, glares from
"the blacks" and the squares and the revolutionary vanguards.
Things change:

February 11, 1967

Riot, three streets down from Richie's school. They had to
sit under their desks, cover their heads with their hands.

"Everything was so loud, Mom. I think the whole world was screaming." Cora told me to get in the bathtub (with the kids) if I heard gunshots. How lovely that it's come to this.

February 16, 1967

How's this for a Valentine's Day gift? Doug bought me a house in "Woodacre," appositely-named town in the middle of a forest. "It's the sensible thing to do." In a few years, the city schools will be all black and Latin. It's gone too far as it is. He's right, but I can't afford to think about that. "So come home, Rose. This city's been too hot since the Auto Row riots. Where are you gonna be when it blows up?"

Speaking of blow-ups, he had a tremendous one with his wife—so he says. She knew he had a "whore" but the children came as a surprise. She threw a knife at Doug's head, broke the mirror in their apartment. A neighbor, hearing her screams, called the police. She was sedated and taken to hospital. Rumors <u>flying</u> through the office. Many glances and evil eyes directed my way.

"You can change your name, wear a ring. We'll take wedding pictures, if that's what you want. It's nobody's business what's on file in City Hall." But the agency... "Never mind about the agency. Don't you want a break? My God, I'd take one if I could."

The runaways are everywhere now. I see them on the way to work: boys and girls in costume, stepping dreamily out of childhood, glowing beacons for every snake-eyed pusher, masher, and hustler in the city. Watched a boy on a motorcycle, all ropey arms and skeleton smiles, with a peachy high school girl mounted on the back. Her tiny pink hands encircled his waist, her face the picture of dumb trust. They were gone before I could reach her.

I wince at Grandma's casual racism. So much for a coalition of the oppressed. Back in 1967, February fades into March. None of the women at work talk to her now. More runaways, more menace in the air, more drugs: "offered 'speed, 'ludes, dope, grass' on the way to the supermarket by man in dirty trench coat and newsboy cap." Doug threatens to kidnap Richie and Zelda.

Rose goes to a meeting for "Revolutionary Transcendence." I'll let her describe it to you:

April 9, 1967

Attended a meeting for "The Doomsday Garden," new politico-spiritual group right off Haight Street. The house is painted white, with a strange image painted over the door: an ouroboros with thirteen black rays inside it, all issuing from a center point. Copious amaranth blossoms spilled over the garden railings. Also in the garden: figs, dates, fennel, dogbane, marigolds, daffodils, nasturtiums, white and red roses. Young people dressed in long robes tend to the plants. Boy, about seventeen, handed me an overripe bell pepper. Delicious! "Yes'm, thank you, we grow them right here in the backyard." I didn't know that bell peppers could grow in the city. "They can grow here. Anything can grow here."

The house interior is pure kitsch: gas lights (really!), silhouette portraits, a wooden record player with claw feet, even a big-eyed Alice in Wonderland in the hall. "I love this era—before the great catastrophe," says the ice-blonde at the center of the room. Meet Beatrice Spar: mid-thirties, long white hair, pale pink skin dotted with gold freckles, piercing blue eyes. Look into those eyes and you'd believe anything they tell you: that the sun is silver and the moon is gold, that polka dots contain the secrets of the universe, that your son is the Messiah, that you are the Messiah.

The audience: students and student-aged, scruffy Marxists, a few middle-class educated types, one old woman dressed entirely in lavender linen. The usual, in other words. But for the beautifully appointed furnishings, we could have been in some grubby student union, a Masonic Center, a used bookstore, a café.

Beatrice arranged us in a circle, gave us each a note to hold using tuning forks. "Listen to the fragment of eternity trapped inside you." Ornate, multi-layered chords filled the air, dipping and bending and rising together, until all our cheeks were wet with tears.

Our voices filled the room. The house echoed in its humming boards and joints. After an eon, Beatrice bade us look out the windows. A tremendous crowd had gathered there, people of every description, all crying too. Two boys, stoned faces turned up moon-like toward the house, locked eyes with me. One pointed to me, whispered something to his friend. I looked down.

We were glowing, all of us. The silhouettes seemed to move behind glass. New shapes, new patterns, revealed themselves in everything, from the grain of the wood to the soft movements of Beatrice's hair. Even in the folds of a jacket on a chair, I saw the order of the universe. Love surrounded us, love far eclipsing the pathetic human show of love. (No, drugs were <u>*not*</u> *involved, thanks very much!)*

Time vanished. The song was only reality, the one point of light in this world of shadows. The pretenses of ordinary time slipped away, helpless, under the assault. When it ended, everything had changed, though nothing had disappeared or visibly altered. Beatrice walked up to me, held my hands in hers.

"Come back tomorrow," she said. "Don't hide your light away."

I promised to, in the moment—but the moment's passed. I've slipped back into ordinary time, pale shadow of eternity. I'm afraid it's impossible. Between the children, work, Doug—but I will be back. I'm sure of it.

April 10, 1967

Cora said this afternoon she's moving to Sacramento soon, to help her daughter with the new baby. Asked her not to tell Doug, or he'll start pushing the housewife plan on me again. He wants us to "visit" Woodacre, but I doubt he'd drive us back.

Gunshots just before dinner. Put the children in the (empty!) bathtub, served them mac and cheese there. Pretended it was a silly joke. The world is cracking apart.

Dream last night: a black sphere, surrounded by an ouroboros, fire crackling through its scales. Where's an analyst when you need one?

April 14, 1967

Letter from Libby at Doomsday Garden. Tells the story of their founder's vision: the Garden of Eden in the middle of a forest, surrounded by the snake, then the garden barren and the sun black. It reads like she copied out something she doesn't quite understand.

April 16, 1967

Doug came by today to see the kids. Zelda squealed with delight, jumped up and down. Richie ran in tight little circles, shrieking "Daddydaddydaddydaddydaddy!"

Doug wanted to take the children to the park, but there were thousands of hippies, freaks, and teenyboppers milling about. Doug drove us to Sausalito instead. His mood spread to the children, who were cross and teary through lunch. He asked if Cora was still "hanging around." Yes, Doug, your children don't vanish while we're at work. Did not tell him of her plans to leave the city.

Another letter from the Doomsdayers, written in child-like print on drawing paper. "I sense you are a wise sol with tremendis powers of persepsion and a vast store of knowllege. You have great gifts that must not go to waiste in the dull illusions of the matterial world" —is one quote from the letter.

April 22, 1967

The dreams have grown stranger and more insistent. Scared to sleep for fear of them. Told Cora and Doug I need to see the doctor. Hate to lie, but if I didn't go today I'd go mad tomorrow.

All doubt vanished when I saw the house. Beatrice took

my hands as I walked through the door—"I knew you'd come back." Cried with joy. The solution to all my problems is here. I knew it all along.

Everywhere in the house, young men and women passed, holding hammers or shears or buckets, off to mend the roof or weed the garden or touch up the paint. A few young women did the laundry in the yard, talking and laughing, while one hung the clothes up on the line. Men and women, ink smudged on their hands and faces, worked feverishly in the print room, setting type for this week's issue of the Doomsday Express. *In one room I saw girls writing letters by hand. Maybe one of them was Libby.*

Beatrice handed me a stack of magazines, ordered me to sell them on Haight St. Before I knew what I was about, I was walking down Clayton. "This is ridiculous," I thought to myself, to no effect. I passed through crowds of unwashed teenagers dressed as movie hoodlums and gypsies and fakirs, in overalls and jean jackets and face paint and military coats with flowers through the button-holes. Mingled scents wafted through the air: grass, incense, burning sage, sweat, new paint, frying dough, bubbling fat. The Beatles, the Stones, sitar music, noodling guitars, KFRC drifted through open windows. Bells jangled on a young man's ankles as he walked (harlequin suit, mod-ish boots, green eyes wild with private knowledge). The wind blew overhead and the birds sang in the trees. Could not stop walking, not for any promise or threat.

Every moment I was fearful of discovery. I was dressed in my "square" clothes. I'd done my hair up like Ronnie Spector. I was even wearing makeup. What if someone from Paradise Voyages saw me? I should have painted my face, let my hair down, worn my flower-print dress (did you pay the bills, or buy yourself a pretty dress?). I felt ancient in this open-air temple of youth. A few tourists bought magazines, the women careful not to touch my hand. One "Son of Man," a Jesus-lookalike with a guitar, tried to pick me up with a song about time flying, living and loving, crying and crying, baby girl—you know. Oddly exhilarating, like being on stage…more than a few men stopped and asked me how much and not for the paper. "If you gotta ask, honey, you can't afford it…"

Two teenaged boys bought a few issues. Said they recognized me from "the happening a few weeks ago." Meet Lee: wild, curly brown hair, artist's hands, animated Jewish face, big black pea coat and tight jeans. Imitates Bob Dylan in style but not in affect. Lee is direct, excitable, full of anecdotes, made us laugh with a story about fishing in Tahoe with his old man. Showed us some drawings in his notebook, portraits and nature sketches, says he plans to publish comics "when I get everything situated." Meet his friend, Claude: pinched accountant's face behind curtains of hair and John Lennon glasses. Off in his own universe, laughs at random, says little; wears a bowler, pinstripe pants, suspenders, bright purple shirt. A sweet-looking unwashed girl handed us flowers, which the boys put in their lapels and I put in my hair. Neither bought magazines, though Lee was full of questions (that I couldn't answer) about the magazine's printing process.

A cop came along, demanded I show him ID and a permit. I shrank. I might have skated by, but Lee argued with him about "free speech," a crowd gathered, and the cop grabbed my arm and handcuffed me. Much howling as he led me away. Hands grabbed at us, tried to rip us apart.

Quaked the entire way to the station. My mother's old warnings about cops getting "frisky" with young girls ran through my mind. The cop, looking at me in the rearview mirror like rancid meat, didn't help. I knew I'd get my picture in the papers tomorrow, Doug would find out, the office would find out, if I didn't get fired...

And the children? What will happen to them? They were safe with Cora today, but what about tomorrow? What if Doug finds out that I skipped work to fraternize with hippies? Would he take the children away? Could he?

In the station, they took my fingerprints and mugshot. Rough but no one mashed me, thank God. Maybe they thought I was some rich man's daughter, ha ha ha. Made my one phone call to Cora, told her I'd be "a little late"— horrible lie, less horrible than the truth. To my surprise, they let me go, no bail, nothing. I walked down the long corridor to the front, expecting to see disapproving Doug, and saw instead—Beatrice!

"It's outrageous," she said. "I called Jack the second I heard. Don't worry about a thing."

"Jack?"

"Yes, dear, Jack Shelly. The mayor?" She led me by the elbow out the door. "Come on. Let's get out of this pigpen."

Beatrice drove me to the Doomsday House, talking the whole way, glowing with joy and energy. "What a lovely flower in your hair. Do you think we become flowers after we die? My father always said so." I didn't want to leave, and they didn't want me to, either. Came home in bad *spirits. Saw the leaking heater, the little bundle of bills tucked under the coffee can. Is this the future I want? Or is there another future out there, waiting for me?*

The rest of April's entries cover familiar themes: work, the children, growing unrest. Rose and her children join the Doomsday Garden on May 1st ("Quitters of the world, unite! Left Paradise Voyages, and Douglas, for good. Now living with the Doomsdayers. Cora to move in with her daughter soon, couldn't be more perfect timing.") Another entry, from May 7th, fills in more of the details:

We work from 5 a.m. until nearly midnight, washing, scrubbing dishes, cooking big pots of pasta, cleaning rooms, and then, just when I thought I'd get time with R + Z, time to sell magazines, to sing, to scream and yell at some perfect stranger. Luckily there's always something for the kids to do: tend the garden, listen to lectures, read from the "Communal Comicbook Collective Pile," play in the playroom, learn all sorts of new skills: how to knit, use the printing press, cook eggs, weave with a loom.

People stream in daily, many high, near-starving, or both. Too many mouths to feed, and no magical subdividing loaves or fishes to feed them with. I spend hours with the other women cooking food. When that's done, would I mind writing something on the psychic state of America? No, Beatrice, of course not. Only had time to write this because Zelda's sick and I'm watching her while she's asleep. "Time traveler" across the hall yells "Billy, Billy, Billy." Always tired, always more to do. Parenting hundreds of children, and a new one "born" every day.

A few brief entries follow throughout May: Richie loses a tooth; ex-banker decompensates during a chronos encounter; long drives North, South, and East to get barley, lentils, apples, rice; the house hums so loud that the children can't sleep. Rose writes "Herb Caen-style columns about the end of the world" for the Doomsday Express. Her author portrait is her mugshot. Lee Simon starts drawing pictures for the paper. Claude becomes one of the "eggheads" working in the garage. Rose pastes a brief excerpt from one of her columns into the diary:

> *Cries of "Revolution!" sound in the streets…*
>
> *Disease, malnutrition rampant in so-called cradle of West-ern Civilization…*
>
> *Police break up "Messiah mob" — dueling prophets fight with clubs, blackjacks in Golden Gate Park…five Jesus Christs, two Virgin Marys, three Vishnus, seven folkies, and a hot dog salesman among the injured…*
>
> *Vietnam War to Affect Business Outlook: full employment, solid consumer spending, steep rise in business investment. "Expect Income Increases," says the man in the papers…*

Rose falls in love with an egghead, "Darling." Darling is also a Berkeley alum. It's not clear if her affections are returned, though one passage, from an entry on May 25, holds my interest:

> *The house hums. The boards and walls vibrate under your hand. Whirring, grinding, hammering sounds from the garage, day and night. No one will answer questions about it. True life exchange:*

Me: At least tell me what you're trying to do in there.

Darling: I told you, it's a delicate situation. If the government knew what we were doing...

Me: You're not making bombs, are you?

Darling: Rose...

Me: You know, the government can't make a wife testify against her husband.

He smiled at that, said nothing. Truly a man of few words.

Rose mentions a brainwashing session—called a "chronos encounter"—a few days later. She's alluded to these before, but never explicitly chronicled them, save here:

I know the drill already: people stand in a circle around you, yelling—no, SCREAMING for hours on end. This one broke me to my foundations. Everything I'd hidden lay exposed: my relationships with my parents, my children, with Doug, my petty jealousies, my "pretensions of grandeur," as one put it. But after it was all over, they embraced me. Cool water of relief flooded through me. That feeling of dirtiness that began back in college, that I pretended and pretended and pretended wasn't there, washed away.

I learn new terms. "Eating your own tail" means you're chasing an illusion. "Clearing a process" means, vaguely, to get over a hang-up. "Lady Keane" is one of Beatrice's more flattering nicknames. "The Snakehole" is the term of art for the ouroboros with the thirteen black rays at its center. "Choir practice" is a flippant term for their singing rituals.

June 8, 1967.

Apparently, Doug's been looking for me. Somebody showed me a Missing poster with my face on it. We decorated it with Day-Glo paints and hung it up on the clothesline next to the wash. Richie asks, "Is Daddy coming soon?" I wonder.

Three days later, Rose's unnamed boyfriend lets her peek inside the garage:

Dusty. Close air, tasting strongly of copper, iron, chalk, grease, and sawdust. Boards lines the walls, covered with figures and equations. Dark rust spots on the floor. Metal arcs, rings, pipes, riveted joints, and coils fill the room. The humming seems to issue from a black sphere (onyx?) at the center. Young men pace, frown, adjust knobs, confer with each other through signs and notes.

I look at the paperweight, now lying on my bed. It's a black sphere alright, maybe made of stone. I hold it up to the light, turn it over, look at it directly. Light reflects off its surface, but it's otherwise completely opaque. It's not humming.

The entries get sparser and shorter, sometimes just a sentence or two ("Zelda turned three. Richie hiding food." "Initiate pulled a knife during C.E."). Plans to buy a commune fall apart. A girl gets kidnapped on the sidewalk outside the house. Richie, standing at the window, sees the whole thing.

I put the diary down. Reading this draws me close to this world, so close that I can almost touch it. And it's not a pleasant world. It's a carnival ride where the levers creak and the gears smoke and the music never stops.

July 7, 1967

Performance on front lawn. Claude played a Mod-ish Uncle Sam (sky-high platforms, striped red-white pants, star-spangled vest, great big brass medallion, top hat) trying to colonize the Garden of Eden. "Naked" Adam and Eve hidden with strategically placed leaves. Much laughter and applause.

Served lunch to the egghead set. Lots of talk that's Greek to me—except I could learn Greek. Much talk about the Lister-LeNormand Hypothesis—the one Darling told me about. It's based on a few letters found in different estates and archives, police evidence notes, a few telegrams and "secret" experiments. Somehow they want to "fill in the gaps," which are considerable. Beyond that, mysteries abound.

A letter came from Doug today. He offered me everything I ever wanted on a plate, and I saw right through the trap at the center. Will keep it as a reminder.

Doug's letter is tucked in between the following pages. His neat, elegant handwriting travels in straight lines across the unlined paper. Paradise Voyages' logo, a stylized compass on a cloud, is printed in green at the top.

My Rose,

I have tried to visit you, but have been rebuffed each time. Strange that we both live in this small city, and I've never seen you or the children in person.

Gloria and I have parted in all ways except on paper. She

will never give me a divorce (as Catholic as Sylvia Tietjens, and just as intractable), but she accepts reality. I persuaded her to move to her mother's house while I sold the condominium. I believe she'll stay there. Where else can she go?

I have also changed my will. If something happens to me, everything goes to you, Richie, and Zelda. Gloria will get just enough to keep you out of court. She doesn't know about this, and I'm afraid she would fight you for every penny if she did. Please call my attorney when you can. His business card is in this letter.

My love for you has not diminished with time. It is your face I see every night in the borderland between sleep and waking, your body I miss lying next to mine. I long to hear your voice, to see your shining face and the faces of our children. I took the liberty of buying plates painted with red roses, to remind me of you in my loneliness.

No one can blame you for running away. I look back at my own behavior with astonishment and shame. You are the mother of my children and I treated you abominably. For that I apologize, without reservation. God knows, I don't deserve half the patience you showed me.

Please come back, Rose. The house in Woodacre is yours whenever you want it. Give your children the gift of a good life with their mother and their father. It isn't too late.

Doug

"How's it going?"

Leah's standing in the connecting doorway. She nods to the notebook, and letter, in my hands. I give her a brief rundown of what I've learned.

"Gloria Snowberger." Leah laughs. "That's *perfect.*"

"Perfect how?"

"I can see her gravestone. 'Gloria Snowberger, Beloved Wife'—with a dainty little cross over the name. No—a cross with a dove."

"You're a monster." Bright anger flares inside me. Leah's eyes narrow.

"Excuse me?"

"She couldn't have kids. Her husband left her for another woman. Do you think anyone loved her when she died? Do you want her life?"

Leah looks down, ashen-faced.

"I know what it's like to love someone who loves someone else. Who loves that other person through you. Every moment together is a fresh wound."

A veil falls from Leah's eyes. "You mean that kid who died in Phoenix?"

"Prescott." I push myself off the bed. "What's for dinner?"

"Dinner? It's hella early."

Leah's eyes burn through me as I walk out of the room. She follows me into the kitchen, where I rummage through the cupboards. "What are you making?"

"Chickpea vindaloo. It's vegetarian. Spicy, though."

"How spicy is spicy?"

"Spicy enough that Dad won't steal it." Leah snorts, hiding her laugh behind her hand.

I pour the chickpeas into a large pot while Leah rummages in the junk drawer. Leah turns to me, holding a cassette.

Joni Mitchell: Ladies of the Canyon. Grandma Rose played this every time she babysat, which was pretty much every day until I started preschool. From the first chords of "Morning Morgantown," I'm transported to a forgotten world of innocence and ease. I feel young again, younger than I ever remember feeling. I watch the chickpeas bob and whirl through the boiling water.

I show Leah how to grate ginger. We joke about a Bollywood dance number centered on making vindaloo. Leah's Lata Mangeshkar impression is better than expected. I take the chickpeas off the heat.

"Who's Lata Mon—what's her name?"

"Mangeshkar. She's sung thousands of Bollywood songs since the sixties. That clear, high-pitched voice you just did— that's her."

"I guess that's my fallback career," Leah says, absently stirring the pot. "If being an artist doesn't work out, I can always sing Bollywood." She side-eyes me.

"I guess it's a plan," I say, taking care to keep my voice neutral. "You could always—"

"What are you doing?" Mom says from the doorway. Leah and I brace for trouble.

"Making vindaloo."

"What's—" Mom's voice catches. She stands motionless, her gaze fixed at some point far beyond me, the room, or the present. I avoid Leah's questioning look. Mom shuts her eyes, shakes her head, and walks to the pot. She leans down, smells it, and stands up, confusion still written on her face.

"It smells…spicy," she says, laughing nervously. "Where'd you get the recipe?"

"Internet," Leah says for me.

"You've both finished your—"

"Yes," Leah and I say in unison. Mom throws up her hands, walks to the door. She turns back at the doorway and stares, wonderingly, at the vindaloo.

Leah rants about the recall election while I dice the potatoes. "The whole thing is so childish," she says. "Who's running—

Arnold Schwarzenegger and a porn star? This is supposed to be about who's the right person to run the whole state, and they're turning it into a popularity contest. Democracy is fucking broken."

"It can get so much more broken than this."

"How?"

I tell her a little more about Trump's campaign and its crazy-making pace, with outrage following outrage day after day. I try to paint a picture of the huge crowds, the breaking news headlines, the suffocating omnipresence of Trump and Trump's words. I explain Twitter. Leah rolls her eyes.

"Maybe in a hundred, two hundred years, the human race will finally get it together. Maybe everyone will be dead by then. What do you think?"

A memory bubbles up from the depths: Leah, and I, laughing in the kitchen, while Dad made us biscuits in funny shapes. I fish another pot out of the drawer.

"Why won't you tell me what I am when I grow up?" Leah says pettishly.

"You said you didn't want to know."

"I did *not* say that…I don't work in an office, do I?"

"No."

"Where do I live?"

"The city."

Leah's eyes light up. "Where? The Mission?"

"I don't know."

Leah's smile falters. "You just said…"

I press my palms into my eyes. "You're a junkie. Homeless, or close to it. You never really make it, as an artist or anything else. It wasn't romantic."

Leah laughs.

"It's not a joke. It's—"

"I bet I don't even go to college." She chuckles sourly. "I knew the SATs were a waste of time."

"You go to college."

Leah sighs, from relief or despair or possibly both. "Which one?"

"Swarthmore."

"Nice."

"Not nice. You nearly died from a cocaine overdose. They kicked you out."

"And then I became a junkie?"

I turn up the heat under the chickpeas. "You, uh, you went to rehab, tried Sonoma State, dropped out, went to rehab again..."

Leah leans on the palms of her hands.

"Some psycho met you at a Narcotics Anonymous meeting, locked you in his house. He did things to you, sold you to...you were never the same after that."

Leah's hollow laugh fills the room. She picks up a ladle and stirs the chickpeas.

"You don't need to do that. They're off the heat—"

"What was his name?"

"Whose name?"

"Mr. Psycho Pimp. If I know his name, I can avoid him, right?"

"I can't remember. I've tried, but—"

"You are *so* full of shit, Amy." The ladle thunks on the pot. "That picture in your locket? I bet you made it in Photoshop."

"You know I didn't."

Leah closes the distance between us, hands outstretched. She grabs my locket, pulls it away from me. I scream. My hand digs into her face. I reach out for the pot, trying to tip it over before she can.

"Don't you dare break this!" I scream. "This is a gift from *God*!"

Leah laughs.

"Don't fight in the kitchen!" Mom shrieks from the doorway. We freeze. Leah releases my locket. I step back, nearly stumble into the countertop. "See," Mom says, pointing to me. "*That's* what we're trying to prevent. If one of you slips, you could burn your face off."

"Sorry," we say in unison.

"You've both finished all your homework?"

"Mom!"

"All of it, really?"

"I already *told* you—"

"Fix your attitude," Mom says. Her eyes linger on my chest. I look down and see the locket, now in plain view. Mom meets my eyes with a puzzled look. "Papa gave me that necklace. Where'd you find it?"

"It was on my pillow."

"I've looked everywhere for this," Mom says, moving toward me. Her hand reaches out for the locket.

"I'm not going to college," Leah blurts.

Mom's hand hovers in mid-air. She turns, the locket forgotten. "I'm sorry?" she says, her voice deadly calm.

"Ray got me a job at Borders—"

"Have you ever *had* a job? Let alone one for minimum wage? You're in no position to decide—"

"You can't make me go, Mom."

Mom follows Leah out of the kitchen and into the living room. Their muted argument filters through the walls. The curry paste is almost finished when Leah comes back. *Thank you,* I mouth. Leah closes the kitchen door.

"You owe me," Leah murmurs. She takes the spoon from

my hand and tastes it. Her eyes bug out. "Spicy," she coughs, reaching for a glass of water.

"Spicy food's great once you get used to it. My first job, after college, there was this lunch thief—"

"Stop." Leah's scrunched her eyes shut, hid her face in her hand. "Don't talk about work like that. You still sound like a kid."

"How should I say it, then?"

Leah takes another drink of water, stares absently into the saucepan.

"I bet Dad's massacring a Double Whopper right now," I say.

"I bet you're right."

"He's killing himself."

"What are you gonna do? Follow him around, slap the cheeseburger out of his hand? He made his choice."

"Have you made your choice?"

Leah frowns into the middle distance. "Do I have one?"

CHAPTER TWENTY-FIVE
ORIGINAL WORK

A PICTURE OF me at Chuck E. Cheese appears on Court TV. I'm the one thread connecting Kathleen to Becca and Erin. Was I really sleepwalking in day clothes? How did I find her body, when the police can't? What exactly do I know?

A locust swarm of shutters clicks around us. Dad eases the car out of the driveway, parting the sea of black-clad bodies and camera eyes. Flashbulbs blind me. We inch past the garishly-painted media vans hogging Blackwood Drive.

Dad comes to a stop at the bottom of the hill. A van pulls up alongside us, a camera pointed out its front window.

"Go," I say, slumping in my seat.

"This is a stop sign, Amy, I have to—"

"Please."

The locust retinue follows us from Woodacre to Forest Knolls, where we're greeted by an even bigger crowd. Voices, muddled by the windows, assault me from every direction.

"Amy, Cheryl *Shrsfn* from ABC7—"

"Mr. Snowberger, how does it feel to—"

"Say you're *erfhgrfns*—how do you—"

"—sure you're *mfnrk*—"

"—any connection to—"

A few reporters follow us into the parking lot before a policeman chases them off. We enter the traffic circle, pull up to the curb. A hush falls over the crowd as I get out of the car. Kids lean out of first- and second-floor windows to stare at me. They whisper to each other, eyes locked on my face. I walk up the steps, eyes fixed downward.

The classroom falls silent as I walk in. I take a seat near the back, keeping my eyes fixed to the floor. Hector Villanueva scootches away from me, his chair legs screeching against the linoleum.

"Dude," Sean whispers.

"Don't *dude* me," Hector whispers back, "I'm not..." The rest is inaudible.

Camera crews are parked on the periphery of the school. Helicopters whir overhead, taking live video of our school rooftop. Anything to get a scoop.

"It's on every major news station," Jessica Truesdale stage-whispers to Emily. "Becca's mom was on KQED."

"Mom won't let me watch it," Emily says, chewing on her fingertip. "It's such bullshit. She let me watch 9/11." Jessica casts a long look at me, then whispers to Emily, hand cupped around her mouth.

The entire morning passes like this. Students part before me as I walk, stare at me as I go to my locker, look away when I look at them. I'm walking under a glass jar, a moving exhibition. Fragments of rumors reach my ears.

"—*holding them for ransom, but they can't prove*—"

"—*gave blowjobs to the whole basketball team*—"

"—*summoned Bloody Mary when*—"

"—*her dad isn't a made guy, though, because they're*—"

"—*sister's drug debt*—"

"*heard* everything—"

"—*puts a spell on everyone she hates*—"

"—*bad luck charm. If you talk to her, if you even look at her, terrible things happen. Be*-lieve.*"

My locker door feels cool against my forehead. I close my eyes.

"Hey," a voice says at my ear. I jump. Sean and Andrew stand there, backpacks slung over their left shoulders. "Are you okay?"

"Never better." I push myself off the wall, then nearly stumble into them. Both boys jump, then act like they didn't.

"I didn't know about your party until this morning," Sean says. "Dad said he lost the email—"

"What's that?" Andrew says. He's pointing to my locket, now dangling out of my shirt.

"This is the, uh, sacred heart of Jesus." Sean stares. Andrew's face twists in a look between disgust and disappointment. I cover the locket with my hand. What if it falls open somehow? What if they want to touch it? What if one of the girls overhears, tries to tear it off my neck? What if they *see*?

"Do you have someone's picture in it?" Sean asks, unconvincingly faking casual interest.

"Only mine. So far, anyway." Sean's face lights up, and I realize I've smiled at him knowingly. Invisible grime coats my skin. I tuck the locket back in my shirt.

"I thought you were Jewish," Andrew says.

"I'm a…lapsed Catholic, I guess. Very lapsed. This came from my great-grandfather."

"He's Catholic?"

"Buddhist. He just couldn't resist anything shiny. Like a crow, you know." Mystified pause. "I'm *kid*-ding. Of course he was Catholic."

Sean and Andrew laugh nervously.

"Where *is* everybody?" Lisa says, bounding up to us. She shoots me a suspicious look. "There were, like, ten kids in my math class."

"All the popular kids are gone."

"Except Bretlyn."

"Bretlyn doesn't count. She pays them to be friends with her."

"How much?"

"A hundred dollars a week."

"Holy shit. Can I be her friend? I give amazing compliments. My rate's very competitive—"

"Cassidy isn't here," I say, realizing it as I say it. Sean, Andrew, and Lisa look at each other. "What?"

"You don't know?" Lisa says.

"Know what?"

Lisa leans forward, her eyes sparkling with the foretaste of great pleasure. "Cassidy went to *jail*," she murmurs. "Her whole family did."

"For what?"

"Selling drugs."

Andrew scoffs.

"No, seriously. My Dad lives across the street from her. There were a dozen cop cars outside her house last night. Five cops tried to wrestle her brother into the back of an ambulance. He *broke* his handcuffs—"

"Holy shit."

"What did he do?"

"He's fucking crazy. I hear him screaming sometimes. I think they've been making meth—that's why Cassidy wears all that gross perfume, to cover up the smell."

"Meth smells way stronger than perfume," Andrew says, emphatically shaking his head.

"Where was Cassidy?" I ask. Lisa shrugs.

"I didn't see. Her brother got away, though. Last I saw, he was running naked into the woods, with five cops chasing after him."

"Wait, he was *naked*?"

"Hey, Lisa, where's Bart?" a boy calls out as he walks down the hallway.

"That stopped being funny in third grade," Lisa yells at him.

"Where's Bart," Sean chuckles. "Man, that's great."

Lisa's face crumples like wet tissue paper.

"One minute to class," Mrs. Rice bellows from her doorway. Her eyes catch, then linger on mine.

Mrs. Rice glares at me as I sit down. She doesn't release her gaze for five seconds, ten. I look down, my ears burning.

If Lisa can be believed, or halfway believed, then Cassidy's safe from her brother. That doesn't mean she's safe. Maybe she's staying with Téa in a hotel. Maybe she's in a nice foster home, not one where the other kids burn your arms with cigarettes. Maybe family's taking her in. Maybe Slice vanished into the woods, forever. Do her parents even know what's happened yet? Do they care?

"I have something serious to discuss," Mrs. Rice says, jolting me out of my thoughts. "Every year, at least one student thinks they can take a short cut. And every year, I catch them."

Her eyes fix on mine again. What the hell is she talking about? I look to my neighbors on either side. They meet my gaze with blank stares.

"Everyone thinks they can cheat the system, and everyone is wrong. The system always wins. Amy, will you come up to the front."

My chair legs squeak against the linoleum. The space

between Mrs. Rice and me seems to lengthen as I walk to the front. Mrs. Rice picks up a paper from her desk. Handwritten on binder paper.

"Read this," she says, handing me the paper. She's crossed out my name with red marker, written a giant "F" across the top. I start reading, my voice scratchy and high.

"Rhea Silvia: Myths and Realities in Roman Life," I read. "A Vestal Virgin, raped by the God of War—" A snicker passes through the room "—Rhea Silvia, mother of Romulus and Remus, represents the union of contrary archetypes: divinity and defilement, holiness and war, virginity and motherhood. Her presence in the Roman imagination tells us a great deal about how the Romans saw themselves..."

Semi-intellectual dogshit, in other words. The sort of thing I used to vomit out at 4 a.m. after wasting the night on YouTube. Mrs. Rice's eyes bore into me. The fluorescent lights hum overhead. I look up at the end of page one.

"Do you expect me to believe that you wrote that?" Mrs. Rice says.

No. I expect you to believe that an angel appeared and demanded I take dictation.

"Yes," I say aloud.

"I don't think so," she sing-songs. "Next time you want to plagiarize, steal from someone on your own level."

Nervousness radiates off the class like static off an old T.V. set. This is one of those situations you replay over and over, for months, sometimes years, afterwards. *I should have said this. I should have done that.* But I'm here right now, and my mouth's welded shut. All that growing up I did, just to clam up in front of my seventh-grade history teacher.

"When you copy other people's work, you rob two people,"

Mrs. Rice says to the class, holding out two fingers. "You rob the person you copied, and you rob yourself—"

"I wrote this, Mrs. Rice. I didn't copy anything."

Mrs. Rice turns to me. She asks me to repeat myself. I do. She looks down her nose at me, her tongue lolling in her cheek. "Then why did you say you copied it?"

"I didn't."

"Yes, Amy, you did."

"What specifically did I say?"

The class holds its breath. Mrs. Rice shifts her weight. Her face is dark and pinched with anger. "The school has a plagiarism database," she says, her voice dangerously low. "I checked your paper, and it came up dirty."

"Prove it."

Rage flashes over her face. "You will *not* call me a liar in my own classroom," she says. If it were the two of us, she would hit me. My hands shake so hard the paper bounces.

"You're wrong."

Mrs. Rice straightens and points imperiously to the door. "Donadio. Now. Before I do something we both regret."

I'm walking to the door when she utters her parting salvo: "Pray to whatever God you believe in that he doesn't hold you back next year."

My hand closes around the doorknob. *Don't say it,* I tell myself, but my body turns without consulting my mind. The words are out before I can catch them.

"You're only mad because I'm smarter than you. You could never write this. And this *sucks*."

The class gasps. Mrs. Rice lunges for me, braying something I can't hear, because I'm already at the end of the hall, my feet flying under me.

Running is the best part of being thirteen. I can run, feint, turn corners, take stairs two or even three at a time, with almost no effort. I might even look graceful doing it, like a rabbit running from a wolf. I bound into the front office. Mrs. Rice huffs in thirty seconds later, lunges for me—then sees the secretary. Mrs. Rice stalks past, throws open Principal Donadio's door, slams it shut behind her. A wounded bellow fills the office. The secretary and I exchange forced smiles.

I take a seat by the door. The secretary turns back to her computer. Mrs. Rice's tirade continues.

Why did I say that? That one insult could send me to wilderness camp, for months or even years. It wasn't even that good. I lean back, look at the motivational poster on the wall. *CHALLENGE*, it says, below a photograph of a man climbing a sheer cliff. *It is not always the strongest people who win, it is the people who never back down from a challenge.* Let's hope that's true.

Mrs. Rice exits the office, smiling beatifically as she glides away. Her eyes cut to mine with a look of triumph.

"Amy," Principal Donadio says from his doorway.

Principal Donadio's office is a tiny, white-walled room with a window overlooking the field. A class in red shirts does burpees outside, more or less in sync with Miss Barnett's whistle. I hand him the paper. He leans back as he reads it, his chair squeaking under him.

"I wrote it by myself," I blurt out. "I didn't even show it to anyone." He looks up at me, mildly surprised. "Mrs. Rice said she had proof that I copied my paper, and I asked to see it. She didn't prove it because she can't."

"You think she's lying to you?"

"She's mistaken. I copied nothing."

He stares at me for a few seconds, tapping his pen on the

desk. He looks back at the paper, flips over the next page, then the next. "So, you wrote this, huh?"

"Yes, sir."

"What does 'atavistic' mean?"

"The reappearance of a trait or practice that's been dormant for a while. 'An atavistic revival of pagan belief.'"

Donadio raises his eyebrows and frowns, like Steve Van Zandt conceding a point. He places the paper on his desk, looks up at me, leans forward in his chair. "You've had the worst week of anyone at this school," he says. "Don't you think?"

"I don't know."

"You don't know?"

"I don't know everyone's business. There must be kids who look fine on the outside, but they're not."

"Of course. Let's walk through it anyway, shall we? First you ran away—which scared everybody to death, including us. A few days later, you're the last person to see Erin and Becca alive. That night, you find a dead body in the woods." His eyes bore into mine.

Miss Barnett's whistle shrieks outside the window. I let the silence linger. "I probably had the worst Monday morning," I venture.

"How's that?"

I tell him about the reporters outside my house, about the ones who followed me into school, even into the parking lot. I fill the silence with my words, to avoid asking the question I can't quite form in my own mind, let alone say aloud. When I pause for breath, it comes to me.

"Is this story *really* on the news? I know it's in the *Chronicle* and the *IJ*, but…is it like the Casey Antho—like, uh, Scott Peterson? Is it all across the country, or…?"

The pen stops twirling in his hand. He writes something

on a white slip of paper, then holds it out to me. "Give this to Mrs. Rice." He pulls back the paper, every wrinkle raised on his forehead. "I won't give you detention this time, and I won't call your mom. But if this behavior becomes a pattern, we'll have to discuss your future at Forest Knolls." He holds out the paper again. "You're going to have to deal with a lot of difficult people in life. Sometimes you have to go along to get along."

I open the white paper in the corridor. *NOTED*, he's written, in large block letters.

CHAPTER TWENTY-SIX
FUCKING FOR GOD

"Why didn't you order sprinkles?" Dad asks. We're sitting in the back of the ice cream parlor, wearing ballcaps and sunglasses, trying not to be seen. Dad picked me up in Aunt Zelda's car to foil the media. He took a few twists and turns through Fairfax while singing the James Bond theme. I'm pretty sure the guy sitting in the front window, in a tight polo and khakis, is a tail of some kind.

I swirl the half-melted ice cream around the bottom of my cup. *Dad's made his choice,* I remind myself, as he bites into his chocolate-dipped cone.

"You love sprinkles. When you were in first grade, your favorite was rainbow sherbet with extra sprinkles. Do you remember?"

I bite my cheek to keep the tears away. "Dad, when's the last time you saw a doctor?"

Dad puts a hand on my shoulder. "Two hours ago. I see them every day, actually. I keep eating apples, but it does no good."

"When did you last get a check-up?"

"Three months ago, maybe?"

"What'd he say?"

Dad thumps his chest. "Strong as an ox and fit as a fiddle. As always."

I look down. Dad pats his belly affectionately. "This keeps me warm through the winter. And it keeps the ladies under control. If it wasn't for this, we'd have to pry them off with the jaws of life."

The girl behind the counter covers her laugh. I wonder if she recognizes us from the news. Maybe she'll take our picture and sell it to a tabloid. I sink into my seat.

Dad, catching my expression, reaches out and ruffles my hair. "Cheer up, emo kid," he says, surprising a laugh out of me. "What are you worried about?"

"You. Cassidy Clark. The Vandergrafs, Becca, Erin, the press...whatever's out there that wants to ruin our lives."

"Nobody wants to ruin our lives. The last week has nothing to do with you as a person, okay? Sometimes bad things happen and...that's all there is to it."

For a moment, I see Dad as he was—as Richie, six years old, crying at the center of a chronos encounter, reading to Zelda in a room full of runaways, hiding bread beneath a dirty mattress.

"You don't have to do it alone," I say, putting my hand over his.

"I don't have to do anything." All mirth vanishes from his face. He takes his hand away.

"Dad, please. Remember I told you about my dream about the future? I think—"

"That's enough, Amy. Pick your grades up. Join a club. Finish your chores once in a while. Then we can talk about my problems."

Two women walk into the shop: granola yuppies (caramel

highlights, craft fair bracelets, Bohemian skirts) somewhere in their thirties. One's pushing a stroller.

"…everyone says that about their own kid," says the one pushing the baby. "but I swear, he's trying to *talk* sometimes."

"Aww."

"I thought, okay, I'm really going bananas now. So I recorded it. After two seconds, Will turned it off. He said it sounded like a demon."

"*No.*"

"Yes!"

"What'd it sound like?"

The mother fiddles with her purse. She takes out a mini-tape recorder, filling the parlor with a tinny, canned air sound. After a few seconds, there's a tiny voice, more like a croak, making the same sound over and over: "*Hehhh. Hehhhhh. Hehhhhh-pffff. Heh-pfff.*"

"Isn't that wild?"

They walk further and further into the store, stopping just before our booth. I peek inside the stroller and see a tiny, squishy baby with a smattering of red hair. The baby stares at nothing with an intense, puzzled frown. The recording continues. The mother smiles down rapturously at her son. Her friend's smile wavers.

"*Hehhhhh. Hehhhhhhh-pfffff. Heh-pfttthhhh.*"

"Are you ready to order?" asks the girl behind the counter. The baby grunts.

A dim memory struggles to the surface of my mind. I remember driving to Woodacre on the last night of my adult life, passing Cassidy's old house, seeing…seeing…what?

"Heh-pthhh?" the baby says, its scratchy voice rising in inflection. "Hehpth hepth hepth herrlllppthhh…" Garbled syllables come out, syllables that almost sound like words. He bursts into explosive, hopeless tears.

"You're okay, Baxter," his mother sing-songs. "You're okay."

Baxter. Cassidy and I drove past a boy in a Burger King crown, red hair and dark eyes. *Baxter, wait up!* And now he's—

No. We're in Fairfax. All the people who went back in time are from the San Geronimo Valley. All turned some multiple of thirteen on August 26th. Zero is a multiple of thirteen, but...it was the 25th when I saw him wearing that crown. Why would he wear it the day before his birthday? Relax, Amy.

"Be prepared," Dad says to Baxter's mom. "It goes by *so* fast. I remember when she was that little."

"Aww."

Tears fall down Baxter's face, now transfigured by agony. Dad takes off his hat and sunglasses, makes faces at him. The mother looks down with an appreciative smile.

"Hey, buddy," I say. Baxter doesn't seem to hear. Everything must be a supersensory blur, too much to process at once.

Dad draws Baxter's mom, Sarah, into conversation. Sarah's husband is a visual effects supervisor at Industrial Light and Magic. Sarah was an esthetician in Mill Valley, before the baby. They've lived in San Geronimo for five years.

"We hiked the trails out there and pretty much fell in love."

"With each other, or the trails?"

"Both."

"Lovely. We're in Woodacre."

"Oh, nice. We're neighbors."

"Do you need a babysitter?" I say.

Sarah pauses, a smile frozen on her face. Recognition sparks in her friend's eyes. She stares at me, taps Sarah on the shoulder. Sarah takes no notice.

"Um, maybe," Sarah says, which is NorCal for "no." "My

whole family is up at the house now. Everyone's making up for lost time."

"Lost time?"

"They weren't there for the birth. By the time I knew what was happening, he was out—what? One second," she dismisses her friend, "Sorry. He came out super-fast. We didn't even get to the hospital until after."

"You had a home birth?" I ask. Sarah's friend is now urgently tugging on her elbow, nodding toward the door. Sarah shrugs her off.

"Not by choice! I was in his nursery when I saw this bright, bright light outside. I thought maybe they were making a movie, because they were playing some intense choral music. Then I felt a strong kick. When I came to, I was lying on the floor."

"Wow."

"Wow is right." Sarah smiles adoringly at her son. "He came out absolutely perfect."

"When did it happen?"

Sarah's friend glares at me.

"Tuesday morning," Sarah says dreamily. "Born just after midnight."

"Hey, Amy, did you hear that? You and Baxter have the same birthday!"

"Happy birthday," Sarah sing-songs, pushing the stroller back and forth.

Tears slide down Baxter's cheeks. He grunts a few times, then sighs. "No," he says, sounding pained, resigned. My soul ices over.

"You've got a little genius there," Dad says.

"I sure hope so."

Baxter's sad eyes haunt me all through the evening. They interrupt my reading and invade my dreams. His eyes are on a movie marquee, in the reflection of a lake, hiding inside a vast network of caves. And everywhere I go I hear his scratchy little newborn voice, the same word repeated over and over: *no, no, no...*

I think of Cassidy. Did I do the right thing, or mark her out for an even worse fate? I tried to help Tom, and drove him to suicide instead. Becca and Erin would still be here if I'd spoken up, or even coughed. I left Kathleen out in the woods, all alone. And Baxter...what can I do for Baxter that won't make everything worse?

I scream into my pillow until my lungs burn for air. When I catch my breath, a pale, unearthly light leaks through the curtains. Faint song from deep in the woods. I cross myself, close my eyes—and it's morning.

5:05, according to my alarm clock. The street's loud, full of people talking, equipment humming, engines idling, vans beeping as they back up. This morning's a Xerox of yesterday: the same scramble, the same slow drive past the vans, the same questions yelled at our car, the same flashbulbs burning my retinas.

"Mister Snowberger, are you prepared to—"

"—given a statement—"

"—Amy, how does it feel to—"

Security guards walk circuits around the campus, walkie talkies sounding on their shoulders. Every blip and crackle sends me back to the forest, feeling Kathleen's cold hand in mine. The hallways echo with squeaking shoes and slamming lockers, not the cacophony of voices I've grown used to. Kids cluster together and talk in low voices. They give me a wide berth.

"She was at the police station all day," Lisa whispers behind me. *"Her parents might go to jail."*

"Who are you talking about?" I say as I wheel around. Lisa shrinks away, won't meet my eyes. She might have been talking about Cassidy, but she's not going to tell me now.

Mrs. Rice doesn't show up for history class. We sit in our seats, doodling, talking, staring into space. Sean and Hector hold a comic book between their seats, giggling as they read.

"Missed a spot," Bretlyn says, pointing at Emily's leg.

"So? I'm a *natural* blonde," Emily says, her gaze dipping to Bretlyn's upper lip. "If you weren't ogling me like a creepy old—"

"You wish. Everyone can see your gross leg hair, Emily."

"Better than a mustache." Emily's gaze dips again. Bretlyn's mouth falls open. A few kids laugh. Bretlyn hunches forward, rests her head in her hands. Emily straightens, pulls out a compact, smiles at her reflection.

Claude Belissan walks in. The class falls silent. He smiles at me, briefly, before writing his name on the board. *Mr. B.* I don't answer when he calls my name.

"How did history begin?" he asks, when he's done taking roll.

A few kids giggle. No one answers.

"Somebody. How do you think history started? I can wait." He does wait—we all do—for a pocket eternity.

Marina Alvarez raises her hand. "With language?"

"That's a good guess, Miss—I'm sorry, your name was?"

"Marina."

"Thank you, Marina." He pauses, holds her gaze. "Do you know what Alvarez means?"

"...Son of Alvaro?"

"And the name Alvaro comes from the Old Norse word 'Alfarr,' meaning 'elf warrior.' Like Legolas in *Lord of the Rings*."

"Nuh-uh."

"Yuh-huh. Look it up."

"Alvarez is *Spanish*," Bretlyn says, holding the last word like a worm between two fingers. Claude doesn't look at her.

"Marina, as the only elf warrior in this class, will you tell us mere mortals why language is the start of history?"

"Because you don't have a history if you can't talk about it."

"Good, good. Anyone else?"

A few hands raise in the air. Marina covers her smile.

"Yes, Mister…Jacobs, right?"

"Right. History starts with architecture," Andrew says. "We have buildings older than the oldest writing. Buildings are a record of how people lived."

"Interesting. But these pre-literate people—did they have a sense of themselves as part of history?"

"Who cares? They're part of it whether they like it or not." The class snickers. Claude stares past us, his gaze abstracted into some private universe. For a moment he holds us in suspended animation. Even Sean and Hector look up from their comic book.

"What's the point of studying history?" Claude says.

"We have to."

"What do you mean, you have to? You could walk out of here right now. You could walk outside of the school. What's stopping you?"

"Parents."

"Security guards."

"The reporters outside. If my mom saw me skipping school, live on TV—"

"What would she do?"

Kids look at each other doubtfully. "Kick my ass," someone mumbles. More laughs.

"I want a good job when I grow up," Marina says. "I see

people working as waiters when they're thirty, thirty-five. If that's me…" She shakes her head.

"That wouldn't be suitable for an elf warrior, would it? So how is studying history going to help you, ah, stay out of the kitchen?"

"'Cause. If I get a good grade in this class, and I get good grades in high school, I can go to college, get a good job."

"What type of job?"

"Business-to-business sales, maybe. I think I'd be good at that." A few snickers.

"*Her brother works at Taco Bell*," Bretlyn stage-whispers to a neighbor. Marina flushes and stares at her lap.

"That's a good reason," Claude says. "My first job was cleaning the deep fryers at a McDonald's. Back when dinosaurs roamed the earth."

No one laughs. Sean and Hector turn back to their comic.

"Do you want to change the world when you grow up?" Claude says. "Do you think it needs changing?"

Uneasy silence.

"No," I blurt out. All eyes turn to me.

Claude smiles a delighted, ironical smile. "Why 'no'?"

"What if I make it worse?"

"What if you could make it better? Wouldn't you at least try?"

Tom's high school portrait flashes through my mind. "No."

"No? So, if I put you in a time machine back to, let's say, 1958. There's nothing about that world you'd try to change?"

"I might buy a root beer," I concede. "I think I could do that without jump-starting the apocalypse."

Claude chuckles. In my peripheral vision, Emily leans toward her friend, hand curled around her mouth.

"Let me ask you something else, then. If Martin Luther King was as scared as you are—and he had good reason to be scared, lots of people wanted to kill him, more than a few tried—but if he was as scared as you, would they still have separate drinking fountains? Maybe black people would still sit at the back of the bus. What do you think?"

"I don't think—"

"You don't think so," Claude says for me, shaking his head. "You think that we can all bury our heads in the sand and all the world's evils will simply disappear." He turns to the class, arm outstretched to me. "It's this attitude that killed millions of—"

"And who killed them?" I say, my voice rising over his. "The Nazis, Stalin, Mao, Pol Pot—they all wanted to change the world, too. They did. Did they make it better?"

Claude's eyes bore through my skull.

"And when those people try to change the world, will you let them?"

Charged silence fills the classroom. The air conditioner hums. I don't dare drop my gaze.

"Nobody ever thinks they're wrong, do they?" I say. "No one's a villain in their own mind, no matter what they've done. When Martin Luther King cheated on his wife, he'd say that he was 'fucking for God.'" The class gasps. Claude doesn't flinch. "That attitude—doing bad for the ultimate good—it's killed millions of people, ruined—"

"So, cheating on your wife is just as bad as—"

"Let me finish, Claude. If you set out to change the world, you give yourself ultimate license to do wrong. It's not really wrong if it's for the right cause, is it? It's 'fucking for God.' And once you're there, it's a short trip from changing the world to trying to control it. To control things that can't or shouldn't be controlled. So, no, I don't want to change the world. Not like that."

Bretlyn rolls her eyes, turns to her friend. *The Simpsons* comic hangs suspended between Sean and Hector's desks, forgotten. Andrew scowls at me, arms crossed. Emily mouths something to her neighbor, twirls her finger by her ear.

"What an articulate expression of defeat," Claude says. "Why try anything, if it might go wrong. Why fix a flat tire, if you're less than an angel."

"That is not—"

Claude laughs. Red mist clouds my vision. I squeeze the edges of the desk.

"Tell us," he says, mirth twinkling in his eyes. "What is your grand solution for the chaos engulfing the planet?"

"I don't have one. Everything I do only makes things worse. I want—I want love, and a family, and a normal life, and I want to do some good. All the evil that I've done, the evil that I've let happen, the hideous weight of this system that I'm a part of—I don't know how to escape that."

"What if somebody showed you how?"

Our eyes meet.

"Mr. Belissan?" Emily says. All attention pivots to her.

"Yes, Miss Padovano?"

"We're supposed to watch a video," she says, pointing to the rig with a TV and VCR. "About the Boston Tea Party?"

Claude's eyes flit to mine. Ironic triumphalism sparkles in them. For a moment, rage swells inside me, and then ebbs away, leaving only despair.

Cassidy's words return to me. *That's such an Amazing Amy answer. If only people started thinking like I do, do what I know is right.* Who was it who thought like that? Images float before my mind's eye: Dad patting his gut, Leah's drug kit, my own mouth, blabbing away while everything inside me begs it to stop. Nothing's changed. All my efforts to get through to Dad, to Leah, to my own hindbrain have failed spectacularly. For all I know,

Cassidy might be living in some horrible foster home, getting screamed at or beat up or even worse. I sink into my chair.

Good thing you don't want to change the world. You can't even change yourself.

Baxter's newborn face enters my mind. *No*, he said, tears falling down his cheeks. I know exactly how he feels.

CHAPTER TWENTY-SEVEN
THE NIGHT SKY

GRANDMA ROSE'S DIARY is in the bottom of my backpack, protected by a cloth and a Ziploc bag. After school, I hide in the back of the library, turn to where I left off.

August 6, 1967

I woke up today knowing we had to leave. Took the kids, went to a payphone, called Doug's home number (no answer). Called the travel agency (no answer). Of course not, today is Sunday, who knew? Walked to Nob Hill. Doug might be at his old apartment. He wasn't. Neither was his wife. Small mercies. Called Mother with my last dime; she hung up when she heard my voice. Housewife, my age, looked at us like we were gum on her shoe. Gave up. Came back. What does this world have to offer us?

Much banging and hollering in the garage. Lee's angry. "We could put a full print shop down there. Instead they're fucking around with something they don't even under-stand." Sharp words with Claude.

Beatrice insists on a chronos encounter for Zelda. Something about the all-important "Scarlet Virgin" and my role as a "guide." Then again, she's so distracted by the garage project and buying the co-op, it'll probably fall through the cracks. Let's hope.

August 13, 1967

The pointless gloom and self-pity of my last entry seems so distant today. The doors of perception have been cleansed. Everything is seen as it is now: infinite. Can truly say I am the luckiest woman in the world. Every day, I discover new things about the universe and our cosmic connections to each other.

Beatrice, in lecture: "How can you doubt, when you've seen miracles?" Like a flame sparking to life. Doubt is the inner voice of the snake dragging us away from eternity. We must let go of the snake before we cross the threshold.

Richie's hiding food in his bed. I asked him about it: get this! He says he can never count on being fed on time. What on Earth? There's food in the kitchen. He shook his head. My double: if he doesn't want to do something, no earthly or heavenly power can make him do it. He went through another chronos encounter, tears streamed down his face, but wouldn't say a word. When will he let go and cross over? I can't make him do it.

August 16, 1967

Now that the co-op's fallen through, things have picked up in the garage. Men (including Him) convene in the hall-ways, make hushed phone calls to Cal and Stanford and MIT. I catch snippets of conversation I don't understand. He says they're going up a "blind alley" at the moment but won't elucidate. Band of tension around his forehead. "Rusty" smell stronger by the garage door.

Lecture today by Beatrice. Fears we are sliding into "pop occulture": horoscopes, tarot readings, love spells, candles. Discussed her father's distaste for the press and all "timely" (as in worldly) institutions. "We must not turn our eyes away from the stars to gaze adoringly at streetlights."

Much ado about nothing at the Doomsday Express. *Lee's illustrations turn bleak as the summer progresses: the snake swallowing the world, the black sphere exploding, the dead garden. Our writers constantly shirk their responsi-bilities, turning in unfinished copy or something that has a profound meaning to them and no one else. Some nice haikus from the letter-writers. Here's one that touched me:*

Eternity stands

Still and dry above the stream

Sun kissing its face

Richie and Zelda misbehaving terribly. Zelda smeared shit all over the walls. I made her clean it up. Richie hasn't said much lately. He spends all his time sitting on the bed or in the bathroom with a brick in front of the door. Not interested in playing anymore. Perhaps he's getting more adult, more serious. It's so hard to tell with him.

I must write in this more but I've been so busy. I'll write in it again tomorrow. I promise.

August 20, 1967

Summer draws to a close. More runaways, drugs, crime, psychosis. Doomsday is coming, in days if not hours. There can be no more doubt.

Fate that I met Doug today. Beatrice and I were walking into City Hall when Doug came down the stairs. We saw each other from across the room. It was as if no time had passed. Was I alright? I looked skinny. How are the children, Rose? Let's go get a bite. I didn't have time to answer before Beatrice hustled me away. How strange to think I lived an entirely different life once. Looked at my mugshot when we came home. Who is that stranger wearing my face?

August 26, 1967

I'm writing this now, scarcely understanding what has happened and why. This time last week, I was, as usual, putting out fires in the press room (horrid metaphor!), writing the Doomsday Express—*or was I out on the street, selling the papers with the new recruits, or posting flyers or, God help me, cleaning again or babysitting seven children while trying to soothe another teenager going through a post-chronos breakdown?*

But that isn't how it will be, not today, not tomorrow, not ever again.

This morning I was washing dishes in the kitchen. The

house began humming again. I could feel the vibrations through my feet. I'd stepped into the hallway, to check on the kids, when an enormous "BOOM" knocked me to the floor. White smoke rose through tiny cracks in the floorboards.

There was no sound, no sense of time, nothing in the universe save the tiny plumes of smoke rising through the air. And then the smells, in one instant: burning wood, burning flesh, molten metals and plastics. I was standing up, without knowing how I stood up.

"Richie! Zelda!" I called out their names, running full-tilt down the hall. They were supposed to be in the playroom. They weren't in the playroom. Two girls were smoking in there, turned away from the children.

"Where are Richie and Zelda?"

"I thought they were with you."

Smoke thickened in the air. They weren't in the half-bathroom. A crowd gathered at the front door, choking off access to the front of the house. Pale lights guttered in the corner of my eye. "Where's Richie? Zelda?" I asked a few toward the back. No one looked at me. The smoke was too thick. I fell back.

I saw it, then, off to my left. White flames rose through what had once been the floor of the lecture room, and were now licking at the walls and eating through the cabinets and paintings. Black smoke billowed from below. A man to my left stumbled and fell into the inferno where the garage used to be.

I covered my mouth with my shirt, held my breath, blinked against the soot, listened for Richie or Zelda's voices above the screams. I felt the heads and bodies of the crowd, desperately searched for them. There was no air to breathe. I'd pass out soon if someone didn't trample me, if I didn't fall into the fire. We would die in here, all of us.

Something told me to look up. A break in the darkness showed me the staircase, daylight streaming from its second-story entrance. I moved away from the crush of people and up the stairs. The air was better there, though not by much. Richie and Zelda were in the front bedroom, Zelda crying, Richie with his arm around her. I grabbed them and opened the window that looks out onto the street. The air felt pure and cold going into my lungs. Zelda coughed ceaselessly under my arm. Both children clung to me. Tears streamed through the soot on their faces.

People were gathered out on the sidewalk. I saw Lee Simon, Claude, and many strangers. Smoke billowed out of the first-floor windows. Screams echoed throughout the house. Where was the fire engine, the police, the neighbors with a bucket or an axe for the hydrant? Couldn't one person cross the street? Could I throw the children to them?

The smoke rose in great plumes around us. I screamed, "Help! Help!" as if anyone was in any doubt what I needed. I could feel the heat of the flames through the floorboards; the iron studs burned the soles of my feet. A man ran toward the house, holding a ladder. He clambered into the garden, coming dangerously close to the fire. He was lifting up his ladder, trying to reach me, when some unevenness in the ground checked him, and he stumbled into the house's front wall. It tore like a piece of paper, and the house swallowed him whole. The crowd gasped.

A fire engine roared down the block. Zelda lay horribly

still against my body. They brought ladders, and unthinking, I cried out "No! No! It'll swallow you too!" But their ladders reached the window. I gave Richie and Zelda to the first man who climbed up. I was about to follow him down when I saw my flower-print satchel on the floor next to me. I hadn't noticed it in the chaos. I grabbed it and slung it over my arm as I climbed down. God must have shown it to me for a reason.

Zelda was pale and still as a doll. An animal cry erupted from my throat as they worked on her. Richie would not let go of me. After a hideous eternity, she opened her eyes and coughed. The three of us cried and held each other. When I looked up, the entire house was consumed by fire. Flames rose through the open window where I'd stood. The house's white sidings were blackened cinders. Flames licked through the wooden beams. The ouroboros survived as a darker shadow over the door. The garden plants curled and died. Someone inside was still screaming.

Columns of smoke drifted upward and disappeared into the cloudless blue sky. The world smelled of ashes, soot, molten metal, cooked meat, burnt plastic, burnt vinyl and—and flowers. Violets, chrysanthemums, plumerias, roses, every type of flower in an overpowering bouquet. No one was screaming inside anymore.

How many dead? Dozens, I'm sure. Didn't see Darling on the sidewalk or in an ambulance. We won't know the full tally for some time, I expect. If you ever wanted to fake your death and start a new life, now's your chance…

I called Paradise Voyages from a hospital payphone. Doug came here inside of ten minutes—didn't know he could drive that fast. Zelda and Richie ran up to him, ecstatic. He failed to hide his tears. "If anything happened to any of you, I couldn't go on." He drove us out of the city. The children fell asleep in the back, Richie holding Zelda in his arms. Somewhere behind us, the house was still burning. Dozens, maybe hundreds, were still in the hospital and the morgue. And here I was, in the passenger seat of a Cadillac. A plastic hippie after all. A coward.

Doug took my hand and smiled his warm, slow smile. I thought of Zelda's still, pale face, and the white smoke rising through the floorboards.

August 29, 1967

Story in all the papers. "Blazing Inferno in the Heart of Hippieland," "Infamous Haight-Ashbury Neighborhood Mourns Its Dead," "Death Toll Climbs to 39 in San Francisco Fire." Darling's name listed among the dead. Can't bear to read any more. We almost died for a dream, a beautiful dream but nothing more.

Richie and Zelda full of questions. Do we live with Daddy now? Will we stay here forever? Both have nightmares. Hopefully they'll forget.

Doug had a surprise for me. He took my mugshot, blew it up into a poster. Made me cry when I saw it. Who is that stranger staring back at me? Yet she feels more familiar than the face in the mirror.

September 7, 1967

Doug, true to his word, has moved in with us—on week-ends. Richard and Zelda Snowberger (their new names) enrolled in the local school. I'm "Mrs. Rose MacLeod Snowberger," according to a letter I received last week. Sensational. Considered ordering monogrammed handker-chiefs to celebrate. Occasionally think about my poor dead Darling—but he would never have given me his last name, even if he'd lived. If he'd lived…

Life in Woodacre is slower than the city. People even talk more slowly here. There are a few communal farms, and other hippie scenes nearby, but they hold little inter-est for me now. Whenever anyone mentions the Doomsday Garden or the fire, I act like I don't know about it. It's so nice to be surrounded by trees.

Drove to the nearest record store while the children were at school. So strange being in a "hip" scene again—same haircuts, same outfits, same poses and expressions, same faces, even. Could have sworn I saw Libby browsing the rock albums, but no, impossible…bought Heather MacRae's "Hands of the Clock" for 25 cents. Title seemed appropriate.

Richie pitched a fit when he heard I was meeting Beatrice. "No, no, no, I am NOT going back!" Even when I explained there was no "there" to go back to, he refused to calm down. Zelda wet herself. Caught her smearing feces in the bathroom again.

Maybe I should finish this diary once and for all, put it in a safe place (along with every memento of the Doomsday Garden) until the appointed time. It's no use to me now. Maybe it never will be.

September 10, 1967

Met with Beatrice. Richie and Zelda were well-behaved, said nothing. Beatrice wants to reestablish herself away from the city and its "madnesses." Can she set up in our house? Our house is much too small, even for the four of us. She sighed.

She is quite broke at the moment, broke and broken down. The Doomsday Garden lost everything in the fire. Insurance refuses to pay out, especially after learning of the unlicensed garage experiments. Newspapers repeat and reaffirm sensationalist lies. Did you know we were part of a "bizarre sex cult" that worshipped Baal? Mayor Shelly won't return her calls. She is not the Beatrice I remember; her spark is gone.

Nothing resolved, but I put her in touch with a realtor, gave her what little money I had. She held my hands in hers, looked in my eyes—bottomless despair in those eyes! "We were looking for doomsday in the newspapers and in the stars. All this time it was underneath our feet."

Realized while writing this—Beatrice is dead. She died in the fire—somebody told me. No. How could she be dead? I held her birdlike body in my arms. She smelled the same, for God's sake. If she's dead, whoever's playing her should get an Academy Award and a job with the CIA. If she's not...

I look outside. A few boys skirmish on the blacktop. Did Rose really forget that Beatrice was dead? Did some impostor meet with Rose, fishing for information—or the sphere? Or did Beatrice really rise from the dead, just to talk to her disciples?

October 29, 1967

After the children went to bed, I played the Doomsday Garden record. I cried. Almost all the singers on this record are now dead. And the room where it was recorded is gone, forever. No one will ever again drop into the lecture hall, or sing with me while scouring the pans, or fuss over the layout of the next issue. It is finished.

I could still hear them singing after the record stopped. A tremendous light came from the woods. The scent of flowers, so strong I nearly choked. First thought: the fire has followed me here. I'll go outside to meet it, so it doesn't take the children.

Claude appeared in the woods and led me to a great circle of singing, their melodies even more beautiful than the ones I remember. I joined them. We sang for centuries, our voices rising like smoke to touch the stars. A verdant paradise appeared inside the circle, with two enormous trees laden with gem-like fruits and flowers. And I saw—

Would you believe it, I saw <u>them</u>! There was the snake, its tail in its mouth, encircling the grove. There was the black sphere shining darkness overhead. It was all as real as the pen I'm holding in my hand.

I no longer fear the future. Why fear an illusion? Eternity waits for us, pulling us ceaselessly to itself. May it swallow us whole.

I close the diary, stare out the window. Two boys linger on the basketball court, calling to each other. One dribbles a ball from hand to hand. A few media vans idle outside the school gates. The late sun casts the school's shadow across the blacktop.

My mind wanders to my bedroom. Back at home, inside my top dresser drawer, is a black sphere, cool and smooth underhand.

I don't open my dresser drawer or look at the black sphere. I try, and fail, to do my homework—who cares what the slope of this line is, anyway? When I come out of my room, Dad's lying on the living room floor. His head, arms, and shoulders are shoved inside the TV cabinet. He's not moving.

"Dad?"

Dad's head bangs against the top of the cabinet.

"Hey Amy," he says. "I'm—ouch, that really hurt—I'm hooking up the old camcorder. Look at this."

A blur of blacks and browns fills the TV screen. Murmured voices fill the soundtrack. The image focuses on Grandpa Doug, now standing in the Stinson house's backyard. There's the shed, right behind him.

"You remember Grandpa Doug, right, hon?"

Grandpa Doug smiles beneath a shock of white hair. This is the man who drew hearts on my Band-Aids, who made me chicken soup when I was sick. How can he be the same man as the one in Grandma Rose's diaries?

The video cuts to Grandma Rose in the Stinson living room, playing a guitar. I know those chords before she starts singing: "The Circle Game." The camera pans to Leah, eight or nine, hugging little me to her chest. Leah sways us in time with the music. We join in for the song's chorus, our young voices rising in harmony. Dad wipes his eyes.

"Let's try that chorus one more time," Grandma Rose says. The camera zooms out, showing Mom, Aunt Zelda, and Grandpa Doug on the other couch. We're all singing.

"Turn it off," I say. Dad doesn't hear me. He stares at the screen, his eyes glazed with happiness.

The song continues as I walk to my bedroom. Outside, vans idle and beep. Voices talk, whisper, yell. Police sirens peal in the middle distance. I open the drawer. The black sphere's still there. *God, give me until tomorrow to figure it out*, I pray as I close the door. *If you can't, don't let it hurt anyone else.*

I wonder what Cassidy's doing right now. Is she safe? Is she with her sister? Did the woods swallow up her brother? Part of me hopes it did.

Afternoon slips into evening. Sirens blare in the middle distance. Artificial lights flood Blackwood Drive, filling the street with a sickly blue glow.

"Dad, did you disconnect the phone?" Leah says, somewhere in the house.

I remember these evenings, sitting trapped in the bedroom, dreading tomorrow, feeling that every day would go on forever. It doesn't last forever, though. Nothing does.

CHAPTER TWENTY-EIGHT
SILENCE

I WAKE UP to a light shining in my face.

"Get up," a voice says. Low, male, loud. Not Dad. I try to scream, to call for help, but I can't. Then another voice, also male, also not my father.

"We can drag you feet first," he says. "Up to you."

My hand closes around the mace in my pocket. I stumble to my feet, hiding my hand behind my back. A woman cries somewhere behind them.

"These men are going to help you," Mom says, her voice choked with tears. She walks past them and embraces me. Her cheek is wet against mine. "It's going to be okay." My hand flexes around the mace. "I know you've been throwing out your medicine," she persists. "The doctor said—"

The connecting door rattles. The flashlight beam swings around. Leah bangs on the door. Mom turns away from me, hurries out of the room.

"Let—me—*in!*"

Mom's voice, now in the hallway. "Sweetie, go back to bed— it's okay—"

"Fuck you!" The connecting door swings open. Leah's holding a baseball bat, her eyes wild. Here's my chance. My window's closed, but if—arms encircle me, too strong to fight off. My feet lift off the ground. I can't bite him. If I fire the mace, it'll hit me more than him.

"What's going on?" Dad shouts from the hallway. Mom murmurs something in response. "*What?*" More murmurs.

Someone screams. Something swishes through the air, then thuds against the man's body. He wheezes as he falls. His arms loosen around me. I push myself free, lunge for the window, open it. The alarm shrieks. Hands grab at me in the darkness. Dad's somewhere behind me, yelling "How *dare* you, Jackie!" Dogs bark.

I fall out of the window and into the bush. I'm still holding onto the mace, which I put back in my front pocket.

I run.

Air burns in my lungs. My heart beats a furious tattoo in my ears. Nettles and leaves poke through my socks.

I run down Blackwood Drive, trying to find an intersection with one of the other streets, waiting at every moment for the glare of headlights, my mother's voice, even for sirens.

There's no one around. The trees rustle in the wind. A few leaves flutter to the ground. The moon shines through the branches above me. A sweet, floral scent fills the air.

I fall, palms first, onto the asphalt. My knee smarts. The wind dies. By the time I get to my feet it's gone. All sound is gone, even my own breath. The trees sway silently overhead.

There's something in my hand. How long has it been there? It's heavy, round, smooth, black—

The gate of a house swings open.

There's a light in the forest. I see it flashing through the trees, waxing and waning in strength. Some unevenness in the ground checks me. I'm through the gate, walking into the woods.

I drop the black sphere, watch it roll through the high grass. I grab my locket, feeling its coldness and smoothness in my palm. *Protect me, please.* I look back up.

Trees surround me, mostly redwoods. *Nothing's changed. Nothing but the trees.* There's not a hint of a path, not a glimpse of a house or a roadway or a backyard. The scent of flowers is unyielding now, coming from everywhere and nowhere at once. A few lonely stars shine through the branches.

There, in my other hand, sits the black sphere, an eye of light glinting on its surface.

CHAPTER TWENTY-NINE
TIME OUTSIDE OF TIME

THINGS MOVE SLOWLY now, slowly and *wrong*. Branches bend before the wind comes to them. I can't hear my footsteps. I can't hear anything.

Stop walking, I tell myself, and keep walking. *Drop the sphere*, I tell myself, and even as I watch it roll away from me, it returns to my hand. An old prayer, learned from Grandma Mimi or my college crush or some movie, returns to my lips. I don't know if I say it out loud. *God, I give you my body as a living sacrifice—alive, holy, and pleasing to you—which is your right to demand. In the name of the Father, and the Son, and the Holy—*

I come back to myself on top of a hill, walking on a trail. Lights glitter in the valleys below. Silvery fields of dry grass undulate between dark patches of trees. Tall redwoods stand in silhouette along the horizon. A cloud glides over the face of the quarter moon. Stars open in the semi-darkness. There's sound now: cars rushing on the distant highway, wind moving through the bushes and trees, my own feet crunching over pebbles.

A sharp gust of wind blows my hair in my face. When I pull

it back, something's changed. The air is different now, pregnant with menace. The heady scent of many mingled flowers fills the air. The rush of cars slowly abates. The stars transform into white flower buds, just out of arm's reach. The moon hides behind a cloud.

Something's humming under the earth, something deep and massive below the level of sound. Music rises out of the ground and into the air, a polyphonic hymn sung by numberless voices. The world falls away.

A point of white light opens in the air. The point takes form as an immense snake, light dancing through its scales. It wraps itself around a dark, faceless body from the legs up, then loops itself endlessly around its neck.

Run, I tell myself, and don't run. My locket feels frighteningly cool in my hand. The singing grows louder, the voices more insistent, more dissonant. There's another sound, separate from the song. A baby crying.

No. I turn around with a great effort of will. I'm prepared to see nearly anything, even my own soul staring back at me. I'm not prepared for Grandma Rose, her eyes overflowing with tears.

"Oh, sweetie," she says, and pulls me into a hug. She smells like she always does: cinnamon, clover, apple shampoo. She pulls away, looks deep in my eyes. Her face shines with reflected light.

Everything's vanished except her, me, and the figures next to us. *It's an illusion*, an inner voice insists. *You're still on the path. The stars are still here. The moon—*

Grandma Rose smiles wider than wide. Tears fill the wrinkles under her eyes. "I'm so happy," she says, and takes the black sphere from my hand.

The path reappears around us. The world is frosted with moonlight. A leaf floats from the ground into the sky. This isn't a dream, a simulation, a Capgras Dimension. Grandma Rose, the snake, the faceless figure, me: we're all as real as the trees.

"I had no idea you were the Scarlet Virgin." The unbalanced smile widens on her face. Her eyes swivel this way and that, not meeting mine. The voices swell. "I don't know why I didn't see—"

A baby screams. The voices rise in an answering chord. When I look up, every flower in the sky has opened, filling the world with silvery-white light. The moon's become a white-silver rose, every petal on its face open and shining.

"You need to be brave." Anguish briefly disfigures Grandma Rose's face.

A confused prayer returns to my mind, bits of things I picked up in college and saw in movies and overheard here and there: *Heavenly Father above, forgive us our sins and those who trespass against us, deliver us from the hour of our death, Hail Mary Our Father Hail Mary Our Father Hail Mary, full of—*

My hand closes around the hilt of a knife. It's enormous, the kind you'd use to skin a deer. Or a…

"This is stupid," I say, or possibly think, as I feel the weight of it in my hand. "Straight out of a B-Movie. *Children of Doomsday. The Thrill of the Snake.* I should be watching this in a dorm room, laughing at the bad special effects…the bright red corn syrup…"

A tiny body squirms in the faceless figure's arms. The baby. I recognize him instantly: sparse red hair, pale skin. *Baxter, wait up!* He stops crying, for only a moment, and blinks up at me, his dark eyes enormous in the unearthly light. I see him as I saw him in 2016, wearing a Burger King crown. I see him as I saw him in the ice cream shop, sobbing in his stroller. His face reddens, pinches. He opens his mouth, lets forth a colossal wail.

Grandma Rose strokes my hair. "Honey, you have to."

"I don't have to do anything. We can go home…"

The snake brushes against my hand. I see hordes of people filling the earth, living and dying and transforming its surface, leaving rubble and sludge in their wake. Never let anyone say you don't make a difference—every car ride and candy wrapper counts. Put that on your tombstone, *I poisoned the planet*, round the decay of that colossal wreck, boundless and bare—

The lone and level sands stretch far away. No footprints. Hardly any life. The odd fungus, cells moving over naked rock. Then nothing, really nothing: lifeless waters, deserts, fossils. Then the swelling sun, lonely red dwarf on the Orion Arm, no funeral, no—

"Sooner than we thought," Grandma Rose says, her voice shaking. "We can't stop it. We can't change it."

"I do the evil that I don't want to do, and I don't do the good I want to—"

"Yes," Grandma Rose says, nodding. "That's exactly it, Amy. You were always so smart." She gulps back tears, presses my hand around the knife. "It won't hurt him. He won't even feel it. When this is all over, we'll be happy forever. We'll be innocent again."

Voices crescendo around me. I don't dare look up. The snake's tongue tickles my wrist. It's cold.

"No," the baby says, in a tiny, reedy voice. Enormous tears, shining in the light, tumble down his face.

God, do something, I pray, willing my hand to drop the knife. *I don't know how to stop this. Kill me, if you have to, please, have mercy—*

Another image comes to me: a clearing, lit by unearthly light, two trees towering above me (*it's an illusion, you're still on the path, don't give in*) and the air, sweet and pure and free of poison. Everything is singing, every blade of grass and pebble and all the glowing, star-like, pale white flowers. White flowers bloom in the black sky. A black flower shines in place of the sun. Colossal, glittering joy overpowers me (*it's not real, don't give in*). There is a place better than this one, a land without shadows, beyond life and death and (*no, no, no, no, no, no*) time—

The snake tries to force my arm up. *God please, stop this, show me*—

You're killing life to save one life, the snake purrs, its voice a velvet hand across my mind. *One tiny little measly life that belongs to eternity. Not to you. If you wait any longer, it will be too late, and everyone will die—Baxter, your grandmother, you, everyone you love, every bird and plant and innocent on the face of the earth. Hurry up, Amy. You're not going anywhere 'til you save the world.*

I raise my eyes. The snake, shimmering around the figure's neck, gives its features a lambent glow. Pale, freckled skin, enormous blue eyes, limp white hair tucked behind its ears—her ears. It's Beatrice Spar, not a day older than she was on that album cover. Pearl earrings gleam on each side of her face.

I drop the knife.

The locket on my chest erupts into heat—blistering, boiling, burning away the skin. Beatrice screams. Her eyes roll down vast dark caverns in her head. Her body collapses.

The light disappears. Numberless voices scream around me. Something swoops toward me out of the darkness. Something inside me rushes to meet it. A vast sound fills the air, then silence.

I sink to the path. The baby whimpers nearby. Relief flows through me. The world slowly reemerges from the dark. There lies Kathleen Vandergraf, even more dead, bony hands holding Baxter to her chest. Her earrings shine in the moonlight.

"Hey, buddy," I say, picking up Baxter. He weighs nothing, his bones birdlike beneath his skin. He curls against me, sobbing.

"Amy," Grandma Rose says, her voice low at my ear. I gasp. Her hand closes around my mouth. "Lie under that bush. Play dead. When you can't hear my voice anymore, run the other way."

I nod.

"I love you," Grandma Rose whispers, and stands up. I crawl to the bush, clutching Baxter to my chest.

Voices rumble in the distance.

"There's the bitch!" Grandma Rose yells. She runs screaming down the path. Footsteps thunder from all directions. I curl into a millipede, shield Baxter with my body. Feet land all around the bush. I hold my breath. They're fading into the distance when Baxter screams.

The footsteps slow to a stop. Baxter wails again, despite my shushing, his cries ringing out in the silence. I stumble to my feet, fight through the bush, and run, as hard as I can, away from the crowd. I make the mistake of looking back, see a few hundred people behind me, staring at me, frozen in place. Then a yell, as if from one throat, rises from the crowd. They're running now, toward me. Toward us.

A dip in the path sends me flying forward. I catch myself with my free hand, nearly drop Baxter. I'm up again and running along a steep incline. A hand grabs the back of my coat.

"No!" I roar. My free hand's already around the mace. I spray blindly behind my shoulder. *God, please.* A voice cries out behind me. The hand lets me go. A moment later I'm running again, the crowd's wail at my heels.

Lights glitter in the valley below. So there *is* a civilization to go back to. My heart leaps at the thought—nasty, brutal, world-ending civilization, with its central heating and power lines and newspapers, its pleasant and unpleasant fictions.

We crest the hill. A small path reveals itself through the brush, leading into a copse. I run through it, crouch behind a tree, hold Baxter to my chest. I put my hand, lightly, over his mouth. "Be quiet," I murmur in his ear. He stifles a sob. People run down the path, getting further and further away from us. Baxter shoves his fist against my hand. There's no food I could give him, except...well, I could try. Girls my age have nursed babies, haven't they? I know, in theory, how it's done.

Baxter sobs against my hand, sucks air in through his nose. My heart leaps into my mouth. I strain my ears against the distant roar of cars, the rustling branches, the crickets and birds. No voices, footsteps, songs or cries. Behind us, the forest descends into the valley, between us and the lights. There may be Doomsdayers waiting for us on the path, but we have to take that risk.

The path is clear, even in the moonlight. It rises and falls in sharp gradients and turns. I have to scrabble up a few hills, praying the dirt won't give under my feet. A plane flies overhead, its red and green wing-lights blinking in the dark. The path forks. Wooden signs at the intersection point the way to Woodacre.

Baxter whimpers against my chest. I can't feed him, no matter how many times I try, no matter how much it hurts. "I'm sorry, buddy," I say, stroking his fuzzy head. "We'll be there soon."

The night wind buffets us. I wrap my shirt around Baxter to keep him warm. The locket irritates the blisters and scabs on my chest. When I come to a high point in the path, I stop for a moment to catch my breath. Moonlight touches every leaf and branch, every pebble and dirt patch. The mountains loom silent and purple against the stars. A few wispy clouds glow along the horizon. Baxter says something garbled, ending in "no." I look down and walk on.

We pass no one on the long path through the forest. We're on a down incline now, only checked by bends in the path. I expect at every moment to meet death or worse. There'll be a mountain lion at the next pass. Better yet, a snake. One of *them*, with a knife. I'm walking as fast as I can when my feet hit gravel. By the time I get to asphalt, I'm running.

The streets are quiet, lit only by garage lights and the odd lamp through a window. I hold Baxter to my chest, running until the wind burns in my lungs. When I get to the mouth of Blackwood Drive, I pause. Rotating blue-red lights spill from the mouth of our driveway. Voices fill the night air.

My legs ache as I ascend the street's steep incline. I scream, chiding myself for not screaming earlier.

"Help! Please!"

The beam from a flashlight blinds me. Baxter squirms in my arms.

CHAPTER THIRTY
SHADOWS

LEAH STOPS IN the middle of the street. Her eyes snag on Baxter, now wrapped in my shirt. "What the *fuck*?" Her eyes move from him to me, from me to him.

"Amy!" It's Mom, running toward me. "Amy, oh my God!" She moves in for a hug.

"Mom, wait! The baby—"

Mom stumbles back, looks from me to the baby, face entirely slack. Officer Franklin's a few steps behind her, her face grave.

"He's not mine," I say, jogging to Officer Franklin. "He needs food," I stammer as I give her Baxter. "Milk or, uh, what's-it-called, formula—"

"Where'd you find him?"

"In the hills."

"What hills?"

"Amy? Sweetie?" Dad's lumbering down the street. His eyes are small and red. For a fraction of a second, I see him as Richie MacLeod, six years old, face streaked by soot. *Blazing Inferno in the Heart of Hippieland. I love you.*

"I need an ambulance," Officer Franklin says into a walkie

talkie, dandling Baxter in her other arm. "We have an infant, possibly newborn, in need of food and medical assistance. Over."

"Is this the, ah, baby that went missing? Over," says a voice on the walkie talkie. Baxter cries, softly, shoving his hand in his mouth.

"Not confirmed. Over."

Leah covers her face with one hand. Sobs rack her shoulders. Dad pulls us all into a hug.

It all comes back to me: the men from the camp, Leah's baseball bat, the confusion and terror and run through the darkness. Did that only happen a few hours ago? Did it happen to me, or to someone else who gave me her memories?

Baxter's face is nearly gray, his eyes half open. "Is that the baby from the ice cream shop?" Dad asks me. Disquiet settles on his face.

Four ambulances roar up Blackwood Drive. Leah goes to the house to find whole milk, half and half, while Mom knocks on door after door, looking for formula. Four paramedics surround Baxter as they take him to the van.

"Is he going to be okay?"

"He's going to be fine," one of the paramedics says. He doesn't look at me as he says it.

"They were gonna arrest me," Leah brags. "I told them, I thought my sister was being kidnapped. What was I supposed to do?"

"No charges?"

"Not yet."

"You're lucky. If you were a poor black kid, you'd be fucked."

"If *you* were a poor black kid, this wouldn't have happened. Those camps don't take charity cases."

Mom clucks her tongue.

"What?" Leah says. "Two body-builder dudes, in Amy's

bedroom, in the middle of the night? What was I supposed to think, *mother?*"

Mother doesn't answer.

The story comes out in dribs and drabs, from my family and the cops and overheard conversations. Baxter Brown, one week old, was abducted from his crib while his parents slept beside him. No signs of forced entry, no suspects. After I ran away, the Marin County Sheriff's Office and the FBI swarmed in, fearing there might be an abduction ring at work. The troubled teen minders were held for questioning. Search and Rescue swarmed through the forest, looking for us. They found nothing. They still haven't found Kathleen.

Officers Franklin and Silveira meet me at the station. I give them the portrait in disjointed snapshots: the knife, the crowd, the songs, the chase. They both take notes. Mom watches me talk with Lenin-esque puzzlement. I can see in their eyes that they don't believe me.

People come in to talk to me all morning: CPS, psychologists, federal agents. They want to know about the blisters on my chest. How did I get those blisters? Do I like to hurt myself, maybe heat up the locket until...? Mom bursts into tears, cradles my head in her hands. I ask to see the priest from Saint Patrick's, in the city.

Leah leaves the hospital and won't answer her phone. Mom calls her frantically, pacing the floor. Dad sits next to me, asks how I feel. I don't feel anything, good or bad. It's like my emotions are off in another room, one I haven't visited for a while. Maybe they'll come looking for me. Maybe it's better if they don't.

The scrum's grown outside our house. We fight our way past vans and cars that try to cut us off, through thickets of photographers, cameramen, MAC-shellacked news reporters, unkempt print journalists. Flashbulbs strobe outside my window. "Pretend they don't exist," Mom says in her frayed cord voice. Inside, we roll down the blinds, tape shut the mail slot. Angry voices knit together, engines idle, fists pound on our door.

The priest arrives in the late afternoon, wearing slacks and a blue shirt with a clerical collar. Mom apologizes for the "hubbub" outside. "I don't believe we've met," he says to me, extending a hand. "I'm Father Greg." He is curiously ageless, the kind of man who looks forty-five from high school until his eighties. We shake hands.

Father Greg and I sit in the backyard, near the tree line. If we sit on the porch, I explain, Mom will go in Leah's room and open the window to listen. A curious change comes over his face when I tell him this, but he says nothing.

After Father Greg takes his seat, I remind him of my confession in a general way. He sighs.

"I've heard so many people talk about their 'future dreams,' especially this week. One woman told me she 'dreamed she became her own mother.' I haven't had them myself."

"They're not dreams. They're glimpses of the future. A future." I laugh without joy. "Finally, we can answer the age-old question: Can man change his destiny? Can he do the good he wants to do, and refrain from the evil he doesn't want to do? And for how long?"

"You've read the Bible."

"Parts of it."

I tell him everything that's happened, from the beginning to today. I show him the locket, the photo inside it, the blisters on my chest. I describe the attempted sacrifice, and my escape.

"You're in danger," he says, his voice soft but insistent. He hands me a large green necklace with a plastic crucifix. I move to loop it round my neck. "You don't put it on," he says, laughing, as he takes it back. He shows me how to pray the rosary, hands me a laminated paper with the prayers on it. I should find a Catholic youth group in my neighborhood, start one if necessary.

"I'd be a pretty terrible leader. I'm still not sure what I believe."

"Faith doesn't come from certainty. You weren't certain you could save Baxter, were you?"

"Where does faith come from, then?"

"From God, of course."

"God didn't stop Adam and Eve from eating the apple. Why'd he even put the tree there? Couldn't he mold them into the kind of people who wouldn't do that?"

"He didn't."

"Why not?"

Father Greg sighs. "Love cannot be ordered or demanded. It has to be given. Which is why God, who loves us so much, gave us the choice. So we could choose to love him in return."

"I can't accept that. Love's not a choice. Does a newborn baby choose to love its mother? Why can't we be like that baby, innocent and protected?"

"Have you asked God?"

"I'm asking you."

Father Greg sighs, looks up through the trees. I remind him of my vision of a dead planet. His eyes grow soft and sad.

"They were trying to open up the Garden of Eden. To live in paradise, forever. They said that was the only way out."

"We'd destroy the garden, too. If he'd let us." He leans back in his chair, gazes at a fat cloud hanging in the sky. "You're quite right that we can't change. God became a man to suffer and die on the cross, because he knew we couldn't change ourselves. Only a miracle can do that."

"What if the miracle doesn't come?"

"It already has." He laughs at my grim expression, his eyes

still sad. "My great-grandmother was certain that doomsday would come in her lifetime. Didn't happen, of course. People have been waiting for the end of the world for at least two millennia. Longer. It has to happen sometime."

After he leaves, I sit outside, feeling the sun on my face. A finch perches on a bush at the edge of the forest. The sun falls behind the trees. The shadows creep further and further into the backyard, heading for the house.

Two hours pass without my noticing. Minutes dilate as I try to brew tea. An hour passes in an instant; the tea turns cold. No one speaks. Dusk falls. Leah fights her way through a throng of media when she returns, shoving a woman to the ground.

"I had to shut off my phone," Leah says, answering a question nobody asked. "So did Ray, Ray's brother, Gordon, everyone." Her eyes alight on me. "Have you seen the news?"

"We're not watching that," Dad says from the couch.

"It's a fucking horror show."

"Language," Mom says robotically.

"Well it is. They're talking about sex cults, black masses, Bohemian Grove—this is mainstream TV, not some cable access show. They had Uri Geller on CNN, for some reason."

We drift off to our respective rooms. Leah wakes me by turning on the light. She hands me the latest issue of *The Moon*. *Elvis Found...in Atlantis Nightclub!* the headline announces. There's the King, strutting in a bejeweled suit, at the mouth of an enormous sea-cave. Behind him, a fish band jams on clamshells and coral harps. Floating mermaids sing into shell-shaped microphones.

She's high, her pupils huge in bloodshot eyes. She can't focus when I talk, so I listen instead.

"Bill O'Reilly showed your picture. I told Dad we should

sue. You're a minor, for God's sake. We're already getting death threats."

"How's Grandma Rose?"

Leah's face falls. I knew there was a reason no one's mentioned her.

"She's missing. A lot of people are. Officer Franklin said it could be suicide contagion. They're looking for her car."

"Is Claude Belissan one of the missing?"

"Who's Claude Belissan?"

I explain. Her eyes bulge, then narrow with anger.

"Why didn't you fucking tell me?" she says.

"I did tell you. At the beach, remember?"

She doesn't. We sit together in silence. I page through *The Moon. In Devon, IOWA*—I stop short. Why is that familiar? The answer rises before I've finished the question. I say his name out loud.

"What's that?" Leah says.

"Devon Jeschke. That's the guy who pimps you out. You meet him in a Narcotics Anonymous meeting, early 2012."

"Twenty…oh." Leah crosses her arms. "Don't worry, I'm gonna cut down. I don't smoke that much, anyways."

After she leaves, I rush through the rosary, feeling ridiculous and insincere. *If God is real, then he knows what's in my heart, and what isn't.* I finish, just to say I finished, and sink onto the bed.

I pick up *The Moon* again, take in the headlines: *Robots Build Killer Scientists; Aliens Abduct Bigfoot; Saddam Hussein Captured At Iraqi Chicken Farm.* I'm near the end when I see the story:

EIGHTH-GRADE "WONDER-KID" SAVES THE PLANET!

A world-ending catastrophe was narrowly averted last week, when an eighth-grade girl foiled a mad scientist's plot to obliterate the planet.

"It was no big thing," said Ashley Yukiyama, 13, of Defiance, Pennsylvania. "He talked a big game, but he was no match for me."

It all started when Ashley noticed strange things happening in her town. People heard strange sounds every night in the woods. A few kids went missing, including her best friend. Rumors swirled of Satanic cults and human sacrifices. But Ashley wasn't afraid.

"God put a sword in my hand," Ashley said. "That's the only way I can explain it. If I didn't fix it, who would? The government? Give me a break."

Ashley did copious research into her town, including past disappearances and local legends. She survived several attempts on her life, but remained committed to getting to the bottom of the story. That's when she discovered that the mad Doctor Lufthausen was trying to birth "a great evil" into the world—and was using human sacrifices to do it.

"I followed Dr. Lufthausen to this clearing in the wood," Ashley said. "I'm sure he would have killed me if I hadn't been prepared."

Ashley gave Dr. Lufthausen an atomic wedgie, while a few cheerleaders watched and laughed. Mortally embarrassed, Dr. Lufthausen flew from her and the town.

"He was totally stupid," Ashley said. "Did he really think he could beat me?"

Dr. Lufthausen could not be reached for comment.

Tom visits me in my dream. He's the Tom I fell in love with: well-dressed, quietly funny, with a mop of brown hair and a lopsided smile.

"But I killed you," I say. He shakes his head, and says something I don't understand. And then he's gone.

Kids stare me down as I walk through the halls. An eighth grader—braces, ruddy cheeks, and no chin to speak of—grins at me as our eyes meet.

"Hey, I heard you—"

A girl shushes him, vigorously shaking her head. She whispers something to him. The smile falls from his face.

Someone's written *BABYEATER* on my locker in thick, black Sharpie.

The rumor, I learn, is that I abducted a baby while high on P.C.P., wandered into the woods, and started eating him. The police found me naked, covered in blood, the baby bleeding from a huge gash on its belly. I then attacked the police, screaming obscenities, and overpowered four officers, only going down when tasered. The baby was missing its penis, stomach, liver, or all three. What I wouldn't give to be called "Amy Snotbooger" again.

"They don't actually think it's true," Sean tells me. "They're trying to get a rise out of you." He's the only person at school that still talks to me. Even the teachers won't look me in the eye.

"I hope so."

Our classes thin out. Jessica Truesdale's gone. James Spar-Desmond moves up to Guerneville. Kids call in sick, then don't come back. A few mention applications to Marin Country Day, Waldorf, Miller Creek.

"This school's a ghost town," Emily Padovano says to Marina. We're in P.E. class, running around the track.

"It's 'cause of the evil in the forest," Marina says. "It's not gone. It's waiting." She sneaks a look at me.

Someone pushes me forward. I fall chin-first onto the asphalt. Miss Barnett blows the whistle.

"Pay attention," she barks. I shoot her my best death glare. An hour later, she breaks her ankle tripping over a tree root. A new rumor flies through the school: *Amy's possessed. She can hurt you with a look.*

I calculate the number of days between today and my high school graduation. Every night I count them down in my silver notebook: *1728, 1727, 1726…*

Mom moves out. There's no announcement, no family meeting; she simply stops coming home, except on weekends and random weekdays. Dad and Mom argue, mostly over the phone, about school districts, furniture, real estate. Mom's more intense when she's with us, as if she's trying to cram a week's worth of quality time into a few short hours. It sets me on permanent edge, not knowing when, or if, she'll be here, filling the house with her stress vibrations, her five-year plans, her all-consuming needs and desires.

"I can't believe he got her to *leave*," Leah says.

Dad joins a gym across from Leah's school, takes up swimming and tennis, goes on his own version of the Atkins Diet. "It's simple," he explains to us, pointing to the salad on his dinner plate. "I don't eat anything beige."

"Aren't those peanuts?"

"Peanuts have dark brown shells, don't they? They're allowed." He winks at me as he takes another bite.

Dad disappears every Friday and Saturday night for bowling league. "More like 'boning league,'" Leah says. Leah all but moves out herself, staying over most weekends with Ray or other friends. "I wish they'd separate for real," she says. "That way, when I turn eighteen, she couldn't see me without my consent."

"She'll pay for your college."

"I'm a junkie, right? I don't need college for that."

Dad and I go to church. We sit in the back, taking our cues from the others when to stand, sit, and kneel, mouthing the words during the songs and responses. A few people do a double take at us, examine our faces. I'm that girl on the news, the "one common link" in all these missing persons cases. No one talks to me, not even during the Peace of Christ.

"That bad?" I ask Dad, when we're back in the car. He shrugs.

"Not bad, just weird. If it makes you happy, though..."

Outside, the world's shrouded in late-morning fog. Two middle-aged women walk down the steps. They look away from us as they pass.

The weeks spin by. Leah's Livejournal gives me a glimpse of the adolescent world I'll never be part of again, even when I'm surrounded by it. *if i hadn't heard this band or met this person or gone to this concert or or or then who would i be?* Leah asks. *a question without an answer, there's no way to know.*

Apparently, I was obsessed with Everclear in late 2002. I dig out one of their albums and give it a listen, but there's still a pane of glass between me and my emotions. I don't want to shatter it.

maybe this is the year i tip over from being a functional addict to a dysfunctional one. hahaha. we'll see.

I read Tom's book. Most of the stories are slight reworkings of the ones he showed me. A few are new: an Etruscan peasant celebrates the birth of his son; a Greek slave tries to teach his spoiled pupil; a guard dog reflects on the lives of the passers-by. The book is dedicated to Holly. I put it away.

We live our lives by new rules. No going anywhere alone.

No answering unidentified phone calls. Don't open the mail. Don't answer the door. Keep the curtains closed. Dad cancels the newspaper, the magazines, even cable. One Friday afternoon, he and Leah haul the TV out to the curb.

"What about movie night?" I ask.

"We haven't had movie night in a month," Leah says acidly.

A reporter from the *Daily Mail* accosts us in the supermarket. Friends and colleagues sell pictures of us to *Newsweek, Us Weekly, People, Time.* Ray's flyers, and excerpts from Oracle Doll, appear in *The Santa Rosa Press-Democrat.* One section runs over and over in my head:

> *Controversy has swirled over the role, if any, of one Forest Knolls student, whose presence is a motif running through these disappearances. This student, allegedly the last person to see Becca and Erin alive, may have found Kathleen Vandergraf's body in the woods behind her Woodacre home. She also found Baxter Brown, who'd gone missing six hours earlier, and delivered him to police.*
>
> *"I'm not saying she's the mastermind," said one local mother who declined to be identified, citing fear of retribution. "But she's involved, and she knows something she's not saying."*

Tom still visits my dreams. His face is blurred now, an impression of a drawing that's been erased. When I reach out to touch him, there's nothing there.

I'm putting away the groceries when Dad hands me a letter. It's from Cassidy Clark, 422 Short Way, Glen Iron, PA. I open it when I'm alone in my room.

Amy,

Did you know Lifetime is gonna make a movie about the Forest Knolls Disappearances? You should call them and make them cast you, you could be a superstar. Just kidding. Thank God my brother's arrest wasn't on TV, I would literally die.

Do you have cameras at your house every day? Emily Padovano told me some of the rumors about you, but they sounded retarded to me. If you were really eating a baby out in the woods, they would put you in a criminal mental hospital, forever. Remember when there was that rumor that I'd eat my used tampons? I didn't even have my period yet!

Speaking of criminal mental hospitals, guess who's not in one. The cops can't find Slice in the woods, but Téa says people have heard him screaming at night. I'm changing his nickname to "Bigfoot" so he won't be real anymore. The cops think he's dead, but we can't legally declare him dead for seven years. I keep hoping he'll come out of the woods completely normal, like he used to be. That's pretty silly, right?

I haven't told you the <u>BEST</u> part!!! My parents got arrested and deported from Switzerland, which I would pay ninety billion dollars to see. They are probably not going to trial because they've got good lawyers, so I might have to live with them again. At least Slice won't be there. I wanted to live with Téa and her boyfriend—yes, she <u>finally</u> moved out—but the judge said no. So I live with my aunt and uncle for now. It's cold here and they're <u>always</u> home. And I don't know anybody at school. And no computer!!! I will literally die!!!

Remember when it was trendy to say you had lucid dreams? Well I had one for real. I was driving along the

California coast and you were in the passenger seat. We were singing, wind blowing hair in our faces. I was pounding the steering wheel. Except, even though I was laughing on the outside, I felt cold, and hollow, and knew that I was only pretending to be happy. Dreams are so weird, right? What was your weirdest dream ever?

xoxo,

Cass

I pin this letter to the corkboard on my wall. I think of Cassidy in the driver's seat, belting out "White Unicorn," but the memory's lost its halo. I can barely remember the song.

I close my eyes. I see Cassidy and Mom sitting at the backyard table, laughing, Cassidy's wedding band glinting in the candlelight. Where will she be in thirteen years? Where will *I* be in thirteen years? The odds of us returning to that moment are astronomical. Fate will tear us apart, unless it has other plans.

CHAPTER THIRTY-ONE
TO THE END

"It's NOT A *Lolita* Lolita look, Dad. Ninety percent of my body is covered, okay? Look how poufy this skirt is!"

"Then why is it called Gothic Lolita?"

"Because it's Japa—"

I close the connecting door. I'm tying my scarf when the door reopens.

"Nice beret," Leah says, eyeing my outfit. She leans through the doorway, a curling iron in her hand. Her face is kabuki white, her eyelashes coated in mascara. She watches me pull the knot slightly off-center, adjusting the tails until they more or less match.

"When'd you learn to do that?" she says.

"A lifetime ago. It's called a French twist. I can show you how to do it, if you want."

"A lifetime...*oh*."

Today is Halloween, 2003. Leah's about to go to Japantown with her friends. I'm about to go to school. I have three tests today, an oral presentation, a headache, and one kind-of friend. At least it's a Friday.

"I don't think this goes with the outfit," Leah says, pouting at herself in the mirror. I reach up to adjust her scarf. She bats my hand away and undoes it herself.

"Amy, Leah, come here," Dad says from the doorway. He's holding a disposable camera. The bottom drops out of my gut. I follow them out to the hallway, slump against the wall.

"Do we have to?" Leah whines, fiddling with her purse.

"Please."

I've seen this picture before. It was printed on a mug, with Leah's face scratched out. Why did I dress up as a French girl again? Why did I dress up, period? I should have remembered, but I didn't. Dad smiles. Leah shifts from foot to foot.

"Say cheese!"

Leah puts her arm around me, pulls me close. That wasn't in the original photo. Was it? I force myself to smile. The flash blinds me.

Half the boys in the school are dressed as Jack Sparrow. Most of the girls are "sexy" nurses, elves, or vampires, until the teachers make them change into their P.E. clothes. Emily Padovano, a "geisha" in a silk cheongsam, makes sure to say "nice costume" to all of them. No one says a word to me.

"*Bonjour*," someone says by my ear. I wheel around, ready for a fight. Sean Hillis stands there, in a black shirt and black jeans, his hair slicked back in a pompadour. He's holding his backpack by one shoulder strap. Andrew—dressed in a toga and a laurel crown—stands ten feet away, watching us with his arms crossed.

"Johnny Cash?" I say. Sean's face lights up.

"You're the only one who got it. Even Andrew didn't know."

"Where's your guitar?"

"At home. But, I am gonna play it at my party tonight, if you want to come."

"Where's your party?"

"At my house. We're gonna build a campfire, make s'mores, tell scary stories. Luke said he'd bring some horror movies, but we don't have to watch those."

"What about trick-or-treating?"

"Nah, that's for kids. We could make milkshakes, but...I dunno. I'm not sure I want all the boys in my yard."

"You could teach them how to do it. For a fee, of course."

I consider going. S'mores and scary stories don't sound half bad. It sounds better than most grown-up parties, to tell you the truth. Mom's supposed to come home tonight, but maybe she won't. Maybe the universe will finally cut me a break. It has to happen sometime.

"I'll be there. You're still on Larch Street?"

"Never left."

Sean smiles and turns away. Andrew says something to him I can't hear. I think of Sean's last Facebook photo, a painful rictus fixed to his face, his hand hovering over his girlfriend's baby bump.

"Sean," I call out, before I can stop myself. Sean and Andrew pause, look back at me. Sean smiles as he closes the distance between us.

"Can you promise me something? When you go to college, pick a major with a job at the end. Even if it's not your favorite thing in the world. All right?"

Sean's smile falters. "What are you—"

"You have those dreams, right? The baby, sending out your resumé, working at the mall—"

"What dreams? What are you talking about?"

"Sean, please. Promise me."

Sean takes a step back, out of my reach. "They were right about you," he says, turning away.

What was that? Andrew mouths at Sean. Sean shakes his head. Andrew laughs as they walk away. Anger and shame flood through me. *Great job, Amy. You just lost your one non-imaginary friend.* I clasp my locket.

School ends. I wait in the library, watch the clock as it turns to four, five, five-fifteen, five-thirty. No one comes. Mrs. Petrelli, deep in a Georgette Heyer book, frowns at me occasionally over her glasses. The janitor walks down the hall, dragging the mop and bucket behind him. We must be the last three people in the school.

I walk to the end of the library, lean on the back wall by the window. I look at the number on my phone, count down to ten before pressing the call button. It only rings twice.

"Hello?" says a familiar Glaswegian voice.

"Mr. Templeton. It's Amy."

"Amy. We've spoken before, haven't we? Have we met?"

"Another lifetime, maybe. Listen, there's a book of Tom's that I want you to have, and I was wondering if—"

"Is it a book he sent you?"

"It's a book that was very important to him."

"You should keep it, then. He'd want you to keep it."

"You really should read this one, Allen—Mr. Templeton."

"It's not his diary, is it? Because he never kept one. Even if he did, he'd rather die all over again than let me read it." He chuckles. In that chuckle, I hear a ghost of the man I knew.

"It's not his diary, it's…well, you'll see."

A long silence passes between us.

"How did you know my son, Amy?" Mr. Templeton says.

I consider not telling him. What good would it do him to

know that his son lived, possibly lives, in a world he can never visit? Something in his voice forbids me from lying. I tell him most of it.

Mom's voice fills my mind as I talk, peppering me with imaginary questions. *What's this phone call to Arizona? Who were you talking to for over twenty minutes? That's a long time to talk to a wrong number. If I call this boy...?* A steely resolve fills my heart. Let her ask.

"I had a dream about him," Mr. Templeton says after I've finished. In his voice I hear the whole of his grief. "He was a few years out of college. He—" Mr. Templeton breaks off. When he starts again, his voice trembles. "He was singing. We were all singing, in this little house by the ocean. There was a silver-haired woman playing guitar, a few people I didn't know. I suppose one of them was you."

The moment rises up before me: the warm white glow of the Christmas lights; the mingled smells of roast turkey, pine sap, red wine, the fire; the smiling faces of the Templetons, Grandma Rose, Mom; our out-of-tune voices knitting together in the air; the waves roaring beyond the bluff.

"I can't remember what we were singing. Every time I try—"

"'The Circle Game.' It's a Joni Mitchell song." I sing a few bars. We sang other songs, "Silent Night" and all that, but I know it's the song he's thinking of. It's the one my mind always returns to.

Mr. Templeton sighs with relief. "That's exactly it...He was good to you, wasn't he? He was always good to the people he loved."

"Yes, he was."

"Oh, I'm glad. I'm so glad he got to—to live, in some way."

"You believe me?"

"Of course. You must have felt it, Amy. The world you left… it's still out there. Tom…" His voice breaks.

I think of Hunter and Halo Duckworth, of Becca Osborne's daughters, of Lucas Vandergraf. Mr. Templeton could spend his whole life trying to find Tom. He might never find him—or, worse, something could find him instead, turn his love for his son toward its own dark purpose.

"Mr. Templeton—"

"Allen, please."

"Allen, can you promise me one thing?"

"Depends on what the promise is."

"I'll put a letter in Tom's book. Before you read this letter, don't…promise me you won't go looking for Tom."

"Why?"

The library shelves blur and bend. I wipe my eyes. "You're right. The world I left didn't disappear. It changed. Maybe it changed into this world. Maybe it became something else. Maybe it's moved on without us; maybe it's suspended in darkness, waiting. Maybe it's right here beside me, even though I can't see it. But we could destroy ourselves looking for it. We wouldn't be the first."

I see Kathleen's pearl earrings, shining with unholy light.

"If I can find Tom, though…"

"You don't need to find it to find Tom. *Omnia mutantur, nihil*…something."

"*Nihil interit.*"

"*Nihil interit.* He isn't gone."

"No, he isn't." Allen sighs. "All right, Amy, I promise. After I finish your letter, though, all bets are off."

"Hey!" someone yells. It's Leah, standing in the library door, waving to me. Blue-black hair falls in ringlets around her face. A streak of black powder's smudged across one cheek. Mrs. Petrelli, disturbed from her reading, goggles at her.

"I have to go," I say into the phone. "I'm glad we got to talk."

"I am too. Goodbye, Amy."

"Goodbye."

Leah hops on the balls of her feet as I gather my things. Her eyes sparkle. She's smiling, a natural open smile from childhood. We pass out of the library and into the hall.

"Hurry *up*," Leah says, skipping and twirling ahead of me. "We're shooting a music video in the park. Some kind of time-lapse, night vision thing. Ray's bringing glow sticks."

"Where's Mom?" I say, wiping my eyes.

"Who cares? Come on."

Fay Ray's car idles in the pick-up circle. The backseat creaks as I sit down. An industrial anthem thunders on the stereo. Ray, dressed as Death from the *Sandman* comics, smiles at me from the driver's seat.

"Nice costume," she says, easing the car out of the circle. "You should totally be in the video, you could—you okay?"

"I'm fine."

The song ends, filling the car with hissing silence. I stare out the window as shrubs, fields, and trees roll by. *Tempus edax rerum*—time, devourer of all things. Every blade of grass will die, replaced or not replaced by another. Everyone in this car will die, succeeded or not by children and grandchildren. And then what? Soon this planet will be void of life, spinning through empty space, without a soul to disturb its mountains, winds, and empty waters.

Only that isn't it—not really. There is another force, above or outside of time, creating and recreating all things seen and unseen. An eternal negation of temporal decay. I can feel it here with me, as close as my own heartbeat. It's in the wind streaming through the window, the music on the stereo, the neurons sparking in my brain. It's in the roses planted on a grave, the bees that feed from those roses, the honey and the honeycomb. It's in every creature's will to live and to make life. What was it the man said? Everything changes, nothing disappears?

Ray parks under a sapling. Gordon and a few boys stand in the middle of the park, frowning over a camera. Ray sprints through the grass, yelling something, a shopping bag thwacking against her leg. I walk to the edge of the park, listen to the wind pass through the trees.

"Hey," Leah says. She's standing next to me, reaching her hand out to mine. I take it.

"You okay? Really?"

"Yeah," I say. "I'm okay now."

Leah holds my hand for another moment. Then she's gone, running across the grass. I run after her, wind roaring in my face.

Leah looks back at me. She's smiling; so am I. For a moment, there's nothing but the wind and the grass beneath our feet, the trees and the sky and the invisible stars overhead.

And then the moment passes.

ABOUT THE AUTHOR

A.O. Monk writes fiction, nonfiction, newsletters, poetry, and occasional blog entries on aomonk.com. *I Am Not Thirteen* is Monk's first published novel.

ACKNOWLEDGEMENTS

I Am Not Thirteen exists thanks to the following people:

Bryony Sutherland, *I Am Not Thirteen's* main developmental and copy editor. She helped make this book far more streamlined and cohesive, to say nothing of the many grammatical errors she found and fixed. I'm especially grateful for her help in closing plot holes and jettisoning subplots that went nowhere.

Leah Todd Brown, who edited an earlier version of this book. Her guidance steered me away from many plot-related dead ends and saved this book from remaining a file on my hard drive.

Ben, my mom, Grady Hendrix, and several writers on Scribophile, who each read and critiqued different scenes from this book. Their feedback was invaluable in pointing out obvious issues I'd overlooked.

My family and my partner's family, who helped us through moves, pregnancies, difficult work schedules, and much more.

Damonza, this book's cover and interior designer. Damonza's professionalism, responsiveness, and high-quality work impressed me at every turn. I'm glad I worked with them.

K.M. Weiland, Joanna Penn, and Mark Dawson, whose

books, websites, and podcasts provided much-needed inspiration and advice. Each gave me important insights into how to write, edit, and publish a book.

The reader—that's you. There's no point writing a book if no one reads it, so you're the most pivotal part of the entire writing and publishing process. I hope you enjoy *I Am Not Thirteen*, now and in the years to come.

CPSIA information can be obtained
at www.ICGtesting.com
Printed in the USA
LVHW040952250219
608648LV00003B/86/P